THE LEOPARD UNLEASHED

THE LEOPARD
UNLEASHED

Elizabeth Chadwick

St. Martin's Press
New York

Library of Congress Cataloging-in-Publication Data
Chadwick, Elizabeth.
    The leopard unleashed / Elizabeth Chadwick.
       p.   cm.
    ISBN 0-312-09323-3
    I. Title.
PR6053.H245L46   1993
823'.914—dc20   93-21739
                                                   CIP

First published in Great Britain by The Penguin Group.

First U.S. Edition: May 1993
10   9   8   7   6   5   4   3   2   1

THE LEOPARD UNLEASHED

CHAPTER 1

The Principality of Antioch
Spring 1139

NTIOCH, THE CAPITAL OF Prince Raymond's principality, was for Renard a rude and not altogether welcome awakening. It was easier to skirmish with Turks among the Nosairi foothills than it was to swelter along a crowded narrow street on a highly-strung war-horse in the wake of a camel's decidedly untrustworthy rear end.

Renard hated camels – an aversion stemming from the occasion of his first foot ashore in St Simeon four years ago when one had spat an evil green broth all over his tunic and tried to squash him against a wall. The beast, currently blocking his view, suddenly belched to an abrupt standstill. Renard's stallion flattened his ears, and, half-rearing, plunged sideways to avoid a collision. The camel's Bedouin rider cursed through a mess of black teeth and swatted the animal with a thin-tipped goad. The camel defecated. Renard cursed too as he backed Gorvenal out of range.

William de Lorys, a knight of his retinue, closed hard brown fingers over his saddle pommel and grinned broadly. Ancelin, Renard's huge English shield-bearer, huffed into his blond beard until dimples appeared beneath his eyes. Renard threw both men a glare that only increased their amusement. Beyond them, among his soldiers, someone stifled a guffaw.

The camel lurched onwards, its huge flat feet moving with an awesome, ungainly grace. Renard clicked his tongue to Gorvenal. The stallion pranced skittishly, nervous of the camel and the hemming seeth of humanity as from all sides they were assailed by the hot, ripe city. People, animals; all that they fed upon, dwelled within, or excreted out.

A beggar thrust the oozing remnant of an arm beneath Renard's nose and whined for money. Another showed him blind eye sockets and a mutilated nose, but he had heard and seen it all before and for the nonce was too impatient and saddle-weary to feel anything beyond irritation.

Four years in Outremer, he thought. Sometimes it seemed like forty. From the marcher hills of his birthplace to St Simeon in northern Syria, he had crossed not only oceans and mountain ranges, but the distance between childhood and maturity. He had been a restless young man of twenty-three at the court of his grandfather, King Henry, when he had met Raymond of Poitiers, recognised a kindred spirit, and when Raymond had left for Outremer to become Prince of Antioch, Renard had taken the Cross and gone with him.

As he recalled, his mother and sister had wept, but his father, watching him with a shrewdness that missed little, said that every man was entitled to sow wild oats providing that he learned from their reaping. Renard supposed that somewhere along the way he must have learned. The restlessness still churned through him sometimes, but he was more able to control its turbulence and apply it constructively.

The camel that had been encompassing all of his immediate vision squeezed past two laden donkeys and down an impossibly narrow side-street in the direction of the souk. Renard sighed with relief and, relaxing against his cantle, started to view his surroundings in a slightly less jaundiced light.

His house in the city, sited conveniently close to the palace, was built of white, sun-flashed stone around a cool courtyard with fig trees and a fountain in true Syrian style. There was also a walled garden and another fountain surrounded by banks of flowers and shrubs, and a grove of dark-leaved citrus trees. It had once belonged to an emir, or so Johad his Turcopol steward said.

Now, as he dismounted and the grooms came running to take the horses, Johad appeared at Renard's side. The steward bowed deeply, flashed his master a dazzling smile, and presented him with a cup of freshly pressed fruit juice which Renard took and finished in several swift, parched gulps.

2

'Johad, you're a godsend!' he declared in Arabic with an answering smile, and removed his helmet. His hair clung to his scalp in black, saturated spikes and sweat trickled down into the beech-red grizzle of a three days' beard. Returning the cup to his steward, he went across the courtyard to the bath-house. William de Lorys followed him. Ancelin, whose dislike of fruit juice was only matched by his dislike of taking baths, made an exaggerated gesture of disgust and perspired away in the direction of the kitchen to find some decent household wine.

'Home,' Renard said later as he sat cross-legged on the floor. Dressed in shirt, chausses and the flimsiest of silk tunics, he was eating a pilaff of saffron-coloured wild rice and spiced lamb. 'If I were at home now, I'd be shivering in the thickest tunic I could find with my winter cloak on top of it, and dining on salt beef and rye bread.'

'Better than this muck!' growled Ancelin, spitting a wad of fatty gristle onto the bright rug. 'Camel stew to eat, and camel's piss to drink!'

Grinning, Renard reached Arab-style to the pilaff bowl. 'When in Antioch ...' he said lightly; but although he had learned to enjoy the eastern way of life, he found that it was the thought of the once despised salt beef and rye bread that was making his mouth water.

William de Lorys gave his young lord a considering look. 'What else would you be doing if you were at Ravenstow now?'

Renard snorted. 'God knows! Probably quarrelling with my father about the earldom or wenching myself into disgrace!'

'Now there's a thought!' Ancelin's eyes brightened.

De Lorys picked out a rag of meat from between his teeth and glanced across. 'It wouldn't be as good,' he said. 'The women back home aren't trained like the ones here.'

'*You* can do it half way up a wall with one leg on the roof and the other on the couch if you like. What's happened to good, honest futtering, I'd like to know!'

Renard regarded the two men with amusement but felt no inclination to take sides. There were valid points to both arguments. His thoughts drifted past them towards the huge, starlit darkness outside. What indeed would he be doing at home now? Quarrelling with his father as he had jested? Perhaps. More likely struggling to hold the earldom on an even keel as Stephen and Mathilda between them whipped England into the worst storm for its people since the coming of the Conqueror.

When Renard had left for Antioch, all had been as calm as a mill pond on a summer's day with King Henry as sharp-eyed, parsimonious and cunning as ever, in expert control of all he surveyed – except his own mortality. Within two months of Renard's departure, the old man was dead of a bad eel stew and his lands cast into turmoil as his daughter and his nephew tussled for the throne.

Renard had wanted to come home, but his father had advised against it. Stephen, having snatched the first initiative and with it the Crown, was demanding sureties for good behaviour in the form of hostages from those barons he did not trust, his father among them. If Renard was abroad, then he need neither be yielded up nor refused to the King, and a smiling diplomacy retained.

Renard's two younger brothers were already marcher land-holders in their own right and therefore unlikely to be called to dally in custody at the court. John, his older brother, was a chaplain in the Earl of Leicester's household, and being as the latter was a staunch supporter of Stephen's right to be King, John too stood under small threat of being taken hostage.

Ancelin and de Lorys were still discussing women. Washing his hands in a bowl of scented water and drying them on the towel presented by Johad, he wondered briefly about Eleanor. How old would she be now? Approaching seventeen and more than ready to settle into marriage. She had been willing four years ago, but her body had been unripe even if her mind had not and the ceremony had been deferred until his return.

Nell, he thought, with her puppy-like devotion and her joy in all aspects of domestic duty. A fine wife she was going to make him, and an excellent mother to the enormous brood of children with which she expected him to furnish her. Neither mind nor body kindled at the prospect. Their betrothal was a

4

business arrangement, agreed ten years ago; a duty not onerous, but nevertheless lacking the spark that might have driven him eagerly home to his marriage bed. Here in Outremer, finding a women for the basic need was simple enough. It was the men who died.

Johad served dishes of halva, platters of fresh figs, and a sherbet made from pressed lemons. Renard took a fig. The halva was delicious, but it caused worm rot in the teeth and the taste of honey was occasionally too overpowering. Like this land, he thought. First it tempted you, then it dissolved into your bones, corroding them. Perhaps this was the reason why he was longing for plain Norman fare and the cold, damp spring of the marches that made a fur cloak a necessity. A reminiscent shiver of longing ran down his spine. He drank some of the cold, slightly bitter sherbet.

The discussion about women had ended in a decision to do more than merely discuss. 'Want to come?' asked de Lorys as he rose from the remains of his meal and brushed some stray, sticky grains of rice from his silks. 'One of the men was telling me they've got a new dancing girl at The Scimitar.'

'Have they?' Renard's interest sharpened. The Scimitar was expensive but the girls were usually worth it.

'A Turcopol wench. Blonde in both places.' Aware of his lord's preference for fair-haired women, de Lorys gestured eloquently and grinned.

Renard curved a sardonic eyebrow at him. 'I won't ask how your informant knows,' he said, and indicated to Johad that he could clear away the food.

The Scimitar was bursting at the seams when they arrived, but Renard was well known there, and having been absent for several months, was quickly found a place to sit and furnished with a drink.

A Syrian youth with kohl-rimmed eyes and a painted mouth propositioned him. Madam FitzUrse, the proprietor's wife, swatted the boy away in the direction of some Genoese sailors up from St Simeon and apologised.

'I wouldn't have taken him on,' she said ruefully, 'only

sometimes we get asked, and it doesn't do to turn custom away.'

Renard smiled and raised his cup to her. 'Business is business,' he said gravely.

She regarded him from the edge of a sly, bright eye. 'Here to see our new dancer are you, my lord?'

Renard shrugged indifferently. 'I was dragged out by my men who were desperate to get their hands round some vice after the monk's life I've been making them lead. I am only here to regulate their worst excesses.' And then his eye corners crinkled. 'But if you have a new dancer, I suppose I might watch.'

'Hah!' she snorted and nudged him with a meaty elbow. 'You'll do more than just watch!' Forefinger and thumb came up to rub before his face. 'I'll warn you now, she's not cheap. Cost you half a mark.'

'If she is going to excite me enough to part with half a mark, then I doubt I'll last long enough to justify the expense,' he said with amusement. 'Try Ancelin or de Lorys.'

She looked shocked. 'Would you give your best mare to be ridden by a novice?'

He arched his brow and looked even more amused.

'Besides, they've already found themselves company.' Patting his arm, she went to help her besieged husband who was refilling the pitchers. 'See me later when you change your mind,' she said over her shoulder with cheerful confidence.

Renard stared round in search of his knights. Ancelin was in the act of disappearing out of the door with a red-haired plump Armenian girl who also sometimes danced. De Lorys was arm-wrestling another man for the favours of a yawning, sultry-eyed Syrian woman with a lined, world-weary face and a body, in contrast, as lush as the fertile plain of Sharon. Oasis in the desert. Renard smiled at the whimsy and drank his wine.

Several times he was approached by one or another of Madam FitzUrse's girls, but although he knew most of them by name and some by a more intimate acquaintance, he found himself turning them away, his mind dwelling in rank curiosity on the ridiculousness of paying half a mark to spend the night with a whore no matter her beauty or expertise.

Shortly before the dancing was due to begin, he finished his drink and went outside to empty his bladder, and it was there, in the star-studded darkness of an eastern night, that his present mood of nostalgia was suddenly consolidated with such force that for a moment it left him totally disorientated.

In the shadow of a wall he heard a man's voice, slurred with drink, but unmistakably speaking the Welsh tongue, and a woman answering him in the same language, her voice low, husky and full of anger.

'I will not!' she said. 'The money is mine. I work for it and you're not going to swill it down your gutter of a throat!'

'You little bitch, you'll do as I tell you!' The man's fist wavered up.

'Go swive yourself!' Accurately she spat in his face and ducked under his arm. He made a grab for her enveloping dark robe and suddenly a dagger blade flashed in his hand as he wrenched her round to face him.

'Your face is your fortune, girl!' he snarled. 'Don't tempt me to ruin it.'

Renard set his hand to his own dagger hilt and took a forward pace, but before he could intervene, the girl made a sinuous movement and drew her own blade from within the voluminous folds of her native Arab robe. 'Strike then,' she hissed. 'Let us see who is the faster!'

Small bells tinkled daintily on her ankle bracelets and her feet were bare as she positioned them with feline precision.

Renard's loins and belly contracted with an instinctive reaction to the dangers of a knife fight. The woman was holding her weapon competently, a gleaming nine-inch steel crescent, and the man was staring at her in fuddled anxiety. Renard changed his mind as to the identity of prey and victim.

'Listen, lass, there's no need ...'

'Piss-proud coward!' she sneered, stepped again and struck. Metal grated on metal and in a circular motion spun like a falling star and puffed in the dust.

Weaponless, the man stared and swallowed. The woman laughed scornfully. Her feet wove the ground and Renard caught a glimpse of diaphanous, spangled fabric as she shifted and struck again with the exquisite Saracen blade. Her victim howled and doubled up, clutching at his belly.

Renard decided that it had gone far enough, if not too far, and with a shout, strode towards them.

Startled, the woman looked up and across. Renard received the impression of huge, dark eyes and a chain of coins winking on a smooth, pale brow before she drew the hood of her robe around her face and, knife still in hand, melted into the deep shadows of a stone-arched entry that led into the back of The Scimitar.

'Bitch!' the man gasped, still doubled over. 'Conniving, ungrateful little bitch!'

Renard's spine prickled. He stared towards the dark mouth of the entry and wondered whether he had really seen it happen or if his imagination was running wine-wild.

The man took one hand from his stomach and looked at the dark smear on his palm. 'Bitch,' he moaned again like a litany. 'No gratitude.'

'It was what you deserved.' Renard glanced round. Behind him he heard the tinkle of bells and the soft pat, pat of a drum. The dancing had started. 'Is it bad?'

'Course it's bad!' the drunk snarled indignantly. 'Look what she's done, the whore!'

Renard looked. Then he spluttered. The dagger had indeed caught the fool, but only the tip in a thin, red surface inscription. The mortal damage was to the string holding up the grey, stained chausses and whatever shreds of soused dignity he was striving to preserve.

Renard gave in to his laughter but was not so overcome that he did not see the man shuffling sideways, eyes to the ground. Reflexes entirely sober, Renard moved rapidly and closed his fingers on the haft of the fallen knife – once a serviceable but now sadly out-worn poniard. The grip was dropping to pieces and the blade had been sharpened so often that it was wafer thin.

Angling his wrist, he struck at the wall, the full force of his right arm behind the blow. A blue spark flashed briefly, illuminating the weapon's destruction as it shattered. Within the lean strength of his fingers, the grip came apart. He dropped the pieces on the ground, dusted his hands free of fragments and looked steadily at the drunk.

The man swallowed and fumbled his tongue around his lips. 'I was just leaving,' he said and, clutching a bunched handful of his torn chausses, started hobbling away. He paused once and looked over his shoulder, but Renard still watched him, and with a grunt and a bemused shake of his head, he gave up and shambled off, muttering.

The drums pulsed sensuously. A cricket chirred on the wall beside him and there was a mark in the stone where the dagger had struck. He looked down at the pieces in the dust and felt uneasy. Nothing that could be pinned down and given form or reason, but suddenly he found himself wishing he had chosen not to visit The Scimitar tonight and almost followed the drunkard out into the wide, star-filled evening.

'Renard?' hissed de Lorys from the doorway.

He swung round.

'Are you going to be out there all night? You're missing the new dancer!' He sounded as excited as a child.

The impulse to flee receded. Renard smiled ruefully at his own misgivings and went back within to the crowded press of humanity.

Being tall, he could see over the heads of most men. Ancelin was an exception and in his line of vision, but he eased in front of him, elbowing him in the belly when he protested. And it was then, as he took his first glimpse of The Scimitar's new dancing girl that he received his second shock of the night.

'Is she not a beauty?' muttered de Lorys against his ear.

'Oh definitely,' Renard responded with more than a hint of dry sarcasm. Beneath the mesh head-dress with its headband of bezants, her kohl-lined eyes were huge and dark, and her garments were of a flimsy, gold-embroidered tissue. There was nowhere about her person that a knife could even remotely be concealed.

Her mouth was sultry and as red as blood, and beneath her head-dress, the hair that whipped her undulating body was the

9

colour of sun-whitened corn. Her skin was not the fair or rosy kind that typically accompanied such hair, but as golden and gleamingly smooth as spilled honey.

The dance she performed for Madam FitzUrse's gawping customers was of the usual erotic order, guaranteed to send any newcomer to Outremer out of his mind with lust and fill with delight those who had only a passing acquaintance with the land. Men more experienced might have walked yawning away except that her striking looks held them riveted, and perhaps too, the way she cast her eyes around the throng like a lioness backed into a corner, one paw raised to strike.

The bells tinkled on her ankles. Bells edged the top of her bodice too, and silver zills chinked between her forefinger and thumb. Her hips moved in a sinuous, hypnotic gyration, sweat glinting on her face and within the declivity of her round, proud breasts.

'Oh God!' groaned de Lorys in agony as she whirled and the tempo increased. Her head went back, throat arching, and the head-dress swung and flashed. Torchlight shimmered on spangled flesh and tinselled garments. Her eyes roved contemptuously over her sweating, lusting audience, her pupils as wide and cold-dark as those of a night-hunting animal. She licked her red, red lips and laughed. Her teeth were white, sharp, and perfect, her tongue flickering suggestively between them.

Renard found himself responding and dropped his gaze. On first arriving in Antioch, he had gorged himself on dancing girls, unable to believe his good fortune; gorged until he was sick of the very sight of them and they held no appeal for him. Gradually, as time passed, his appetite had returned, but now he consumed in cautious moderation, and the moment their heavy, evocative perfume began to cloy in his nostrils, he backed off to digest.

He felt that he should be backing off now. The dish before him was certainly edible, but so hot that it would likely scorch the fingerprints off anyone attempting to do so, and half a mark was too steep a price to pay for burned fingers. He shifted restlessly. Men were tossing coins on the floor around her stamping feet. Her fingers fanned over her body, imitating those of a lover and she went to her knees, long thigh muscles stretched and gleaming, breasts heaving and outthrust, hair sweeping the floor as the drums pounded to their climax.

Renard could not help himself. He lifted his lids and looked at her. Her own eyes had been closed, but as the final throb of sound resonated and died, she brought her head forward and met Renard stare for stare and he saw that her eyes were not brown as he had thought, but a blue as rich and deep as the sky beyond the stars.

The Scimitar erupted with roars of appreciation, loud whistles, thumped tables, bellows for more. Coins showered upon the panting, sinuous girl. A wine-flown young idiot who made a grab for her was snatched away by the scruff. She gained her feet in one lithe movement. Her lashes came down. They were thick and black, spiky with soot and gum. The drum beat lightly. She danced among the scattered coins, stooping gracefully here and there to collect them up.

Renard became aware that his throat was dry and his palms sweating. He wiped them on his tunic and, turning abruptly away, forced a path through the avid, still riveted crowd of men. Madam FitzUrse smiled knowingly at him and tipped wine from the pitcher she was holding until it brimmed his cup.

'What do you think of her, my lord?'

Renard took three deep swallows to prevent the drink from spilling. 'She's a good dancer,' he said impassively.

Amused, she leaned across him to mop a puddle of wine from the trestle. 'Aye, she's that, and more if you've a mind.'

'Half a mark.' He cocked her a bright look. 'Why so expensive?'

'Ask her to show you.' She stood up, hands on hips. His voice was indifferent, but that counted for nought. She knew how to read men; her livelihood depended upon it.

'And risk being stabbed in my dignity?' His indifference was suddenly tinged with wry laugher. 'I think not.'

She narrowed her lids at him and then shrugged. 'Ah well, if you're not in the mood, I'm not the one to force you.'

Turning at a command from her husband, she gestured that she was coming, and patted Renard's shoulder in a familiar way. 'Her name's Olwen. If you change your mind, the payment is half to her and half to me.'

Renard sat down at the trestle to drink. Another girl was dancing now, slender and dark as a dockside cat. His view was more than half-blocked but he had no real inclination. Olwen. A Welsh name for a Saxon-blonde girl who handled a dagger like a man and danced like a sinning angel in a brothel and drinking house frequented by the knights and soldiers of Prince Raymond's guard. An enigma to be treated with caution, if not abstained from completely.

He drained his cup, set it to one side, and rose to leave, but it was pushed back at him and refilled with the rich ksara wine. Surprised he stared beyond the lip of the pitcher and a gold-bangled wrist into the dark sapphire eyes of the girl who was pouring. Their colour was emphasised by the gown she now wore – eastern silk but cut in the Frankish style and as deep as midnight. The head-dress was gone and her hair rippled unfettered to her waist in a golden skein.

'Sit,' she commanded, giving him the predatory look of a cat at a mousehole.

Renard stared back, nerve ends coldly prickling. 'Is this free, or do I have to pay half a mark?' he challenged, but subsided as she bid.

Her gown rustled, releasing the waft of an exotic, spicy perfume as she sat down next to him. 'Half a mark? Is that what she told you?' She jerked her rounded chin at Madam FitzUrse who was watching them and chortling gleefully.

'I said I was not interested.'

'You lied.' Her voice was like rough silk, a compound of smoke and cream, and held within its depths a hint of scornful amusement. She extended one perfectly taloned forefinger and drew her nail gently over the back of his hand. 'Men always lie.' She gave him a slow, wild smile.

Her shoulder rested against his. The neck of her gown was decorously fastened but accentuated rather than concealed her figure. The warmth of her perfume rose from between her

12

breasts. Renard became aware that his body, independent of his mind, was gradually being wound up taut like the rope on a mangonel. He could feel the long pressure of her thigh against his and her forefinger in gentle dalliance on his wrist. He started to harden and shifted a little away from her. She glanced down at his crotch as if she could see through tunic and chausses, and moistened her lips.

'Where did you learn to fight with a knife?' he asked abruptly.

She picked up his cup and took a long, slow swallow of the wine. Renard watched her creamy throat ripple and then brought his eyes back to her face. 'I was born with one in my hand.'

'And your name is Olwen?'

'Sometimes.' Lowering the cup, she looked at him. 'And yours?'

He stretched his legs beneath the bench and smiled. 'That depends on the woman.' It was like a sword fight, he thought; each of them trying to strike beneath the other's guard. 'Cullwch perhaps?'

A beautiful, golden-pink tint stained her face and he felt her pulse leaping, running into his like two tributaries of the same river. He moved again, trying to ease the band of hot pressure across his loins.

'You know the tales?' she said.

'My grandfather used to recite them to me. He was part Welsh, and I grew up on the Welsh borders surrounded by bards and story tellers.'

She pushed the drink back into his possession. Her colour remained high. 'My father was a Welshman,' she said in a gentler tone than she had used thus far. 'He came over with Duke Robert, took up with my mother after the siege of Antioch, and stayed. He died when I was eleven.' Abruptly she tossed back her hair and narrowed her eyes. The shield that had momentarily been lowered was back in place and jabbing at him. 'You're clever aren't you?'

'If I was clever,' Renard grimaced, 'I would not be about to place half a mark on this table.'

'You can afford it.' The contemptuous expression returned to her face as she perused his rich silk tunic and gilded dagger belt.

'I am not sure that I can,' he contradicted with a pained smile. 'I'd certainly never buy a horse this way.'

'You wouldn't take a horse to your bed.'

His lips twitched. 'I wouldn't take a knife-wielding virago either . . . not unless she promised to behave.'

She stared at him with wide, hostile eyes. They were a deep, ocean sapphire and he could have drowned in them.

'To behave,' he added softly, 'as befits the circumstances, *Olwen fy anghariad.*' And he watched her through his lashes to determine the effect that using Welsh would have on her. She reminded him of a lioness, was quite likely to maul him, and his blood was surging with a rough heat he had not experienced since the early days of discovering the pleasures of bed-sport.

'Don't call me that!' she said sharply. 'I am not your beloved!'

'Not even for one night of pretence?' Fishing out the coins he arranged them before her on the table, saw with a rueful glance Madam FitzUrse advancing on them, and wondered at his own folly.

'Changed your mind then?' she gloated, face adorned by a triumphant, fat-wobbled smile.

'Lost it more likely,' he retorted as she scooped up her share of the money and secreted it in her ample bodice.

A fight broke out across the room. Renard instinctively turned towards it. Shouts and flying fists, an overturned bench and splattered wine. A woman screaming. Madam FitzUrse hitched her bosom, gestured to two brawny serving men, employed for just such occasions, and waded in to separate and evict the culprits.

Renard grinned and looked back at the girl only to discover that both she and the money had disappeared. With an oath, he shot to his feet, and having cast a rapid eye around the room, shouldered a path through the other drinkers to the back entrance and out into the courtyard where chance had first shown her to him. It was silent and dark, apart from an unsteady drunk attempting to urinate in the gutter and splashing his boots instead. Cursing fluently, he swung round to search elsewhere ... and discovered that she was blocking his way.

'I went to fetch my robe and other things.' She held up a small tied bundle and tilting her head considered him. 'Did you think I had run with your money?'

Renard breathed out hard. 'It had crossed my mind.'

'It crossed mine too,' she half-smiled. 'I suppose you are familiar with the way to the rooms?' Husky scorn edged the question.

Renard held out his hand. 'Your knife,' he said.

Her eyes flashed rebellion and her jaw clenched. Faster than a pouncing cat, Renard caught her wrists and with his free hand sought out the weapon from its neatly stitched sheath within her robe. Half-sobbing, half-gasping, she writhed in his grasp. He dropped the knife, stood on the flat of the blade to keep it safe and dragged her hard against him, body to burning body, their faces bare inches apart.

'A knife is not part of the bargain,' he murmured into her breath, mouth hovering over hers. 'And neither for half a mark is a room in this place. I have a house; it isn't far.'

'Not without my dagger,' she mouthed back at him, and raised herself on tip-toe to stroke herself against him in a slow, enticing friction.

'No.'

The fraction of space closed between them and they duelled in the silent lightning of a kiss. She leaned in towards him, moving with her dancer's grace, a small whimper rising in her throat as he palmed the tip of her breast. She clutched him, parting her thighs as the caress moved downwards, rubbing herself upon his fingers; then suddenly, like a viper striking a lulled prey, she snatched his own dagger from his belt and thrust herself out of his embrace.

'Yes!' she panted triumphantly.

Breathing hard, assailed by anger, irritation and pure, hot lust, Renard fought for control and assessed his chances of disarming her. Probable but not certain, and if he gave in to his temper, he was lost. 'All right,' he said indifferently and stooped to retrieve her dagger from beneath his boot. 'We'll

15

exchange these as lovers' tokens in the morning shall we?' Tone dripping sarcasm, he put the weapon in his belt.

She studied him warily.

He held out his hand. 'Are you coming, or are you going to give me back my money?'

Despite the raucous noise from within The Scimitar, a silence hung around them, heavy as a cloak, almost smothering. The tension mounted, but just as Renard felt he must snap, his dagger disappeared within the voluminous folds of her robe and she stepped up to him again. Laying her palms upon his chest she looked up through her spiky black lashes. 'Well then,' she said throatily, 'will you not show me the way?'

The words were loaded with *double entendre* and spoken coyly like any other dancing girl's. His sense of humour returned, tempering the savagery of his lust.

'I don't know if I can,' he said as he led her into the street. 'We'll never get any further than the stable yard if we keep on fighting over who is going to be the rider and who is going to be the horse.'

Unexpectedly she laughed.

CHAPTER 2

IT WAS EARLY DAWN and the man beside her breathed evenly in sleep. Knees drawn up to her chin, hands laced in their bend, Olwen studied him thoughtfully.

His bones were too angular and strong for him to approach being handsome, but that very strength was arresting and indicative of the steel in his character. He was a challenge. The better men always were. First you brought them to their knees, then you drove the knife into their hearts and twisted.

The morning light gave his dark hair a reddish tint and his skin where it had not been exposed to the sun was Frankish-fair. The lashes lining his lids were a dense black, but his eyes when open were a dark flint-grey lit by vivid flecks of quartz. Superficially he looked as though he belonged to Outremer, but beneath the surface lay his heritage, which was also in part her own.

Her Welsh father and his brother had taken the Cross and sailed for the Holy Land with Duke Robert's Norman and English contingents. Following the capture of Antioch from the Moslems, they had remained in the city as members of the garrison. Her father had met and married a native Armenian Christian, and having begotten four daughters and a son in rapid succession, had died untimely of the bloody flux. The boy had died too, then two of the girls, and lastly Olwen's mother, weakened by exhaustion and a broken spirit.

It had been left to her feckless Uncle Gwylim to keep bread in their mouths and a roof over their heads, neither of which he could do for himself, let alone two orphaned girls of ten and eleven. Olwen had been forced to grow up fast. She had learned to survive by her wits and her knife, and she soon realised the power of her striking looks and how she could obtain

17

money from the men for whom she danced and lay down. Sometimes, like last night, Gwylim would seek her out, begging like one of the creatures at the city gates, his affliction that of the permanent obsessed drunkard. He had been thrown out of Prince Raymond's guard for his drinking. One day it would kill him.

She re-focused on the sleeping man. The scar of a recent wound puckered his smooth bicep. Her gaze travelled lower over the broad pectorals, lean ribs and hard, flat stomach; flickered briefly over the sheet-covered remainder and returned to his face, dwelling on his mouth while she remembered his kisses, the feel of them on her body, the dark hours spent in passion and the passion spent.

It had been surprisingly good for a business arrangement. He knew women's bodies, she thought, and caught her underlip in her teeth as she remembered with embarrassment the failing of her own professional expertise. That first time as he took her, a little rough with lust and several weeks of abstinence, she had been filled with scorn, judging him the same as every other man who had paid money to lie with her – nought but mannerless, greedy haste. Coldly unmoved she had clasped her legs around him and gasped and threshed like a fish in extremis, acting the role to its sordid conclusion. He had been too near the edge to do anything but mutter indistinctly into her shoulder as he drove into her one last time and shuddered, but afterwards, raising his head, he had looked down into her face and said, 'At least do me the courtesy of not pretending. I know the difference.'

And so he had. The heat extended to other parts of her body, weakening her limbs and dissolving them. She remembered the pleasure, the way he hung over her, the sweat trickling down his chest, gluing their bodies together; the alternating swift and slow rhythms. 'And all rivers run to the sea,' he had murmured. 'And all tides beat on a shore.' Ebb and flow, the sound of his voice speaking to her in the Welsh tongue.

Disturbed, she left the bed to find her clothes. She needed to be alone for a while, to settle her mind. As she was pulling her gown straight, he stirred and turned over, arm reaching

18

across the space that was still warm from her body. Olwen held her breath, not daring even to put on her shoes lest the slight sound should bring him fully aware. He sighed, clenched his hand and thrust it beneath the pillow, and settled back into sleep. She let out a relieved breath, picked up her shoes and easing out of the door into the cool morning air, went in search of something to quench her thirst and also a little information about the man in whose bed she had passed the night.

In the kitchens a woman was busy preparing food – leavened bread, goat's cheese and fruit. She was one of the soldiers' wives, a middle-aged Armenian and as ready to spill gossip as a ripe poppy was to scatter seeds. Manipulated by Olwen, she soon warmed to her enquiries.

By the time Olwen returned to Renard, bringing him a cup of watered wine, she had discovered that aside from having the royal Welsh blood of Hywel Dda in his veins, he was also the grandson of the recently deceased King of England and heir to an earldom.

He was awake when she entered the room, hands clasped behind his head, eyes on the first sun streaks dancing on the ceiling. A small lizard clung there, as vividly green as a carving in emerald.

'*Salaam*,' he said, diverting his attention. 'I did not know if you would stay.'

She handed him the wine and sat down on the bed. 'You still have my dagger, and besides, your bed was comfortable.'

He gave her a taut look over the cup. 'Comfortable?' he queried, a quick smile lighting his face as he perused her from crown to toe. 'That is not the word I had in mind. No, don't start bristling at me again, I did but tease.' He reached his free hand and lightly touched her cheek. 'Last night, my Olwen, will keep me warm for a long time to come.'

She raised her lashes. Without the cosmetics she had now washed off, they were a thick, dark gold, darker than the sun-bleached hair cloaking her shoulders but a match for the curly triangle between her thighs. The thought initiated a fresh surge of desire. He put the cup down and reached for her. She arched towards him. When he fumbled at her gown, she pushed his

19

hand impatiently aside, and dragged it off herself, then pulling him down on top of her, spread her thighs, and guided him desperately within her body.

Her total lack of inhibition both surprised and aroused him. Abandoning control, he gave himself up to the violent, driving pleasure, as brief but powerful as a storm wave crashing on a rock. Her nails scored his flesh and her cry of release was wild and high with triumph as she brought him with her, stranded to the shore.

'Christ Jesu!' Renard panted when he could speak. 'Are you trying to kill me!'

She raised heavy lids to reveal blue, pleasure-glazed eyes. A faint smile parted her lips. 'Didn't you like it?' she purred.

He gave a flesh-muffled laugh and lifted his head. 'It is what Ancelin would call "good honest futtering" — yes, I liked it, but I would not make it my daily diet.' He slid out of her and pillowed his head on his bent forearms. His breathing was still erratic but he had cooled enough now for consideration.

Something had changed since last night. Every wriggle and cry had been spontaneous, nowhere a lie. He knew women, took pleasure in giving them pleasure and was well aware that one night was not enough to effect the transformation he had just experienced.

'What would you make your daily diet?' she stretched luxuriously.

Renard half-smiled and ran an idle forefinger between her breasts, over the smooth curve of her belly and down to the curling mound of her cleft. 'Witch,' he said softly. 'I am not sure I want to give you the power of knowing.'

Beneath his searching grey stare, Olwen closed her eyes. Aloud, but half to herself she said, 'It is the first time I have stayed with any man until cock crow.' And moved her body away from the delicate, lazy play of his fingers.

'Is that what you told all the others?'

'I told them what they wished to hear.' She lifted a scornful shoulder. 'If they believed it, that was their folly.'

'And am I foolish too?'

'That depends on what you believe.' She retorted and opened

her eyes again. 'Madam FitzUrse asked me to seek you out. She said that you had been away all winter and she wanted to welcome you home in a fitting style.'

And charged me half a mark for the privilege!' he snorted.

'The more you pay the more it is worth.'

He shot her a dark glance and leaving the bed began to dress. 'Being as you have stayed beyond cock crow, you might as well break fast with me too,' he offered. 'After a night like last night I'm starving, and if you are not, you ought to be!'

'Ravenous,' she murmured, demurely lowering her lids.

His grin became outright laughter.

She tilted her head at him. 'Do you have a wife or a mistress?'

Renard hesitated, belt half-buckled. 'Why, are you angling to fill the position?'

Olwen shrugged indifferently. 'I hazard that others have angled many times before and had their bait refused. I was merely curious.'

He finished fastening the belt in silence. 'I have a betrothed,' he said at length, 'but it is a business arrangement. Pleasure is my own to organise.' And went out into the courtyard.

Picking up her rumpled gown she slowly put it back on, an absent expression in her eyes that spoke of deep thought.

They were in the midst of breaking bread when Johad led a tall, travel-stained stranger into the room and unobtrusively began arranging another place at the board.

'Adam!' Renard stepped over the trestle to heartily hug and clasp the older man. 'What in God's name are you doing here!' And the surprised delight at seeing his brother-by-marriage was suddenly overriden by anxiety. 'What's happened at home?'

Adam de Lacey returned the embrace with a similar enthusiasm before standing back. 'Nothing as yet,' he reassured. 'Have you got a drink? The stuff they served on that galley was straight out of the bilges!' His gaze flickered sideways.

Renard saw him look, saw the infinitesimal lift of the eyebrow and mouth corner, and clearing his throat made a brief introduction as Johad poured wine and retired to a discreet distance.

'Olwen?' queried Adam and gave her a quizzical smile. 'That's a name from home if ever I heard one.'

'My father was Welsh.' Olwen studied him as keenly as he did her and saw a man past youth but only just into his middle years. The lines on his face were, she judged, graven by weariness rather than time. Fanned by new creases caused by staring into a salty wind, his eyes were a light, amber-brown and disconcertingly shrewd as they took in the rumpled state of her silk gown and rested on a purplish-red blotch on her throat.

He bent his attention on Renard while he took several strong swallows of the wine and she saw him take note of Renard's casual apparel and several similar marks on neck and collarbone. 'Home comforts too,' he said drily.

'Some of them,' Renard qualified. 'How's Heulwen?'

'Very well, if a little annoyed at being made a widow for the better part of a year. She sends you her love and bids you not to do anything she would not.'

Renard laughed aloud.

Adam grinned, but quickly sobered. 'Miles is still at home with her because it isn't safe to send him anywhere to train, and I dare not considered betrothing either of the girls. I have had offers from both camps, Maud's and Stephen's. I suppose I ought to give one to each.' He broke a piece off one of the flat loaves and put it in his mouth. 'It is the still before the storm, Renard, and you're needed.'

'When did you set out?'

'January, from Anjou, with letters from Count Geoffrey to his father. Nothing too secret or treasonous, just greetings and news. My main purpose is to bring you home.'

'Letters for King Fulke? You've to travel down to Jerusalem too?'

Adam nodded and washed down the bread with a mouthful of wine. 'I'll probably sail down the coast. It's quicker and I want to be home by the autumn myself. A crusader's lands might be sacrosanct in theory, but it does not always work in practice.'

'My father . . . No, finish eating first, and bathe if you want.

22

There's a tub in the rooms across the courtyard.'

Adam gave him a single bright look and cut free a cluster of grapes from the mound in the centre of the table. 'It might be best,' he agreed. 'Eleanor sends you her love. There's one of her famous letters in my baggage.' He glanced at Olwen. 'She's become a very pretty young woman in your absence.'

'Has she?' Renard stared at the wall behind Adam's head. He had been forewarned by that piercing glance, by the very fact that Adam was here in Outremer. The smell of the goat cheese was suddenly so strong it was nauseating. He pushed his bowl aside, and standing up went to the doorway and looked out on the fountain. De Lorys, groggy-legged, was ducking his head in it and groaning. Renard clenched his fingers in his belt. Distantly he heard Adam murmur something to the girl. He leaned one shoulder against the gritty white wall and watched the sunlight pattern the tiles around the fountain. Now he knew why he had been thinking of the marches yesterday.

Fingers pressured his sleeve. Startled he looked round at Olwen. Already he had forgotten her. She was as unreal to him now as a fevered dream.

Olwen bit her lip. Having lived in the gutter, she knew how to street-fight with a knife in her hand and that when the advantage slipped, it was time to melt away and strike at a different, unexpected moment. Besides, she required time alone to think, to plan, and to control an appetite that was far stronger than she had ever suspected.

'It is best if I leave, my lord. You know where to find me if you have need. I am sorry if your news is not good.'

She saw him make the effort to concentrate, to bring his mind and eye back from the distance to focus on her. 'I am sorry too,' he said with a stretching of his lips – hardly a smile. She remembered their touch on her body, the words they had formed, and a small shudder rippled down her spine. 'Thank you for last night,' he added. 'It was a . . .' he hesitated, seeking the words. '. . . a memory to treasure on a cold winter's night.' He kissed her lightly on the mouth in farewell and dismissal.

Was, not *is*, she noted with a feeling of panic that did not show on her face. She had no intention of being shown a feast hall through an open door only to have that door slammed in her face. 'If you have need,' she repeated softly, and returning his kiss with a light brush of her lips on his cheek, left him.

He heard the rustle of her gown, caught the drifting scent of her perfume, attar of roses and something spicier, and then even that was gone. He went back inside.

Finished, Adam was leaning back from the crumb-spilled table, a cup cradled in his hands. 'Who was she?' he asked. 'Or am I treading on forbidden ground?'

Renard shrugged. 'A tavern dancer. It was my first night at home in Antioch after a round of duties for Prince Raymond.'

'Very attractive,' he said appreciatively.

'Yes.' Renard sat down in the place Olwen had been occupying and once more caught the haunting echo of her perfume. He moulded a piece of bread into a pellet, then broke it apart.

Adam studied his goblet for a moment then looked at Renard from beneath his brows. 'Your father will see another winter snow if he is fortunate, but not beyond.'

Renard stared at Adam and felt his body prickle all over like a frost-breathed surface.

'The damp got into his lungs last year. We had to ford the Dee in the spring spate and his horse put a foot wrong. He was wearing mail and the wonder of it was that he was still alive by the time Harry and I finally managed to drag him out. He took the lung fever and it was only by a miracle and your mother's skill that he survived at all, but there was some permanent damage. He can't take out the patrols like he used to. The first breath of cold or damp air and he starts coughing. Before I left at Christmastide he had begun to bring up blood.'

Renard swallowed. His own lungs stopped working. He struggled a breath.

'It was your father who sent me to fetch you,' Adam said gently. 'Before it is too late ... are you all right?' Anxiously he leaned across the trestle to touch Renard's shoulder.

'Struck by lightning,' Renard answered through stiff lips. 'What do you expect?' He shrugged off Adam's compassionate hand. 'Yes, I'm all right. What else? You might as well tell me

24

now as leave me to recover and then hit me again.'

Adam sighed heavily. 'Ranulf de Gernons is making a nuisance of himself and your father can't hold him any more. Harry's doing his best but ...' He grimaced. 'Well you know Harry. All brave heart and nothing but solid stone in the head.'

'What manner of nuisance?' Renard's tone was abrupt.

'He's nibbling at Caermoel. Claims that the castle stands on land belonging to him, not Ravenstow.'

Renard's eyes flashed. 'That's a lie!' he snarled. 'We have a charter from the time of the great survey to prove it, and reaffirmed by King Henry when he granted Papa the earldom!'

'I know that. There's no need to blaze at me!' Adam raised and lowered his hands in a calming gesture. 'It is the excuse that's important, not the truth. There have been a couple of nasty clashes between Chester's and Caermoel's patrols, and when your father has complained, it has fallen on deaf ears. De Gernons merely laughs and sticks up two fingers, and Stephen does not want to anger one of his most powerful tenants-in-chief over a fly-biting dispute so he just mutters platitudes into his beard and looks the other way.'

Renard said nothing. He put his hands down on the trestle and stared at a white scar on one of his knuckles, legacy of a skirmish with the Welsh when he was scarcely old enough to wield a war sword. The sun-brown skin would eventually fade like a dream, but the scar would remain with him for life.

'De Gernons has also been hinting to the King that a certain betrothal might be broken and placed more profitably elsewhere,' Adam said after a drawn-out silence. 'To his credit, Stephen has taken scant notice thus far, but he's apt to change his mind under persuasion.'

Renard felt a burden settle on him, heavy as a black cloak with a gilded border – the responsibility of a marcher earldom. 'So,' he murmured, 'Ravenstow still stands by Stephen then?'

'For the moment. Your father would rather have Stephen for King than the Empress for Queen, but it eats at his conscience that he swore to uphold her claim while her father was still alive.'

'Everyone swore, and under duress,' Renard grunted. 'What about you, where do you stand?'

Adam's lop-sided smile curled wearily across his face. 'Precariously on the fence, like your father. Were it practical, I would support Mathilda. Her son might only be seven, but the throne is his by right, not Stephen's. The pity is that she is not fit to be regent while he's growing up, and his father is too occupied with matters in Normandy and Anjou to be bothered with England. Also, as matters stand, I'm too close to Stephen's stronghold at Shrewsbury to risk renouncing my fealty. For the nonce I'm a crusader, beholden to neither, and that I find a relief.'

Renard made some swift mental calculations. 'It will take about a month to make ready,' he murmured. 'That should give you time enough to reach Jerusalem and return ... unless you plan to stay longer?'

'There is not the time.'

'No,' Renard agreed and saw that his hands, flat a moment ago, had clenched into fists. 'It will soon be winter, won't it?'

CHAPTER 3

HAND STEADY, OLWEN painstakingly applied a line of kohl beneath and within her lower eyelid, stepped back from the tiny sliver of polished steel to study the effect, and picking up a pot of red paste and a dainty camel-hair brush, started to paint her mouth. A loud, sodden snore stopped her in mid-stroke. She looked round at the couch and scowled at her Uncle Gwylim. Her sister had taken pity on him last night and given him drinking money and sleeping space – more fool her, the stupid slut. Gwener was never going to be anything more than a common soldier's whore; this tiny hovel in the wrong quarter of Antioch, a reflection of her capabilities.

Olwen returned to her preparations. Her sister brushed through the curtain that separated the house into two squalid rooms. She was wearing a gold filigreed bodice that Olwen recognised as her own, and new at that. Gwener had larger breasts and the seams were straining to contain her flesh. Yesterday Olwen might have made a cat-fighting issue of such blatant misappropriation. Tonight, the glimpse of another world in her eyes, she was merely filled with contempt. Bestowing her sister a single, cold look, Olwen returned to her toilet.

Gwener yawned and scratched the pads of surplus flesh quivering on her hip bones. 'Who is he?' She picked up the knife lying on Olwen's pallet and examined it – a man's and of a length useful to either eating or fighting. The grip was handsome but plain, of plaited silk, and the edge was smoothly sharp.

'That is my business.'

Gwener tossed her tangled hair. 'He wasn't there last night was he?' she gloated. 'I've never seen you come home in such a temper before.'

'And is it any wonder when I find you writhing on the floor with one of your greasy clients and yonder drunken sot lying across the door in a pool of vomit!' Olwen smacked down the pot of red paste so hard that it cracked in half. 'He wasn't there last night because he had company – some relative from England.'

'Ah, he's English then.'

Olwen tightened her lips and turned her back.

Gwener stretched like a fat, indolent cat. Her eyes were sleepy and feline, blue like Olwen's, but lacking their size and clarity. 'Nobility?' She fondled the knife in a suggestive, intimate fashion. 'What's he like between the sheets?'

Olwen snatched the weapon from her sister, and seizing a fistful of the straggling, oily hair, jerked back Gwener's head and let the blade glide against her jaw. 'Are you really so desperate to know?' she hissed.

Gwener screeched and struggled. Gwylim's snores ceased in a stertorous series of grunts and he sat up, blinking, disorientated like a day-wakened owl. 'Whassamatter?' he mumbled, knuckling his eyes.

Gwener's wild threshing caused the knife to slip. It was only a shallow cut, but there was quite a lot of blood and it splashed onto the filigreed bodice, ruining it. Gwener flapped like a half-wrung chicken. Gwylim staggered to his feet with some vague thought of separating the girls, tripped over the piss pot that no one had bothered to empty last night, and pitched headlong. A pungent, unpleasant smell filled the room.

An elderly, inquisitive neighbour poked her head around the door to see what all the noise was about.

'She tried to kill me!' Gwener howled, pointing a dramatic finger at Olwen. 'Look, she's still got the knife! I'm bleeding! Oh, God's love, someone help me!'

Olwen threw a rag at her sister. 'Staunch it yourself, you stupid bitch. I wish I'd cut your throat!'

Their neighbour started to jabber her own loud advice and condemnation. Other curious faces clustered the doorway, among them a water-seller's donkey. It brayed, the sound appropriate. Gwylim struggled to sit up, his clothes stinking fishily of stale urine.

Olwen stared round the squalor of the room where she had been born and raised, first in poor decency then in hand to mouth desperation. She detached herself from it like a knife stroke severing an umbilical cord, and stalked past Gwylim. He cowered from the dagger, but ignoring him, she took her best silk gown and another of good linen from her clothing pole and also the black wool robe that she wore when she went out at night to dance.

Gwener howled and dabbed at the nick on her jaw. The neighbour snatched a half loaf from the table and tucked it away inside her shawl. Olwen saw but made no comment. It was not her concern now, nor ever would be again. She had other battles to fight.

Without a backward glance or even a word of farewell, she went out of the door, and the onlookers made way for her like a crowd parting before a queen. She had that air about her as she took the first steps of a decision made two days ago in the bed of a man she had known for the space of one short night.

Stripped to the waist, Renard curried Gorvenal, a task he could have left to his groom, but the rhythmic motion of his arm working the comb over the glossy black hide and the rich, warm stallion smell were comforting.

Adam had left for Jerusalem and he had begun to make his own preparations for leaving Antioch. An Italian galley was riding in the harbour at St Simeon, bound for Brindisi once she had been refitted for the long sea voyage, and her master had been willing to take him, Adam and their retinues providing they could be ready within five weeks.

A chapter of his life was ending with the same scrambled haste in which it had begun. It was an interlude, already almost a dream. He put down the comb and wiped his brow on his forearm. Outside, the light was hot and somnolent. Gorvenal whickered and nudged him imperatively. Renard fondled the plush, white-snipped muzzle and smiled, knowing full well that the horse was snuffling around him for the dates he adored.

'It is a taste you will have to forget,' he told the stallion with a hint of wistfulness as he threw the embroidered saddle cloth over the glossy back.

Ancelin came into the stables in search of a halter he had earlier been mending. 'You're not going out in this heat, surely?' he asked in amazement.

Renard shrugged. 'I need the space,' he said. 'And I've a sort of pilgrimage to make.'

'Oh yes?' Ancelin grinned knowingly.

'Not that kind!'

'You'll fry your brains.' His shield-bearer shook his head and strode out again.

Renard finished saddling Gorvenal and picked his tunic off a pile of straw. It was made of the thinnest, finest white silk, stained now with the marks of the stable and earlier perspiration, but it was only an undergarment to the dark Arab robe that he donned on top of it to quench the sun's rays. For further protection, he wound a turban round his head in true eastern fashion.

When he rode out into the city, he looked more like an emir than a Norman lord, but that was the way of the Frankish east. Foreigners who stayed beyond the length of a pilgrimage were wise to adapt their ways to suit the climate. Those who did not, frequently died.

Following the line of the high city wall, Renard rode past St George's Gate and the Tower of the Two Sisters until he reached the lower slopes of Mount Silipus, its summit crowned by Antioch's vast citadel. His destination was the grotto of St Peter, a cave shrine frequented by pilgrims in droves, but quiet now and cool in the scorching mid-day heat. The priests there knew him and did not intrude as he dismounted, flipped a coin to one of the regular horse boys, and entered the dim, candle-lit cave.

Genuflecting to the altar, Renard knelt to pray. He had come to worship in this tiny chapel on the evening of his first arrival in Antioch, the stars like spangled embroidery on a royal gown, the citadel a crown thrusting to meet them. The grotto had been silent then too, steeped in ancient tranquillity and aglow with the pin-prick candles of a thousand hopes and prayers. Frequently he came here in the quiet times, drawing on that tranquillity as if it was cold water from a well in the desert.

Renard was not of a particularly pious nature but he had always found himself genuinely moved by this little mountainside chapel where St Peter and his disciples had met and prayed in persecuted secret and where the word 'Christian' had first been coined. It gave him a sense of continuity, breathed life into the dry words of sermons that usually sent him to sleep and brought him much closer to God than he was ever aware of feeling on other, more grandiose occasions.

He emerged from the grotto refreshed and filled with a sense of well-being and peace. The sun made him blink, but it was not quite as fierce as before and the light had mellowed from white to pale gold. He walked a little way down the slope to where Gorvenal was tethered in the shade, spoke briefly to the lad and, without mounting, led the stallion by a goat-track further up the mountainside.

Wild thyme, crushed by his boots, flavoured the air. A goat herd passed him, urging his small flock down the mountainside, and their pungent ammoniac smell and the dust they raised added evocatively to the scent of the herb.

Renard found a small, rock-shaded overhang. A lizard darted away into a crevice as he released the bridle to let Gorvenal crop on the scrubby grass. He unslung his waterskin from the pommel, took half a sun-warmed loaf and some grapes from his saddlebag, and sat down to eat, drink and contemplate the vast city spread out before him.

A warm wind gusted into his face, forcing him to half-close his eyes. Behind him Gorvenal champed and snorted. Renard looked at the document he had pulled from his saddlebag along with the food. After a moment's hesitation, he wiped his hands on his robe and reached for his knife to slit the seal. A curved Saracen dagger came to his grip instead. He swore on a smile. His body tingled, responding like an adolescent's to the mere stimulus of thought. Olwen, as golden as a lioness, Olwen tumbled beneath him or riding triumphantly aloft. The biting, scratching, melting surrender. Grinning, he shook his head, took several swallows from the waterskin, and decisively cut open the package containing Eleanor's letter.

Her handwriting was clear and precise and had developed a firm character of its own since the first childishly executed smudged offerings had arrived haphazardly to discomfort him during their four years apart. The content, however, was much the same. The usual domestic chatter. A travelling huckster had got one of the maids with child. One of the serfs had murdered his mother-in-law. The steward's wife at Ravenstow had produced twins – a rambling description of the infants. Renard skimmed over that part impatiently and spat a grape pip into the dust.

There were regrets and a genuine concern for his father's ill health. Eleanor, as he recalled, had a heart as soft as warm butter. He doubted from what he knew of her that a single calculating thought had ever entered her head, which, if this letter were any indication, appeared to be stuffed with feathers.

His youngest brother, William, had acquired a new horse, white with black spots like a duff pudding, speaking of which, Eleanor had discovered a wonderful recipe for preserving fruits. Renard flipped the parchment over and stared in growing dismay at the compact, efficient flow of trivia. Groaning softly, he cast his eyes rapidly over it, then stopped at the last third of the page. There was a description of a jousting contest she had attended and an interesting list of the lords who had been present.

'*Ranulf de Gernons was there. He did well and took more than one ransom, but then he has always been greedy. I do not like him. He looks at me the way a wolf might look at a sheep it wants to devour. De Gernons spent a lot of time with his brother William de Roumare. I do not much care for him either. Rumour has it that they want to unite their lands in one line from east to west. Your father says it is probably true and that it bodes ill for Caermoel and Woolcot, not to mention Ravenstow, as they lie in the path of their ambition.*

'*The wool clip was excellent this year. I have bought two new rams for the Woolcot herds...*'

Renard lifted his head and sighing, pinched the bridge of his nose. Ranulf de Gernons, Earl of Chester and lord of the world, given half a chance. Eleanor's lands lay on his borders as did the northernmost of his father's keeps, Caermoel.

Renard spread his hand, brought it down over his face, and looked at the view stretching away before him without really seeing it. If de Gernons took Caermoel, then he would be able to swallow Harry's small keep at Oxley in one swift gulp, and advance on Woolcot, then Ravenstow, the heart of his father's earldom.

'No,' Renard said softly to the hot, thyme-scented air. Gorvenal swung his head to regard him with large, liquid eyes. Renard abandoned Eleanor's letter, apart from noting that she had signed herself in loving obedience his wife, and lay back on the slope, head pillowed on his clasped hands to think – and fell asleep.

A group of pilgrims toiling up to the grotto woke him some hours later; that and Gorvenal snorting gustily into his face. The sunlight was more diffuse now, turning the Orontes into a river of molten gold. His face was tight, a little sore from having lain so long exposed. It was a newcomer's trick, inexcusable for one so long accustomed to the terrific heat of northern Syria.

He caught Gorvenal's bridle and rode back down into the city, returning to his villa by way of the high-walled garden entrance. The sunlight filtered through the leaves of the citrus trees and the first stirrings of an evening breeze rustled the cypresses and drifted the scent of lavender from the plants growing along the top of the wall.

Gorvenal went immediately to the stone fountain, dipped his muzzle and drank. Renard dismounted and did likewise, splashing the water in relief over his hot face. The horse pricked his ears and turned. Renard, face water-sluiced and blinded, was unaware of the danger until he felt the blade against his ribs. Body and breath both froze. Murder by stealth was a not uncommon way to die out here in Outremer.

The tip indented his skin but did not puncture it. He breathed out again and slowly lowered his hands.

'Fortunate for you that I am not one of the hashishin,' Olwen said scornfully as she lowered the weapon. 'You should guard yourself better. Here, this is yours.'

Renard took his dagger from her in silence.

Her lip curled. 'You have been lying out in the sun too.'

'I fell asleep.' He fumbled at his sheath for the blade currently occupying it.

Olwen sat down on the edge of the fountain, trailed one hand in the water, and with the other accepted back her own Turkish dagger, her eyes on him.

Recovering from the shock, he stared back at her and said coolly, 'That is the excuse dealt with. Are you going to tell me why else you are here?'

She shook back her blonde cascade of hair. 'Why do you think?'

He rested his hands on his belt. 'Because a quarter of a mark is an irresistible sum? Because there is something you want of me?'

Olwen smiled and began slowly unhooking the neck fastening of her gown. 'Or that you want of me, my lord?'

Renard opened his mouth to say that the thought had not occurred to him, that she was mistaken if she believed she could manipulate him, but the words went unspoken and his eyes drifted to the throat of her gown and travelled down the golden declivity between the swelling curve of her breasts. She rose and came to him, twining her arms around his neck and half-nipping, half-kissing his jaw and throat, seeking his lips, her body rubbing.

Renard ceased thinking at all.

It was release and oblivion, an indulgence of the senses that temporarily obliterated the mind, and he did not realise how much he had needed it until he surfaced from the exquisite sensations to become aware of the breeze playing over his sweat-coated muscles.

He propped himself up. 'How did you know before I knew myself?'

Olwen tilted him a smile. 'It is my profession to know, and I learn very quickly.'

Renard rolled over and sat up on the soft grass, a frown

34

between his eyes. 'A profession demands payment. What is your price this time?'

She bit her full, red mouth. 'It wasn't just for gain.'

Gorvenal lipped experimentally at a clump of rosemary and shook his mane irritably at the flies. Renard touched her face. 'I know it wasn't, *cariad*.' He looked at her sombrely. 'But I am not sure that it is something to be continued. It is too hot, too wild to be safe, and it will break one of us, I am sure of it.'

'But you are leaving soon are you not?' She sat up beside him and placed her lips against his throat. 'Where is the harm in a few weeks? You do not have to pay me. I need somewhere to sleep.'

'Surely you have money enough for a roof over your head.' He gave her a wary, disbelieving look.

Olwen pulled a face. 'Until today, I lived with my sister and my uncle – that drunk who accosted me in the courtyard of The Scimitar. I've quarrelled badly with both of them and I'm not going back. Yes, I could afford to rent a room, but I would rather stay with you.' Her lips moved persuasively. 'Please, my lord.'

Renard shifted slightly away and scraping his hands through his hair, tried to assemble his scattered wits. In little more than a month he would be on board a pilgrim ship bound for Brindisi. Surely there was no harm in playing with fire for so short a time. It would suit them both, giving her time to find new accommodation and him the relief and release from tension that just now he needed so strongly.

Standing up, he extended his hand to her. 'You can stay for tonight,' he temporised. 'After that, well, we'll see.' And knew that he was deceiving himself.

Olwen smiled at him meltingly.

CHAPTER 4

The Welsh Borders
Summer 1939

THE FIELDS OF THE DEMESNE were like an expanse of green-coloured sky clumped with creamy-white bleating clouds – the sheep that were, as the name of the main village suggested, Woolcot's main source of wealth. Gold upon the cloven hoof.

On top of the knoll, Eleanor drew rein and stared out over both land and sheep with a proprietorial eye. 'It will be a good clip this year,' she said to her companion. 'There were a lot of twin lambs too. I'm glad I bought that new ram.'

'You know almost as much as your bailiffs and shepherds, don't you?' laughed Heulwen de Lacey, Eleanor's future sister-in-law, a strikingly attractive woman with brilliant aquamarine eyes and flame-gold hair.

Eleanor returned the laughter. 'I suppose I do. Papa was always telling me how much the sheep were worth and now that he's gone it's like a sacred trust, an honour to his memory.' The curve of her lips became wistful, a little wry. 'Besides, they are the better part of my dowry, the main reason the arrangement was made. A castle to defend the land between Ravenstow and Caermoel, and the sheep to pay for its upkeep.' She plucked at a burr in Bramble's mane. 'I sometimes have the ridiculous daydream that Renard will want me for myself, or even worse that I will be as important to him as the very breath he draws, like your husband is about you. Stupid isn't it?'

Heulwen studied Eleanor. Her hair was loose today beneath the veil, held away from her face by two twined, slender plaits. It was jet black and slightly coarse in texture and framed winsome, elfin features dominated by hazel eyes that were the green-flecked gold of turning leaves. She was pretty but by no stretch of the imagination could she be termed beautiful, and Renard had always displayed a marked preference for fair-haired opulence in his dealings with women.

'Renard is fond of you,' she said awkwardly.

'Oh yes, I know that.' Eleanor turned her gaze from contemplation of her wealth to rest it measuringly on Heulwen. 'Before he left for the east with Prince Raymond, he gave me a red bridle hung with bells for my new pony, and ruffled my hair. He's fond of me the way he would be fond of a pet dog.' She shrugged. 'It could be much worse. I've never seen him whip a dog. Do you know what I gave him?'

Heulwen shook her head.

'A bracelet of my plaited hair woven with gold thread. I was daydreaming at the time.' She smiled bitterly. 'You should have seen his face!'

'Eleanor ...' Heulwen laid her hand on the girl's sleeve, unsure whether to comfort or reason.

'Oh, it's all right.' Eleanor tossed her head. 'I was still a child then. I didn't understand.' She wrinkled her dainty, tilted nose. 'Do you know, I could not think of anything to write to him when Adam took the Cross. I just set down the first things that came into my head – panicking on parchment, I suppose. He probably thinks that he is going to get a sheep for a wife as well as in payment of my marriage portion!'

'He will discover differently when he sees you,' Heulwen soothed. 'I should think that the situation being what it is, you'll be wed as soon as he sets foot in England.' Her eyes clouded. 'I only hope that Papa will be well enough to see you married.'

Eleanor shook the reins and started the mare down the slope. 'He has been very ill, hasn't he?' she murmured. 'Even with the coming of the warmer weather I notice that his cough has little improved.' She was very fond of Earl Guyon, had come to regard him as a father in the years since her own father's death, and was concerned by his recent poor health.

'He doesn't have the time or opportunity to rest it. No

sooner does Mama get him settled by the fire than someone wants him, or a problem arises, and even if he cannot ride out with the patrols he has to brief them and listen to their reports. It eats at him that he's so confined when before he lived such a vigorous life.'

'He is not the best of patients,' Eleanor agreed wryly, having helped at his sickbed during the crisis time immediately after his near drowning.

Side by side they rode towards the flocks and did not speak again, each troubled by heavy thoughts.

Eleanor was questioning a shepherd about an outbreak of sheep fly among the herd and absently fondling his good-natured dog when Heulwen murmured and pointed. Riders were splashing across the shallow ford of the river beyond the flocks and advancing purposefully towards them. Eleanor quickly gestured her groom to boost her back into the saddle, for she knew it was not one of her own Woolcot patrols.

Heulwen stared hard for a moment, then relaxed her grip on the reins as she recognised the red chevrons adorning the leading rider's shield. 'Rest easy,' she said. 'It's Harry.'

Eleanor gave a sigh of relief and kicking Bramble's flanks, cantered her through the herds to meet the approaching men.

Harry, one of Renard's brothers and four years the younger, slowed his destrier and brought him round. The shield by which Heulwen had recognised him was dinted and Eleanor saw that his horse was freshly cut about the chest and fore-quarters.

'Eleanor, greetings!' he saluted her in a light, boyish voice completely at odds with his stolid, powerful appearance. 'May we beg a night's hospitality at Woolcot?'

'Of course! You know you are welcome at any time. What in the name of all the saints have you been doing to yourself?'

He followed the direction of her worried gaze and screwed up his face. 'We skirmished with a band of Earl Ranulf's mercenaries. They were helping themselves to some cattle from the Caermoel herds.'

'What!'

'Oh, it's nothing new.' He removed his helm and used the

cuff of his gambeson to wipe sweat from his eyes. They were a round, innocent tawny-grey, quite unlike Renard's. His hair was straight and gingerish-brown and his moustache resembled a dead mouse. 'It saves de Gernons feeding them if they can steal their food from someone with whom he has a grudge.' He nodded a greeting to his half-sister as she rode up to join them, and flashed her a brief smile.

She had heard the tail-end of the conversation and asked, 'Did Chester's men escape then?'

The shoulders he shrugged were wide and square, his neck a squat extension. 'Unfortunately so. Doubled back on me. I'm no good on a trail. They had to leave the cows though. I thought I'd ride down this way and make sure your flocks weren't being molested.'

Eleanor shook her head. 'All's been peaceful here.'

Harry rested one square, strong hand on his thigh, guiding his stallion with the other. 'Renard has always been much better at this sort of thing than I am,' he shrugged, glancing wistfully at Eleanor. 'If he and I were dogs, I'd be short and pot-bellied, tripping over my ears while I followed a stale scent, and Renard would be hot and graceful on the trail like one of those long, lean Arabian hounds.'

'Harry, you shouldn't . . .'

'But it's true!' he protested.

'At least you come when whistled for,' Heulwen patted her brother's shoulder. 'No, that's not really fair,' she temporised. 'Renard was going to return home two years ago and Papa stopped him because he didn't want him used as a lever on his loyalty.'

'But now there is no choice,' Eleanor said as they paced back towards the comforting solidity of Woolcot's walls. Her young face tightened to reveal the fine bone structure beneath the adolescent roundness and the stubborn will that ran as a quiet, deep undercurrent to her gentle nature.

Harry watched her, but when she looked round at him, sensing his stare, he made himself busy with a loose stirrup iron and persuaded himself that the dull ache in his breast was merely the weariness of battle's aftermath.

CHAPTER 5

The Principality of Antioch

'I SAID I AM WITH CHILD,' Olwen repeated. 'And it is yours.' Renard carefully stoppered the bottle of oil and put down his sword and the rag with which he had been cleaning the blade. 'You can't be.'

Olwen set her hands on her hips and tossed her golden sheaf of hair. 'My flux is more than two weeks late. It is never late. I feel fat and sick.' She spoke with calm finality. 'I know.'

Renard swore softly and rising to his feet paced to the end of the room and stared at the crucifix nailed there. 'You can't be,' he said again.

Olwen glared at his turned back and contemplated thrusting a dagger between his shoulder blades. It went no further than the mind. You did not murder your promise of wealth and security. 'And I assure you that I am,' she said coldly. 'I suppose you are going to tell me that it never entered your skull when you took your pleasure that I might quicken?'

Renard swung round, his expression dangerous. 'I took *my* pleasure?' he demanded angrily. 'It was you who begged your way into my bed. Do not blame me for what was mutual! Did it never enter your skull either?'

Bright grey eyes hit blue, and the blue retreated, but in strategy, not defeat. Olwen heaved a sigh and said on a quieter note, 'Very well, I admit that the blame is at least half mine, but it changes nothing. What am I to do? Soon I shall be unable to dance, or take men into my body to slake their lust and earn my living.' She said it deliberately and felt a twinge of triumph as she saw him flinch. 'In two days' time you are leaving for ever. The last thing I need for a keepsake is a huge belly and no means of making my living. Will it disturb your conscience when you lie in your marriage bed with your new wife that I am begging in the gutters of Antioch? Will it prey on your soul when you look at your heir swaddled in fine linen and rocked in a carved cradle that somewhere else you have a child living on the edge of starvation?'

Renard seized her wrist and dragged her against him to silence her. His grip pressed the edges of her bangles painfully into her flesh. She did not fight him, but drew in close to his body instead, knowing that he was easier to handle thus.

'You use words like you use a knife too!' he said harshly.

She saw the anger in his eyes, felt the tension shuddering his body and was excited by it. It was delicious. Playing with fire, caressing it, shaping it to the dream you desired and knowing that if you made a mistake it would burn you to death. 'Renard, take me back to England with you,' she murmured, looking at him through her lashes and stroking him gently with the downward pressure of the heel of her free hand. 'I am carrying your child ... your son.'

Renard closed his eyes and swallowed, struggling for the control he no longer seemed to possess. Her skin and hair smelled like a lemon grove in the midday sun. He was aware of the expert persuasion of her fingers and the rapid response of his treacherous body. 'Olwen, I cannot. I'm not just going home to take an earldom on my shoulders, I'll be getting married as fast as the priest can utter the vows!'

'But it is a business arrangement, yes?' Her lips brushed against his throat.

'Yes.' He snatched her caressing hand away, aware that he was already ripe to bursting point. 'But that does not mean I'm not fond of Nell. I don't want to hurt her.'

'You'd rather throw me to the wolves instead?' Her tone dripped acid.

'I didn't say that. Oh Christ's wounds Olwen, I don't know. I can't think when you're this close to me. I lose all sense.' And to prove it, he took her face in his hands and kissed her deeply.

41

'You don't have to hurt your wife,' she tempted against his mouth. 'What she doesn't know ...'

'... She would soon find out,' Renard said wryly and retained enough sense to break away before it was too late. 'Women always do.' He gnawed his lip and looked at her. 'I could arrange to give you money now if you stayed in Antioch.'

'I don't want to stay here.' Her eyes flashed. 'Here, I am a dancing girl, a high-class whore. In England I can invent my own past — a crusader's widow, a wealthy pilgrim travelling with an armed group for safety. Why,' she added mockingly, 'you could even find me a rich husband if we both tell the right kind of lies.'

'I suppose I could,' he answered, tone parodying hers, and wondered how Eleanor would react to the existence of this predatory lioness of a woman in his life if he chose to keep her with him. He required leave to think without the disturbing closeness of her body tempting the weakness of his own.

'Besides, I want to see my father's homeland,' she added on a slightly less challenging note as she played him on her line.

'Renard, have you ... oh.' Adam de Lacey paused, and clearing his throat, made to go away again.

'No, it's all right. I wanted a word with you anyway.'

'Oh?' He gave Olwen a thoughtful, tawny look.

'We'll talk later about this,' Renard murmured to her. He kissed her again, this time with the lightness of dismissal, but she knew that no such lightness existed in his mind.

'It is very simple,' she said. 'If you leave me behind, you might as well put a dagger through my heart now and throw me in the Orontes.' And turning on her heel she stalked out.

Renard stared after her. Adam uttered a low whistle. 'Woman trouble?' he enquired, and picked up Renard's sword to scrutinise the oiled edges.

'She's with child,' Renard said starkly.

Adam sighted along the fuller with one eye closed. 'She knows it for certain?'

'So she claims.'

'Yours?'

Renard flashed him a startled glance. 'You think she's foisting a cuckoo on me?'

'I didn't say that.'

Renard drew and let out a hard breath but said nothing.

Adam put down the sword. 'No,' he said after a pause for consideration. 'I would say that more than likely it is yours, and more than likely it is deliberate. Women of her trade know how to avoid that kind of trouble. Even now there are potions she could drink if she so willed.'

'You're very knowledgeable for one who's lived so pure a life,' Renard said sarcastically.

Adam gave him a rueful, lop-sided smile. 'I am married to your sister and that makes up for whatever I missed in my youth.'

Renard snorted.

'Heulwen learned the herbal arts from your mother – all of them. Why do you think we only have Miles and the twins? And not because we frequently practise continence or Onan's sin. Mark me, that girl of yours knows all about the application of moss soaked in vinegar and beeswax plugs, else she would have fallen long before now.'

Renard stared at Adam as if he had never seen him before. 'Dear God,' he said softly.

'I agree a little prayer at the same time doesn't go amiss,' Adam said dryly. 'What are you going to do?'

Renard scraped his fingers through his hair and sighed. 'I wish I knew. I could leave her behind, but if I did my conscience would gall me like a hair shirt for the rest of my life. Whatever the manner of her scheming, I cannot throw her back onto the street and leave her to face the consequences.'

'You could buy her off.'

'She says that she wants to see her father's country, and that once in England she can make a new life.'

'As an acting mistress or as a brood mare to be pensioned off when she foals? You'll have too much on your trencher already without a sour serving of domestic war in your own household.'

'I know, I know!' Renard snapped and kicked bad-temperedly at a cracked floor tile. A chip flew off and skittered across the room. 'How is Eleanor likely to take to Olwen's presence?'

Adam rubbed his jaw. 'I don't know. She's a practical lass for all her soft heart. Probably she will accept Olwen and the babe with a reasonable grace providing you don't stick them directly under her nose or spend all your time in Olwen's bed ... but I only say probably. She has been trained by your mother who once took a knife to a courtesan who overstepped the bounds with your father.'

Renard laughed humourlessly. 'I doubt that Eleanor with a knife in her hand, or even my mother come to that, would be any match for Olwen. If I was wise, I'd bring her to England, make sure she was safely delivered, and then pay her to keep her distance. The problem is, Adam, I know I'm not capable of keeping mine.'

Outside, listening, Olwen pressed her head against the wall and smiled, her hand upon her belly which was as flat and taut as it had always been.

CHAPTER 6

The Welsh Marches
Autumn 1139

JUDITH, COUNTESS OF RAVENSTOW, genuflected to the small altar and stood up. Her knees were stiff from kneeling too long, although the discomfort began to ease as she moved slowly to the chapel door. She was fortunate and as yet did not suffer from the severe aches and pains of encroaching years unless the weather was unusually damp, and it had been a dry autumn thus far, praise God.

In the ward some women were dipping rush wands into a vat of warm tallow to make lights for the dark months ahead. Another group from the kitchens was organising itself with woven baskets to go out berrying on the common grazing. Judith listened to the chatter of the women and wished that she could share their high spirits. Berries were a late harvest gift, excellent preserved or stewed with apples and spices, or served tart with the roasts. They were also a reminder of how swiftly the year was advancing; how swiftly time was running out like grains of life sliding down the neck of an hourglass.

Two children came skipping across the ward towards her, a fat nurse puffing in pursuit. Judith regarded her twin seven-year-old granddaughters. Juditta, her namesake and the older by half an hour, was the taller of the two, with her mother's red-gold hair and her father's tawny eyes. Rhosyn was more daintily made with fine features drawn in shades of olive and brown.

'May we go berrying with Hilda and the others Grandmother?' Juditta pleaded breathlessly. 'We'll wear our oldest gowns, I promise.'

Judith considered the two upturned smiling faces and then

the beet-red countenance of their gasping nurse. She almost smiled herself, but succeeded in keeping her amusement unshown. 'Berrying?' she said. 'When I see you have been bedevilling poor Adela into a state of collapse?'

Juditta dropped her lids to the rumpled, dusty hem of her gown and shuffled her feet.

'Sorry Grandmother,' said Rhosyn, giving her a gappy, incorrigible grin.

'I said that they weren't to disturb you madam, that you were at your prayers,' Adela panted defensively and pressed her hand to the stitch in her side.

'But we saw you across the bailey so we knew you must have finished,' countered Rhosyn triumphantly and smiled up at her nurse before looking again at her grandmother. 'Please may we go?'

Judith stared at the kitchen women with their baskets. 'I suppose so,' she said after a long pause for deliberation. 'But don't wander away from the main party. Stay near Adela or Hilda and do not even think of going near the river!' She widened and flashed her eyes.

'Yes Grandmother!' they chorused in unison and whirled.

'Walk, don't run!' cried Judith, and bit her lip, torn between pain and laughter as she watched them cross the bailey to one of the towers, dragging their poor nurse along as though they were a couple of hound puppies on a leash. She could remember how it felt to be scolded for running when she should have walked, could remember sneaking off to the stables or hiding in the guardroom where she had cozened de Bec, the constable, into teaching her how to use a dagger. So near and yet so far away. It was the same riverbed but different water. She was in her fifty-sixth year and Guyon would be sixty-nine in the spring. Only sometimes spring did not come.

The girls returned with Adela and joined the berriers. Their laughter was as clear and careless as the light chime of bridle bells. Rhosyn waved to her as they walked towards the outer bailey. Judith smiled and waved in reply and followed them at a slower pace until she reached the plesaunce.

Guyon was there, sitting on his favourite turf seat beside the rose hedge and playing tables with the girls' older brother, Miles. The boy heard her first with the quick ears of the young. He was almost eleven now, his voice starting to deepen, although it would be some time yet before it broke. He gave her Adam's slightly tilted smile and a look from beneath his brows.

Judith sat down on the turf seat next to her husband. 'Who's winning?'

'Grandpa, he always does,' Miles said without rancour.

A dark V of geese skeined the clear sky. Judith followed their flight with narrowed eyes until they were almost out of sight, then looked at Guyon, only to discover that he was already looking at her.

'Bearing south.' His voice was husky, a legacy of his near-drowning last year. 'It will be a difficult winter.'

'Your throw, Grandpa,' said Miles.

Judith looked away over the late summer bursts of colour lingering in the herb beds. Marigold, chamomile, yellow hawkweed and purple devil's bit.

Guyon threw the dice, studied the board and made his move. Then he looked at his wife. 'Stop fretting,' he said softly. 'Renard will come.' He closed his hand over hers and squeezed.

She sighed ruefully. They knew each other too well to be able to hide anything for long, or even to want to hide anything. 'Yes I know. It just seems an age since his last letter reached us from Brindisi, and it is such a long and dangerous road.'

'No more dangerous than England,' Guyon said bleakly.

Judith watched his mouth tighten and set. He had put on flesh during the dry, hot summer, but she knew that as soon as the damp weather returned, the harsh, racking cough would burn it away within weeks, stripping him down to the bone. Every time he even cleared his throat she was afraid. She had brewed up horehound and feverfew syrup, had all the ingredients for hot poultices and plasters ready. Sometimes they eased the worst of the symptoms, but they did nothing to cure them.

'I wish my father hadn't had such a passion for eel stew!' she cried with sudden vehemence.

Guyon looked at her and laughed, then coughed.

'Eel stew?' Miles pulled a disgusted face. 'I hate it. So does Papa.'

'And so do I,' said Judith, thinking of the dish that had sent King Henry untimely to his grave, and probably Guyon too. If only they had been given a few more years of his iron-handed rule while his young grandson and namesake grew to maturity, then there would have been none of this wrangling over a crown that neither Stephen nor Mathilda were fit to wear.

Guyon coughed again. She was desperate to leap to her feet and run to fetch her medicines. Past knowledge prevented her from any such mistake. If he thought she was fussing he would baulk, and probably out of sheer pig-headedness would push himself to prove her wrong and make himself very sick indeed. She had learned to be either extremely circumspect or teasing about it these days, never maternal. Even so, she could not bear to sit still on a knife edge waiting for the next cough.

'I must go and write to your mother and Eleanor,' she said to Miles, and with that excuse, rose to summon a maid, but in the event, it was the shrieking, excited maid who summoned her.

On the common grazing Rhosyn sat down on the bleached prickly grass and sucked at a blackberry thorn that was embedded in one of her purple-stained fingers. Her mouth was purple too, and her gown, fortunately an old homespun. She had dragged its encumbering length through her belt like the other women, her undergown too, and her legs were bare to mid-calf. If Adela saw, Rhosyn knew that she would be in trouble, but the nurse had twisted her ankle on a half-buried stone and was sitting guard over two full baskets of the fruit on the low bridge over the brook that further down fed into the Dee.

Juditta yelped as a nettle pricked her tender, exposed skin and then swore an oath she had once overheard her father use to one of the grooms.

'You're not allowed to say that,' Rhosyn stuck her nose sententiously aloft.

Juditta scowled. 'I can say what I like.'

'I'll tell Grandmother.'

'You're always telling tales. She won't listen.'

'I didn't tell when you ...'

'What's the matter, my young mistresses?'

Both girls turned and stared guiltily up at Hilda, the senior kitchen maid. She was neck-craningly tall to a child's eye, as broad in the beam as a merchant galley, gave respect where respect was due, but was not in the least intimidated by differences of rank. Juditta and Rhosyn had watched her knead dough at the huge, scrubbed trestle near the bread oven and knew the power in the fleshy pink forearms and thick hands.

'I've got a thorn in my finger,' said Rhosyn, drooping her lip and fishing for sympathy.

'Look how many berries I've picked.' Juditta quickly held up her basket, determined that her sister was not going to get all the attention. 'And a nettle stung me.'

'Rub it with a dock leaf, over there, look, and then pull your gown down a bit; that way it won't happen so easy.' Hilda tucked a stray wisp of greying hair back into her wimple and stooped rather breathlessly to examine Rhosyn's finger. ''Tis not in deep. Belike your grandmother will be able to get it out and put some salve on it when we go back.'

Juditta discarded the screwed-up dock leaf, a juicy green stain on her rubbed leg, and stared towards the floury main road. 'Hilda, look!' she cried. 'Horsemen!'

Hilda followed the child's pointing finger to the distant but swiftly approaching riders. 'They're none of ours,' she muttered with alarm, and grasping Rhosyn's arm, hauled her to her feet. 'Go on, child, get you back to Ravenstow as fast as your legs will carry you. Mistress Juditta, go with your sister now!'

Juditta ignored the woman and shaded her eyes against the hot, golden beat of the sun.

'Mistress Juditta!' Hilda wallowed towards her like a sow in pursuit of a wandering piglet.

'It's all right.' Juditta wriggled away from the woman's restraining hands. 'It's Papa! It's his shield and he's riding Lyard. I'd recognise him anywhere!' And as if her skirts were not already raised to an indecent level, she drew them higher still and began running towards the party.

Hilda screeched after her but to no avail. She lumbered round to detain Rhosyn, but heels flashing like those of a startled rabbit, she too evaded the maid and headed at a direct run for the horsemen.

Renard reined down as he saw the girls approaching. For a moment he thought that they were serfs' children but quickly dismissed the notion. Serfs' children would not run yelling at a strange troop of riders. To the contrary, they would run yelling in the opposite direction and warn everyone else.

Adam pulled Lyard round. 'The hoydens!' he growled with a mingling of anger and amusement.

'Surely not ... They can't be!' Renard's eyes rounded with disbelief. 'Juditta and Rhosyn?'

'I'm afraid so,' Adam said ruefully, and taking Lyard out of the company, cantered the last twenty yards to reach his nearest daughter before she could reach him amidst a press of iron-shod jittery horse-flesh.

'Papa!' she cried, and held out her arms for him to lean and sweep her up onto his saddle. Her arms half-choked him. She smacked kisses on his cheek and the corner of his mouth and wriggled herself delightfully secure by which time Rhosyn had arrived at her father's stirrup and was clamouring to be lifted up. Adam thought that it was fortunate Lyard was no longer young and full of nervous fire or they would probably all have been thrown. He found he could not bring himself to scold them.

'Mama's not here,' Juditta said. 'She's gone to visit Eleanor up at Woolcot, but she'll be back before Michaelmas.'

'Will she?' Adam felt a small twinge of disappointment but did not let it show on his face. It was only selfish and Woolcot was but a day's ride away, not half the world as Jerusalem had been.

'I don't like your beard.'

'Don't you, puss? It was easier to grow than to shave off while we were travelling. Your Uncle Renard's got one too.'

'Uncle Renard?' Rhosyn, seated behind her father, arms

50

squeezing his waist, looked at the riders he had left to meet them. A man was staring across at them. His smile was very white against a skin that was almost as brown as her homespun gown, and bracketed by a full, beech-red beard. 'Is that him?' she pointed.

'Don't you remember? No, I suppose you'd both be too small.' Adam wheeled the sorrel and trotted him back to the line.

'Who is the lady?' whispered Juditta.

'Her name's Olwen. She's travelling with us,' Adam said, telling the literal truth. Time enough for revelations later. 'Rhosyn, it's rude to stare.'

'But she's very pretty, Papa. I wish I had hair like that.'

'But then you wouldn't be mine. Here Renard, what do you think of these two hussies?'

'I think they have more than doubled in size.' Renard laughed and tweaked one of Rhosyn's black braids.

'Grandpa does that to me too,' Rhosyn said and gave him an extremely suspicious brown stare.

'Does he now?'

'You don't look much like him.'

'It's probably the beard,' he said equably and turned to the other child who was not watching him but Olwen with the kind of fixed fascination only to be found in young children who had yet to learn the artifice of manners. 'As I remember, you're Juditta?'

Her eyes came back to him, Adam's eyes but differently tinted by the reflection of copper hair, brows and lashes. 'Yes.' Her small, round chin came up. 'I'm the eldest.'

'So,' sniffed Rhosyn from behind the safety of her father's bulk. 'You'll get wrinkles sooner than me!'

Renard grinned. 'Not for the sake of half an hour,' he chuckled.

Adam tightened his grip on Juditta as she drew breath to do battle. 'Is this how you have been taught to behave? Will you shame yourselves and me before family and visitors?'

Both girls fell silent beneath the tone of his voice. 'Sorry, Papa,' murmured Juditta, lowering her lashes to purple-stained fingers. Rhosyn laid her cheek against his back and gave him a squeeze.

Adam was always amazed at how different in character his daughters were. Juditta when reprimanded would apologise and either conform or disappear to sulk in private. Rhosyn was all woman, flirting and coy, cozening forgiveness by manipulation. It was impossible to come down on her with a heavy hand when she smiled and hugged him.

'Come,' he said with a rueful look at Renard. 'We'll ride on to Ravenstow and let them know Renard's on his way, shall we?' He slapped the reins against Lyard's neck.

Renard shook his head and laughed into his beard. 'They wrap him round their little fingers,' he said to Olwen.

'Women are born with their weapons already honed, otherwise they would be defenceless,' she replied with a look from the corner of her eye.

Some of the humour left Renard's expression. 'You were certainly born with an abundance!' he said softly, his voice like a blade gliding stealthily from its sheath.

'The gift matches the need,' she retorted. 'Are those the Welsh hills over there?'

He looked, narrowing his eyes against the sun. 'Yes. That line of trees marks the border dyke. Where was your father from?'

'Near Ruthin.'

'That's north of here. Closer to Caermoel than Ledworth and Ravenstow.'

They rode on in silence. Olwen gnawed her lip and looked at her lover's broad, hauberk–clad shoulders. Their relationship was as volatile as a barrel of hot pitch and occasionally she had the disquieting feeling that the passions invoked were beyond all control. Had they all been on Renard's part, it would not have mattered, it was her own responses that troubled her.

On the road from Brindisi when her flux had come at the appointed moment, she had feigned a miscarriage. As it happened, she had indeed been mildly ill at the time with a stomach upset from eating tainted meat. The results had been convincing, particularly as she had been overtaken by a storm of grief, as if the child had been real and not a figment of her imagination. Certainly Renard had believed her dramatics, had been so gentle and tender with her that she had wanted to lash out at him from the depth of her guilt. That release had not been feasible. She wanted to keep him, not drive him away. Her anger had turned inwards against herself, but every now and then some of it would surface and she would be unable to keep from deliberately baiting him.

When they reached the keep defences, the people were out in force to greet them. Serving maids, scullions, soldiers, hound-keepers, the blacksmith and his apprentice, the falconer, knights, squires and serjeants, all pressed forwards, cheering. There was a lanky boy in a fine linen tunic who strongly resembled Adam de Lacey. There was also a young woman with fat, honey-coloured braids, a toddler balanced on one hip, another child ballooning beneath her homespun skirts. Renard leaned over the saddle to speak to her and her colour rose.

Olwen narrowed her eyes and as it came to her turn to pass the woman, she changed her grip on the reins, jibbing her mount sideways, forcing her to dart back out of the way. The woman gasped, and as she met Olwen's eyes her pretty colour faded. Olwen rode on. A former mistress she surmised, and busy in his absence if the child and advanced pregnancy were any indication.

The bailey was thick with people jostling and clamouring, cries of delight and welcome on their lips. Renard felt the euphoria sing through his blood. His eyes filled. He blinked rapidly and slid from Gorvenal's back. Three grooms argued over who was going to tend the stallion, but before Renard could open his mouth, were reprimanded by his mother's authoritarian voice; and then she was facing him.

'Jesu!' she said, looking him up and down. 'Adam has brought me home a Saracen!'

'It's a good disguise, isn't it?' he replied with a lightness of tone that was contradicted by the look on his face. 'Sometimes I even forget that there's a man living behind the mask.'

And then they were in each other's arms, hugging hard, kissing and weeping with a mingling of joy and sadness.

Judith, practical as ever, sniffed, and wiping her eyes took a step away to study the whole of his long, lean form. 'Is a beard part of the mask too?' she asked.

Renard fingered the luxuriant growth on his jaw. 'It was more convenient to let it grow while we were on the road. If you promise not to cut my throat, I'll let you barber it off.'

'I'll do my best.' Her laugh was shaky. 'But my eyesight is not as good as it was!'

'Rubbish!' said Guyon from behind her. 'It's still sharp enough to pluck a needle from a haystack!'

Renard looked at his father. He had expected to set his eyes upon a walking skeleton or a hunched, incapacitated bundle of pain. Guyon was neither. Thinner, yes. There were marked hollows under his cheekbones and his eyes were more set back in their sockets and pouched with wrinkles, but if so they were still a glowing brown and there was not a great deal more grey in his hair for the sake of four years.

Renard wondered briefly if Adam had been wrong and merely panicking, but as he and his father embraced, Renard felt against his palm the roughness of the older man's breathing and heard a faint, whistling wheeziness that would only need an injudicious sprint across the bailey or to be caught out in a downpour while hunting to turn it into a severe congestion.

'You made good time,' Guyon said as they parted. 'We did not expect to see you for another month at least.'

'The summons was urgent. I came as fast as I could, and the good weather has been a blessing.' He turned with his father to face the keep.

'Yes, it has,' Guyon said softly.

Judith had not turned with her husband and son but was regarding the young woman who had dismounted unaided from a brown mare and was staring at Renard's back with an almost hostile expression in her deep blue eyes. Blonde hair tumbled over her shoulders and breasts, loose as a maiden's or a virgin's, although Judith knew that she was neither. Adam had very briefly told her that Renard had a female travelling companion. His brows and expressive mouth had said far more than his few words, but now Judith was wondering how to deal with the situation.

Renard's associations with women before he left for Outremer had always been passingly casual. The nearest he had ever come to forming a permanent bond was with Roslind, the falconer's daughter who had borne him a little girl. The infant had died in the epidemic of spotted fever the summer before he left. Since then Roslind had married the farrier's journeyman and settled well to the yoke. Renard, it seemed, had moved on to more exotic fare, and if he had brought her all the way from Antioch, then it was more than just casual.

'Renard's absence has certainly not taught him any manners,' she said to the girl in a carrying voice. 'It seems that we must introduce ourselves.'

Belatedly, Renard whirled round. Both women were watching him expectantly, and his face grew ruddy beneath his tan. He cleared his throat. 'Mama, this is Olwen. She has travelled with us from Antioch. Her father was a Ruthin man who took the Cross with Duke Robert and settled out there ...' He hesitated.

'... And I am your mistress, aren't I?' Olwen added in her sweetest, rolling purr, then looked at him with mock anxiety. 'That was what you were going to say?'

Renard gave her a furious look. His lips moved in the silent mouthing of a word that was far from affectionate.

Beside him, Guyon was aware of his wife's rigidity. Between Renard and the girl, the tension was so powerful that it threatened to ignite the air. Quickly he stepped into the space where flame would fall.

'Come within and be made welcome,' he said formally to Olwen, giving her the kiss of greeting and peace and flickering a brief, eloquent look at his son. 'Time later for all else. Today is a day for celebration.'

CHAPTER 7

I T WAS VERY EARLY, not quite dawn when Judith discovered Renard seated at the huge chopping trestle in the keep kitchens. There was a beaker of milk at his right hand and he was eating a slab of rye bread topped by a thick slice of cold salt beef.

'I see time has not moderated your appetite,' she said tartly as she fetched a cup and sat down beside him. 'You ought to be as fat as a bacon pig!'

Renard stretched his legs and leaning back, raised his shirt to show her his flat, muscle-banded stomach. He smacked his palm on it. 'I challenge you to find an ounce of spare flesh!' he said indignantly. 'We've been on pilgrim rations for four months and travelling so hard that we've hardly had time to eat them!' Lowering the garment, he returned with gusto to demolishing his bread and meat.

Judith poured milk from the pitcher. 'Your companion weathered the journey well to say that she miscarried your child on the way.' Her tone was barbed with the disapproval that had been evident ever since the rudiments of Olwen's story had been relayed at table the previous evening.

Renard's mouth was too full to make answering mannerly and it gave him the time to raise his defences and prepare to do battle. He had known this was coming ever since last night, but there were things that could be said in public and other things that were best left to the fire-lit darkness of an early kitchen where the only ears to overhear were English and would not follow the rapid Norman French.

'Do you love her?'

Renard sighed. 'I do not know,' he said when his mouth was empty. 'When we are together it is like being in the heart of a thunderstorm. We strike sparks off each other all the time.'

An aroma of fresh bread filled the kitchen as one of the cook's apprentices paddled a batch of loaves out of an oven. Over at the stone sink a scullion clattered utensils together and whistled loudly. Judith watched the work go forward, noting its alacrity, doubtless the result of her presence. 'Tell me about her,' she said.

Renard swished crumbs off the table with the side of his hand.

'There is not much to tell. She's a tavern dancer from the hovels of Antioch. Her father was Welsh, her mother native. She uses a dagger better than most men and her body better than any woman I have known before.'

'And you have full experience of that,' Judith snapped.

'Mama, I'm not a monk, nor of a monk's temperament,' he said with a hint of irritation. 'Done is done, and a lecture is not going to unwind any of this coil, or cause me to change my nature.'

A dairymaid clattered in with another pail of milk and was followed by an older woman swinging two necked chickens by their feet.

'I'm sorry.' Judith leaned her hands on her forehead. 'My temper is very short these days. Your father was coughing badly in the night and I haven't slept much.'

'Neither have I,' Renard said, suddenly contrite. 'My mind has been turning like a butter churn.' He made a wry gesture. 'That's more than half the reason why I need Olwen. It's impossible to think of anything else when I'm ...' He made an eloquent shrug serve for the rest.

'You must decide what you are going to do with her.' Judith's tone, weary at the edges, held a note of urgency. 'You have seen how it is with your father. I know that we haven't had opportunity for a full discussion yet, but you must know from Adam what de Gernons is saying and doing. Your marriage has to come soon before true winter sets in.'

Before there is no time for weddings or celebrations ... he thought ruefully. It hung between them, a black, cavernous certainty.

'Yes I know. Don't worry. I won't bring Olwen to my wedding.'

'But neither will you put her aside?'

Renard contemplated his cup, picked it up and in several strong swallows drained the milk. Then he looked at his mother. 'I think not,' he said with finality. 'And if you had seen Eleanor's last letter to me you would understand why. Oh, I daresay she will make a superb chatelaine and mother, everything that I know Olwen will not, but I doubt she will ever be capable of firing my blood to scalding point, and sometimes I need that kind of release.' He pushed himself to his feet. 'I'd better arm up if I'm taking out the patrol.'

Judith stared up at him, young and lithe and in the half light, the beard shaved off, suddenly looking so much like Guyon as she had first known him that it almost broke her heart. 'Renard, have a care.' Her voice quivered.

'On the patrol, or in my dealings with women?' he enquired lightly, but she could sense the checked irritation.

'Both,' she rallied on a snap. 'And you can count me among the women.'

The light in the west brightened to a rosy gold as Renard took the household knights and serjeants out of the keep and on a wide-sweeping patrol of the demesne. The breeze was cold, but not unpleasant, and blew away the last vestiges of sleep from Renard's brain. He began to enjoy the feel of the powerful horse beneath him, the slide of leather through his fingers, the musical sounds of armour and harness, and the rough jesting of the men in the early air.

He moved up the border to visit two fortified manors, beholden to Ravenstow. Thomas d'Alberin at Farnden complained that the Welsh had been raiding.

'Nay, not Rhodri ap Tewdr,' he responded to Renard's sharp query. 'We haven't had any trouble that way for ten years now, not since the agreement of Milnham.' He folded his hands upon his belt-supported paunch.

'Welsh levies from further north then?' Renard finished the cup of wine he had been served by d'Alberin's equally plump wife, leaving the sludge of lees in the bottom. Returning it to her with a preoccupied smile of thanks he gathered up the reins. Their son, christened Guyon in honour of their overlord, was a doughy boy of nine or ten who did no justice to his namesake as he leaned against a wain in the yard, mouth full of honey tart.

Renard considered Sir Thomas. 'When do your forty days' service fall due? Remind me.'

'Between Candlemas and Easter, my lord. I usually do garrison duty at Ravenstow.'

'Hmmm.' Renard eyed the man's paunch. 'If the Welsh are slipping through you had better tighten your vigilance. My own patrols will visit regularly.'

Sir Thomas was not unaware of the pointed quality of Renard's stare and drew himself up, inhaling to make the damage look less than it was.

'Send to Ravenstow immediately at the first sign of trouble.' Renard shook the reins.

'It is a pleasure to have you home, my lord!' The words ended in a gasp as d'Alberin was forced to breathe out and let his spare flesh wobble and settle on his belt again.

Renard glanced sharply, but the man's face, apart from being slightly pink with effort was as plain and honest as a lump of cold pease-pudding. Probably the soft fool meant it, and Renard did not know whether to thank him or laugh in his face and disillusion him. In the end he did neither, just nodded briskly and clicked Gorvenal to a trot.

Renard spent the rest of the morning garnering information about the extent of the Welsh raiding, inspected a couple of barns that had been plundered and set on fire, and rode thoughtfully up the border to eat and rest the horses for an hour at Adam's mainholding of Thorneyford before returning through the safer heart of the earldom to Ravenstow.

The sun in the mid-afternoon was hot and the perspiration began to trickle delicately down Renard's spine. It was a different kind of heat to Antioch, he thought. Out there the sun parched a man to the consistency of boiled, hardened leather. Here it melted him in a puddle of his own sweat.

In the fields gleaners were out among the stubble as they picked their way across the barbered golden strips. Beyond the fields the land rose slightly and ran into a small belt of oak and beech forest that was gradually being eaten inwards by assarts as the population of Hawkfield expanded. A new area of ploughland was being cleared even as Renard and the men rode into the trees, a young peasant swinging his axe at one of the sturdy trunks. Seeing the horsemen, he paused to watch them approach and pushed the hair off his soaked brow. An older man, working beside him, groaned and pressed his hands into the aching small of his back before tugging his wispy forelock to the soldiers.

Renard dismounted to talk. The knights gave each other long-suffering looks, and fidgeted, gently stewing in the cauldrons of their armour.

The younger man tentatively offered Renard a stone cider jug and a slightly grubby hunk of maslin loaf. Renard declined the latter, but drank thirstily from the jug. The cider was coarse, almost as rough on the throat as usquebaugh. Coughing, he passed a remark in English that caused the two peasants to grin and watch with approval as he took another long swig.

He enquired pleasantly about the assart. His English was accented, a little rusty from four years at the back of his mind, but he spoke it well enough to be understood and in turn to understand what the two men replied. One particular remark made by the older man caused Renard to lift his brows and stare thoughtfully into the sun-flickered gold and green autumn forest beyond, a half-smile on his lips.

Within ten minutes he had earned their respect. Within twenty, they were eating out of his hand. His escort once more exchanged glances, revealing mingled reactions of admiration, rueful pride, and genuine alarm.

'My lord, is it wise to rub shoulders with the serfs?' asked one of the men when once more they were riding through the trees. 'Will they not get ideas above their position?'

Renard shifted his shield as its pressure began to chafe a sore spot between his shoulder blades. 'I know what I'm about,' he said with quiet confidence. 'You cannot buy loyalty either with coin or with fear. It is like mastering a horse,' he grinned, 'or a woman – gentle but firm, and applying the pressure in the right place at the right time.'

The knight laughed, eyebrows dancing, and Renard, with little effort, bound yet another disciple to him in loyalty and thought of the woman he had not yet mastered, and was not sure that he ever would.

'Lord Renard!' Ancelin's voice was terse with sudden warning.

It was not just his shield-bearer's tone that caused the hairs to prickle erect on Renard's spine. He shifted his shield again, rapidly bringing it down onto his left forearm, and started to draw his sword. Then he stopped with the weapon half out of its sheath. His mind flew while his body grew roots. He could feel the tension in his men, was aware of someone behind him, audibly swallowing into a deadly silence. Amid the tumbling, turning leaves the light angled off arrow and spear tips and eyes dark as berries, watching them from behind the concealing foliage.

Renard's breathing, which was as light and shallow as an untimely grave, suddenly deepened. His chest expanded. He slammed the sword back into its sheath, and setting his hands to his helm, struggled it off.

'William!' he roared. 'Come out now, or I swear to God I'll thrash you to within an inch of your miserable life!'

There was a long pause. The swallower swallowed again. A horse shook its head and harness jingled. From behind the cover of a smooth-trunked silver birch, and looking like some spirit of the woods, a young man stepped out. He was a little above average height and as rangy and lissome as a colt. His clothes were made of linen and buck skin, coloured the buffs and golds of the autumn woods, and an elm bow dangled negligently from his fingers.

'*Croeso*,' he said on a flourish and a bow. When he stood erect again there was a smile on his lips and dancing in his brilliant green-blue eyes. 'You rode straight into our trap.'

Four other grinning young men emerged from the trees and lounged, their bodies brimming with arrogance, their eyes slightly uncertain as they flickered between their leader and Renard.

Renard's mouth tightened, but his irritation was mostly self-directed. After a moment he controlled it and vaulted down from Gorvenal to close the ten strides between himself and his youngest brother and embrace him heartily.

'Scare me like that again and I'll break that bow of yours over my knee and collar you with it!' he promised, shaking the youth.

'I couldn't resist it!' his brother laughed, punching himself out of Renard's grip. 'Pwyll saw you sitting with those two cottars while he was getting a stone out of his horse's hoof and came to warn the rest of us!' He looked curious. 'How did you know it was me?'

It was Renard's turn to grin. 'The old man mentioned that he had seen you pass through earlier and if there had been anyone more dangerous waiting to ambush us in these woods the alarm would have been sounded long before we fell prey. It's too small a wedge of forest for any raiders to enter it without being seen on a day like this with all the gleaners out and folk clearing assarts.'

William gave a quick tilt of his head in rueful acceptance. 'It still put a look of dread on your face though,' he said, gleefully.

Renard grabbed a fistful of his brother's profuse black curls and tugged them in a not altogether fraternal way. 'I will put a look of dread on yours in a minute, you wretch!' he growled.

William wriggled like a fish and almost twisted free. Renard recognised his strategy and used a fast countermove, taught to him in Tripoli by a Turcopol mercenary. William's shoulder blades struck the ground with bruising force and the air whistled from his lungs. He stared up at Renard, blue-green eyes immense with surprise.

'How did you do that?' he gasped when he had breath enough to speak. 'Show me!'

'Not now, Fonkin.' Grinning, Renard addressed William by the pet name of his childhood. It meant little fool but was a term of endearment rather than an insult. 'Wait until we're back at Ravenstow.' Stooping, he grasped a handful of William's jerkin, pulled him up, and dusted him down, then ruffled his palm over the springy black curls to rectify the damage of his earlier grip. 'I thought you'd grown beyond all reason but half of it's your hair, isn't it? You're as wild as a Welsh-man!'

'Better than being an Arab, or half of each, if what I hear about your mistress is true?' He gestured to one of his companions who smiled and sauntered off to fetch their horses.

'What?' Renard demanded. 'How do you know about that?'

William smirked at the disconcerted expression on his brother's face. 'Not now,' he parodied. 'Wait until we reach Ravenstow.'

'William, so help me God . . .!'

The youth turned to take the bridle given to him and fondled his spotted stallion's cheek. 'It's easy enough,' he shrugged. 'You paid off one of your men at Shrewsbury. He met up with the carrier who services Ashdyke and I had the news while you were still snoring in your bedstraw yesterday morning. I was coming up to Ravenstow to greet you.' He paused then added, 'Is it really true that you've brought a dancing wench home to comfort your nights, or is it just embroidery for the sake of an audience?' He settled himself in the saddle, a leggy boy of almost nineteen with pure, severe bones and a cat-like slant to the startlingly coloured eyes.

Renard swung into his own saddle and clicked Gorvenal forward alongside William's mount. 'Yes,' he sighed. 'It's true, or at least more than is usual of such tales.' And found himself telling William everything, for despite their earlier needling and the ten years that separated them, they had always had a close affinity. Their minds worked to a similar pattern. Renard would not have dreamed of speaking thus to Harry, only four years his junior but so unimaginative and one-paced that holding any kind of discussion with him was a sheer, frustrating waste of time.

'And don't ask me what I'm going to do with her or I'll throttle you!' he concluded.

'I shouldn't think you would need any advice on that score, not unless four years have altered you!' William retorted with

63

a grin, but then he looked thoughtful. 'You can't keep her at Ravenstow.'

'I know.' Renard busied himself adjusting his stirrup.

'A nice cosy hunting lodge somewhere then, or a private house in the town.' He cocked his head when Renard did not respond. 'I'd like to see her dance. Is it also true that . . .?'

'Oh, it's all true!' Renard interrupted with a grim laugh. 'Just be thankful that you haven't been corrupted. Are you still living half in Wales?'

William darted Renard a curious look. It was almost as if he was unsure of himself, running on quicksand, and that, for Renard, was a very rare occurrence. Perhaps Outremer really had altered him.

'Some of the time,' he said cagily. 'I'm mostly at Ashdyke. It's the stronger of my two holdings and a fraction nearer to Wales should I need to run for my life or make myself scarce.'

'What do you do about your forty days' service?' Renard enquired with interest. 'Stephen won't brook you running over the border every time you're summoned.'

'Oh, that part's easy,' William said airily. 'I send the King what he's owed – two knights, fully accoutred, to serve for the whole period and apologies that I'm too busy dealing with the Welsh to attend in person. The men I do send are usually the oldest, laziest, or most bad-tempered in the garrison and the same goes for their horses.'

Renard spluttered.

'Papa's done it too, but he has to be more careful. Two suspect knights astride broken-winded nags from a small tenant like me doesn't really matter, but twelve from Papa's holdings and four times that number of footsoldiers and archers is a somewhat more serious offence.' Thoughts of Stephen led him on to another grumble. 'I've had to graze my stud herd on the Welsh side of the border with Rhodri ap Owain's permission to stop Stephen commandeering half of it for remounts. He sent twenty mares to Papa's stud herd for covering. Papa was furious. He said that Beaucent had enough work to do already with the Ravenstow mares without servicing a score of Stephen's jades too!'

Renard bit his lip.

'You can stop laughing!' William warned. 'That black you're riding is ideal for the King's intentions. If Stephen can't have you in his army, he'll have a damned good try for your stallion!'

Renard sucked in his cheeks. 'He can have his services for a price,' he murmured, and slapped the sleek raven hide.

'What sort of price? The head of Ranulf de Gernons on a platter?'

'Something like that, although unfortunately Stephen's not susceptible to dancing girls, is he?' Renard kicked Gorvenal into a canter.

Wrapped in a fur robe and sitting close to the fire, Guyon looked up from conversation with his steward to see the blonde-haired beauty his son had brought home standing uncertainly in the arched entrance that led from the sleeping quarters. It was well into the morning, all the trestles had been cleared away, and the uneaten food either returned to the kitchens or given to the needy at the castle gates.

'And if you think it wise, my lord ...' The steward halted in response to Guyon's half-raised hand and followed the direction of his stare. 'Oh,' he said tellingly.

'Oh, indeed,' Guyon murmured and told a loitering maidservant to bring Olwen over and then fetch some food from the kitchens. Olwen advanced on the two men with her fluid dancer's walk and accepted the stool that the steward fetched and unfolded for her with a cool nod of acknowledgement.

Guyon, trained to look beyond superficial defences, saw the rapid pulse beating in her throat and the way that her hands shook before she folded them in her lap. She was wearing the blue silk gown that she had worn at table last night. It suited her magnificently, but silk was a fabric for high summer and hotter climates and she was trying hard not to shiver.

'Come closer to the fire, child,' he said, making room for her, and when the maid returned with some bread, honey and ale, sent her to fetch a spare cloak. 'The climate will seem different to you,' he added, making conversation as Olwen began to eat.

'I will grow accustomed to it, my lord.' Despite her nervousness she ate without difficulty. A hand to mouth existence had made that ability a necessity of survival.

Guyon rubbed his jaw, unsure what to make of her. He knew that Judith was worried about the hold the girl had on Renard and whether to let it run its course or actively interfere. Difficult, when faced with this beautiful enigma and a son who in four years had changed from boy to man.

'Although while she's here,' Judith had said to him grimly as they lay in bed last night, 'she may sleep in the bower with the other unattached women and Renard will preserve the decencies even if I have to tie him up and knock him senseless!'

The maid returned with a cloak made of Welsh plaid and presented it to Olwen. She put it on, finished her meal, and looked around the hall.

'Renard isn't here,' Guyon said as he saw her search. 'He rode out with a patrol at dawn.'

Olwen clutched the edges of the cloak together and compressed her lips.

He took pity on her. 'It might be a good idea to use this opportunity to organise some warmer clothing for you. Come above to the sewing room and the Countess will see what we have in our coffers.' Commanding the maid to find Judith, he pushed himself to his feet.

The steward eyed him doubtfully. The Countess had settled her lord by the warmth of the fire and was going to be vexed that he had moved. Probably she would blame the girl, although it was none of her fault.

Olwen followed Guyon from the hall and up the winding stairs. He paused for a moment beside a window slit to gain the breath to go on and pretended, despite the fact that he could hardly speak, that he was showing her the view.

She stared over the ploughlands towards the dark smudge of forest and the Welsh hills beyond. The smell of damp stone invaded her nostrils and lungs and she contrasted it with the memory of the sun-baked dustiness of Antioch.

'Is it all yours?' she asked, after a while, wanting to know if one day it would all be Renard's.

The seams at Guyon's eye corners deepened with grim humour. 'The hills are sometimes Welsh and sometimes Norman,' he wheezed. 'Just now they're both, the Norman part belonging all except my keep of Caermoel to Earl Ranulf of Chester.' He braced one forearm on the stone, pressed the other against his ribs. 'He'd like the rest of what you see too. That's why Renard is out on patrol.'

'Earl Ranulf of Chester?' she repeated. 'He is your enemy?'

Guyon snorted. 'Anyone who stands in his way is his enemy. We're not on the best of terms with him, never have been, but we've got by in uneasy peace until now. This war between Stephen and Mathilda is making him more powerful by the moment. Both sides want him so he holds them both to ransom. The more power he obtains, the more he wants and the more he flouts the law to get it.'

Olwen's expression became deeply thoughtful. 'Is he old in years to have gained so much power?' she queried as they continued slowly up the stairs to the next level.

'Unfortunately, no. There's no chance of him withering off the tree yet. He has less than ten years' advantage over Renard.' He paused again for respite and coughed harshly before leading her along a gallery and into Judith's sewing room.

The Countess was there before them and her tight lips and rigid spine told their own story. 'So help me God!' she snapped at Guyon. 'You spend all night coughing and then have no more sense than to leave the warmth of the fire and climb stairs! Have you run mad?' She glared at him and then at Olwen.

'And if I have, it is my entitlement,' he said to her calmly before swallowing down another cough. 'I'd rather be mad than caged any further than I am.'

Judith continued to frown but she did not seek to argue beyond her first outburst, knowing that it would probably provoke him to worse folly.

'Olwen needs warmer gowns than this.' He gestured to the blue silk. 'We have the fabric, do we not?'

Arching one brow, Judith looked Olwen coldly up and down. 'Yes, we do,' she said and went into the room. Olwen hesitated, but Guyon gestured her to follow his wife within.

Another window looked out onto the bailey. Going to it, Olwen gazed down at the bustling activity. Behind her she heard the Earl speaking to his wife in placatory tones and her murmured but vehement responses followed by the sound of a coffer lid being thrown back. When Olwen drew up the courage to look round again, the Earl had gone and the Countess was examining a length of fawn wool.

'No sign of moths,' she gave it a shake. 'There should be enough here for two undertunics and a bliaut if we use this blue as well.' And in the same breath added, 'It is no use watching and waiting at the window like that. Renard won't be back until vespers at the earliest. And tomorrow will be the same, and the day after that, and the day after that.' A ball of string in her hand and some shears, she advanced on Olwen to take her measurements.

Olwen stood tense but still and let the older woman work. Every now and then Judith would stop and put a knot in the string to mark the length from shoulder to wrist, or back of neck to hem, and then cut off the relevant strand.

'If you think you are the core of Renard's life you are wasting your time,' Judith added in a hard voice when she finally stepped back, the measurements completed. 'This is the core, this stone, this land, bred into him blood and bone and soul. All you are is a means to vent the heat and soon even for that need he will have a wife.'

Olwen tossed her head confidently. 'I realise that Renard has duties that do not involve me, but duty is not pleasure, and I know more about that than his bride ever will. If I so choose, she will be no match for me.'

'If you so choose!'

Olwen gave her a contemptuous, almost pitying smile.

Judith turned abruptly away to the pile of fabric on the coffer. There was a red mist before her eyes and the temptation to lunge at Olwen with her sewing shears was almost overwhelming. She pressed her hands hard down on the coffer, fighting for control and realised that it was no use. She could not remain in the same room. Swallowing, feeling physically sick, she stormed out.

For a while Olwen did not move, but when at last she did, it was to return to the window slit and lean against the wall, her eyes on the distant lands belonging to Ranulf of Chester.

CHAPTER 8

R ENARD SIGHED, TOSSED THE QUILL onto the heap of
parchments beside him on the table, and rubbed his
eyes. The hound dozing beside the brazier raised its
head and thumped its tail on the floor. Renard snapped his
fingers and held out his hand and the dog padded over to nuzzle
him with its moist, black nose. He thrust his fingers into the
wiry grey coat and made a fuss of the animal. It was a brief
comfort, a momentary diversion from the difficult task of
sorting out which of their vassals owed what and when in
terms of military service, and making up for the inevitable
shortfall around harvest time, which was nigh on impossible.
Some lords, taking a page out of William's book, were not
averse to sending the most shoddy goods they could get away
with.

A dull ache of fatigue throbbed behind his eyes. It was the
middle of the night, everyone asleep but himself and the dog,
and he had to be up at the crack of dawn to take out another
patrol. Later it would not matter, he could delegate the task,
but for the nonce he needed to make himself known as a leader,
had to impose his own codes and methods on men who either
did not know him, or still thought of him as a feckless youngster
who had done nought but jaunt about Christendom at the
earldom's expense. Renard had no intention of wasting his
breath on argument. Actions spoke by far the louder, even if
they were wearing him out.

He ruffled the dog's coat, and reaching across the table to
the flagon, refilled his cup with the indifferent Norman wine.
Then, with another heavy sigh, he drew a fresh sheet of parchment towards him and began to set down the results of his
rough calculations in a neater hand that FitzBrien the Constable

would be able to understand and act upon. He knew that there were bound to be some disagreements and he would have to prepare himself for some hard negotiating. At least, he thought, as he drank the wine and wrote, his forthcoming marriage to Eleanor would be a convenient meeting ground for all the vassals and tenants to air their opinions, form new ones and pay their dues.

The wedding day had been set for the first of November. It had been mooted in a letter taken up the march by Adam when he went to collect his wife from Woolcot, and his return had furnished Eleanor's reply — brief this time and to the point, in full agreement of the date and welcoming him home. The handwriting had been a trifle shaky and the ink had spotted the parchment here and there, but with joy, nervousness or fear, he did not know, nor at this moment, he admitted, really care.

Pressing the heel of his hand against his forehead, he leaned his elbow on the trestle and continued to write. The dog lifted its head and a soft growl rumbled up from the depths of its throat. 'Quiet, Cabal,' he commanded, frowning in concentration.

A shadow passed before the candle light and startled he looked up.

'May I?' Without awaiting his reply, Olwen picked up his cup and took a swallow of the wine. Her hair, pillow-tousled, spilled in pale rivulets over her loosely tied bed robe. The silky skin of one shoulder gleamed as did the smooth upper curve of her breast. Perching herself on the table's edge, she put her free hand down to balance her weight and leaned sideways and slightly forwards to give him more than just a glimpse of her cleavage.

He put down the quill, carefully set the ink horn out of reach, and folded his arms to regard her warily. 'What do you want?'

'Can't you guess?' She tossed her head at him. The wine glistened on her lips. She licked them slowly. Renard tried to stare her out and discovered that he could not, and when he lowered his gaze, it was caught by the swell of her breasts.

She said, 'You have been avoiding me, you know you have.'

'I've been ...' He cleared his throat and started again. 'I've been too busy seeing to the affairs of the earldom. And I cannot just walk into your chamber as you have walked in here now. It is a matter of common courtesy to my mother and father,' then added acidly, 'I don't suppose you know much about that.'

She gave him a bored, feline stare. 'No, I don't.' Yawning, she slipped from the table, but only to come round and sit down next to him. 'But I know a great deal about other things. You've been trying to pretend you don't want me, but I can see straight through you.'

Renard looked rueful. 'You're wrong. I haven't been pretending at all. I do want you, Olwen ... too much.'

'Ah,' she murmured, stalking him with claws unsheathed. 'Proving to yourself that you can abstain if you have to.'

He shrugged his mouth, conceding her the point. She looked at the parchments and tally sticks strewn upon the table and then through her thick lashes at Renard. 'This man you all keep talking about, Ranulf de Gernons? Is he very powerful?'

'Yes, on his own territory. He wants some of ours to add to it and there is a personal grudge between us going back ten years.'

She teased her hand up his thigh, kneading gently. 'Do you fear him?'

Renard hesitated. Her hand moved higher and his senses swam, overriding reason. 'I fear his ambition,' he said in a distracted voice. 'And his greed. The man himself ... No, I do not acknowledge him my master.' Gasping, he caught her hand. She gave him a bone-melting look and slowly eased her fingers from his grasp and unfastened the loose knot on her bedrobe. It fell open and she shrugged it down baring herself to him. Round, full breasts, the nipples puckered by the cold of sudden exposure, slender waist, taut belly and generous hips framing the gate to heaven ... or hell. Renard could no more resist the lure than a wasp could resist the jar of honey in which it would ultimately drown.

He grasped her naked shoulders and crushed her against him,

fingers seeking and tightening in her hair, mouth taking hers. She yielded utterly for a moment, then clawed him and tried to make her escape. He caught her back by the wrist. She tried to bite him. On both sides it was more battle than play. Growling and stiff-legged the dog circled them. Then he barked. Renard stopped, aware that in a moment they were going to have an interested audience of disturbed sleepers and summoned guards.

Carefully he released Olwen and turned to command Cabal down and into a corner, then, breathing hard, he looked at her. She returned his stare and a slow smile parted her lips. Her eyes were as dark as liquid sapphire as she laid her palms on his chest and pushed him gently back down onto the bench and straddled herself across his thighs, lips descending on his.

Heavy-lidded, breathing once more on the level and mind functioning above instinct, Renard watched Olwen retie the bedrobe and rake her fingers through her tumbled hair. She was avoiding his eyes as if embarrassed. He had had to stifle her scream of pleasure against his hastily raised palm. It was as if she resented the violence of the response he evoked in her – no less violent than his own. His teeth ached from gritting them against his own voice and his body was still liquid with aftermath.

'God's life,' he said sombrely. 'Olwen, you turn me inside out.'

She flicked him a brief glance full of caution and something deeper. 'Will you say the same thing to your wife?' she challenged.

He snorted. 'I doubt it very much.' A faint smile. 'Nell's too innocent to even remotely imagine the things you do to me, or I hope she is.' The smile became a wry chuckle.

'But you could teach her?' Olwen licked her finger and rubbed at a flea bite on her wrist.

He shrugged. 'Perhaps. I don't know what sort of pupil she would make. Some things are inbred. Beyond a certain point they can't be taught. Not jealous are you?'

She withered him with a look. Renard's eyes narrowed in

amusement, some of it at his own expense. Rummaging among the heaped parchments on the trestle, he picked one up, glanced, and handed it across to her.

'What is this?' She looked blankly at the gilded capitals of a professional scribe, the strong brown ink strokes beneath it and the attached seal. To her unlettered eyes they were just meaningless patterns on a page.

'A charter granting you lifetime rights to the manor and demesne of Hawkfield and an annual sum of twenty-five marks to be paid each year at Michaelmas. It's all couched in legal terms but I'll read it to you if you want.'

Her eyes became huge and dark and still. 'Please,' she said, with a gesture.

Renard almost made a sarcastic remark concerning her lack of trust, realised what her retort would be, and contented himself with a pointed look before reading to her the fine details of the charter. It had been his mother's suggestion, and he would have thought it inordinately generous of her had she not declared that the sooner Olwen was away from Ravenstow, the better for all concerned, particularly herself.

Olwen stared down at the document in her hands and felt disturbingly ambivalent. A manor, servants, money – distant stars longed for from the gutters of Antioch, but now that she held them in her hands, she felt more desolate than triumphant and did not know why.

'It still needs witnessing,' Renard said when she did not speak. 'Your cross or thumb print and mine and my father's signatures. It can be done tomorrow and I can take you to Hawkfield as soon as you're ready.'

'In haste to be rid of me?' she attacked.

'You know I cannot keep you here at Ravenstow,' he said tersely.

Olwen scowled at him. 'It is acceptable to have a mistress, but ill-bred to flaunt her beneath your family's nose?'

He bit his lower lip and felt it curve despite himself into a sudden grin. 'You are probably right at that,' he conceded, rubbing the back of his neck.

'And is that to be my payment for all this generosity?

Accommodating your needs whenever you choose to take a diversion while out hunting or on patrol?'

'By mutual consent.' His smile became almost mischievous. 'I won't constrain you to anything you don't desire of your own free will.'

Her colour was high. 'Stabling for a mare, occasionally to be ridden?' she demanded. 'Do you expect me to hang over the paddock fence quivering for your approach?'

'Knowing you,' he said drily, 'I'm more likely to find myself bucked off in the midden.'

Reluctantly Olwen was forced to return his smile as she remembered their first meeting in Antioch and how he had said they would never get any further than the stable yard until they had decided who was the horse and who was the rider. He had yet to learn that a parameter set for one occasion, unlike a charter, was not binding on a lifetime.

CHAPTER 9

As THE FIRST LIGHT of dawn greyed Hawkfield's court-yard, William dismounted from his spotted stallion and stared round at the few yawning servants shambling about their first duties. 'Where's Lord Renard?' he demanded of the scratching, gummy-eyed groom who came to tend the horse.

'Dunno, m'lord,' he mumbled. 'Still abed I think.'

'Still abed?' William repeated flatly. His jaw tightened and he signalled his men to dismount. The hall door was barred. William thumped on it with the hilt of his sword until a serving woman opened it. He barged past her into the darkness which was dimly lit by the fire from the central hearth, the former only just being resurrected to day-time use by a puffy-faced wench.

In the bedchamber located behind screens at the end of the hall, Renard's eyes snapped open, and cursing he sat bolt upright.

'What's wrong?' Olwen murmured without bothering to open her eyes. She burrowed and snuggled, her hand caressing his thigh. An hour ago it had been on a part of him even more intimate as she coaxed him into smouldering need and then white-hot conflagration.

'You know full well!' Pushing her hand aside, he began scrambling rapidly into his clothes.

'It's not my fault if you go back to sleep instead of getting up.' She rolled over, half-raised her lids, and extended fingers and toes in a replete feline stretch.

Renard scowled at her but omitted to retort. As she said, the blame was not hers, but he knew full well that she had meant it to happen. Otherwise why tease and prolong and provoke to so powerful a culmination that it drowned all consciousness? And the way she had lain against him afterwards, soothing and stroking him into sleep, knowing damned well that he was supposed to be meeting his brother at the crossroads north of Hawkfield before the full crack of dawn. It was his own fault. He should have spent the night at Ravenstow, not arranged to set out to meet his new bride straight from the warm bed of his mistress. And now he was going to be late.

Outside there was a squawk of protest from one of the maids, and the curtain separating bedchamber from hall was rudely clashed aside. Riveted mail flashed in the rushlight.

'Are you going to malinger there all day?' William demanded, disgust written on every feature of his handsome young face. 'We're supposed to be meeting Eleanor before noon.'

Renard fumbled into his braies and hunted out a cross garter. 'Oh stop looking so damned righteous and fetch me a drink!' he growled.

Olwen slowly sat up, not bothering to draw the sheet around her body. William stared at her silken shoulders and arms, at the seductive curve of her breasts stranded by her glorious hair, at the look she gave him, inviting, provocative and mocking.

'Fetch it yourself!' he snapped and stalked out into the hall.

'Oh dear,' murmured Olwen sweetly. 'He *is* in a temper isn't he?'

Having scrambled into the rest of his clothes, Renard began to struggle with his hauberk. 'Can't you leave that tongue of yours sheathed for once?' he snarled.

She tut-tutted, and making not the slightet effort to help him, watched him with amusement. 'By the looks of you, he's not alone in his rage.'

By the time Renard finally succeeded in donning the garment, he was so furious that he was unable to speak and the awareness of her silent laughter, the way she was making him look a fool, was a galling mortification. Mouth compressed, he jerked up and latched his swordbelt, lashed his scabbard thongs to their eyelets, and made to leave the room.

'What, no fond parting kiss?' she mocked.

On the threshold he paused, knuckles clenched upon the wall, mastering the desire to stride to the bed, drag her from it by her beautiful hair and horsewhip her. 'Stop playing with me, Olwen,' he said through his teeth. 'I'm not a tame hound to jump through hoops at your bidding.'

'I know,' she said throatily.

He struck his fist once against the wall and, without looking round, walked out.

Olwen rolled onto her belly, and smiling, closed her eyes.

The first few miles of their journey up the march to greet the bridal party travelling down towards them were loaded with tension and brooding temper. Renard set a vicious pace, and Gorvenal, half Arabian and lighter boned than a full destrier, flew over the ground and left the escort lumbering. William had to spur Smotyn hard to keep level, and after one particularly bad stumble, shouted at Renard to slow down.

'You're going to founder us all!' he snarled.

'Don't blame me if you can't keep up!' Renard retorted, but drew rein and looked round at the men strung out behind, and knew that the blame was indeed his. It was not horses or men he was riding into the ground but his own foul temper. If any serjeant or knight of his had led the troop in such a sloppy formation as he now saw, he would have blistered that man's ears from his skull and docked his pay. He breathed out hard and ran the bridle through his fingers.

'Christ, Renard, take a grip on yourself!' William's voice cracked with anxiety. 'The whole future of the earldom's in your hands. You can't throw it away because of a ... because of a ...'

'... Half-breed dancing girl?' Renard finished for him, with a mirthless laugh. 'Jesu, if you knew how easy it just might be.' He watched the men ride up.

William looked at him. Renard's features were now schooled to tight-lipped impassivity, grey eyes narrowed into the wind. William's gut ceased to lurch with fear and the tightness across his shoulders eased. Just before the leading knight reached them, Renard slapped William's mail-clad arm. 'My wits had gone wool-gathering and left my temper in sole command,' he said with forced lightness. 'I'm all right now, you can stop fretting.'

Which meant, thought William, that the temper was of a necessity throttled down, not that it had magically evaporated like this morning's autumn mist into the brisk air. He watched Renard muster the men, jest with them about his haste to greet his bride, watched him organise them into a tight escort, van, centre and rear-guard to his liking and then settle companionably among them to ride at a sensible, disciplined pace. It was more than just the girl, he thought. It was the responsibility for Ravenstow. It was the sight of their father dying by fractions before his eyes. It was the constant living on a blade's edge. What wonder that he should seek oblivion in the arms of a woman who was a reminder of the lost freedom of Outremer. What wonder that he should object to being roused and thrust face to face with duty.

William was suddenly thankful that as his father's youngest son, and unlikely to succeed to the earldom, he still had the freedom that Renard was being forced to forfeit.

The wind surged like an ocean, roaring through the trees and leaching them bare in trailing swirls of copper, gold and brown through which the horses waded and crunched as though they were treading shingle.

Eleanor shivered within her coney-lined cloak, her best one, trimmed with ermine tails, and stared up at the boiling grey clouds. The wind spattered rain into her face so hard that the droplets hurt her. She gripped her hood around her face and fidgeted uncomfortably in the saddle, her woman's parts chaffed by the long day astride.

'Not far now,' Adam de Lacey said to her with a sympathetic smile. 'Are you nervous?'

Eleanor explored the cold, hollow feeling in the pit of her stomach. 'A little,' she admitted tentatively. 'It seems so long ago. We'll be strangers – married strangers within a week.' She tried to smile at him and failed.

Adam leaned and lightly clasped his hand over hers on the reins. 'It will be all right, Nell,' he said compassionately. 'I know it's going to be difficult at first, but you'll adjust, you'll see.'

She nodded stiffly and wished that it was Adam she was marrying. He was gentle and kind and seldom out of humour. He would have time for her, time she already sensed Renard would not.

Adam's wife, who would have been greatly amused could she have but read Eleanor's mind and who might have given her some sound advice about men in general, said to her husband, 'You should see her wedding gown. It's so beautiful that it looks as though it has come straight out of a jongleur's romance. She had spent hours stitching it, you know. I even put a few in the hem myself – where they would not show of course!'

Adam grinned. His wife's clumsiness with a needle was a family jest of long-standing. She occasionally succeeded in cobbling together a shirt for him or Miles, and short shifts for herself and the girls, but that was the supreme limit of her ability.

Eleanor bit her lip, and blushing looked down at Bramble's dark mane. She had sewn all her dreams into her wedding garments, but was beginning to wish that she had been less obvious. There was a tunic for Renard too, the rich embroidery, a play on his name. Renard, an unusual form of the more common Rainard and taken from his Norman great grandfather who had borne the colouring and vulpine cunning of a fox – le renard.

They had corresponded briefly over the matter of the wedding. His letter had been terse and cold, bearing no imprint of the young man she remembered. No humour, not even a glimpse of the carelessly affectionate hand that would pat a dog's head in passing. It was more than just nervousness that tensed her stomach; it was fear.

Adam made excuses for Renard, saying that he had little time for courtship and dalliance just now, but as he spoke, he had avoided her eyes. There was more that he was not saying, but Adam was adept at keeping his mouth firmly closed. Eleanor had decided of her own intuition which was seldom wrong (at least as far as sheep were concerned) that to Renard this marriage was a necessary, but far from welcome intrusion into the pattern of his life: a duty to be consummated and dispensed with as quickly as possible.

Tears blurred her eyes and she sniffed a trifle too loudly.

Harry leaned round from where he rode on her other side. 'What's wrong?' he demanded anxiously.

Eleanor shook her head and forced a smile through her own weak self-pity. 'Nothing,' she reassured him. 'Just the wind stinging my eyes.'

Hamo le Grande was the leader of a troop of mercenaries in the pay of Ranulf, Earl of Chester. He was a hard-bitten soldier who had been fighting for money since his early adolescence. His career now spanned almost thirty years of battles, skirmishes, and varying degrees of atrocity ranging through minor plunder and looting, to rape, murder and the razing of entire hamlets. It was a rough, uncertain way to make a living and only the strongest and most fortunate survived to the years that Hamo now wore like a lead collar around his throat, dragging him down. Time was against him. He knew that the next ten years would either see him settled in a more permanent occupation or dead in battle.

He rubbed the fingers of his right hand over his thick silver and black beard, found a crumb, and absently teased it out. Below the ridge on which he had paused to rest his stallion, his paymaster's lands blended with those of the enemy – Ravenstow. A few miles to the north on a finger of land pointing into Chester's earldom lay the keep of Caermoel with its ownership bitterly disputed. Earl Ranulf wanted it, but was not yet ready to make his move. Other, more important pots were simmering on his hearth, such as forging contacts with the rebels in Bristol and poking his nose into affairs at Lincoln, but he had given his patrols and the Welsh levies of Cadwaladr ap Gruffydd rein to raid and forage where they would.

Hamo moistened his lips and gazed at the lands, imagining himself the lord of one of these border fiefs. He had been indirectly promised a holding of his own if he proved worth his salt, or failing that, a castellan's position in one of the Earl's many keeps. It was a dream that goaded him, sitting on his back like a gargoyle, while he fought to pitch a tent in the streaming rain of a dark November bailey, while snug within the keep the lord he served sat on top of a roaring fire, gorging himself on bloody venison, drinking dark, rich wine, and fingering the maid servants.

'Do we go in?' asked his second-in-command, a small tough Welshman who spoke appalling French.

Hamo gave him a withering look. 'Don't be stupid, boyo!' he mimicked. 'Of course we go in! Who's to stop us? Henry FitzGuyon?' He laughed, exposing a mouthful of chipped white slabs.

'He held us off last time.'

'Only because he caught us in the middle of a herd of cows and a third of us on reconnaissance elsewhere,' he dismissed. 'There's a village a few miles down. Anyone fancy roast pork?'

The village consisted of no more than half a dozen daub and wattle huts clustered around an even smaller ramshackle wooden church. There was very little to raid, but the villagers had not yet begun the autumn slaughter and there was pork to be had, the young ones plump and succulent. The sound of their squeals was deafening and drowned out the screams of the human occupants as they either fled or died.

Hamo allowed his men to quench their thirst on the villagers' cider, but not to the point of intoxication. A pack horse was laden with spoils and provisions. What they could not carry they killed or burned and then they rode on, their passing marked by the crackle of flame and a pall of smoke darker than the sky.

An hour later Hamo was just contemplating turning for home via a quick harassment of a flock of sheep he could see dotting the horizon when he caught sight of the riders joining the main road below from the rutted drover's track that led to Woolcot. Hamo slitted his eyes and rapidly counted. There were eight knights and a like number of mounted serjeants.

'Women, look you!' cried his second with a wolfish grin.

'Shut up!' Hamo snapped, his own gaze fixed upon the red chevrons on the leading knight's shield, and a little behind him, riding with the women, the gold lozenge on blue background of another knight.

'God's teeth,' he blasphemed softly. 'It's Henry FitzGuyon and Adam de Lacey.'

'Who are the women then?'

'How should I . . .?' Hamo began on a snarl, then stopped, expression suddenly tense. 'One of them's red-haired, that'll be de Lacey's wife. Those two behind are maids, you can tell from their dress, and they're joining the road from the Woolcot track, so the other must be Eleanor de Mortimer − Renard FitzGuyon's betrothed.' Discovering her identity as he spoke it, his eyes brightened with the hunting instinct that was never far from the surface. 'And what would my Lord of Chester give to have her in his hands?' Hard on that enquiry came the thought that despoiled goods were far more likely to go to the despoiler than to a second party, particularly if that despoiler had already been promised a fief of his own.

'Are we going to take them on?' The Welshman's voice was rough with nervous excitement. Henry FitzGuyon might be as dull as an ox, but he was also as solid and strong as one in a fight and de Lacey had a reputation in battle that stretched from the Welsh borders all the way to southern Anjou.

'If it were man to man I'd opt for caution, but they're hampered by the women, and it's the women, or rather one woman we want. We'll catch them going into those trees further down, hit them in the centre before they know what's happening, cut out the woman and use our bows to stop them pursuing.' His teeth flashed in a brief, hard smile.

The glint of sunlight on mail rivets caught the corner of Harry's vision. He jerked round so quickly that he ricked his neck and the sudden streak of hot pain, coupled with the inability to move his head, prevented him from scanning the horizon. When he was able to look again, the sun had retreated behind clouds and there was nothing to be seen.

'What's wrong?' Adam asked, as they rode into a scrubby willow coppice lining the moist valley bottom.

'Nothing. I thought I saw something on the hill but it was probably just the sun reflecting off that stream up there.'

83

Rubbing the back of his neck, he winced.

Adam decided nevertheless to tighten up their formation and turned to give Sweyn the order, his words becoming a bellow of warning as the horsemen crashed suddenly upon them, hitting them dead-centre, just as Hamo had planned.

Eleanor screamed as a weight smacked onto Bramble's crupper. Hard mailed arms snatched the reins from her hands and spurred heels rammed into the mare's flanks, sending her at a bolting gallop through the trees. A branch whipped Eleanor's face. Her world tilted and see-sawed as the mare ploughed through the slushy mud and started to strain up the slope. The man seated behind shouted at the horse and kicked her again. Eleanor wriggled and immediately his right arm clamped vice-like around her waist.

'Don't even think of it, my lady,' he said against her ear.

Adam slammed his shield into one man's face, cut at the mercenary on his right, and pressed Lyard forward in front of Heulwen's mount.

'They've got Eleanor!' Harry bellowed with a hacking slash at his own opponent. The blade bit into the man's shield arm and lodged in bone. He screamed. Harry's breath grunted out with effort as he wrenched his blade free and spun his stallion in the direction of the escaping mercenary. He found himself accompanied by several of the enemy, but none of them were particularly bothered to engage him, and in the moment that he understood why, an arrow thumped into his upper right pectoral and sent him reeling from the saddle. He hit the ground hard and heard the shaft snap. Fluid filled his mouth. He lost consciousness, the last thing he saw Adam's sorrel stallion buckling beneath a rain of arrows and Adam trying desperately to scramble free of the saddle before he was rolled to death.

Hamo and his troop made their escape. They could have pushed their excellent good fortune and stayed to fight, but Hamo had possession of what he wanted and the men who remained were still formidable opposition even if they were not now seeing fit to pursue.

★

Renard slowed Gorvenal from lope to walk as he reached the crossroads where the pre-arranged meeting with Eleanor and her escort was to take place, and discovered himself the first to arrive.

'You could have spared me another hour abed, Fonkin,' he remarked, dismounting to stretch his legs and gaze into a windswept distance of half-naked autumn trees that obscured the road from view. A squirrel scampered across their path. Renard's boot sole crunched on a hazel shell. He stooped to pick it up and split away the casing to reach the nut.

William squinted at the dull haze of the sun. 'It's not that we're early,' he said, 'but that they're late, and that's very unusual for Adam.'

Renard shrugged and ground the nut between his teeth. 'But not for Harry. He'd miss his own funer . . .' His eyes narrowed to follow a startled flight of birds wheeling suddenly above the tree tops.

'That will be them now,' said William as Smotyn sidled restively, nostrils flaring to test the wind. 'And there's a mare among them if I'm not mistaken.' He grinned and nodded at Gorvenal who had arched his crest and tail in display, sharp ears pricked. He nickered gruffly. Renard swore beneath his breath, hastily caught the black's bridle and scrambled aloft, drawing in the reins until the stallion was on so tight a curb that he could barely move his head.

The sound of galloping hooves was accompanied by a dull vibration.

'In a hurry whoever they are,' murmured William.

Renard set his hand to his hilt. 'It can't be Adam, there aren't enough horses.'

Around the bend and into their sight pounded a grey palfrey going at full stretch, astride her a young man in a half coat of mail whom William recognised immediately.

'It's Gerard, Adam's squire, and that's Heulwen's mare!' he cried in alarm as the youth galloped up to them, reined her back on her haunches, and all but fell out of the saddle. The mare staggered and her head went down, her sides pumping like bellows.

'Lord Renard, Lord William, grave news!' the squire gasped out. 'We were hit by a mercenary troop five miles back! They snatched Lady Eleanor and made off with her. Lord Henry's sore wounded and Lord Adam's horse killed beneath him. . . . They sent me . . . lightest man . . . fastest horse . . . fetch you!'

'Blood of Christ!' muttered William, his face white and stricken.

Renard set his jaw. 'All right, lad, well done.' His eyes moved from the youth to the road, while his hands worked at the reins to control Gorvenal whose priorities were governed by pure instinct. 'I'll have to leave you with the mare. When she's recovered enough, ride on down to Ravenstow and raise the alarm there.'

'Yes, my lord.'

Quickly Renard grilled the squire for the finer details and fixed them in his mind as he rode for the place described. Again Gorvenal started to outstrip the other horses, but this time no-one hailed him back.

He found Heulwen kneeling beside Harry, one of the knights' cloaks pillowed beneath his head, Heulwen's and his own draped across his body.

'Renard, thank Christ!' Adam exclaimed as he flung down from the saddle.

Renard spared a brief glance for his brother-by-marriage, saw that he was nicked and bruised but not seriously injured, and knelt quickly beside Heulwen.

'Is it bad?'

She gave him a desolate look. 'He fell on the arrow and broke the shaft. The head will have to be dug out and it's in deep . . .' She drew a shuddering breath and choked down a sob. Such a wound was almost certain death, and if by the remotest chance he survived, he would never wield a sword again.

Harry's lids with their sparse sandy lashes flickered and lifted as he heard Renard's voice. 'I saw them coming,' he said hoarsely. 'I saw them coming and I ignored them!' His eyes were hazed with pain and there were gashes in his lower lip where he had bitten down.

Heulwen made a small, helpless gesture. 'He saw the flash of armour just before they attacked and he keeps blaming himself for dismissing it.'

'Idiot,' Renard said in a voice gritty with emotion. 'From what I hear it wouldn't have made that much difference.'

'Except between life and death,' Harry said wryly and laughed, then gasped through clenched teeth, body going rigid.

'Harry, lie quiet,' Heulwen murmured. 'It's no use to rail.'

He nodded, complexion grey, and swallowed. 'Renard, get Eleanor before anything happens to her. I'll never forgive myself if it does.' He closed his eyes.

Renard stood up. The wind was stinging in his eyes, mingling with tears. He caught Gorvenal's bridle and remounted.

'I sent one of my men after them,' Adam said. 'He's a good tracker, trained by your grandfather. He should be able to keep them in sight. He's leaving signs for you to follow.'

Renard nodded jerkily. 'Send William after me when he arrives. I'll leave you to get Harry to shelter. Take my remounts when they come. It was de Gernon's men, I suppose?'

Adam shrugged. 'Your guess is as good as mine. They were well led though, not just rabble and de Gernons has long had his eye on destroying the union between you and Eleanor.' He shook his head. 'I would have stopped them if I could, but you can see what their archers did. We could not pursue in force. It was well thought out. I was in half a mind to bring Miles and the girls on this trip. Thank Christ I left them at Thorneyford.'

Renard rode away. Gorvenal snorted and shied from the corpse of a destrier, arrows quilled in throat and chest – Adam's sorrel, Andalusian, and after Heulwen and the children, the pride of his life.

Renard felt Gorvenal heave beneath him as he ploughed through the mud and took to the wooded slope. He knew how it felt to have a horse killed beneath you. He had only been fifteen years old when his destrier had been gut-shot by a Welsh arrow during a skirmish and he had had to finish the horse himself with his dagger. The memory haunted him even now. Putting his hand in reassurance on Gorvenal's warm black neck, he saw in his mind's eye that other horse of his youth screaming and threshing on the ground, the look in its eyes as he went to it with the knife ... the look in Harry's eyes. For a moment he bent over the saddle as the anguish became a physical cramp. The spasm passed and was replaced by a cold, implacable rage. He honed his gaze to the ground like a sword blade to a throat and sought the trail.

CHAPTER 10

WHEN ELEANOR'S FIRST SHOCK wore off, it was replaced by furious outrage that she should be thus handled on her own territory, and when she truly realised the enormity of what was happening, the outrage in its turn gave way to terror. The man who held her had a wrestler's grip. The rivets of his hauberk hurt her as she was squashed back against them, and his breath was hot and rank on her cheek.

Her mare started to labour beneath the double weight and a brief halt was called while her abductor remounted his own sturdier stallion. She was bundled kicking across the pommel and they were off again at a lumbering, jerking canter, heading for the forest that shrouded the border between Ravenstow, Wales, and the Earldom of Chester.

They forded a wide stream and water splashed up into her face and soaked the hem of her gown and cloak. The horse stumbled and Eleanor's breath caught on a cry of alarm. Hamo peered round into her milk-white face with its taut, stubborn jaw and wide, blank eyes.

'Never you fret, wench,' he growled. 'I won't let you fall. You're too valuable a prize.' The growl became a soft chuckle and his fingers splayed across her buttocks.

Eleanor gritted her teeth, tried to wriggle away, and desisted as his grip dug painfully.

'Ranulf de Gernons will be mightily pleased to offer you his hospitality, so pleased that he's going to reward me with a fine young wife and a rich fief ...'

His breath chuckled out close to her ear and belatedly she took his meaning. 'Never!' she spat vehemently. 'You'll never get me before a priest!'

'Oh, one way or the other it'll be managed,' he said amiably. 'With or without your consent, smiling or senseless, it makes no matter to me. The Church approves of men who repent the sins of their lust and make proper amends. Yes, I see you understand.' With a satisfied grunt he concentrated on guiding his horse up the far bank of the stream.

Eleanor swallowed a retch, understanding only too well. Rape to assert his immediate claim and then marriage to appease the Church and secure her lands. She looked at the ground rushing past beneath them and felt the hard band of steel, muscle and bone securing her to the man. With the panic of a trapped animal she began a futile, frantic struggle. He swore, guided his mount with his thighs, and taking his left hand from the reins, raised his fist and struck her semi-conscious.

Eleanor knew that he had hit her, and she was also aware of the motion of the horse and the man's exasperated cursing as he shifted her limp weight to a more manageable position, but there were black stars before her eyes, a blossoming numbness where her jaw should have been, and her limbs had become disconnected from her brain.

Towards dusk they stopped in a clearing to rest their blowing horses and water them at a forest brook. The ground was carpeted with a mass of dead leaves and more were twirling down to join them in a fitful golden rain.

The men fetched oat cakes from their saddle rolls and unslung their wine skins. A cautious fire was lit, not sufficient to draw notice to themselves but enough to roast slivers of pork from one of the piglets they had taken earlier in the day.

Hamo dismounted and dumped his half-conscious burden on the ground, and taking out his own rations, sat down beside Eleanor to eat.

Her fingers closed around the moistness of newly fallen leaves. She opened her eyes and stared at a sparse amber canopy, lofty and indifferent to her fate, turned her head and saw the bearded mercenary leader watching her, his left cheek bulging with food and his eyes dense blue slivers glinting between seamed pouches of flesh.

'Wine?' he offered.

Eleanor averted her head. She heard him laugh and then the sound of him washing down his mouthful of food with strong gulps from the skin. This was not happening she told herself. In a moment she was going to wake up in her own bed at Woolcot and thank all the saints in heaven that she had endured nothing worse than a particularly vivid nightmare.

The fire crackled softly and the merest streamer of smoke drifted upwards. In the dusky silence all the autumnal colours of the forest were suddenly so sharp that to look at them hurt her eyes. Her jaw throbbed. She touched it gently and discovered a tender, swollen lump. Inside her mouth there was a ragged line of bitten flesh.

'You should not have fought me,' said Hamo with righteous satisfaction. 'You'll learn not to. I don't brook disobedience in a woman.'

Eleanor dropped her gaze to the rumpled folds of her thick woollen riding gown. She felt cold and shaky, wanted so much to cry that her throat ached, but not for the world would she let her pride break before this odious routier who held her prisoner.

Hamo grunted and, continuing to chew his food, studied her. Pale with shock and her face distorted by the violence of his blow, she was not even remotely pretty. The hair that was straggling free of its braids was as black as jet and coarse and her eyes were a muddy, indeterminate shade somewhere between brown and green. Her body, however, was pleasing; he had had opportunity enough to handle it over the last few miles. High, round breasts, a willowy waist he could span with his two hands, and haunches lithe and firm from the active life she led. His mind imagined and his loins quickened.

Gulping down his last mouthful, he wiped his hands on the hem of his gambeson and stood up to remove his sword belt and then his hauberk. 'We might as well get it over with now,' he said coarsely. 'The sooner it's done, the sooner you're mine.' He stooped to grasp her arm and jerked her to her feet. 'Meurig, Saer, come over here a moment, I need witnesses.'

Grinning, the two men detached themselves from the fire and sauntered towards their leader. Eleanor struggled against the hand clamped on her upper arm but she might as well have tried to move a mountain. His grip was as solid as a rock. She tried to bite him and he laughed, slapped her away, and hooking one leg between her ankles, swept her effortlessly to the ground.

'Hold her down,' he commanded Meurig and Saer. They moved with alacrity to obey, excited at the thought of witnessing the rape of a high-born virgin. Eleanor fought them grimly, threshing and struggling until her limbs grew hot with fatigue and the power drained from them. Her skirts were dragged up out of Hamo's way. She watched him fumble within his garments to free his turgid organ and whimpered and shook her head, begging God to let her wake up.

'It's not a dream,' Hamo panted as he knelt in the leaves and began to prize apart her clenched thighs. 'Here, let me show you.' And positioned himself for the thrust home.

Eleanor started to scream like a coney caught in a poacher's snare.

'This way,' William whispered and stepped between the trees and through the underbrush with the lightness of a young doe. His Welshmen moved with him, insubstantial as shadows flickering from trunk to trunk.

Renard could track; it was a skill his half-Welsh grandfather had taught him, but compared to William who possessed an innate talent, he knew he was as clumsy as a wild boar in the undergrowth and about as short-sighted. William moved like a wraith and even when the tracks petered out seemed almost capable of smelling the way.

'What do you think ...'

'Sshhh, we're very close now!' William held out the flattened palm of his hand to Renard. 'Can't you smell their fire?'

Renard sniffed. Faintly he did indeed catch the drifting scent of wood smoke but would not have been aware of it without William's half-scornful remark. A tree root tangled around his foot. Carefully he stepped over it and moved on, following exactly in his brother's footsteps.

'There.' William crouched on the balls of his feet and pointed through the trees. He made a spreading-out motion to his men and indicated with sign language that one of them should go back and bring up the reinforcements consisting of Renard's troops who were not forest-trained and would have given away any scouting party with their noise.

Renard crouched beside his brother and concentrated on the drifting wisps of the camp fire and the men squatting or standing around it. He signed 'thirteen' at William to indicate their numbers and mimed a query for he could not immediately see Eleanor.

One of the Welshmen signalled to William.

'The other side of the big oak,' he translated on a breath to Renard. 'There's another man with her, eating and drinking.'

'Fourteen to five then. How many can you take with your bows if we move in?'

William pursed his lips and rubbed them along the cool, polished elm of his bow stave. At length he held up six fingers, increased them to eight. 'If we're lucky,' he added and, delicately fingering an arrow from the half dozen thrust through his belt, put it to the nock. 'Alive or dead?'

'How merciful do you feel?'

'Alive then,' William said in a cold, soft voice. For practice, he flexed the bow and sighted at one of two men who had left the fire and were strolling towards the large oak tree. They disappeared from range and suddenly the imperative cry of a startled blackbird shrilled out from the Welshman nearest the oak.

'What's happen . . .' began Renard, but whatever else he had been going to say was drowned out by Eleanor's screams. 'I hope that man of yours is a fast runner,' he muttered instead as he drew his sword.

William used the blackbird's cry three times to signal attack. Then he sighted again and let fly. The shaft thumped into his victim's chest, knocking him from his feet. He twitched, hands clawing at the feather shaft, and did not rise again. William nocked a fresh arrow and sent it in fluid pursuit of the first. The second mercenary was running and only winged, but his sword arm was rendered useless.

Renard ran around to the opposite side of the clearing and

was in time to save the young Welshman who had trilled the alarm from being broached by the blade of a bearded routier. Another man lay arrow-dead close by and a second one, bleeding hard, was struggling to remove a barbed arrow head from his pierced arm. The bearded one wore no hauberk, only a quilted gambeson that was still rucked up around his hairy thighs. He had no shield and Renard's blade almost immediately reached his throat.

'Yield,' Renard panted, holding back the death thrust.

'What for?' Hamo laughed grimly. 'So that you can swing me later?' And he lunged onto the blade. Whiplash swift, Renard twisted his wrist so that the wound went only half as deep as Hamo had intended. The cut welled blood rapidly, but not enough to kill. Renard used on him the same tripping technique he had once used on William, and as the mercenary went down, slashed and unwound one of the cross-garters from the chausses hampering the man's knees and used it to truss him up as efficiently as a dead deer brought home from the hunt. Then he looked round.

Eleanor was watching him, her back pressed rigidly against the oak trunk, fist to mouth and her skirts in disorder around her upper thighs. 'Are you all right?' he asked brusquely and flicked a rapid look to the fighting beyond.

Swallowing, she managed to croak a syllable that might have meant either yes or no. Renard, not having time to comfort or soothe, took it for the former. 'Good lass,' he addressed her as though she was a dog he was training. 'Stay right there. I'll be back as soon as I can.' And without more ado he plunged into the fray.

Eleanor shivered, teeth chattering, and hugged her arms. He had spoken to her with the impatience of a man forced to speak, seeing her as nothing more than an impediment. He did not even look like the Renard she remembered. His face was thinner, shed of its final puppy flesh and almost as brown as potter's clay, and the glint in his eyes had displayed neither kindness nor humour.

Hamo stared at her with baleful eyes, the blood running into his beard, his hands and feet working to try to untie Renard's rapid knots. She thought she saw some slack in his bonds and a new wave of terror surged over her. She pushed herself up against the trunk of the tree. Her legs wobbled uncontrollably. She went down again, grazing her knees, whimpering, then from the corner of her eye caught sight of Hamo's dagger and swordbelt, the long poniard still in its sheath. Crawling towards it, she set her fingers to the grip, eased it free, and turned to face her dread.

Hamo's eyes widened and he tried to roll among the leaves away from her. She saw that his wrists were bleeding and that Renard's knots were holding fast, but she did not release her grip on the poniard lest she also release her grip on sanity.

Swords clashed, scraping her eardrums. She saw Renard take a blow on his shield and counter strike with a rapid, hard back hand at his opponent's right knee. The man fell with a cry, the limb shorn through. Renard left him where he lay, not bothering to finish it, and ducked beneath the swipe of another opponent, buffeted his shield sharply beneath the man's chin and knocked him senseless.

Strangely detached from reality, Eleanor watched her future husband and thought of a ritual dance she had once seen performed at a harvest celebration. Death and fertility. Sowing the ground with blood. Virgins and sacrifices. Hysterical laughter welled up in her throat. She choked it down and found it turning into a sob.

The ground began to roar, to shake. She looked blankly at the bearded captive. He returned her stare, then groaning, closed his eyes and pressed his forehead into the fallen leaves. Horses thundered beween the trees, heralding the arrival of the Ravenstow knights and serjeants, and the tide of battle turned in Renard's and William's favour.

Renard leaned against a tree and took several deep, grateful breaths. A dull pain throbbed in his right side where a sword hilt had butted into his ribs and his arm hurt with the strain of sustained action. He was aware of them as minor background sensations as he surveyed with grim satisfaction the damage wrought upon one of Ranulf de Gernons's best mercenary contingents, probably the same group that had been harrying the Caermoel lands all spring and summer. He thought of Harry, then, belatedly, as his breathing eased, of Eleanor, and with a soft oath hastened across the clearing to find her.

There was a dagger in her hand and her eyes were wild and strange. His gut contracted and the hairs prickled erect down his spine. He had a momentary vision of Olwen as he had first seen her outside The Scimitar, light-footed and deadly.

'Nell, give me the knife,' he said softly, and held out a cautious hand as if to a wild animal.

She blinked at the sound of his voice and looked at the marks of his sword grip still imprinted upon his palm and fingers that by their tapering length should have belonged to a minstrel not a warrior, but she was learning to live with inconstancy. His hand touched her icy one with the contact of blood heat. Carefully he sought around her fingers to the grip of the knife and took it from her unresisting grasp. 'It's over now,' he said and drew her against him, free hand going to her hair.

Eleanor heard the gentler note in his voice and felt the familiar touch of his hand on her head, soothing the child she had always been to him, and knew that she was about to consolidate that opinion. Her eyes filled with water and her throat closed. Pressing her face into the gold velvet of his surcoat, she clung to him and wept like a lost infant.

Renard looked down at the crown of her head and felt her shuddering run through into his own body. He grimaced and even as he held her, murmuring reassurances, glanced across at William who was directing their rapid preparations to leave. They had time, but not sufficient to delay.

Hamo was hauled onto a pack-horse. A groan jerked from him as his breechless buttocks struck a horsehair saddle cloth. Eleanor gasped and squeezed her eyes shut at the sight of his nakedness. 'He was going to rape me and then claim me as a marriage prize from Earl Ranulf,' she gulped. 'I thought . . . I thought that it was really going to happen!' Her grip tightened on Renard and she trembled so violently that he thought her bones would tear through her flesh.

He held and soothed her for a while longer, and when the trembling eased slightly, cupped her face in his hands and forced her to look at him. 'Nell, we have to leave. We're in Earl Ranulf's territory and if we meet another of his patrols it would be the end of us; we haven't enough men. I don't expect you to ride your own horse. Come pillion with me ... Yes? Good girl.' He gave her a quick hug of encouragement and lightly kissed her clammy forehead.

'Don't leave me again!' she wailed in a panic-strangled voice, and clutched his arm convulsively as he turned away.

He swallowed his impatience. 'Gorvenal's tethered across the clearing. I'm only going to fetch him.'

'Renard . . .' Sobs choked out of her. She was beyond coherent thought, only knew that he was walking away. Renard's own thinking processes were perfectly clear, reaction reserved for when it was safe to react. The quicker they were out of here the better. He stopped, swung her up in his arms, and carried her the rest of the way to his stallion. She wrapped her arms around his neck and half-throttled him. He had to prize her off before he could mount up and when he lifted her into the saddle, she locked herself to him again as if he were the only rock amidst miles of quicksand. Renard wondered bleakly if she knew that the rock was made of quicksand too.

CHAPTER 11

E LEANOR FED A TWIST of raw, carded wool onto her
spindle, twirled and let it drop, and repeated the move
with an expert sleight of hand that required very little
mental concentration. The motion, however, was familiar and
soothing, occupying her hands and anchoring her to stability.

Within the bed over which it was her turn to sit in vigil,
Harry was sleeping uneasily. He was dosed to the eyeballs with
willow bark and poppy syrup and his wound was packed with
mouldy bread and a dressing of bandages smeared with honey.
Judith said that it had been very difficult to dig the arrow head
free. 'Like butchering an ox in the kitchens,' she had said in
her usual forthright way, and then burst into tears. 'I hate
November.'

At the time it had seemed a strange *non sequitur*, but since
then Eleanor had remembered that Judith had lost her first son
Miles in November when the White Ship went down. King
Henry had died in that month too and the door had blown
open to wolves such as Ranulf de Gernons.

It was too soon to know if Harry would live or die, and, if
the former, how much use he would have in his right arm.
Not a great deal, she suspected, by the look of the gaping
wound she had helped to dress yesterday. Everything was too
badly lacerated. Everything . . .

She plucked wool from the carded mass at her feet and
twirled it onto the distaff. The first night and day of her arrival
at Ravenstow were a merciful blur. She was not even sure that
she could recall the events leading up to that arrival. There
were shadowy images, nightmare figures dancing rampant in
blood and the echoing sound of her own weeping loud in her
ears; Renard's arms in comfort around her and the look in his

eyes. It was the last recollection that caused her to shiver. He did not want her. Blinkered by her innocence she might be, but not blind.

A hot bathtub, salve for her bruises and one of Judith's sleeping draughts had dealt with most of the physical trauma of her ordeal, and despite her earlier hysterics, Eleanor's gentle nature was also resilient. There were others in far worse cases, she told herself when she was visited by an attack of self-pity, and the ending could have been so different. If Renard and William had not been so swift and decisive in their pursuit, she might be lying in a marriage bed of an entirely different making than the one to be hers in two days' time.

As it was, those of Hamo's men who had survived the initial fight had been hung on the town gibbet. All of Ravenstow had turned out to watch the hangings. Guyon had arranged it for market day so that as many people as possible could witness and cheer. Hamo himself was not among the half dozen men entertaining the crowd with their death throes. While being granted a brief spell of daylight in the ward, he had escaped while his guard was distracted by the sight of a woman washing her legs beside the well. Having grabbed and untethered a standing horse, he had ridden hell for leather out of the gates. By the time pursuit was organised, it had been too late. Hamo had escaped both net and noose.

In disgust, Renard had flung up the march to Caermoel to survey the keep with an eye to strengthening it against Chester's greedy eye. That had been four days ago and there had been no messenger as yet. The wedding guests had begun to arrive and there were only two days left. Eleanor felt the tears threatening again, and quickly plied her distaff.

The curtain parted and a face peered round. She sniffed and managed a smile for John, Renard's older brother and a priest in the Earl of Leicester's household, home at Ravenstow to officiate at their wedding. Leicester was here too, bearing blandishments and good wishes from the King to his somewhat reluctant vassals at Ravenstow and inviting them to court for the Christmas gathering of the faithful.

John came to the bed. 'How is he?'

'Sleeping.' Eleanor stated the obvious because there was not a great deal else to be said. 'At least the wound fever hasn't set in, but it's still very early.'

'It's a pity he wasn't born with my eyes,' John murmured in the subdued tones of the sick room.

Eleanor smiled and looked puzzled. 'What do you mean?' John's eyes were his most arresting feature – a melting, deep brown, set beneath black, strongly marked brows. They were also so myopic that he was liable not to see objects in his way until it was too late to avoid them. It was a family joke that John had more scars on his shins and ankles from tripping over things than the rest of them had from all their battles put together.

'He'd have been the priest then. You don't go to war if you can't see. Harry would have made a good priest too, he's so good-natured and innocent – more innocent than I'll ever be.'

'He may yet take his vows,' she said grimly and came to stand beside him. 'I doubt he'll have much use in that right shoulder even if he does make a good recovery otherwise.' Leaning, she smoothed the coverlet with an almost maternal hand.

John saw and assimilated the gesture and wondered if he should warn her against being similarly maternal with Renard. She was likely to have her hand bitten off if she was.

'Did you come here to see Harry, or is it me you wanted?' she asked at his continued silence.

'A little of both really. I wanted to make sure that you are familiar with all parts of the wedding ceremony. It's all been rather rushed, and now this.' He gestured at Harry. 'If there's anything about which you're worried or uncertain, you only have to speak.'

He was looking at her steadily with compassion in his enormous brown gaze. She brought her chin up and managed to return the look with equal steadiness. 'I know my part,' she said stoutly. 'All you need do is pull the strings and I'll sit, kneel, stand, say what has to be said and do what has to be done.'

He bit his lip at the quality of her tone beneath the quietness.

It was not hysteria, but certainly something akin to it. 'Listen Nell . . .'

'Why don't you go and talk to Renard when he returns from his latest jaunt?' she interrupted bitterly. 'I'm sure he's in more need of advice about the ceremony than I am.'

John cocked his head. 'It would be more than my life is worth,' he said wryly. 'From what I hear, Renard's about as amiable just now as a barrel of hot pitch. I thought I might get more sense out of you, and you are the one who will be in the best position to keep him from exploding all over the rest of us.'

Eleanor stared at him in astonishment. 'Me? He doesn't know me. He doesn't even want to know me! He thinks I'm witless, a clinging, drizzling ninny.'

'Oh Nell, that's rubbish!' John laughed and set his arm across her shoulders.

'It's not,' she said grimly. 'I behaved like one. Renard was very patient with me, but I knew what he was thinking.'

'Then that augurs well because none of us ever do.'

'None of us ever do what?' Renard asked, walking through the archway into the room and dumping his helm and gauntlets on the coffer. His eyes were alight, dangerous glints of quartz in their darkness.

'Ever know what you are thinking,' John answered amiably and gave Eleanor a reassuring hug. 'And by the way you're scowling at a priest, a virgin and a sick man, I don't believe I really want to. Is it confessable?'

Renard glared at him, but then, amid a three days' dark stubble of beard, his lips started to curve. 'Oh, it's confessable all right,' he said somewhat grimly. 'But not in the present company. How's Harry?'

Eleanor spread her hands in a slightly nervous gesture. 'No better, no worse, my lord.'

He raised his brows at the soft intonation of the two final words and the blush that stained her milky skin. 'No wound fever then?' He stooped over the sick bed. 'He's hot.'

'A little, but nothing serious. I'll have a tub prepared for you.'

He looked round at her and stood up. 'Do I smell that bad?' His tone was barbed.

Her colour deepened to a dusky rose. 'No, my lord. I only thought that with the Earl of Leicester present and the other wedding guests ...' Her voice trailed off beneath his stare. Lowering her eyes she swallowed.

'Of course, you're right,' he said sarcastically. 'A bridegroom shouldn't come reeking to the feast. By all means prepare a tub. Scent it with bay and rosemary and spikenard and whatever other concoctions you can find in the coffer. We don't want to offend the Earl of Leicester's nose, do we?'

'Renard!' John reprimanded sharply.

'If you'll excuse me then, I'll go and see to it.' Lowering her gaze, lips compressed, Eleanor almost ran from the room.

'There was no need for that.' John glowered unfavourably at Renard from beneath his brows. 'She's only concerned for your welfare.'

Renard thrust his right hand into his hair, grabbed a handful, and released it. 'I know, I know,' he growled out on an exasperated breath. 'But the moment I walk in she starts twittering about bath tubs!' He gave a caustic laugh. 'Christ, the future of the earldom is in jeopardy and all I get is, "do I want to bathe"?'

'It was the offer of comfort and you'd do well to accept it. Half a candle notch with your eyes shut in a hot tub would do wonders for your temper. You haven't even greeted me properly yet, and after a gap of four years!'

Renard gave him a shame-faced grin and embraced him, then stood back. 'Take no notice. I'm glad to see you, but I'm not so sure about Robert of Leicester. Did you have to bring him?'

John shrugged. 'I asked him for leave to officiate at your wedding and he decided to invite himself too. More in the cause of diplomatic persuasion, I think, and he cannot abide Ranulf de Gernons. You want to think about that.'

'I'll see if I can find the time,' Renard said laconically and looked again at Harry. 'I don't think Leicester's revulsion can ever reach the depths of mine.'

A maid servant came into the room and dipped a curtsey to the two men. 'Mistress Eleanor has sent me to keep vigil over Lord Harry.'

John smiled at her and gestured to the bed, giving her full leave.

'Where's Mama?' asked Renard.

'Resting. She took the night watch with Harry, and Papa insisted that she went to bed until vespers at least. Papa's in the solar with Lord Leicester and Adam. His cough seems better than it was. Having you home has made all the difference.'

Renard looked down and beat dust from his travel-grimed clothing. 'I'm not surprised!' he snorted. 'I'm the one running my arse into the ground now.'

The words were spoken in a brittle tone, but without malice and John did not take him up on them but said instead, 'I hear you've got some solace at Hawkfield, an eastern dancing girl no less?'

'Hell's death!' Renard hissed, eyes flickering with irritation. 'That news has travelled faster than a dose of corn cockles through the bowels. Does Eleanor know?'

'Not as yet, at least I don't think so, but you'll have to tell her soon.'

'I know.' He tried to close the subject by walking towards the curtain, unhitching his swordbelt as he strode.

'Let her down lightly,' John pleaded. 'I know you have a lot on your mind, but for other reasons so has she.'

Renard sighed. 'All right, I'll try,' he murmured, 'if only to stop you from preaching me a sermon.'

Renard stepped into the bath water, noting that it was neither scented, herb-scattered, or anything else. It was, however, very hot and made him gasp and clutch at the sides of the tub.

'Are you trying to boil me!' he demanded indignantly.

'It will soon cool, my lord. You undressed more quickly than I expected,' Eleanor said meekly. 'I'm sorry. Shall I put in some more cold?'

'No, leave it now.' Gingerly he relaxed and looked at her. She was like a young deer, taut, quivering, poised for flight –

a tall, slim girl with enormous, haunted eyes and a dainty tip-tilted nose. Her lips were full and looked as though they would be quite kissable when set in a different expression. 'You were not so formal four years ago,' he said. 'Or have you forgotten my name?'

She blushed and shook her head and looked at her toes.

'It was a long time ago,' he mused. 'I used to slap your rump and ruffle your hair, but we've each gone beyond that kind of familiarity now, haven't we?'

'Yes my lo ... Renard,' she mumbled.

'Where's the soap?'

She brought it to him and he saw that her hands were shaking, and her chin dimpling with the effort of holding onto her composure. Guilty irritation washed over him, and then a wave of compassion. He sighed. 'I'm sorry if I was bad-tempered, Nell,' he said quietly. 'My mind was dealing with more difficult matters. You were right about the bath.'

Eyes still focused groundwards she turned away to fiddle with the towels that were laid out. 'My thoughts were only for your comfort.' It was the customary duty of the wives and daughters of a great household to see to the well-being of all new arrivals to the keep, be they visitors, friends or family. The offer of a bath tub and comfortable clothing was always the first hospitality. Eleanor had performed the function of hostess so many times now that this particular occasion should have come as second nature. The fact that it hadn't and that she was intensely aware of him, naked and in a volatile mood, was extremely unsettling.

'Yes, I know.' He began to wash. There was an awkward silence. More out of desperation to break it than anything else, he asked her how the flocks up at Woolcot were faring.

Her reply commenced in a quavery voice. He did not look at her as he washed, but occasionally intercepted with a question. Gradually her tone brightened with a spark of confidence. He discovered that the discussion, far from boring him, was a diversion from mental worries of vassals and supplies, stratagems and defences, sickness and death.

'I have ideas for the wool clip too,' she said, as he stepped from the tub and she handed him towels from an arm's length distance.

'Oh yes?' he said dryly, but Eleanor, not looking at his face, heard only the sarcasm without reading the humour.

'I ... I know they will be yours to deal with as you see fit after our wedding. I wasn't presuming. I ...'

Renard ceased drying himself, tucked the towel around his waist, and took hold of her shoulders. 'Stop making excuses and apologies Nell and we'll get along much better.'

'I thought that you were annoyed.' He was so close that she could not think properly. There was a huge queasy knot where her stomach should have been, part fear, part something else. She wanted to touch his skin, run her hands up his forearms and over the smoothness of muscle until she linked her fingers around his neck. Of course, innocent girls did not do such things uninvited, but when they had lived under Countess Judith's tuition, they knew about them all the same, even if not in graphic detail.

'I was teasing.' He tipped up her chin. 'Next time, just answer me back. I promise not to beat you.'

Blushing furiously, she broke away from his light grip.

Renard frowned slightly at her obvious discomfort and picked up his braies. 'So then, what are you going to do with the wool clip if not sell it to the Flemish?'

'Oh, some of it will still go to Flanders, we need that security.' She started to breathe more easily now that there was space between them. Her eyes flickered briefly to his groin but he was flaccid, neither threat nor promise in what hung there. The memory of Hamo's probing, swollen flesh was revolting, but the thought of accepting Renard was different, frightening and exciting at one and the same time.

'And the rest?' He had not missed the direction of her rapid glance, nor her momentary distraction and suddenly had an inkling of intuition as to the source of her flustered behaviour. Near rape was not going to give her a taste for bedding with an impatient, bad-tempered stranger.

'I thought of weaving and dyeing it at Woolcot to sell in Ravenstow and Shrewsbury and the other nearby towns.' After handing him chausses and cross-garters, she fetched a shirt and tunic from a pole near the brazier where they had been airing.

'That's already being done elsewhere,' he pointed out, 'although it would probably bring in some profit.'

'No, I don't mean homespuns, I mean high-quality fine cloths for those who usually buy from Flemish looms, but of course mine will cost that much less without all the transport tariffs.'

It was an audacious idea and not one on the face of it he would have expected to come from Eleanor. 'Where are you going to find the skills?' he tested as he wove the cross garters up his legs and tied them. 'Do we have them locally?'

'We do now.'

He looked up as she came over to him. She was confident again, a gleam brightening in her hazel-green eyes as she expounded, and her face a warm, rosy pink. 'Who possesses the skills that our weavers and dyers lack?'

'The Flemings,' he responded promptly.

She nodded. 'And what kind of mercenary does King Stephen employ in high numbers?'

'Incompetent ones?' Renard could not help commenting with a grin, but then he sobered. 'Flemings, I think I see what you mean.'

'Some want to retire from service, others are injured out of it. Many have families whom they want to see settled while they are at war and there are bound to be a good many with the skills I seek. I've found one experienced weaver and a dyer already and settled them on land in the village.'

Renard grasped the shirt she handed him and after a moment remembered to put it on.

She looked at him anxiously. 'What do you think?'

'What do I think ...?' He laughed and dug his fingers through his hair. 'Eleanor, I think I've been looking at a fish out of water suddenly gliding into a lake.'

'But ...'

'Yes, it's an excellent idea!'

She gave him a radiant stare, compounded of the puppy-like adoration he remembered and something else besides.

'Your tunic is a sample of the kind of cloth I'm hoping to produce,' she offered shyly.

Renard took the second garment from her hands. The fabric was smooth and soft and of a rich, dark blue, embroidered over in the same colour thread to give it an understated but undeniably rich appearance.

'It's from this year's clip,' she said. 'I used whinberry for the dye and a Flemish loom to weave the piece. I hope it fits you because I had to go by the measurements taken four years ago, although I did add some extra width to the shoulders.'

Thoughtfully he looked at the shirt he was already wearing. 'You made this too?'

Her small gesture was defensive. 'I become bored without a use for my hands, and I enjoy needlecraft.'

Rapidly reassessing his first impression of her, he put the tunic on. The fit was excellent and he saw that the embroidery consisted of tiny sheep and coils of grass and even a shepherd and a dog. 'You took no small time over this,' he said softly, a hint of awe in his voice.

'It is my wedding gift to you.' She blushed again. 'I know you must have serviceable tunics aplenty and Outremer silks, but you will need some warm court garments too. Besides, I wanted to see how the cloth would look as a finished garment. There's another tunic too, but you're not allowed to see that yet.'

Her expression became enchantingly shy, almost mischievous. She darted him an upward look through her lashes in totally innocent provocation. His breath caught. Before he could rationalise the move, he had slipped his arm around her waist, pulled her against him, and bent his mouth to hers.

Eleanor had been kissed by men before – her father, her vassals, Earl Guyon, Renard's brothers in rumbustious play at the Christmas feast, by Renard himself in a like, playful mood, but this sensual, deliberate intimacy was different. She had imagined it often enough, but the reality was out of her control and all in Renard's, the pressure of his lips delightful and frightening.

Sensing her uncertainty, he started to withdraw. Eleanor did what she had wanted to do earlier and ran her palms up his sleeves, across his shoulders, and laced her fingers in his hair. Their lips remained joined, hers parting as she pressed forwards against him and heard the catch in his throat, the change in his breathing. His hands tightened on her waist and she was suddenly aware of a pushing hardness against her abdomen and of strange lightning flickers of sensation between her thighs.

Renard's hand curved down over the small of her back, stroked there for a moment, then ventured lower, pressing her into that imperative hardness, releasing and pressing again. The kiss broke on a mutual gasp. Eleanor shuddered, thought about tearing herself away from the danger and instead buried her face in his neck with a half-sob and clung to him. Renard held her and closed his eyes. The sensations radiating from his shaft were so strong that he felt more pain than pleasure, and the pressure of Eleanor's body, the slight movements she was making were only intensifying his need – an instinctive demand for release that had no immediate hope of being satisfied.

Putting his hands up, he removed hers from around his neck, and still holding them, took a step back and a deep breath. Eleanor went as red as fire and dropped her lids in confusion. She had liked the feel of his arms around her and the touch of his lips, but the inevitable power channelling through their bodies had been a shock, the difference between observing a river in full spate and being tossed into it.

Releasing her, he turned away and began to buckle on his belt. 'It was only meant to be a kiss,' he said with a wry shrug. 'But sometimes one thing leads too quickly to another. I'm living on a knife edge just now and what I need to ease the tension is . . .'

She stared at him with round eyes, half-knowing what he meant and half-curious.

'What I need, I can't have. Hell's death!' he growled, thoroughly discomfited. 'How did we ever get onto this from wool production! I'd better go, the Earl of Leicester will be waiting.'

Lower lip trapped in her teeth, she watched him leave. One of the maids giggled behind her hand that it was going to be a fine wedding but nothing compared to the wedding night.

Eleanor rounded and snapped at the girl to hold her tongue and, for something to do, picked up Renard's discarded clothing to send down to the laundry. His shirt smelled of stale sweat and something far less identifiable and far more unsettlingly pleasant. Her body quivered with the memory of that kiss, the feel of his hands on her and the pressure of his engorged manhood. The sharp sensations still arrowed and darted in her loins, making her uncomfortable. The thought of the remedy made her hastily bundle the soiled garments into the arms of a waiting maid and seek a task with less evocative associations.

Robert Earl of Leicester was thirty-five years old, a handsome man with heavy-lidded grey eyes that missed very little despite their sleepy appearance. Renard greeted him with a smile that did not conceal any of his wariness and sat down on a vacant skin-draped stool near the brazier.

'I don't blame you,' Leicester said, amiably cynical. 'If I were you, I'd be looking at me that way too.'

Renard laughed and relaxed slightly. 'Everyone's hunting everyone else,' he said ruefully. 'You spend so much time looking over your shoulder that finally you disappear up your own backside.'

'The Earl has invited us to guest with Stephen at the Christmas court,' Guyon said huskily and cleared his throat. 'But I think he can appreciate that in the present circumstances it is impossible.'

'The King was hoping particularly to greet you,' Leicester said smoothly to Renard. 'And your new wife. Has she ever been to the Christmas court? It may be her only opportunity before she is burdened with little ones.'

Renard glanced speculatively at the Earl. 'Will Ranulf de Gernons and William de Roumare be there?' he asked.

'Probably, although with them, nothing is ever certain.'

'Apart from their greed.'

'Apart from their greed,' Leicester confirmed, grimacing.

Renard rose from the stool and paced the room. A woman's distaff lay on top of a pile of carded wool in a wide willow basket. He thought of Eleanor. His loins, independent of his mind, still pulsed with subdued sensation. He swung round. 'Then I'll come.'

'Renard . . .' Guyon began, and broke off, coughing. Adam moved from his seat in the candle shadows and quickly poured him some wine.

Renard turned to his father. 'Papa, if you had been that keen to see Mathilda wear a crown you'd have done more by now than just sit on the fence. You were persuaded to swear for her twelve years ago by Robert of Gloucester, but it was always a forced oath.'

'Mathilda has a son,' Adam pointed out, his voice calm but with a gleaming edge to it like the bite of good steel.

'Who could either save or sink us depending on how he matures, and don't say he cannot be any worse than what we have because it wouldn't be true.'

'I was not going to moot anything of the sort,' Adam said mildly. 'I was just going to remind you that the oath was not to Mathilda alone, but to the heirs of her body.'

Leicester scowled at Adam. 'Perhaps you ought to be with the rest of the rebels in Bristol,' he suggested, lip curling.

Adam spread his war-calloused palms. 'I make no bones as to where my sympathies dwell, but my family's interests and my lands come first. If Shrewsbury was to be regained by the Empress, it might be a different matter. For the nonce, I'm content to fence-sit and see what else Miles of Gloucester can accomplish apart from tucking Worcester, Hereford and Winchcomb beneath his belt. He's quite a thorn in Stephen's side, isn't he?'

Leicester's attempt at swallowing down his anger was audible. He glared at Adam who glared implacably back.

Guyon, struggling for breath tonight, gathered himself to intercept before the atmosphere became too volatile for it to end in anything less than a serious quarrel, but Renard pre-empted him.

'It's me you want, isn't it?' he said to Leicester. 'I have said I will come to court and bring Eleanor with me, and as you know I am not constrained by oaths to anyone. For the rest, an agreement to differ might be best. My mother's very proud of that screen. It's Lebanese cedarwood you know, straight from the Song of Solomon, and if it gets damaged while you're each trying to persuade the other, you'll have a war of an entirely different kind on your hands, one you'd lose.'

Robert of Leicester subsided with a reluctant chuckle and held out a broad, fleshy palm to Adam who sheepishly smiled and took it. Renard exchanged looks with his father and, widening his eyes, puffed out his cheeks in relief.

'Don't make me laugh!' Guyon wheezed and took a sip of wine. 'Did you look in on Harry?'

'He was asleep.' Renard's mouth levelled and tightened. 'I'll be seeking reparations at court.'

'You won't get them,' said Leicester. 'Leave well alone. 'Only an idiot kicks a wasp's nest when he's been stung.'

Renard said nothing, but his face closed. He sat down again restlessly.

'Did you raid while you were up at Caermoel?' Adam asked.

'I thought about it, but there wasn't enough time. I was too busy at the keep itself to hare about the country with a burning torch in my hand.' He looked at Leicester, poured himself some wine and made himself busy with it.

'And you're not going to talk about what you were doing in front of me?' said the Earl with a good-natured smile.

'No.' Renard returned the smile somewhat savagely. 'You saw the bodies on the gibbet as you rode in? Beautiful adornments for a wedding feast. I only wish that Ranulf of Chester was dangling among them.'

That evening as Ravenstow settled down to sleep, Renard showed his father a parchment upon which were rough sketches of suggested alterations to the castle at Caermoel. 'Not the keep as such, let that stay,' Renard said, finger advancing across the sheet, 'but extend the curtain wall across this part and build towers here and here to guard the approach, and also put some at intervals along the wall. I have also added plans for two more well shafts to be dug in these areas.'

Guyon stared at the plans in amazement. 'Are these your own ideas?'

'Borrowed and improvised from places I saw in Outremer. *Sayhun and Kaukab al-Hawa.* They're better than anything we've got.'

Judith looked over their shoulders. 'Expensive?' she queried.

'Depends what you set against it,' Renard shrugged. 'Not really. I can probably raise a relief from the vassals – with Papa's permission,' he added quickly. The physical responsibility for the earldom might now lie with him, but the verbal control was still his father's.

'I remember when the walls first went up,' Judith said mistily. 'It was in the early years of our marriage. You were conceived and born there.'

'And you don't want to see it all change?' He looked round at her.

'It was a long time ago,' she said with a briskness that covered the sudden depth of her emotion. 'Too long.'

'The changes are all to the good,' Guyon murmured. 'Providing you can do it without beggaring us.' He smiled at his wife. 'I remember those times too!' his tone was both rueful and poignant. 'Half a mind to the passion and the other half worrying about what to do if the Welsh made a full-scale assault. It's too strong for the Welsh now, but Ranulf de Gernons could probably take it if he made a determined siege.'

Renard tapped the parchment. 'Not when these have been implemented. I'll engage engineers and stone workers and start the work immediately.'

'Before you go to court?'

'As soon as all this nuptial fol de rol is over. I'll leave this with you.' He headed towards the door of his parents' bedchamber.

'Nuptial fol de rol?' Guyon repeated as his son reached the curtain. 'Renard, go gently with the girl. It might not be to your taste, but do not spoil it for her.'

Renard's shoulders stiffened and his hands clenched at his sides.

'It is my prerogative to deal you crusty advice,' Guyon added

112

with a mixture of humour and warning.

'And mine to do as I see fit,' Renard retorted, but relaxed his stance. 'Don't worry, I'll be as meek as a unicorn in a virgin's lap.'

'You don't expect me to believe that!'

Judith fixed him with a gimlet stare. 'Did you visit Hawkfield on your way home?'

'No I didn't.' He fingered the heavy crimson wool of the curtain. There was hunting on the morrow for fresh meat and he intended returning by way of Olwen, but he was not about to make such an admission to his mother who would not see his need in the same light that he saw it himself. She was still looking at him suspiciously. He could feel her eyes boring into his spine. Without turning round he bid her and his father good night and quickly made his escape.

'I knew you would come,' Olwen said. She stood in the doorway and watched Renard dismount in the gathering dusk. His courser hung its head and rested on one hip. Salty sweat caked its shoulders and flanks and there was a bloody score across its chest where a branch had whipped during the chase. Renard was in a similar way to his mount, burrs and snags in his cloak and a dried cut on the hand that delivered the reins to a groom.

'Water him, but not too much, and wipe him down but don't unsaddle him,' he instructed the man. 'I'm not staying long.'

'How long is not long?' Olwen asked, leaning against the door jamb and folding her arms.

The November wind rustled dead leaves across the court-yard. The coming night smelled cold. The warmth behind Olwen beckoned Renard and the faint, spicy aroma of food he had not tasted since leaving Antioch. A slight smile twisted his lips. In Outremer he had longed for salt beef and rye bread. Now it was the smell of lamb pilaff that was enticing him. 'As long as it takes,' he murmured, and drew her into his arms.

Her loose hair felt like silk, her mouth was warm and experienced like her body and he could have taken her there

113

and then on the threshold. 'Not long then,' she said against his lips, and slipped her hands down. 'My, my, you are eager aren't you? Perhaps we could just finish it here and you could be on your way to your bride.'

Renard grasped her hand and brought it back up and ground her back against the door post. 'Yes, we could, couldn't we?' he snarled, forcing his mouth down on hers. An involuntary cry rose in her throat and was stifled by the kiss. The wood pressed into her backbone.

He heard the smothered protest and felt her body crushed up hard against his. His anger turned inwards against himself and with an oath he released her. She remained braced against the door post, panting hard and glaring at him. Deliberately she wiped the back of her hand across her mouth. Scowling, she drew away from the door and went into the hall. Her manner was, however, of scornful invitation, not rebuff.

Renard scraped his fingers through his hair and wondered why he was not riding homewards with the rest of the hunting party with the kills from an excellent if rough day's sport. He looked towards the door, half-meaning to stride back out and catch them up. Then he looked at Olwen and knew that the other half was the stronger and the reason he was here in the first place.

They sat down to a shared bowl of lamb pilaff, flat bread, and the potent, cloudy local cider. Perhaps the skirmish had warned her not to trifle with Renard's temper that night, or perhaps the way he had looked at the door as if he would walk out on her, for she made no more attempts to bait him and her tongue when she answered his questions while they ate was civil, if stilted.

He noticed that the servants trod warily around her and the atmosphere made him feel uncomfortable, as if a nocked bow was aimed at the space between his shoulder blades. One of the younger girls, clumsy with nervousness, splashed cider onto Olwen's gown and received a stinging slap out of all proportion to the offence.

The girl retreated, trembling. Renard said nothing, just looked at Olwen, and beneath his stare, she coloured and dropped her lids. He found himself thinking that whatever the crime, Eleanor would never have struck a servant like that. He pushed his bowl away and drained his cup.

'You haven't finished your food.'

'I lost my appetite,' he retorted and stood up.

A frisson of fear tingled down her spine. She had thought to be content with everything she had gained, but perversely found herself dissatisfied, wanting more, and her growing frustration was taken out on the servants and on Renard now that he was here. But supposing he did not come again? Left her here to rot? She had seen it in his eyes. They had so little in common apart from the bed. Gesturing another maid to remove the remains of the meal she decided that it was time to invoke that common ground before it was too late.

'Do you not still hunger?' she murmured, eyeing him from between half-closed lids as she slowly unhooked the neck opening of her gown. Her actions were slow and deliberate. 'I thought this is what you came for.' She tossed her hair, sending a blonde ripple down her spine. Leaving him, she undulated slowly towards the bedchamber. On the threshold, she looked over her shoulder and parted her lips.

Renard thoroughly intended to walk out, but found that he could not. His feet refused to move in the direction of the door, but independent of his conscious will took him towards the screen. Olwen smiled and disappeared into the depths of the room. Like a moth drawn to a candle flame, Renard wove across the hall, and entering after her, dropped the curtain.

Propping herself up on one elbow, Olwen watched the candle-light play over Renard's back as he set about finding his clothes. He twitched when she put a languid hand on his skin. She had revelled in the effect she had on him, had enjoyed toying with him until he was on the verge of madness, but tonight, for her, the final pleasure had been elusive, hovering just out of reach.

'When will you come again?' she enquired.

Renard moved his shoulders. 'I don't know. After the wedding I've to return to Caermoel, and from there to the Christmas court.'

Olwen veiled her eyes. 'Will the Earl of Chester be at court too?' She made her voice neutral, as if she was indulging in conversation for the sake of it while he dressed, but her heart was thumping in great, heavy strokes.

'All the tenants-in-chief will be there, except the rebels of course. They'll be in Bristol.'

She knelt up, put her arms around his neck and snuggled her cheek against his. 'Take me with you?'

'I can't. It's official and Eleanor will be with me to be presented to the King and Queen.'

Olwen frowned at him and flounced onto the rumpled bedclothes. 'Am I supposed to stay in this poky, back-of-beyond byre for the rest of my life?' she demanded bitterly.

'You could have remained in Antioch to dance for your living,' he reminded her as he put on his braies and chausses. There was a livid mark on his thigh where she had bitten him.

'Yes, I could!' She rolled over away from him. Tears of frustration and rage prickled behind her lids. 'At least I would not be dying of boredom!'

He flickered her a look full of impatience. 'This land is yours. Far from being a "poky, back-of-beyond byre", it's prosperous and productive, one of the best beholden to Ravenstow, and if you had wit or wisdom about you, you'd nurture it, not mock and sneer. I need not have given you anything at all.'

'Oh, generous indeed!' she scoffed. 'Put a hoe in my hand and expect me to be overcome with gratitude!'

It was the look in her eyes and the tone of her voice, rather than her actual words that did the damage to Renard's temper. In a move that was whiplash swift he whirled and grabbed her, pushing her down. For a moment it hung in the balance. He had never in his life struck a woman before. It was against all his training. A man who beat a woman unmanned himself. He struggled, his whole body trembling as she goaded him towards the edge of a different kind of passion. She curved her thigh along the length of his and he saw the bloom of naked hunger in her eyes. His body answered hers, but this time he denied the temptation, and breathing hard, almost sobbing, thrust himself away from her. Without stopping to put on his remaining garments, he gathered them up in his arms, and because his voice would not serve him to speak, stormed out in damning silence.

Panting, body strung as taut as a resonating harp, Olwen stared after him. She heard the shouts of the grooms and the neigh of a horse, the drumming of hooves and then silence. The heat of lust and temper cooled from her skin, leaving her cold, as if she had been sitting too long at a hearth where the fire had gone out.

CHAPTER 12

ELEANOR SMILED PROUDLY at the gasps of awe, envy and delight as her wedding garments were laid across the bed. The undertunic with its tight-fitting sleeves was of a soft, wine-coloured wool, exquisitely stitched but unembellished, a plain foil for the overgown of moss-green velvet. The hem, throat and hanging sleeves of the gown were trimmed with bands of the red and both were oversewn with thread-of-gold in a tapestry of intricate detail. Foxes, leopards, sheep and horses curved around trees that stood against keeps, stylised to represent Ravenstow and Woolcot. In a garden stood a man and woman, hands clasped together, the man's tunic embroidered with tiny foxes, the woman's with grazing sheep.

The women wedding guests stroked, examined, and exclaimed over Eleanor's skills and a warm glow lit within her at their praise. A laughing remark was made about the couple in the garden. Eleanor blushed, unsure now that she wanted that particular part of the garment on public display and knowing that it was far too late to unpick the stitches.

Despite the braziers and the fire in the hearth, the room was still cold. The heat imbued to Eleanor's skin by the bath water was fading, and clothed as she was in nothing but her short shift, she started to shiver. Judith, her eyes dark-shadowed by permanent worry and lack of sleep, was preocccupied, but Heulwen noticed Eleanor's teeth clicking together and with a concerned murmur picked the under tunic from the bed and helped her to don it, followed by the gorgeous wedding gown.

'If Adam and I ever find anyone rash enough to take on our hoydens, I hope we can call on you to sew their gowns too,' she said as she fastened the lacings.

'Of course.' Eleanor smiled at the two girls, each in their best tunics, who were watching her, eyes round and awestruck as a veil of gold tissue was arranged over her hip-length cloud of black hair.

'You look like a princess!' Juditta breathed.

'Will Uncle Renard look like a prince?' Rhosyn enquired, and wriggled away from Dame Adela who was trying to tweak her chaplet straight.

Heulwen laughed. 'You know he will. He'd look like one if he were clothed in rags; he has that way about him. But then he's the grandson of a king, and nephew of an empress.'

'Harry is the one who most resembles his grandfather,' Judith said neutrally.

'Physically yes, but not in terms of presence,' Heulwen argued, then bit her tongue and lowered her eyes. 'Sorry Mama. It's not fair to keep holding up Harry and Renard for comparison. They're so unalike.'

Judith sighed and set another pin into Eleanor's veil. 'I suppose it isn't, but I know what you mean. Harry's nature is far too simple to have come from that side of his breeding. Your father says that he's like his Great-uncle Gerard, without the brains.' Her voice shook slightly.

Eleanor touched her gently. 'At least he hasn't taken the wound fever or stiffening sickness,' she tried to comfort. 'I know he has been hot, but nothing that willow bark and feverfew cannot contain. And if his nature is simple, it's also cheerful. He will make a good recovery, I know he will.'

Judith's preoccupied expression sharpened into focus on Eleanor, but she found not a hint of platitude. The girl actually believed what she was saying and Judith had to remind herself that Eleanor's nature was gentle and straightforward, completely lacking the ability to dissemble.

'And I'm sure you are right,' Judith said in a softer, more personal voice and tenderly embraced her, wondering at the same time if Renard, less familiar with Eleanor, would see the pride and stubbornness of spirit, or just the surface docility. After Olwen, Eleanor could either be as uninteresting as plain bread at a feast, or a welcome relief from a highly spiced diet.

Thomas d'Alberin's plump wife was simpering and giggling like a silly girl as she helped one of the other women to scatter herbs over the bottom sheet of the bed, the sheet that tomorrow would be blotched with the scarlet proof of Eleanor's virginity. She paused, her hand full of dried forget-me-nots, and called cheerfully to the bride, 'Which side will you be sleeping tonight? Nay, but I don't suppose you'll actually do much sleeping. When Thomas and I were wed, I couldn't sit comfortable for a week afterwards!' She winked and scattered the forget-me-nots. 'You be sure to lie just here if you want to bear your lord a fine son before next Michaelmas.'

Eleanor gave her a fixed smile, the heat glowing into her face.

'Pay no heed,' whispered Heulwen. 'It's all in jest. Just answer back and stick out your tongue.'

'That's as difficult for me to do as sewing is for you,' Eleanor said ruefully. 'I can't.'

Heulwen considered her with a frown. 'You're not scared about tonight are you? I mean after what happened?'

For a moment Eleanor thought that Heulwen was talking about the embrace in the wall chamber two days since and only belatedly realised that she was in fact referring to the attempted rape.

'What? Oh no ... well, only a little. More butterflies than terror.' She gave a small, philosophical shrug. 'Renard's skilled at dalliance, isn't he? There'll only be one fumbling innocent in that bed tonight – me.'

Heulwen exchanged a glance, surreptitious as she thought, with her stepmother, but Eleanor was quick and caught it. 'I may be innocent,' she said with dignity, 'but I'm not ignorant. I know there were women at court and at home before he left for Antioch, and I do not for one moment believe he was celibate while he was out there ... What is it? What have I said?'

Heulwen avoided Eleanor's bright hazel stare.

'Child,' Judith murmured. 'If you know my son's nature then you will be prepared for whatever the future may throw at you . . . and strong enough to weather it, I pray.'

It was a strange thing to say and Eleanor felt a tingle of alarm run down her spine, but had no time to examine or probe further because a squire came enquiring if the bridal party was ready for church and there was a sudden flurry of giggles and last minute adjustments and the sweeping on of thick, furred cloaks. The thought was pushed from her mind, but hovered to one side of it with the indignation of an unlooked–for wedding guest left standing in the cold.

In response to Harry's croaked command, Renard turned in a slow circle. 'What do you think?' he grinned. 'Awe-inspiring, isn't it?'

'Don't mock,' Harry said weakly and then pointed to his pillows. 'Prop me up, will you?'

Renard obliged, and as he moved, heard a seam in his wedding tunic give a slight crack and was almost relieved to know that it was not perfect.

The main colour was a deep red wool with cuff and hem trimmings of green and the whole of it decorated with a twining forest of thread–of–gold among which foxes ran, sat, played and fought. Eleanor's skills as an embroideress were without question. It would make a superb court robe, but Renard was not entirely comfortable with such ostentation no matter the amount of thought and care that had gone into its creation.

'I wasn't mocking,' he said as he sat down on the stool at the head of the bed. 'It *is* awe-inspiring. If King Stephen sees me in this, he'll think I'm using the claim of my grandfather's blood to set myself up as another contender for his crown – and that I'm a popinjay into the bargain.'

Despite himself Harry chuckled, then caught his breath as the movement in his chest and shoulders sent the pain coursing through his wound. 'You don't wear rings or oil and perfume your hair like the Bishop of Winchester, and you don't stuff the toes of your shoes with horsehair and decorate them with bells,' he objected.

'Ah, but these are early days yet,' Renard grinned, and then sobered to study his brother. 'At least, even if you're not well enough to be stretchered to church to witness the wedding, you're on the mend. No wound fever, so the women say. Mama's mouldy bread always seems to work. How do the arm and shoulder feel?'

'I've got some movement there, but it's very weak and it hurts like all the devils in hell to move it. I'll have to toast you with my left hand.'

'At least you'll be at the feast. Last week we did not know if it would be held to mark your funeral instead of my marriage.' Renard rose to leave.

'Renard . . .' Harry's voice was husky. He did not yet have the strength to raise it. 'You're a lucky bastard. Don't abuse it.'

Even enfeebled and distorted by physical pain, the emotion in Harry's voice came through, and Renard stared at him in dawning astonishment.

'Go away.' Harry closed his eyes.

For a moment Renard remained where he was, just staring. He supposed that it was not so unlikely. Harry's was the kind of nature to thrive on Eleanor's gentle domesticity. All too easy for brotherly affection to deepen into something much more dangerous.

'Does Eleanor know?'

'I'm not that stupid. Besides, it is you she has always loved.' His eyelids tightened. 'If I wasn't so sick I wouldn't be telling you this. Private . . . none of your concern. But if you forsake her for that dancing girl you brought home with you, I'll kill you myself!'

'How did you know about . . .'

'I've got ears to hear. People talk over my head and think because I'm ill that I'm unaware . . . You didn't come back last night until well after compline did you?'

Renard was by now heartily fed up with people telling him to be kind to Eleanor. He could not, however, in the present circumstances, vent his irritation in a bad-tempered outburst on Harry. Composing himself he said, 'I'll do my best by Eleanor but I'm not going to give you reassurances about my "dancing girl" because I'd probably not honour them. I'll explain later when you're in a better condition.' He looked round as Adam came into the room holding out a cloak.

'Ready?' he asked.

Renard nodded and swinging the garment around his shoulders stabbed in the round Welsh pin.

Adam looked from one to the other, sensing the tension. A frown was scoring two deep lines between Renard's brows and Harry's skin was beaded with feverish sweat. A maid came from the corner of the room with a bowl of lavender water and began gently to wipe him down.

Adam jerked his head. 'What's wrong?'

'Nothing,' Renard said lightly. 'What could be wrong on a day of joy such as this?' His brow cleared and he smiled, but his expression was as cosmetic as the fine wedding garments masking his hard, warrior's body.

'Wassail!' The traditional cry echoed round the hall in the Anglo-Saxon tongue.

'Drink, hail!' came the response, and cups and goblets were raised and drained and not for the first time or the last.

Eleanor stared round Ravenstow's great hall at the progression of her wedding feast. Flown with wine, Rhodri ap Tewdr, Welsh prince, wedding guest and family friend, was subjecting them all to an impromptu rendition of *Dingodad's Speckled Petticoat*, much to Juditta's and Rhosyn's delight. It was at least a child's song and a deal less explicit than some of the others that had been requested of the professional minstrels in the gallery.

Renard grimaced as the notes quavered towards the beams. 'If I were a maid and he serenaded me thus, I'd run for my sanity,' he leaned to murmur in her ear.

'It certainly doesn't seem to have done him any harm by his wife,' Eleanor contradicted. 'How many children do they have now? Ten in as many years?'

'It's probably the only way she can get him to shut up,' Renard said, then muttered an oath under his breath and started to get up as fighting broke out between one of Rhodri's Welsh and a knight of Leicester's household.

Rhodri was too far in his cups to do anything except stare reproachfully at the commotion interrupting his song. William plunged into the midst of the mêlée to separate the combatants before fists could become armed with knives and a full-scale war developed, and hauled the Welshman away by the scruff of his leather jerkin. John quickly set about calming the knight to a muttering simmer. Renard subsided onto his chair. Brawls were a not uncommon hazard of wedding feasts when the wine was plentiful and people were brought together who would not always choose to be in each other's company. Stephen's Christmas court would likely be beset by similar or worse problems.

Eleanor watched Renard reach to his cup and swallow. The evening was well advanced and although mellowed by the wine he was by no means drunk, staying sober with an obvious purpose in mind. She picked up her own cup and sipped at the contents, aware that she herself was more sober than perhaps a new bride should be. There had been dancing earlier, and thirsty after exertion, she had gulped down a full cup of the strong Anjou wine. Her head had started to spin and unsure of the sensation she had drunk scarcely anything since, perhaps a mistake. Through her lashes she continued to look at Renard. The tunic suited his darkness and she had been deeply satisfied by the responses of the guests when they first saw the bride and groom together, uncloaked at the wedding mass – two halves making one whole.

Renard turned his head and caught her looking at him. Her breath quickened and shuddered. Down the hall, shouts once more rose towards a crescendo, and with difficulty were subdued, the culprits dragged out into the sleety night to literally cool off.

Renard decided that it was time to set the next act in the charade into motion, one to which he was not averse. Eleanor looked very fetching. The crimson and green suited her well and the tight lacing of undergown and tunic accentuated her figure. The looks she had been giving him, full of nervous curiosity and the warmth of the wine had stirred his blood.

She might not have the skills that Olwen used to such exquisite effect, but her very innocence was stimulating.

Next time she flicked him a look, he trapped her with his own stare and leaning forward, kissed her. Eleanor's eyes closed. So did Harry's where he sat propped upon cushions in a high-backed chair and his good hand dug into the plaid of the blanket covering his knees. Renard's own eyes were open and he saw his brother's reaction. On a surge of pity, he withdrew from the kiss, for its signal had already been recognised by the more eager of the wedding guests, A raucous cheer went up. He felt Eleanor stiffen and draw away from him, her pupils so widely dilated that her eyes looked black. He formally kissed her hand and giving her a reassuring smile, rose to leave. The women converged upon her, led by Judith, and bride and groom were separated for the bedding ceremony.

Harry declined to be carried upstairs by some well-meaning but drink-fuddled guests to witness the ceremony. He said that he was tired. He said that he did not want to be jostled about. He said that he would rather wait downstairs in the company of a flagon. By the time they returned, the flagon was empty and Harry was full to the point of oblivion.

Eleanor shivered as the women stood her on a sheepskin rug near the hearth of the main bedchamber and began disrobing her. First the tunic, then the undergown, followed by soft shoes of green leather and the fine woollen hose and garters, and finally her short linen shift so that she stood naked, bathed in the fireglow, her hair crackling around her hips.

Some of the women were eyeing her dubiously and discussing whether or not her hips were wide enough for successful childbearing, their voices over loud with the wine they had drunk. Heulwen silenced them crossly while Judith draped a bedrobe around Eleanor's goose-fleshed shoulders and drew her to the bed.

Memories of her own wedding night crowded Judith's mind. She had been a couple of years younger than Eleanor and terrified of the coming ordeal, never having known anything but abuse from men. It had been this very chamber and a night like tonight with snow threatening in the wind and the women around her offering advice that was meant to be practical and kind but that had only increased her dread. One of them had given her a pot of dead nettle salve, telling her that it would soothe her abused female passage. Another had told her not to worry; the bigger the man and the more it hurt, the more likely she was to conceive a boy. By the time the men had come into the room, Guyon naked among them, she had been almost insensible with terror.

Eleanor's situation was different. The girl had known since childhood that she would marry Renard. Her father had been strict with her but not brutal, and when he died she had grown to maturity among her future family at Ravenstow. The fear was bound to be less, but even so, Judith knew that at this precise point in the proceedings, it was all too easy to become overwhelmed.

Eleanor grimaced and wriggled on the strewn, dried flowers. The scent of lavender rose from the bolster and pillows and there was a strong herbal smell from the crushed plants beneath her. She looked at Judith and smiled ruefully but said nothing. Her throat was too tight and she felt a little sick.

'It will be all right, I promise you,' Judith said as she prepared the traditional cup of spiced hippocras — another aid to potence and fertility. She tossed her head at the loudest of the women. 'Take no notice of them unless it's to feel sorry. They'd take your place if they could.'

'I'm not worried,' Eleanor croaked. 'I only wish that ...' She stopped speaking and clutched at the coverlet as noise sounded in the antechamber, approached the inner room, and suddenly burst upon the women in a cluster of less than sober men, Renard being jostled among them.

Robert of Leicester was laughing so hard that he could scarcely finish the joke he was in the midst of telling. '... And the squire says to the whore, "The priest told me that if I ever sinned with a woman I'd be turned to stone, and look, it's started happening!"'

Loud guffaws and drunken bonhomie. Someone slapped Renard so hard between the shoulder blades that he winced and staggered.

'Steady on!' cried someone else. 'It'll be your blood that flows, not the bride's if you render him incapable!'

More laughter. 'It's a blessing that bitch yesterday didn't bite him any higher up!' chortled de Lorys, and then howled as Adam dug an elbow viciously into his ribs. 'What did you do that for?'

Naked among the throng, Renard shrugged himself free of their grasping hands. 'The only blessing I want now,' he said, 'is that of a priest on this bed. Where's John?'

'Eager to get to business are we?' grinned Ancelin.

Renard looked round, both amused and irritated. 'Not "we", Ancelin ... At least I don't understand from the vows I took that you're anywhere involved in this.'

The remark was greeted with ribald shouts of laughter and Ancelin became the recipient of the shoulder slaps.

'Send him to Hawkfield in your stead!' slurred de Lorys at the top of his voice. Adam dragged him out of the throng and elbowed him again, this time in the diaphragm, effectively silencing him.

John thrust his way to the forefront, complete with silver vessel of holy water and a sprinkler. Although not drunk, he was very merry and his brown eyes were aglow with mischief.

'What's the remedy, Father, if Renard should find himself turning to stone?' asked Leicester, nudging his chaplain.

John rubbed his jaw and pretended to consider. 'Well now,' he deliberated. 'A dipper of cold well water blessed by a priest and poured over the offending member works wonders, but the best remedy by far is to put it in a warm, dark place and leave it there all night ... if you know where to find one.'

De Lorys was too busy being sick in the antechamber to mention Hawkfield a third time. Leicester screwed up his face as if pondering the problem, then looked at Eleanor in mock, exaggerated understanding, his act greeted by loud guffaws. Eleanor blushed a fiery red and refused to raise her lids beyond the hands that tightly gripped the coverlet.

Judith caught Renard's eye and made a small gesture at the doorway. He saw that she was desperately hoping he was not as wine-flown as the rest of the men. Merry he certainly was, but nowhere near intoxication, and his mother's concern and Eleanor's strained expression recalled him to responsibility. The trick was to know how far to go without stepping off the edge, although sometimes other people pushed you over it. He thought of the bite mark on his thigh, Olwen's deliberate branding. The wavering candle light concealed the worst of it, thank Christ, but he would have bruising for days to come, and not just of the flesh. Olwen knew how to set her claws into a man's soul and tear it to shreds. He shut her from his mind and abruptly stepped forward, hands held palm outwards to the chuckling crowd. 'Enough!' he cried. 'I have to leave it in all night so the good father says and it's half-way to cock crow already.'

There was more laughter at the innuendo placed on the words 'cock crow' and jests about rising at dawn and then rowdy cheers and barracking advice as Renard climbed into bed beside his flustered new wife and John solemnly blessed and thoroughly sprinkle-soaked them with holy water.

Guyon's voice was hoarse tonight, raw with phlegm and he was unable to raise it and clear from the room the reluctant revellers who wanted to squeeze the last drop of enjoyment from the situation. William's light baritone was useless and John had developed a severe attack of hiccups. Robert of Leicester, however, had a bellow on him like a rutting stag and muscle-thickened arms that gathered up, swiped into line, and ushered most effectively.

'I trust you'll remember this favour,' he twinkled ambiguously at Renard as he stood on the threshold.

'I'll ask you to stand godfather to any child that comes of this night,' Renard said dryly.

Leicester chuckled. 'I'll hold you to that, with the Countess and all these ladies here as witnesses.'

'Was that wise?' Judith murmured as the women kissed Eleanor and filed out.

Renard jerked his shoulders. 'He's Chester's counter-balance, equally as powerful. If I don't cultivate him then I've got to cultivate the other. Besides, I like him.'

'But he is firmly committed as Stephen's man.'

He looked at her keenly then veiled his eyes. 'Yes, Mama, I know.'

'But . . .' Her lips tightened.

'It is my wedding night,' he reminded her.

Judith looked away. Renard had taken his father's black leopard as a blazon for his own shield, but adapted it from the couchant to the snarling rampant. If she had ever had her hand on its leash, the beast had long since torn free and now confronted her, narrow-eyed and dangerous. 'Yes, so it is,' she agreed softly and leaned to embrace Eleanor and then more tentatively her son, wished them well, and left, her step slightly unsteady, although Eleanor could not remember having seen her drink more than two cups of wine all night.

'What's the matter?' she asked Renard as the curtain dropped behind Judith, a door closed, and they were suddenly and silently alone.

'Oh nothing.' He eased the pillow against his spine. 'She doesn't like to see my hand hovering over a chess board knowing that she cannot influence my next move. We've always argued. She can't wrap me around her little finger the way she can my father and it worries her.' He smiled grimly. 'Still, it's thicker than water. If we fight, it's not through hatred, rather the opposite.'

The silence settled, as heavy as the fine quality Arras curtain and the door that separated them from the rest of the keep. Renard picked up the cup of spiced hippocras and grimaced. 'Do you want some?'

She took it from him. 'Don't you like it?'

'Loathe it,' he replied. 'I don't know how Papa can drink it.'

'It's supposed to warm your blood.' She took a quick sip. It was sweet, spicy with cinnamon and nutmeg and not unpleasant to her own palate. She took another swallow and stopped. My lips will taste of it, she thought, and he said he loathes it.

'My blood doesn't need warming,' Renard said softly, watching the candle light play over her skin and smiling at the way she kept the bed clothes modestly tucked around her breasts. She was shivering slightly, and as he touched her arm and took the cup from her, he felt the slightly rough texture of gooseflesh along her arm. 'But yours does.' Setting the cup down on the coffer, he turned and gently pressed her down on the mattress.

'Oh,' said Eleanor, wide-eyed, and swallowed.

He drew the coverings over and around them, swathing them in linen and thick, stitched-together furs, and putting his arm across her cold body, drew her close to share his warmth.

'Oh,' said Eleanor again as she felt his heat, and then a movement between their bodies, a sleepy stirring against her abdomen and thighs. She tensed, trying to flinch away from its growing hot intrusion but constrained to stay where she was by the weight of Renard's forearm on her hip bone.

'Lie still, Nell,' he murmured. 'I'm not going to hurt you.'

'I know . . . It's just that . . .' She got no further for he silenced her mouth with a gentle, almost fraternal kiss and stroked the sensitive valley of her spine and the curve of her buttocks.

'There is no cause for haste,' he said softly. 'You have to learn to walk before you can run.'

The coldness started to melt from her limbs. Renard's hands and voice were soothing. She relaxed slightly against him, and then a little more as she realised she was not about to be pounced upon and devoured. Drowsiness began to steal upon her as she was stroked, the day's tensions easing from her. She closed her eyes and snuggled into the warm, strong contours of his body. Her breathing slowed and deepened as she lazed in the pleasure of his fingertips.

Renard brushed his lips over her throat and the silky curve of her shoulder. He encountered a thick strand of her herb-scented hair, and raising his head to look into her face saw that he had soothed her too far. She was hovering on the verge of sleep if not already over its first threshold. He imagined the response of the wedding guests could they but witness this scene and laughed to himself at the irony. All the jesting, the knowing looks. No hope of a warm, dark place now. His mother would be pleased. No child for Robert of Leicester.

'Oh Eleanor,' he said helplessly to her unconscious form, and shaking with silent laughter, put his head down beside her, his arm still across her body. His half-curious erection subsided. He was not in any need; Olwen had seen to that. At the time he had thought it was better so. In hindsight, perhaps not. Too late. He closed his eyes and matched the rhythm of his breathing to Eleanor's, and within five minutes was himself asleep.

Pain woke Eleanor with a jolt, and when she tried to escape from it, it only hurt the more. The night candle was still burning on its pricket and the fire in the hearth was a dull red glow through grey logs of ash. Unable to get up, and still more than half-asleep, she started to struggle and cry out.

Alarmed, Renard shot up, thus removing his weight from her spread hair and the cause of her pain. 'What is it?' he stared round blearily.

Eleanor gasped with relief. 'I couldn't move. You were lying on my hair and I dreamed that I was trapped.'

Renard grunted and lay back down to recover his senses. He glanced at the night candle. It had burned well down on its pricket but not far enough for dawn. 'Is there any wine?' he asked. 'Not the hippocras, something honest and ordinary.'

'I'll see.' Shrugging into her bed robe, she padded over to the table that stood near the narrow window slit. He watched the heavy swing of her blue-black hair and yawned.

'It's watered,' she said as she poured from flagon to cup and tasted on her way back to him.

'No matter.' Sitting up, he took it from her.

Eleanor gave him a look from her eye corners before stooping to brush the scratchy fragments of dried herbs from her portion of the bed with the flat of her palm until the sheet was smooth and white – an ordinary sheet, its very blankness significant. By now it should have been stained with the proof of her virginity.

'I can say with complete truth that this is the first time a woman has ever gone to sleep on my attentions,' Renard said lightly, trying to dispel the tension he could sense in her.

She bit her lip. 'I didn't realise how tired I was. I did not mean to.'

Renard swirled the wine reflectively in his cup. 'It doesn't

131

matter,' he said with a shrug. 'I suppose I could have been more persuasive, but I didn't want to frighten you, and besides, I was tired myself.'

Her gaze fell on the tell-tale bruise marring his thigh and she found herself unable to look away. The remarks de Lorys had made about a bitch biting him fell into place with what Judith had said earlier when they were dressing for the wedding.

Made uncomfortable by the quality of her stare and feeling the sting of guilt, he shifted and drew up the covers. 'Get back into bed, Nell, it's cold,' he said.

She cast him a bright, almost challenging look. 'It was after the hunt, wasn't it?' Her voice was raw with pain. 'You were late returning and I could smell attar of roses on you.'

Renard bit the inside of his mouth, aware that there was no point in denying the accusation. 'I needed the release,' he said. 'I didn't want to be rough with you tonight.'

'I see,' she said in a choked, defensive voice. 'You were only thinking of my welfare. You are very kind.'

'Oh, in the name of Christ!' he muttered in exasperation as she started to cry. 'Eleanor, don't.' He took hold of her jaw and forcibly turned her so that he could brush away her tears on his thumb. 'I admit it was stupid of me, but at the time I thought it was right.' Slipping his hand beneath her thick sweep of hair, he stroked her neck, drew her against him, and kissed her gently. Her lips parted, responding even while she wept and her hands came up to clutch at him, fingernails scoring his shoulders. The pressure of the kiss increased at her insistence and when he made to pull away, her hold tightened.

'Now,' she whispered against his lips. 'For the sake of my pride, now, before there is nothing left.'

Renard felt her trembling against him, the rapid shaking of her breath and heartbeat, the coldness of her skin as she shrugged out of the bed robe. His body responded to the frantic demand of hers, and putting his hand on her breast, he covered her with his warmth.

★

Eleanor's eyes had been squeezed shut against the pain. It had eased a little now, but it still hurt. Releasing her breath, she tried to relax her tense body. Beside her she was aware of Renard's similar tension. He swore softly, but whether at himself or her she could not be sure.

'It isn't always like that,' he said after a moment, his voice sounding weary. 'I thought that you were ready.'

Eleanor bit her lip. The weak pleasure that had coursed through her limbs two days ago had been entirely missing. She had felt nothing at his touch, only a desperate need born of insecurity to unite their bodies, one within the other – and it had been a total disaster. She had tried not to cry out, but the first pain of penetration had been so violent that she had been unable to prevent the scream that rose in her throat, her body arched against his, taut with agony, too tense to receive and welcome what she craved the most.

At least it had not been prolonged. About the same time that it took a ram to mount and fertilise a ewe. Eleanor wondered if she had conceived and hoped so. After this he would not want to bed with her again unless necessary, nor did she relish the thought herself. Every one of the six searing thrusts with which he had taken her maidenhead were branded on her memory in bloody pain. She raised the covers and then herself to see if the sheet was stained with sufficient proof of her virginity, and discovered the linen damp beneath her.

'If there's no blood, I'll go surety for your innocence,' Renard said wryly in a certain amount of discomfort himself. His foreplay had been met with wild impatience, almost irritation, and she had slipped beneath him, parted thighs not just inviting, but demanding. It was then that he had discovered she was far from ready; so tight and dry that penetration had been agony for her, painful for him, and after the first few movements he had seen no sense in continuing the torture and withdrawn, the act incomplete. Eleanor was too inexperienced to know the difference and he was not about to maim either of them with a demonstration.

Eleanor grimaced at the red smears on the inside of her thighs, the blotched sheet, and let the covers fall. 'I suppose I am not a patch on her,' she said in a low voice.

'What?' He looked at her blankly.

'The other woman; the one at Hawkfield who bit you.'

Renard's eyes were gritty with fatigue. All he wanted to do was turn over, go back to sleep and pretend that tonight had never happened. It had and he couldn't. His conscience would not let him. Sitting up, he dry-washed his face and groaned, then lowered his hands and looked at her. 'I was going to tell you about her before, but I didn't want to spoil the wedding for you. Skeletons have a way of leaping out of cupboards at the most inappropriate moments, don't they?'

Eleanor swallowed. She felt trembly and cold. It was not that she expected Renard to be faithful to her – that was just the dream. She had grown up among his family, had watched him from a childhood distance as he flirted and dallied on feast days, had seen him kissing Roslind, the falconer's daughter. She had been prepared, if not willing, to accept casual infidelity, but on the eve of her wedding and immediately beneath her nose, it hurt.

'What is she to you?'

Renard grimaced. 'A thorn in my side.' He took his half-finished wine from the coffer. 'If she hadn't been with child, I'd never have brought her from Antioch in the first place.'

Nausea added itself to Eleanor's other various discomforts. 'She's with child?' she repeated numbly.

'Not now. She miscarried on the road from Brindisi, but I couldn't abandon her in the middle of nowhere the state she was in and she was still determined to travel to England.' Briefly he told her about himself and Olwen, paring the narrative down to the sparsest facts and reasons.

'So you brought her back to England and installed her at Hawkfield,' Eleanor said in a dull voice.

'Would you rather I kept her at Ravenstow?' His gaze lifted to her face and flashed brighter grey at her tight-lipped silence. 'Well, would you, Nell?'

'I would rather neither.' She busied herself with finding and donning her crumbled bed robe. That was bloodstained too, she noticed with distaste, and wondered why she was fighting.

Leaving the bed she went to sit down before the hearth, her back to him, and rubbed her cold shoulders with equally cold hands. Marriages were made for convenience, she told herself. She and Renard were joined for the sake of their lands, and if begetting an heir to those lands was even half as painful as tonight's experience, then this Syrian gutter-slut was welcome to all his attentions.

'It can't be neither,' he said. She tensed, hearing him leave the bed. 'It has gone too far for that, Nell. Just don't read too many portents into it. It is you who are my wife.'

'Hah!' she spat bitterly. 'Bought and sold for a meaningless vow and a parcel of land!' She clenched her jaw as his hand came lightly down on her shoulder and she felt his breath against her cheek.

'I don't blame you for being angry, but it's late, and you're overwrought,' he murmured. The breath became a gentle kiss. 'Can we not start afresh in the morning?'

He was used to cozening women, she thought, stiffening herself against the light touch of his hands and lips. Staring into the fire, she watched it fall into ashes. 'If you want,' she murmured in a blank, dutiful voice '... my lord.'

CHAPTER 13

Salisbury
Christmas 1139

THE HORSES THUNDERED PAST the on-lookers, hooves tearing clods from the moist December grass. Breath smoking from wide-flared nostrils and muscles flowing like fire, they devoured the length of the race-course crudely marked out on the tourney field. A bright chestnut boasted a half length lead over a powerful ash-grey with black points. At the grey's hindquarters a bay strove to gain ground, and a length behind, an ugly brown was fighting to maintain contact.

The fair bearded man in a cloak trimmed with ermines clenched his fists against the fur and muttered anxiously beneath his breath as the chestnut eased further in front. 'Too soon, he has taken him too soon.'

Beside his king, Ranulf de Gernons twisted the tail of one long black moustache around his forefinger and smiled in his mind if not on his face. It had been a simple enough matter to bribe the boy astride the royal courser to waste him on the first stage of the race. The grey would probably have won anyway, but being as several bags of silver were riding on the outcome, Ranulf had preferred to make sure. It was money that Stephen could afford to lose. The Bishop of Salisbury's demise less than a month ago had left the King in delighted possession of everything that was in the old weasel's strong boxes. It was the reason the court was spending Christmas in Salisbury instead of gathering at Windsor. Stephen wanted to take account of and secure the bishop's massive wealth for himself.

Robert of Leicester hunched his shoulders against the gnawing wind and watched the coursers swirl around the post at the far end of the designated sprint. Like horse, like owner, he thought wryly. Stephen's chestnut had the swiftest turn of foot but only in a very limited burst; de Gernons's grey was powerful, showy, and unpredictable. His own bay, an honest worker, had no exceptional talent, and the brown would still be running one-paced long after all the others had dropped.

He flickered a glance across the field towards a young nobleman who was holding the bridle of an elegant black stallion and talking earnestly to one of the King's Flemings. Renard FitzGuyon of Ravenstow. A pity he had not been here earlier when the race was organised. Neither chestnut nor grey would have stood a chance against the black's pace as demonstrated over Ravenstow's hunting grounds during the two days of celebrations following the wedding feast.

The thunder of hooves swelled in a crescendo towards the waiting men. Stephen's horse was sweat-darkened and visibly labouring. The grey pushed its nose in front. Stephen's disappointed groan was audible. Ranulf de Gernons continued to finger his moustache and say nothing, but his eyes glittered. The horses tore past their owners in a wind of ragged manes, tails and tearing breath, the earth shaken by the force of their speed.

'Congratulations, Ranulf.' Stephen managed a tepid smile at Chester. 'I would have sworn on my life that Automne was going to win. A good thing I didn't, eh?' It was supposed to be a jest, but it fell tellingly flat.

Leicester was driven to folly by the half-concealed smirk lurking behind Chester's moustache. 'It's a great pity that FitzGuyon's black wasn't competing, Ranulf,' he drawled. 'Your grey would have been left standing for certain.'

Ranulf's eyes sharpened to dagger points. He swung his heavy, bovine head in the direction Leicester indicated. 'Call that a horse!' he snarled. 'I've seen bigger dogs!'

'Fast though, and the size is deceptive. FitzGuyon's a handspan taller than you and the beast bears him well.'

Ranulf spat on the grass to demonstrate what he thought of Leicester's opinion. 'You've been soft on that trouble-making whoreson ever since you went to his wedding!'

'We're talking facts, not personal opinions.' Leicester's voice was mild, his eyes hard. 'You want to forget old scores. You've got more irons in the fire than Caermoel and Woolcot.'

Ranulf glared but had the good sense to tighten his lips rather than open them. It was common, if unspoken knowledge that he only adhered to Stephen's cause because he desired the return of the former family possession of Carlisle and whatever else Stephen would grant him for his 'loyalty'.

Ranulf's boy dismounted from the blowing but not winded grey and he stumped huffily away to speak to him.

Stephen watched his groom lead the chestnut around to cool off and bit in agitation at his thumb nail, eyes full of disappointment. He had been certain that his horse would win. Scowling, he looked round for the chestnut's rider, but the lad had made himself scarce.

His drifting gaze fell upon Renard FitzGuyon and the horse he was idly fondling as he talked to the Fleming. It was a courser, pitch-black in colour except for its hind legs which looked as if they had been dipped to the hocks in milk. The stallion was long-boned and rangy with the high-flagged tail and dished face of the Arab. An eastern type, typical of the kind brought home by returning crusaders. Stephen thought that de Gernons was right; bigger dogs did exist, but there was plenty of lung room in the well-sprung ribs and the lean lines suggested speed. His scowl cleared.

'I'll make you another wager, Ranulf!' he yelled over to the Earl. 'Your grey against FitzGuyon's black!' And without waiting for Chester's confirmation, set off across the field.

Renard left his conversation with the Fleming to make a hasty obeisance as the King strode over to him and clapped a powerful arm across his shoulders. Stephen's enthusiastic proposal filled him with more than a seasoning of doubt.

'Sire, there is already enough bad blood between us. Whoever wins, it will only increase the enmity.'

'Are you refusing me?' Stephen snapped.

Renard drew a breath and hesitated for a long moment on the peak of it. 'No, sire,' he said, when at last he let it go.

'Leicester's lad can ride him for you. He's the lightest boy and he's got an angel's touch on the reins. Come on, man, don't be such a wet trout!' He shook Renard exuberantly.

Renard could hardly refuse. Besides, it was something he more than half-wanted to do. Barring a freak accident, he was as certain of Gorvenal's victory over the grey as any man could be. The thought sent a churning sensation through his gut. He also knew that it was folly and if Stephen had the sense to look beneath the surface he would see it too. The problem with Stephen was that he saw his own ungrudging, generous nature in every man he encountered, never realising it was a false reflection.

Renard shrugged, acquiescing against his better judgement, and led the horse across the field. Ranulf of Chester gave him a glare which he coldy returned. They had both been at court since yestereve but thus far separated from each other's presence by the throng of earls and barons in similar attendance on the King. This was their first eye to eye confrontation since Renard had gone to Antioch. The main enmity stemmed from an incident more than ten years old now. De Gernons had been showing off a new and vicious hunting dog. The beast had run amok, Renard had killed it with a jousting lance and there had been trouble. Nothing had changed.

'Is your grey rested enough, my lord?' Renard asked his rival with neutral courtesy. 'I would not want to claim a false victory.'

Ranulf's neck started to mottle with angry patches of red that filtered into his stubbled jowls. 'He'll leave that pony of yours standing!' he sneered, squat fingers toying with the jewelled hilt of a long dagger at his belt.

'Force is not everything, my lord. If you doubt it, go to Ravenstow and look at what remains of a troop of mercenaries caught raiding on my lands.' Renard turned to watch Leicester's boy spring into the saddle and bit the inside of his mouth, already knowing that he should not have gratified his temper by that small spurt of viciousness. Poison from a festering wound, he supposed.

Chester's fingers tightened convulsively on the dagger grip. 'You had no right . . .' he started to grate.

'Neither did they,' Renard interrupted without turning

round, but he was intensely aware of the glare focused on the space between his shoulder blades. He checked the girth for something to do with his hands. 'It is not in my interests to seek a quarrel with you, but I will bite if provoked.'

Chester dragged on his moustache and his eyes began to water, always a sign of impending rage.

Stephen's hand came down heavily on the Earl's thick shoulder. 'Come now, Ranulf!' he cajoled. 'It's the season of goodwill. Time to abandon old grudges and make peace!'

De Gernons shuddered beneath the broad, spatulate command. A mangled expletive stumbled off his tongue but he held his body in check. Stephen gave him an encouraging slap that was immediately added to Ranulf's long list of old grudges which were never abandoned, indeed, were an integral part of his nature.

An interested group of courtiers had gathered around the starting point as the horses were brought round and lined up. De Gernons's grey stood well over sixteen hands high, the solid power tempered by strains of Barb and Spanish. Gorvenal's sire had been a desert-bred Bedouin stallion, his dam a mare of Andalusian blood. In consequence he was much smaller and lighter than the other horse, but Renard had few qualms. What was lacking in weight was made up in speed.

Each youth fretted his mount back on its hocks, awaiting the King's signal, and when Stephen dropped his raised arm, both horses sprang forwards like shafts from a triggered arbalest.

At first there was no discrepancy. The sheer power of the grey's initial thrust from the starting line put him a length in front, but as they approached the wooden stake marking the turning point, it became obvious that the black owned the fleeter turn of foot. The horses swerved neck and neck. The lighter Arab had the advantage of manœuvre and began to draw ahead as they started the home stretch.

De Gernons's boy knew the penalty for failure, could already feel the stripes smarting across his back and the boot connecting with his ribs. Fear became panic as the black continued to overtake him, and in desperation he cut his whip at Leicester's boy.

The youth gave a cry of pain and jerked his arm from the rein to ward off a second blow. Gorvenal's stride slackened. He wavered, pecked slightly on an uneven piece of ground, and veered into the grey. The whip cut again. The grey's solid weight barged Gorvenal out of stride and almost brought him down. Chester's horse regained the lead.

Sobbing with pain and outrage, a bright weal swelling on his white cheek, Leicester's boy gritted his teeth, dug his heels into Gorvenal's flanks and drew him wide, asking of the stallion everything that he possessed.

Ranulf de Gernons's premature smile froze. He gaped in utter disbelief as his grey courser, the pride of his stable, was overhauled and taken on the line by a spectacular burst of speed from the black.

Stephen crowed his delight aloud, as tactless but genuine as a small boy. 'What do you think of FitzGuyon's pony now!' he chortled to Earl Ranulf.

'A fancy toy to be shown off at fairings and the like!' Chester snarled. 'That's no honest mount!'

'Oh, come now, Ranulf!' cried Stephen.

'But then it wasn't an honest race,' Renard observed tartly as he went to Gorvenal. 'Are you all right, lad?'

The boy nodded and gingerly touched the swollen stripe on his cheek. 'Yes, my lord. He's got fire in his feet. No side-swipe from a whip was going to stop him!'

Renard gave the boy a silver coin and examined Gorvenal for signs of damage.

Incensed by having lost the wager and Renard's remark, Chester started forwards with a snarl on his lips, but bounced off Leicester's wide velvet chest. 'Peace, Ranulf,' he growled. 'You're beaten, you know it, so accept with a good grace for once.'

De Gernons thrust himself out of Leicester's grip. 'Don't lecture at me, Beaumont! You're not as holy as you think you are!' Then, glaring at Renard, 'Enjoy your petty triumph. Hide behind Beaumont and his ilk. I'll winkle you out of your shell yet on the end of my sword. We have some unfinished business, you and I.'

'Caermoel is Ravenstow's,' Renard said, voice a calm façade to fear-mingled fury. 'Copies of the charter are lodged with the monks at Shrewsbury and in Chester itself if you care to look. You'll not find a single point lacking.' He turned to Stephen. 'Perhaps you would like to study the charter yourself, sire, and confirm it?'

Looking at Renard, Stephen was reminded of the old king. Not so strange, for it was in the blood and the actual bond closer than his own. He had been delighted when Robert of Leicester had managed to persuade Renard to attend the Christmas court. Although there had been no open display of rebellion from Ravenstow, neither had there ever been any tremendous enthusiasm of loyalty and Stephen knew for a fact that Earl Guyon's son-in-law, Adam de Lacey, was possessed of strong rebel sympathies. It behoved Stephen to treat the young future earl generously. The dilemma was how much he could dare to afford.

He could vaguely recall Caermoel being mentioned before. De Gernons disliked the intrusion of the keep within territory he considered his own. It served to prevent the Welsh from raiding, but it was also a watch-tower on some of his more questionable activities.

'Charter?' Ranulf spluttered furiously. 'Maurice de Montgomery bribed that land from old King William at the time of the great survey!'

'Obviously he was setting a precedent,' the tone of Renard's retort was caustic.

Ranulf shoved violently past Robert of Leicester and before anyone could stop him had closed with Renard and seized a handful of his tunic. Renard promptly used the street-fighter's trick he had shown William in the forest. A slight refinement and an adroit twist of his arm prevented him from being pulled over as his victim toppled like a tree.

'Enough!' Stephen roared, horrified, but aware of a treacherous glint of satisfaction, indeed amusement, at the sight of his most powerful tenant-in-chief sprawled thus. He concealed it in a show of blustering royal displeasure.

Chester opened his mouth to roar out curses and threats. Renard, in contrast, kept his clammed shut, eyes glittering with all that went unsaid. Indeed, some of the anger was self-directed. He knew that he should have kept a closer guard on his tongue which was frequently his worst enemy. It was just that Ranulf of Chester had the ability to rile him beyond all caution. He reacted with his gut, and instinct was always the hardest thing to control. Renard had intended Stephen to ratify the Caermoel charter, but quietly, not in a blaze of public display like this, with the main contender at his feet, howling for blood.

Stephen stared from one to the other. The spark of amusement faded, leaving him angry and a little frightened. He hated being backed into corners by his barons. The former king, his Uncle Henry, would never have permitted it to happen, and if by some mischance it had, would have extricated himself by sheer, cold charisma. Not possessing that same strength of character, nor the ability to cower men with a single look, Stephen was at an immediate disadvantage.

Chester regained his feet. From the way he was standing, it was obvious that he had torn a muscle in the fall.

'There will be peace between you,' Stephen said, eyes flickering between the two men. 'The matter of the Caermoel charter will be fairly examined and in whomsoever's favour I find, I will hear no more on the matter. Now clasp hands and have done.'

Neither man moved a muscle. Stephen seized Renard's right hand and Chester's and forced them together. 'Clasp and have done!' he repeated, his colour as ruddy as wine.

Chester bestowed a look of contempt on Stephen and, with a shrug that was pure insult, did as he was bid.

A half-turned ring bit Renard's flesh as de Gernons squeezed. Renard made no attempt to compete. Now was not the time or place, but he had no doubts that the handshake was confirmation of a war begun in earnest.

Stephen smiled and the angry flush dissipated from his brow and cheekbones. He took men at surface value, upon their superficial gestures. One of his main failings was that he trusted like a child. 'Good,' he said forcefully, and gripped his fingers on Renard's tense shoulder. 'Now, about that black of yours. I realise you would not sell him whatever sum I offered, but might I ask the favour of his services at stud?'

CHAPTER 14

MATHILDA, STEPHEN'S QUEEN, bore the same name as her husband's rival, the Empress, but was affectionately known to close friends and family by her childhood name of Malde. Adored by her husband whom she adored in return, she was definitely the more strong-willed and purposeful of their partnership, and she most certainly did not trust like a child.

This morning, she was holding a court of her own composed of the wives and daughters of the barons who were out with their horses on the tourney field. She looked down at the piece of fabric in her hands and then at the young woman sitting demurely beside her. 'It is truly a beautiful piece of work, child. Your own, you say?'

'Yes, madam, woven from our own Woolcot fleeces.' Eleanor watched the Queen's hands smooth appreciatively over the rich green length of cloth. Eleanor had woven in a border of darker green, cross-banded with thread-of-gold. With the Christmas court in mind, she had set the project in motion the moment she had returned to Woolcot from her marriage feast, and immersed herself in it most thoroughly. While she was busy at the dye vats and the loom she did not have the time or inclination to brood upon life's disappointments.

'There is enough for two gowns, madam,' she added, as the Queen gestured and the material was spread out to its full size. 'Or perhaps tunics for your husband and sons.'

The Queen glanced fondly at a boy who was playing with a bratch hound, tossing a leather ball for it to catch in its mouth. Prince Eustace had his father's wiry blond hair but her own bright, dark eyes. Prince William, only just two years old, had thrown a tantrum and been removed by his nurse and put in his crib to sleep. 'Tunics, I think,' she said. 'It is very thoughtful of you, Lady Eleanor.'

Eleanor murmured a disclaimer. It was more than thoughtful, it was calculated. If people knew that King Stephen himself wore cloth of the Woolcot weave they would be more inclined to buy. It was also a very personal gift and therefore likely to please the Queen.

Malde gestured to her maids to refold the cloth and cast a look sidelong at the slim, raven-haired girl attending upon her. 'I was sorry to hear of your father-in-law's continued ill-health,' she murmured. 'The King has always regarded him with respect.'

Eleanor kept her eyes upon her clasped hands while she tried to translate the Queen's meaning. Whatever Stephen said could be taken at face value. His wife, however, was woven from different fabric entirely. She was Stephen's backbone, the manipulating force behind his crown. Eleanor decided that as she was a new bride, wide-eyed and wondering at the rich complexity of court life and temporarily deserted by her husband, Malde would most likely offer a listening, sympathetic ear and expect confidences in return.

'It is indeed a great pity,' she agreed sweetly, lifting her lids to show Malde pools of limpid innocence. 'Although he has been a little improved since my husband's return from Antioch.'

'I am pleased to hear it, but it is still disappointing that he cannot be here himself and the Countess with him.' She patted Eleanor's hand in a maternal gesture that was genuinely meant even if other motives were lurking in the background. 'Nevertheless we are very glad to welcome his heir and new bride.' Very glad indeed. There had been the distinct possibility that Renard FitzGuyon would spend Christmas at Bristol instead, cementing ties with his uncle, Robert of Gloucester. 'Your lord has been very busy we hear since his return from crusade?' she added gently.

Eleanor sighed. 'Yes, indeed, madam. He has scarcely stopped to breathe, let alone eat and sleep since he came home.' But what he had been doing was Renard's own business and Eleanor was not about to be any more specific.

'Poor child,' Mathilda said. 'Has he been neglecting you?'

Eleanor clenched her fingers in her gown. She felt herself blushing and swallowed. Not if her life depended on it could she have replied to that one. Not neglecting. Avoiding. After the débâcle of their wedding night, he had returned to Caermoel to supervise the start of the new fortifications, escorting her as far as Woolcot. They had spoken little for there had been little to say ... or perhaps too much.

'All men neglect their wives. In their absence we have to make lives of our own,' Malde said gently.

'I am not complaining, madam,' Eleanor replied in a careful voice.

'No, I can see that Renard should be proud of your duty,' Malde said, wryly amused by Eleanor's cautious responses.

The leather ball, slimy with the hound's saliva, smacked the floor near the women. The dog bounded past, swerved and spun and caught it up in its slavering jaws. Eleanor recoiled slightly. Ever since seeing an alaunt run biting mad in her childhood she had nursed an aversion to large dogs no matter how friendly.

Prince Eustace ran up and caught the hound by the collar, prised the ball from its jaws, and threw it with a certain maliciousness of aim at the two harpists playing softly in the background. He shot his mother a sly glance to see if she would reprimand him.

She made a token gesture, shaking her head with a frowning smile. 'Wait until you have sons,' she sighed to Eleanor. 'Nought but boisterous trouble, I warn you now!' Her eyes were full of pride.

Eleanor smiled tepidly. It would not be before next winter if she did. That first disastrous coupling had not resulted in any seed taking root. At Woolcot, ten days after their marriage, she had begun her flux at the allotted time and had been more than a little dismayed. When she thought about it logically, she knew that children were seldom begotten on the strength of one isolated mating. She had also realised in hindsight that the ordeal she had suffered was not typical. She knew that the pleasure existed because she had felt its sensuous weakness with Renard two days before their wedding. Finding it again was the dilemma.

'If you did have a babe,' Malde pursued, 'whom would you choose for godparents? It is such an awesome responsibility.'

'Oh, Renard has already asked Lord Leicester in anticipation,' Eleanor said brightly. It was something to which she could admit without worrying that she was doing her husband a dis-service, for Robert of Leicester was in high favour with the King and Queen. She knew that Malde was probing to try to discover the true direction of Renard's sympathies, but Eleanor did not believe that he had anything to conceal. He was essentially too busy strengthening the earldom against attack to think about fomenting rebellion.

'Ah.' The Queen's attention suddenly diverted from Eleanor. 'Here come the men from their sport.' Her dark eyes lit on her husband and her breathing visibly quickened. So did Eleanor's as she looked at Renard, although her own emotions were more ambivalent.

He was wearing the blue tunic she had made for him, already a firm favourite of his and worn frequently in marked preference to the wedding tunic. She had taken note, and a new robe begun for him in a charcoal-grey Italian velvet was trimmed with thread-of-silver in sparse circumspection.

One of the Queen's ladies, a vivacious russet-haired beauty who had been standing near the door, stepped across Renard's path, and with a sly look over her shoulder at Eleanor, held a mistletoe kissing bunch over his head. Not being aware of her until the last moment, Renard stopped so abruptly and so close that he almost knocked her over. Eleanor saw a look of irritation flicker on his face before the courtier's smile concealed it. Setting one arm around the girl's waist, he drew her to him for an obligatory but perfunctory kiss. She said something to him. He arched his brow and murmured a curt reply that sent her flouncing away.

'Heloise can never resist other women's husbands,' one of Malde's older ladies whispered wryly to Eleanor. 'Particularly when they are as dangerously charming as yours.'

Eleanor blinked. Dangerously charming? Was that how other women saw Renard? She had never really examined the thought herself. In childhood she had looked up to him with adoring awe, the ten years between them a vast gulf of expectation and experience, their daily exchanges those between adult and child. As her body matured she had dreamed unsettling dreams that left her hot and restless, seeking she knew not what. At one and the same time Renard had become more accessible and more distant, and her marriage had only consolidated the contrasts.

She looked at him as he approached. He had strong rather than handsome bones, thick, black hair, narrow eyes the colour of a winter sea, and a smile that made her knees go weak, independent of all dreams and all barriers. Was that what the woman had meant by dangerous charm? He had stopped smiling now and she could tell from the manner in which he was bearing himself that he had recently been very angry.

His greeting to the Queen was civil enough but he made it obvious that he had no intention of dancing attendance on her and her women for longer than was strictly necessary. Even so, the tale of the horse race and all its accompanying drama had been related and embroidered upon at least twice by other barons before he finally succeeded in making his escape.

'Did you really knock Ranulf de Gernons off his feet?' Eleanor enquired as he lifted her down from the palfrey in the courtyard of the house they had rented for the duration of the Christmas feast.

'I'm afraid so. It has gone too far and too fast.' His hands rested a little longer on her waist than was necessary, but when Eleanor darted a glance up at him, his eyes were preoccupied and she might as well have been that russet-haired court hussy for all the notice he was taking. 'Stephen should never have tried to make us shake hands. It was the last straw I think.' Shaking his head, he released her and turned towards their dwelling.

'Does that mean you'll be returning to Caermoel?' Her voice was neutral as they went up the outer staircase to the small solar and bedchamber. They had rented the house from a

merchant, who, with an eye to profit had transferred himself
and his family to his wife's parents for the Christmas period,
temporarily relinquishing his home for a tidy profit.

The merchant's sharp business brain was attested to by the
trappings of prosperity that adorned his home. Eastern rugs
hung on the walls and the coffer against the wall had obviously
been carved and inlaid by a master craftsman. Eleanor paused
beside a beautiful cherry wood cradle and gently tapped the
rocker with her foot.

Renard sat down on the bed they had brought with them
on the baggage wain and watched her at the crib. Her
expression was guarded and he could not tell whether it dis-
guised regret or longing, or if she just did not care. 'Yes,' he
sighed, 'it means I'll have to go back to Caermoel. I can stay a
few days at Woolcot if you want, and of course we'll travel
by way of Milnham and Ravenstow.'

'Is war imminent?'

He lay back, tucking his arms behind his head. 'I'm not the
only thorn in Ranulf de Gernons's side, and certainly not the
largest or most painful. More than Caermoel, he wants Carlisle
from the Earl of Huntingdon. I have a little space of time I
think, at least until spring. Sieges in winter are always more
demoralising for the attackers than the attacked.'

'How will you raise the money?' Eleanor asked. 'Go in debt
to the Jews?'

He looked thoughtfully at the scuffed toes of his deer-hide
boots. 'No need. There is enough income from the market and
river tolls at Ravenstow and Ledworth to cover the initial cost,
our marriage relief helped to swell the coffers, and Stephen has
just given me a more than generous amount of silver from the
Bishop of Salisbury's fortune against the future services of
Gorvenal on some of his mares.'

An odd sensation quivered in Eleanor's stomach as she stared
at his lean length stretched out on the bed. 'Will you visit
Hawkfield too?'

He frowned and made an impatient sound with his tongue.
'I hadn't thought about it.' Raising his eyes from contemplation
of his boots, he returned her stare. 'I suppose I'll visit to see

how she's faring, more for Hawkfield's sake. She called it a poky, back-of-beyond byre and threw a temper because I wouldn't bring her to court. It doesn't augur well.'

Eleanor turned away to remove her cloak, shielding her face from him.

He studied her rigid spine. 'I won't stay long, I promise you.'

'Just long enough to ...' She bit her tongue and wrenched the pin out of the cloak, bending it.

Renard left the bed. 'We're back where we started, aren't we?' he said wearily, 'with the ghost of our wedding night.' He stretched his hand towards her. 'Look Nell ...'

Eleanor's maid knocked on the door and poked her head around it. 'My lord, there's a Fleming here to see you. Pieter of Ypres. He says you have invited him to dine?'

Renard's outstretched hand went to his forehead. 'God's teeth, I'd forgotten!' he cursed. 'That affair with de Gernons put it right out of my head. All right, Alys, give him some wine and tell him we're coming.'

'Yes, my lord.'

They heard her pattens clattering back down the stairs. Eleanor looked a question. 'Pieter of Ypres?'

'I met him this afternoon at the horse fair, although I knew of him already from his cousin William d'Ypres.'

Eleanor paused in a swift tidy of her hair to regard him with surprise. 'Isn't he one of the King's senior captains?'

'*The* senior captain,' Renard corrected.

'You want him for Caermoel?' Eleanor guessed and gave up the unequal struggle to control her hair. Unwinding her braids, she combed them out. Loose hair was not generally worn by married women but it was permissible in one's own household and Eleanor knew that it suited her much better than the braids.

'No.' Renard gave her a look glinting with mischief. 'I want him for you.'

'For me?' Eleanor stared at him. 'Why? Do you mean as a body-guard in your absence?'

'No, not as a body-guard. He isn't a soldier, Nell, he's a master cloth finisher – in exile for murdering his daughter's husband. Apparently, he caught him thrashing the girl in a fit

151

of drunken temper and gave him a taste of his own medicine. He went too far and the young man died. His family are very influential among the merchant fraternity and Pieter had to flee here and take shelter with his cousin.' Renard kissed her cheek and went to the door. 'I told him that if he wanted employment in his own trade, you had a useful proposition to put to him.'

'What!' Eleanor gasped.

Renard laughed, highly pleased with himself and returned from the door to slip his arm around her shoulders and draw her towards it. 'Was I wrong? You said that you needed people of the trade.'

'No, not wrong,' Eleanor said vaguely. 'It's just that you sprang it on me.' Her mind raced with sudden possibilities. A master cloth finisher . . .

'If the fish bites you pull him in,' Renard said as they went down to the main room on the level below. 'I didn't know myself until this morning when we were chance-introduced. Your hair suits you like that.' He touched it gently.

Eleanor stammered a reply she was not later to recall and felt her face grow as hot as a furnace.

Master Pieter was a florid, stocky man and probably well-fleshed when stress was not stripping the flesh from his bones and playing havoc with his stomach. He spoke excellent French with only the slightest trace of a Flemish accent, and although he deferred in courtesy to Renard's rank, he was not in the least cowed by it.

A man of his hands, he was accustomed to the presence of women in everyday trade too and scarcely checked at the hurdle of accepting that Eleanor and not Renard was truly the driving force behind the wool project.

Peeling an apple with a silver fruit knife, Renard sat at the board and listened to his wife and Master Pieter discuss the intricacies of the wool trade.

'Yes,' Eleanor responded to a point raised by the Fleming. 'I can see that these new mills for fulling the cloth would be better than treating it in tubs as we do now. We have a good stream to hand at Woolcot and I think I know an ideal site. Would it cost a great deal to build one?'

'No more than a standard flour mill, my lady.'

'I daresay we could run to the expense,' Renard volunteered, watching the apple peel spiral towards his trencher. 'The clip was good last year. I could probably spare masons and carpenters from Caermoel for a couple of weeks in the early spring.'

'Might I also suggest, my lord, that you bring in some of the new Flemish looms too? The best houses in Flanders have started to use them. Two weavers to a loom instead of one, and the size of the frame makes the cloth that much broader.'

Renard made a non-committal sound, but when Master Pieter raised his cup to drink, bestowed Eleanor a swift wink. She smothered a smile.

Master Pieter took a long swallow from his cup. 'What about alum for mordanting? I know where to obtain it for a bargain price. Of course you'll have to pay transport costs, but if you can arrange to bring in other items on the same galley, you can offset those ...'

And so the discussion progressed, covering abstracts and hard points of fact. Eleanor spoke of wages, working terms and responsibilities with such hard-headed acumen that Renard's proud amusement gradually gave way to astonishment. He stared at her with glazed eyes, his jaw hanging slack, and only remembered to tighten it when he raised his cup and missed his mouth.

Later, when Master Pieter had gone, having accepted employment and as pleased with himself as Eleanor was at hiring him, Renard stood in their bedchamber and in thoughtful silence pulled off his day tunic. The evening at the palace was to be a formal affair in full splendour and he had perforce to dress for the occasion. His older brother, Miles, who had drowned on The White Ship, had always enjoyed gilding the lily, and Adam was not averse to striking a pose if the occasion demanded, but Renard always felt like a fop.

A maid was laying out the finery – their wedding garments with the fox and sheep theme. The thread-of-gold twinkled in the light from the candles. Renard unlaced his shirt and watched Eleanor as Alys, her personal maid, helped her to remove the undergown and bliaut she was currently wearing.

'Will he do?' he enquired.

'Oh yes, more than that!' Eleanor cried and advanced on him buoyed up with confidence. 'I think I'll be able to trust him to run the weaving sheds at Woolcot.'

Renard nodded. 'That's what I thought – although I never realised you had so much knowledge yourself.'

'I suppose I've been garnering it since I was little,' she said with a dismissive shrug, then added impulsively, 'Renard, thank you. It was very thoughtful of you.'

She had called him by his name, not a careful 'My lord'. Her face was sparkling with enthusiasm, becomingly flushed. The low neckline on her short shift displayed the shadowed hint of the cleft between her breasts. Her hair was a black cloud, crackling around her shoulders with a life of its own and he was suddenly surprised into wanting her, his physical response a direct result of his interest in the intricacies of his mind.

Cautiously he stepped closer. 'Your good is mine if profit comes of it,' he smiled and played with a tendril of her hair, following it slowly and lightly down her body.

'But you have matters more important on your mind. I never expected you to ...' Eleanor stopped speaking as Renard's knuckle brushed like a feather over her breast. His hand travelled down her lock of hair, stopped at the curling end, and transferred to her hip. Fingers extended, he pulled her against him. 'Don't live by expectations, Nell, they'll let you down every time,' he murmured and kissed a line down her temple and cheek until he reached her mouth, and setting his lips on hers, stroked them gently with the very tip of his tongue.

Eleanor shivered but did not freeze or draw away. His hand was warm through the fine linen of her shift as it lay on her waist. Her own hands were pressed lightly against his chest. He was holding her gently and she had only to push at him to break the contact. Remembering the pain and humiliation of her wedding night, she hesitated. His touch on her waist was nice, the tickling sensation of his tongue pleasant in a disturbing kind of way. She spread her fingers, encountered the linen of

154

his shirt and then the warmth of his skin through the unfastened laces. Moving her hand higher, she circled his neck. Her other arm dropped to his waist, sought under his shirt to the springy muscles of his back. Her lips opened beneath his.

He stroked the side of her breast, increased the pressure of the kiss and rubbed his thumb lightly back and forth over the peak of her nipple. Eleanor made a small sound in her throat and pressed herself closer to him, revelling in the feel of his skin against her fingertips. Fear trembled along her nerve endings but it was only a minor ingredient in a brew of other equally elemental emotions. The room was cold but she was warmed by the heat emanating from their joined bodies.

After a moment, Renard reached to the drawstring of her shift and delicately unplucked the knot. His mouth left hers and trailed down her throat to the pulse beating rapidly on the verge of her collar-bone. He sucked on it, then explored lower, fingers gently drawing the linen aside.

Eleanor gasped at the sensations but was not yet totally in thrall to them. 'Renard, wait!' she said breathlessly. 'The maids!'

'What?' He raised his head. She could feel the rapid thud of his heart against her cheek. He made a peremptory gesture and the two women curtseyed and hastened out of the room, one of them stifling a giggle against her cupped palm.

'I . . .' Eleanor blushed a fiery red. 'Everyone will know,' she whispered, imagining the looks as they descended the stairs afterwards.

'And expect it,' he answered, smiling. 'We're a newly-wedded couple.'

Eleanor swallowed and pressed her hot forehead against Renard's throat.

'You look good enough to eat when you blush like that,' he murmured and returned to what he had previously been doing, lips questing down over her milky skin. Taking his hand down to the hem of her shift he placed it lightly on her thigh, describing tiny circles, radiating outwards and upwards beneath the linen.

It had been a long, long time since he had needed to use the skill of slow persuasion to seduce a woman to bed. With Olwen there had never been any need. She had always been ready and it had always been a battleground, the limits set by the amount of stamina that each of them possessed. This was another discipline entirely, calling for the same skills, but a completely different method of application.

Enjoying the novelty and the slow arousal of his own senses, he played with her, kissing, nibbling and stroking. Her breath caught in her throat and she made small sounds, twisting against him. His fingers travelled further up her thigh and sought inwards. He felt her stiffen as he touched her. Murmuring reassurances against her ear, he nuzzled and nipped at her lobe and coaxed her gently, his other hand rhythmically pressured on the curve of her buttocks, holding her against him. When she began to gasp and clutch at him convulsively, he stopped what he was doing and brought her to the bed.

Below stairs, Alys told her husband who was also employed as Renard's cook that she did not believe their lord and lady would be attending the court that particular night.

Not best pleased, he grunted and folded his flour-smeared arms. 'I've only made pottage for tonight,' he grumbled, cocking an eye at the fat bacon and vegetable stew simmering in the cauldron suspended over the central hearth.

'Oh, like as not they won't be down to eat either,' Alys said knowingly and picked up a piece of mending. She nodded at the cauldron. 'Put in some dumplings just in case. My lord is not so grand that he won't stoop to pottage.'

He grunted again and scowled. The couple upstairs had evinced little interest in each other these past two months and why they should do so now when he had settled to the thought of an evening's leisure aggravated him intensely.

Alys smiled into her sewing. Saer was never content unless he had something about which to grumble. Renard's absence at court would have been cause to mutter that there was no point in him keeping an itinerant cook when all he did was dine elsewhere.

'At least matters between my lord and lady are improving,' she said.

'Improving?' Saer queried sourly as he gave the pottage a quick stir. 'He ain't the kind to dangle from a woman's girdle longer than the time it takes to shorten it with a babe.'

The needle flashed. 'My lady hopes for children, and my lord, whatever is said of him, is not blind to kindness.'

Her husband snorted. 'As far as it suits him.'

'Which is more than most masters. Think yourself lucky you're not beholden to the Earl of Chester for your wages,' his wife said tartly and bit off the thread, severing the conversation at the same time.

Above them in the candle-lit brazier-warmed bedchamber, Eleanor bore Renard's weight, that which was not taken on his forearms, and with eyes closed, savoured the dwindling ripples of a pleasure so intense that it had twice driven her to the edge of oblivion. The potential still hovered in the background. She rotated her hips beneath him, searching out the last quivers of sensation.

'Greedy,' he murmured kissing the tip of her nose.

She smiled lazily. 'I'm fattening myself against the lean times.'

'Fattening?' He ran one hand lightly over her hip bone, waist and rib cage to the swell of her breast.

Belatedly Eleanor realised that there was more than one interpretation and in the next moment decided that she did not mind if he misconstrued it. 'That as well. I might be more fortunate this time.'

She felt him tense slightly. 'Yes, you might,' he said after a pause, his tone neutral, and rolled over onto his back.

Eleanor lifted her lids to look at him. His expression was wry, but he had relaxed again. Her own body felt languid, satisfied if not replete. He had been right, it did get better. There had been some pain, but of the kind that only added to the pleasure.

On the last occasion – her wedding night – Renard had been in complete, cold control of every faculty even though it had been she who forced the pace. This time her body had moulded smoothly around him and she had heard his sigh of pleasure and the catch in his breathing as she arched her hips and thrust

157

to meet him. Later, surfacing from the intensity of climax, she had been aware of his ragged breathing, the fierce grip of his hands, and known that somehow she had pushed him beyond refinement and into the last driving moments of need.

There was more to be learned. She knew that she was innocent, and was also shrewd enough to realise that her very innocence was sufficient to hold Renard for now, but what of the future? How did she compete with a tavern dancer whose very livelihood was pleasing men? Remembering the expertise of his foreplay, she wondered what would happen if she touched him instead. Her eyes flickered over his body. She knew what she wanted to do but was afraid of his reaction to such boldness.

Watching her expression, a mingling of nervousness and sensuality, Renard was stirred to new arousal. 'We don't have to go to court,' he murmured, lightly brushing a strand of hair from her shoulder. 'Ranulf de Gernons will be there, and we'll only quarrel again or worse. I danced attendance on Stephen all morning and you suffered interrogation by the Queen. I think we are entitled to a little time to ourselves.'

'To do what?' Eleanor widened her eyes as he took her eager, hesitant hand and put it where she had not quite dared. Soft as warm velvet and blood-hard he filled her hand.

'Anything you want,' he said. And showed her.

'Pottage?' Renard looked at Alys.

'Saer did not think that you and my lady would be eating in the hall tonight,' Alys excused, bobbing a curtsey.

'Tell him it's all right,' Eleanor reassured the maid. 'I know how much he takes matters to heart.' She flickered her husband a cautious glance, hoping that he was not going to make an issue of it, but still too unsure of his character to know for certain what he would do.

'He says that pottage is fit only for servants,' Alys volunteered, 'that he is ashamed to be giving it to you.'

'And am I not a servant of the King?' Renard said on a slightly bitter note, then added with a smile, 'Besides, my great grandfather was the bastard of a common tanner's wench.

Peasantry's in my blood. Tell Saer I'd rather eat pottage than court fare any day. He should serve it more often.' Picking up the polished horn spoon, he dipped it into the lentil-thickened mixture.

Eleanor glanced at him sidelong as Alys left them. 'You were telling her the truth weren't you?' she discovered. 'You really do prefer pottage.'

He reached to the dish of crumbly salt between their two places. 'I suppose if I was forced to live on it day in day out I might weary, but it makes a change to all those spicy sauces and meats so stuffed and smothered that you can't even begin to guess which animal they came from!'

Eleanor busied herself with her own food, her expression thoughtful. She toyed with the germ of an idea. If Renard preferred to eat simple food and wear understated garments, might that not apply to other aspects of his life too? The restless side of his nature sought variety, she was aware of that, but the force of that restlessness varied like a tide and was probably linked to the twin fountains of boredom and stress.

Eleanor thought back over the years she had spent in Countess Judith's care and recalled the various little ruses enacted to keep Earl Guyon dancing on a string. They would not necessarily work on Renard who did not dote on her the way the Earl had doted on the Countess, but there might be some way of adapting them to her own situation.

'What are you thinking?' The curiosity in Renard's tone was tinged with just a hint of sharpness.

Eleanor jumped. The betraying colour flowed into her face. She took a hasty spoonful of the pottage so that she would not have to answer him, and promptly burned her mouth. Her eyes watered. She rolled the soup round her mouth until it had cooled enough to swallow. Her mind remained distressingly blank of a plausible answer. Unlike the Countess she did not have the ability to bend the truth to her own advantage. Raising her chin a notch, she drew a deep breath and faced him. 'I'm not going to tell you, it was private.'

Renard cocked an eyebrow. 'Fair enough,' he said, and with difficulty subdued the urge to laugh. She had claws after all, he thought, just did not know how to use them. 'As long as you're not plotting my death, I don't mind.'

'I would have to be mad to cut off my nose to spite my face.'

Accustomed to the temperament of his mother and sister, he thought at first that she was teasing him and laughed. When she gave him a startled look, he realised his mistake and also the fact that she had spoken the truth. If he died untimely she would be a rich and vulnerable widow. Suddenly it hit him as never before that he was the driving force behind the earldom. Without him, Ravenstow would devolve upon Harry's willing but incompetent shoulders, or else go to William. The latter would be horrified at the prospect of such a burden and too mercurial to settle to the yoke. It was him to carry the line or no one.

'Yes, you probably would,' he murmured, all amusement flown, and in the ensuing silence attended rather grimly to his meal.

'What's wrong, what have I said?'

'Nothing. You just jolted me into realising I'll have to make provision for you in the event of my death. A word with John won't go amiss. The support of the Church will be essential.'

'If I am forced into another marriage, you mean.' She met him look for look, not fearlessly perhaps, but with a steady understanding.

'You have seen how it is at court. A fair weather wind that will blow cold the moment you look away.'

Eleanor's jaw tightened and a spark kindled in her eyes. 'No one is going to take Woolcot away from me,' she said with an intensity of feeling that surprised her as much as it did him.

'You may not have a choice.'

'Oh, not at first.' She tossed her head. 'But I know how to build and I know how to wreck. I'd rather destroy the Woolcot herds than see them fall into a raptor's hands.'

Renard gaped at her, spoon suspended in mid-air while he tried to reconcile his view of her as soft-natured and gentle with this determined creature thrusting her chin at him now. It was not all vain talk either he realised with a feeling of unease. He abandoned his spoon in the pottage. 'You really would

160

founder the herds rather than give them up, wouldn't you?'

'Yes.'

He stared at her.

'Of course,' she added, 'that would be by way of revenge. If a new husband was prepared to live and let live, then I would make him a proper and dutiful wife.'

A memory echoed in Renard's mind – his own voice full of grave amusement as he saluted Madam FitzUrse at The Scimitar with the toast 'Business is business'. 'Good Christ,' he said wryly. 'I used to think you were as soft as unsqueezed butter, but really you're as hard as stone.'

Eleanor broke a piece of bread off the loaf in front of them. 'I'm neither,' she said, 'I just don't know how to lie.'

Renard saw that her fingers were trembling. Studying her, he was aware of the contrasts of softness and determination in both face and character, the innocence and the clear, hot flame of a passion that had outmatched his. 'Sometimes it is easier to lie than tell the truth,' he said with a grimace. 'Especially to yourself.'

CHAPTER 15

THE WATER DRIPPED FROM the ladle over the hot stones. Steam hissed and surged around the seated, towel-draped men who were laughing at one of Robert of Leicester's seemingly endless supply of bawdy jokes.

'I don't believe that position's possible!' guffawed Waleran of Meulan, Leicester's twin brother, and returned to his bench from sprinkling the hot stones. 'What do you say, Renard?'

Renard grinned and spread his hands. 'Don't look at me, I'm innocent.'

'After four years in Outremer? You're a bigger liar than he is!' Waleran sat down heavily. He was beginning to run to fat and the hot, moist atmosphere was making him decidedly uncomfortable. Not that he would have admitted it for the world. This steam bath built by the disgraced and recently deceased Bishop of Salisbury was the height of luxury. A plunge in a quiet river pool or a quick dunk in the castle tub were the usual and infrequent ways that Waleran chose to clean himself. A steam bath-house like this hinted strongly at indulgence, especially when a flagon of the best wine was being passed carelessly from hand to hand.

Renard was accustomed to this particular form of bathing. Antioch possessed several such institutions, the attendants there much more handsome than Waleran of Meulan if you liked that sort of thing, and women available if you didn't. They were places to gossip and relax at ease with your peers – places to plot and arrange as Stephen was plotting and arranging now.

Leaning against the wall, lids half-closed, he watched the King take a swallow from the flagon and pass it in turn to Leicester. No cups, Renard thought. A subtle move, enhancing the camaraderie that had been nurtured during a fast-paced day's hunting. Other barons had been with them too, but some had preferred to patronise one of the conventional bath houses in the town where women were to hand, and others preferred not to bath at all, following the creed that sweat was best left to cool on the body, its smell worn as a badge of hard toil. Ranulf de Gernons had been one of the latter.

'Listen.' Stephen nudged Renard. 'I had a look at your charter.'

The flagon came round to Renard. He drank, making more show than actual swallowing and studied Stephen's pink, earnest face. 'It's valid. Your grandfather's seal is upon it and that of William Rufus,' he said evenly as he passed the wine on to Leicester.

'Oh yes, it's valid,' Stephen murmured. 'Malde and I had a long discussion about it.'

And Malde's opinion would be the deciding factor, Renard thought.

'She did wonder if Ranulf felt he had rights in Caermoel because the castle was originally built by your father and Hugh d'Avrenches as a joint venture.'

Hugh d'Avrenches, Ranulf's great uncle, had been the Earl of Chester forty years ago when the keep at Caermoel had first been built. He and Guyon had not only been allies, but also good friends.

'I know that they shared the building costs,' Renard said, 'but my father bought out Chester's interest not long after the battle of Tinchebrai. Caermoel has been wholly ours since the year of my birth.' Leaving the bench, he took his turn to drip water on the stones. The steam hissed up creating a grey veil between himself and Stephen. 'If Ranulf claims otherwise then he's lying.'

Stephen fiddled with the frayed end of his towel and looked perplexed. 'You must understand the difficulty of my position. Ranulf's loyalty is so precarious that I cannot afford to tip the scales too far. I don't want him or that brother of his galloping down to Bristol to offer their support to Maude.'

'On the other hand,' Leicester rubbed his thumb beneath his nose, 'neither can you afford to let Renard take his own grievances to Bristol. Besides, you don't really want to see a change of garrison at Caermoel, do you?'

'Neither of those,' Stephen looked genuinely shocked. 'Of course not! The charter is valid and must stand.' Through the clearing steam he looked at Renard. 'I am asking you to respect the reasons for not making a public announcement of your right to the land. You have witnesses here in Beaumont and Meulan, let that be enough.'

Renard considered, then nodded stiffly. 'But if Ranulf of Chester comes anywhere near Caermoel, I will set the marches alight to stop him.'

'I would expect that. All I am asking is that you do not provoke him.'

Renard snorted. 'I provoke him just by breathing.'

'Don't breathe then,' Meulan suggested flippantly.

Renard grimaced and threw a towel at him.

'Or breathe when he's not looking,' Leicester's gaze met Renard's in frank understanding. Dark grey and light grey, both shades of the same colour. Between them the steam coiled and their bodies glistened with droplets of sweat. Leicester handed him the flagon. Renard drank. From being cold at the outset, the wine was now warm and flat. He passed it to Stephen who was eyeing him and Leicester, obviously unsure whether to read more than just sour humour into the latter's remark.

Leicester promptly started to tell another joke, one he had been saving for just such a moment. Stephen choked so hard on the wine that he forgot everything except his struggle to breathe.

Welcoming her unexpected guest in from the cold, Eleanor tried her best not to look surprised or suspicious as she ushered Matille, Countess of Chester, towards the warmth of the hearth. Alys was sent scurrying to fetch hot spiced wine and Eleanor whisked her sewing basket and some mending from the chair beside her own and bade the Countess sit down.

Matille thanked her and did so, but declined to remove her cloak. 'It is so cold,' she added. 'I think that soon we shall have some snow.' Her gaze roved around the compact but pleasant room. 'I suppose your new husband has gone hunting with the others?'

'Yes.' Matille was Renard's cousin, the old King being her grandfather too. She had hair of an attractive beech-leaf red and her eyes were stormy grey like Renard's. The set of her mouth and jaw also attested to their common royal Norman heritage. 'Did you want to see him?' A silly question Eleanor thought even as she asked it. If Matille had wanted to see Renard, she would have come at a different time.

'Only to congratulate him on his wedding and tease him a little.' The Countess smiled. 'And I can probably escape from Ranulf long enough at court this evening to do that. Never mind. At least I can congratulate you.' Half-rising, she leaned across and kissed Eleanor's cheek.

Eleanor wondered if she knew that because of Earl Ranulf the marriage almost hadn't taken place and Harry had been disabled. Chester might not have told her, but women had a network of other ways of collecting news. It was, however, a subject too delicate to broach on the strength of one meeting.

Alys returned with the hot wine as the Countess settled back in her chair and spread her skirts to the fire's warmth.

'It is probably all for the best that they've gone hunting,' Matille added. 'They can ride off some of the energy they'd otherwise spend in arguing and I certainly don't want to be closeted with Ranulf all day. He grumbles and swears and behaves like a loose bull in a market place.' She looked keenly at Eleanor. 'And Renard's no better. He can be a devil incarnate when he's bored. We used to play together as children and if he had no task to steady him he'd run wild until Judith despaired. Small wonder that he and Ranulf quarrel so much.' She took a sip of the wine and made an appreciative sound.

'It is more than a clash of characters,' Eleanor responded quietly, hands in her lap. 'Renard has never set out to deliberately antagonise your husband. Why should he? By rights Ravenstow and Chester should be allies. It has always been so in the past.'

'Oh indeed, I agree – apart from what you said about deliberately anatagonising.' She put her wine down on a small

gaming table. 'From Ranulf's viewpoint Renard has humiliated him several times in public.'

'The first move has never been Renard's.'

'No, I grant you that. My husband is frequently the
aggressor, but Renard has by far the quicker tongue. He makes
Ranulf look like a wallowing Martinmas hog, which he
isn't.' She paused for breath and her eyes hardened, looking
inwards. 'He's as cunning and dangerous as a lean wild boar and
Renard's going to get gored if he doesn't take care.' She
refocused on Eleanor who was widely alert, her breathing
shallow as if she was facing a wild boar herself – or a wild
boar's mate.

'I'm very fond of Renard,' Matille continued, and stretched
to clasp her hand over Eleanor's. 'I do not want you to think
that I'm threatening either of you, but I hope a friendly warning
will not go amiss. Whatever influence you have with Renard,
use it, as I will use mine on Ranulf.' Her mouth curved wryly
as she reached for her wine again. 'The bedchamber is a good
place to start, and it goes without saying that the announcement
of a pregnancy works wonders on a husband's generosity.'

Behind a blank expression Eleanor thought that Renard was
the one adept at bedchamber persuasion, and that to bring an
atmosphere of barter into what was a shared pleasure spoke of
whoredom.

'It does help, of course, if the child is male,' added Matille
with a sigh. Both the offspring she had borne Ranulf were
girls, now aged four years old and one. In between, there
had been an early miscarriage. Ranulf had not endured his
disappointment with equanimity, indeed on the occasion of
Lucy's birth last Christmas had ranted and raved about annul-
ment and divorce. It was all bluster, she knew. Her father was
the Earl of Gloucester, his position far too prestigious for
Ranulf to do anything as damaging as putting her aside. Not
that it would worry her if he did. Matille enjoyed her wealth
and titles, was even mildly fond of Ranulf in his better moments
and tolerated him with resignation for the rest of the time, but
there was no great passion between them.

'I will talk to Renard,' Eleanor said neutrally. She could see

166

the sense in what Matille was saying, just knew that she would go about it in a different way.

'Will you? Good! We women must help each other all we can. Certainly we never get any from our lords and masters!' Relaxing, she unfastened her cloak. 'This spiced wine really is excellent. You must give me the recipe . . .'

Under canvas in the grounds of the palace of Salisbury, Olwen considered her costume and the effect it would produce on the men of Stephen's court when it came her turn to dance. The coin head dress and gold bezant earrings, a belt worked in thread-of-gold and set with lapiz-lazuli and crystals, and foaming from it, skirts in three shades of blue.

She had joined a troop of performers in Shrewsbury who were travelling down to Salisbury in the hopes of being hired to entertain Stephen's Christmas court. Having proved to their leader that she could dance beyond the wildest imaginings of any man alive, she had been accepted into the group. When one of the members had attempted the limit of his own wild imaginings on her she had demonstrated her equal skill with a dagger and made it clear that she only desired to join them because it was safer than making her way down to Salisbury as a woman alone. She also pointed out that with her exotic talents the troop stood a far higher chance of being employed to entertain the King. Alfred, their leader, a quiet, laconic man, saw sense in her reasoning for all that it was based on her own needs, and with an eye to profit had accepted her among them for the duration at least.

As once before in Antioch, Olwen applied the kohl to her eyes and the carmine to her lips with only the aid of a splintered piece of mirror and curtained dull light. Aaliz and Jehanne, Alfred's wife and daughter were tuning up the lute and crwth it was their particular skill to play and Jehanne kept humming a small tune to herself, perfecting the rise and fall of the notes. Outside Alfred and his two sons were limbering up with a series of jumps and tumbles, a small dog in pied jester's costume leaping exuberantly with them.

'What will you do after tonight?' Aaliz asked curiously of

Olwen. Putting down the lute, she began combing her glossy black hair. 'Will you stay with us?'

'That depends.' Olwen's reply was distorted by the motion of her lips as she carefully painted them. 'I'm hoping to find myself a patron tonight.'

As ever, Aaliz was amazed at the transformation wrought by the painstakingly applied cosmetics. Olwen's blonde beauty had become sultry, exotic, and brooding. A night flower releasing its intoxicating scent to lure a thousand moths. 'Oh yes?' she laughed shortly. 'Piece of advice for you. King Stephen loves his Queen and she for certain won't brook a dancing girl making a play for her crown.'

'I know,' Olwen said in a cool, offhand voice. 'It was not the King I had in mind.'

'Who then?'

Olwen gave her a 'none of your business' shrug and continued with her toilet.

Aaliz tightened her lips and turned away. A strange one and no mistake. Friendly overtures were either ignored or rebuffed. Occasionally Olwen would deign to be gracious, but only at her whim. Aaliz knew that, despite all the extra coin the troop had earned since the girl had joined them, she for one would not be sorry to see her leave.

Olwen flicked at her lashes with a small, black-laden brush. A queasy feeling not unrelated to triumph lurched in her stomach when she thought of dancing before the King and all his senior barons tonight; of having them at her mercy to pick and choose as the fancy took her. Her loins were pincered with small, sharp stabs of sensation. She doubted that even the most likely candidates – the Earls of Chester, Huntingdon and Leicester – would be better lovers than Renard, but the power they wielded would be aphrodisiac enough to compensate. With Renard there had always been a betraying glimmer of affection to hold her back.

Sometimes in an unguarded moment she would think of him and feel her throat tighten, but if she wept it was only as others would weep at the passions of a minstrel's tale, and then awake to face reality. He would be there tonight, unaware that she was not still at Hawkfield. Beneath the triumph, adding to the excitement, an edge of fear shivered deliciously down her spine at the thought of how he would react.

Licking forefinger and thumb, Eleanor sought to poke the wire of the gold and garnet earring through the hole in her lobe, a grimace of concentration on her face.

Behind her Renard was stretched at ease on the bed. He was already dressed for the court in the embroidered fox tunic and was absently examining a new hawking gauntlet he had bought. 'Cousin Matille,' he said softly, responding to her mention of the visit. 'People used to mistake us for brother and sister when we were children. I don't think I've seen her since Herleve's christening, and that was before I went to Antioch.'

'She's got another child now, Lucy, after Ranulf's mother.'

'Mmm?' He twisted the glove this way and that. 'Was it purely a social visit, or did she have other pots to simmer?'

The second earring between her fingers, Eleanor looked round at her husband. 'How did you know?'

He smiled grimly. 'Matille's pleasant enough, but she's too wrapped up in her own life to enquire about the lives of others unless it suits her purpose.'

'I think she was trying to make excuses for Chester's behaviour and to warn you against baiting him. She said this dispute between you was not all his fault.'

Renard snorted and threw down the gauntlet like a gage. 'Oh no,' he scoffed. 'It is like the tale of the bear-ward who said when his bear was accused of biting a child that the child should not have put its arm in the beast's mouth!'

Eleanor secured the second earring and advanced to the bed to pick up her fur-lined cloak. 'I am only repeating what she said. She wanted me to persuade you to be more conciliatory towards Chester. As you say, she is probably wrapped up in her own life, but at the moment, from what I gathered, her husband's temper is making it very difficult.'

Renard took up his own cloak and secured the pin. 'Conciliatory?' He smiled in a manner that owed more to his grandfather, King Henry, than anything of his own. 'Yes, I think that for tonight at least I can be pleasant to Ranulf.' Drawing her against him, he kissed her mouth and then her throat beneath the flashing garnet and gold earrings. 'Stephen has confirmed the Caermoel charter. Ranulf can go whistle for it all he likes.' His arms tightened as he hugged her.

Eleanor returned his embrace, but amid the delight there was also fear. 'Does Ranulf know?'

'Not yet.' Releasing her, he led her to the door. 'And by the time he does, that keep will be so strong that if he tries to bite, he will only break his teeth.'

The night closed cold claws around them and Eleanor shivered as they went down the steps to the courtyard.

The Christmas feast was well into its latter stages. The boar's head had been served as had the stuffed and reassembled swans and peacocks and a whole porpoise swimming on an enormous platter of glistening raw fish roe garnished with oysters.

Now people were desultorily picking at the sweetmeats — fruit and nuts, small tarts, honey cakes and comfits. Dogs scrounged beneath the tables, discovering amidst the scraps the odd reveller who had underestimated the potency of the wine, the occasional hand fondling discreetly beneath a neighbour's tunic or gown, and one individual in solitary enjoyment. Someone being sick in a corner. Someone else noisily breaking wind. The usual social pleasantries of a sprawling royal feast. Servants and squires moved unobtrusively around the throng, clearing away used trenchers and dirty platters, refilling cups, and bringing round finger bowls and towels.

During the business of serious eating, the entertainment had mostly been of the musical kind – instrumentals of harp, crwth, and bagpipes. Two women, mother and daughter to look at them, had sung some pretty, twee French love songs. The man with the bagpipes had performed a couple of table-thumping soldier's ballads and a much appreciated bawdy epic from the Scots borders.

Eleanor had watched the tumblers, jugglers and acrobats while Renard immersed himself in a discussion with Robert of Leicester and his twin brother, Waleran of Meulan.

Leicester's wife, Amicia, had engaged her in fitful conversation. She was plump and lazy, even the effort of speech seeming to weary her, but her eyes, behind drooping lids, were shockingly alert. And they were not the only ones on the prowl. Several times Eleanor caught Matille of Leicester looking at her with a conspiratorial smile on her face which she rather tepidly returned, and the Queen's gaze was hawk-sharp on everyone, seeking out any nuances of false behaviour that might have spoken of impending treason. Eleanor stoutly concentrated on the entertainment.

The acrobats were both clever and amusing with a delightful little black and white dog dressed up to look like a court fool, and she was sorry when they finally made their exit, the dog frantically wagging his stumpy tail and yapping excitedly. Two different members of the troop took their place and bowed before the royal table to the King and Queen. One was a young, slender man with a drum hung around his neck. The other, a woman, wore a full, black robe that looked as if might have been misappropriated from a Benedictine monk. She had loose, corn-blonde hair kinked from tight plaiting and bound back from her brow by a head dress of gold coins. Her sultry mouth was painted a rich, blood-red.

'An eastern dancer,' confided Amicia of Leicester in Eleanor's ear. 'From the court of Prince Raymond in Antioch, although if you believe that, you'll believe anything. She's probably never been further than the Billingsgate fish wharf in her entire life.' She yawned with cynical boredom.

Eleanor felt as if she had swallowed a lump of cold stone. An eastern dancing girl, one from Antioch was already for her the source of too much pain. She flashed her gaze to Renard but he was deep in conversation with his fellow earls, slender fingers weaving as he emphasised a point. She tried to catch his eye, seeking reassurance, but Leicester leaned forward to interrupt him and his great solid back blocked any hope of eye contact. Before the dais, the dancer had cast off the black robe and revealed a costume of full, slit skirts attached to an embroidered bodice by transparent blue fabric embroidered over with gold stars, and across her hips a wide, decorated belt. Fixing some small silver cymbals to her fingers she waited for the youth with the drum to seat himself cross-legged on the floor to one side of the dais.

Attention started to wander from sweetmeats and conversation. Men gaped at the costume, unable to believe their eyes or their good fortune. Women stared too in censorious amazement. The girl smiled scornfully at all and sundry with the exception of Ranulf of Chester whom she favoured with a look he could not mistake. Then she whirled in a circle, twirling the skirts up and around her long, graceful legs, and began to perform.

Biting down on her lower lip, Eleanor watched the girl move and realised that the words '*eastern dancer*' were a totally inadequate way of describing her art – the hip-rolling mimicry of copulation with its overtones of promise and undertones of contemptuous denial. The sensuous undulation of flesh. And yet there was grace and beauty in the performance too; in the way the fabric of her skirts lilted and flowed with her movements, in the artistic description of her arms and the precise positioning of her feet.

'. . . And anyway,' Leicester said to Renard. 'When you think about it in those terms it's obvious that . . . Good God!' His mouth dropped open in perfect imitation of the earlier served porpoise.

Renard had already seen, raising his head and losing all thread of the conversation as the first, familiar pat, pat of an eastern drum resonated around the trestles. In utter disbelief he watched Olwen strike lightly from one hip to the other, and undulating, rotate her way slowly in his direction.

'Hell's gates, but I wouldn't mind getting my leg over that!' gritted Meulan, his voice thick with lust.

'You and every man present, eh Renard?' Leicester laughed and elbowed his ashen companion in the ribs. 'Mind you, I forgot. You're used to that kind of thing, aren't you?'

If his life had depended on it, Renard could not have answered. His gorge rose as she continued to advance on him. Never before in his life had he felt so angry or humiliated. He grasped his eating knife and thought about killing her.

She paused before the three of them, circling her hips, taunting. Her eyes mocked Renard, as she silently reminded him of Antioch. Her hands moved slowly down over her golden body, paused, teased, moved away. Leicester choked. Laughing, she danced her way along in front of the tables until she came to the place where Ranulf of Chester was sitting, his eyes — and everything else — out on stalks. She did not taunt him. She blatantly invited.

Renard jerked to his feet, aware of nothing but molten rage. His goblet crashed over and he upset a dish of pears in mead. Sticky, pale gold fruit glistened on the board. The thick syrup dripped into the rushes. He set one hand on the table and vaulted across, dagger brandished.

Eleanor blocked his way. Her face was limestone white, her eyes huge and dark. 'In God's name, if you are going to make me a widow, let it not be here and over a whore!' she said through bloodless lips, and put her hand upon the taut tendons of his wrist.

He raised that wrist to swipe her aside, caught sight of the dagger he was brandishing and felt the world suddenly coming back into focus around it. The breath shuddered out of him and with it the blind edge of his temper. He sheathed the dagger. Eleanor's knees buckled with relief and she swayed, forcing him to grab hold of her and brace her up.

Behind him the drums were reaching a crescendo and the shouts of encouragement were the ripples preceding climax. He did not look round, but all the same he was horribly aware, his scalp prickling, his loins coiled with ice. His heart thumped in rapid, hard strokes and he felt sick. Eleanor had steadied, but she was still dreadfully pale and shaking like a leaf. As much for his own sake as hers, he took her outside into the courtyard.

Frost bejewelled the walls, sparkling like powdered amber and topaz in the smoky light from the torches, and the air cut like jagged crystal as it was inhaled. A rat scuttled into a pool of torchlight and was lost again in shadow. The sound of laughter drifted like smoke and a couple of squires hurried past on an errand. Renard looked down at his hands. His right palm was still imprinted with the grip of the dagger.

'It was her, wasn't it?' Eleanor croaked in a maimed voice. 'There cannot be two such.'

There was a bitter taste in Renard's mouth. He turned aside and spat. 'Oh yes.' In the aftermath of white-hot rage he felt drained and weary. 'It was Olwen. We quarrelled before the wedding. I thought she was baiting me into a temper for her amusement, to heat her blood. I never thought for one minute that she would ... Christ's wounds!' He broke off and struck the wall on a renewed surge of emotion, not so much anger now as shock and humiliation; the knowledge that every move of hers had been calculated since that first night in Antioch.

Eleanor's teeth were chattering violently with cold and reaction too, and her eyes were glassy with tears. 'I want to go back to the house,' she quavered at him.

The laughter grew louder, intruding on them. One laugh in particular detached itself from the background, rich and triumphant in response to a suggestive remark made in a throaty, feminine voice.

Ranulf of Chester emerged from the hall, his cloak across his shoulders and shielded around the blonde-haired woman clinging to his side. They disappeared in the direction of the stables, and obviously they were not going riding unless it was of the beast with two backs.

Renard swallowed and swallowed again. There was a cold hollow where his stomach should have been.

'Please,' Eleanor said huskily, her frozen hand on his sleeve.

He looked down. Olwen's laughter rippled the air. 'Let's go,' he said through blade-thin lips.

Eleanor lay in bed and listened to the silence. Despite the weight of the covers and the fact that she was still fully dressed she was chilled to the bone, no warmth in the bed beside her from which she could draw comfort. Her teeth clicked together. She stared into the darkness which was relieved by the tiniest glimmer of light from the guttering night candle. Her eyes ached and then started to burn fiercely, the only part of her that was hot. Rolling over, she pressed her face into the bolster and sobbed, hands clenched in the linen and furs.

At last the storm abated. The bolster was wet and uncomfortable and her throat was sore. Gulping and sniffing, she turned upon her back and stared up into the darkness, her mind filled with images of that evening, images she wanted to block out but could not. They tumbled and churned feverishly. The expression on Renard's face; the expression on Olwen's as she took her pleasure; the knowledge of how that pleasure had been taken before in private and was now exhibited in public.

Eleanor sat up and pressed the heels of her hands into her sore eyes. It was late, very late. Renard was downstairs, had not yet seen fit to come up. He had said that he would not be long. That had been several hours ago. They had each needed time alone, she understood that, but her own need for solitude had come and gone an aeon ago.

Still sniffing she left the bed. One of them upstairs, one of them down and no words spoken, only a deepening chasm of silence. She looked down at her wedding dress and was tempted to take her shears to the convoluted embroidery and the lies it portrayed; tempted but unable to bring herself to administer the *coup de grâce*.

The brazier had gone out. The night candle sputtered. Eleanor rubbed her arms and paced the room. Another piece of sewing caught her eye, the silver thread on the hem reflecting the candle's dying flickers. It was the tunic she was currently sewing for Renard. Turning, she stared at it and gradually it occurred to her that a needle was capable of weaving more than one tale and of creating more than one garment – that a needle could repair and refurbish.

Fetching a kerchief from her baggage chest, she wiped her eyes, blew her nose and, setting her jaw, went down to the hall.

Renard was sitting by the fire where Matille of Chester had sat that afternoon – a lifetime ago. He was staring down at a chess piece taken from the gaming table beside him and was turning it over and over as though it were a physical manifestation of his relationship with Olwen and he was trying to understand the grooves incised on its cold, polished surface.

'It is very late,' she said tentatively. 'I have been waiting for you a long time. Will you not come to bed?'

He raised his head to look at her, and after a moment sighed and put the chess piece carefully back down on the board. She saw that he had been holding the black queen.

'It's not love,' he said with a swift gesture. 'I never felt that for her. I wasn't even at ease in her company unless we were in bed, and even there it was a battle.' He shrugged bitterly. 'I suppose that I have never been rejected by a woman before. I'm choking on pride, Nell, on the fact that she should have chosen to leave me for Ranulf de Gernons.'

Eleanor faced the warmth of the banked hearth and rubbed her icy palms together. 'Do you think you are the only one with wounds?' Her voice was as quiet but intense as the red heart of the fire. 'I watched her dance, taking her pleasure on us all, feeding on our responses. I do not believe that I will ever feel the same way about love-making again.'

Her curly hair was loose around her, screening her face from him as she fought to steady herself.

'There's a world of difference between making love and siege warfare,' he said, and rising from the chair put his hands lightly on her shoulders. 'With you I don't feel as if I have to guard my back in the act, nor do you turn to ice when it is over as if you hate me or have begrudged the responding.' A slight, wry smile ghosted his lips. 'You fit well into the hollow of my shoulder, Nell.'

Eleanor stared into the fire. She did not want to fit into the hollow of his shoulder. She wanted him to look at her the way he had looked at Olwen and forget all about control, as he had forgotten at the Palace tonight.

'Nell?'

She turned to face him, new tear tracks glistening on her cheeks. Muttering an oath, he took her in his arms. She clung to him. Against her damp face the gold thread on his court tunic was abrasive.

'Perhaps I needed this to happen,' he muttered into her hair. 'Perhaps I had to learn that all you get for playing with fire is badly burned.' Bending his head and angling hers up, he kissed her. Eleanor hesitated and then with a small gasp responded, her lips parting beneath his and her body yielding from its rigidity. Anxiety and desire swept through her bones, melting them. She pressed against him.

Renard broke the kiss and raised his head. 'Listen.' Releasing her he went to the window that looked out onto the street and unhooked the ox hide shutter. Eleanor heard the scrape of hooves on cobbles, the champing of a horse and the jingle of harness.

'Who is it?'

'Edmund.' The harshness of his voice said everything that the single word did not. He repinned the shutter with precise care and went towards the door.

'Sweet Jesu,' Eleanor murmured, putting her hand to her mouth. Edmund was the youngest son of Ravenstow's constable, his trade that of messenger when haste was required, and there could only be one message that would bring him to Salisbury's gates in the dead of a cold winter's night.

'When?' she heard Renard ask the young man. The cold darkness blowing through the open door was frightening. She shook a maid awake and sent her to the stables to find a groom to take the sweating horse.

'Two nights ago, my lord,' Edmund rasped and knelt at Renard's feet, half in obeisance, half in exhaustion, his eyes dark-ringed in a face tight and pale with strain. 'I've ridden three horses into the ground reaching you.'

Renard stooped, pulled him to his feet, and bringing him into the hall, pointed to the chair by the hearth. Alys, her face puffy with sleep was poking the fire to life. 'How did it happen? He was in reasonable health when we left for this feast.'

Gratefully Edmund accepted the drink that Eleanor poured for him. 'On the same day that you rode out, my lord, a merchant bound for Shrewsbury sought hospitality with us overnight. He brought some kind of contagious ague with him. It starts with a sore throat and shivering fever, then a tight chest and a cough capable of cracking the ribs. For those already weakened . . .' He broke off and spread his hands in a helpless gesture. 'Roslind lost her new baby and old Gamel the hafter died on the same night as your father. Half the garrison's down with it too.'

'What about the Countess?' Eleanor asked, her thoughts on Judith and the state she was likely to be in already without being struck down with this sickness, whatever it was.

'She was all right when she sent me with the tidings,' Edmund said. 'Shocked, yes, and as pale as a ghost, but quite within her senses.'

'My mother is not the Countess any more,' Renard said to Eleanor in a dull voice. 'You are.' He signalled down the hall and sent the responding servant to go and rouse the rest of the household.

'You mean to set out for Ravenstow now? In the middle of the night?' Eleanor clutched his sleeve, less to detain him than in shock at his words. She was not ready to be a countess.

'As soon as the baggage wain can be packed. Where's Saer? I doubt there's any bread, but tell him to boil up something hot for the men before we set off.' His mouth twisted grimly. 'Ranulf de Gernons had the advantage over me tonight. Now it's my turn to take advantage of him. He won't be stirring this side of prime and by the time he does we'll be long gone from any designs on ambush and murder that might be lurking in his mind. You'd better fetch me parchment and quill before you pack them for travelling. I'll need to write to Stephen and explain our haste. Edmund can sleep here and take it to the palace in the morning.'

Eleanor nodded. She would have been disturbed by the cool briskness of his speech and manner had she not known the emotions they masked. Instead of leaving at his bidding, she put her arms back around him and gave him a hard, convulsive hug.

Renard put his hand on her hair, stroked it, tightened his fingers around some of the curly strands, then released her. 'Go on,' he said gruffly. 'There is much to be done.'

She glanced up at him. He turned away, beckoning to Ancelin who had just staggered sleepily into the hall, but not before she had seen the glitter of tears in his eyes.

CHAPTER 16

The Welsh Marches
February 1140

THE STINK OF BURNING HORN filled the farrier's small corner of Woolcot's crowded bailey as he pressed a red-hot horseshoe onto Gorvenal's near hind hoof. Although unable to feel the fierce heat of the glowing iron, the stallion hated having shoes fitted and tried to snap and kick. His endeavours were thwarted by the confining English frame in which the farrier had sensibly secured him.

'Hold him, lad!' the sweating man grunted over his shoulder to the youth standing at Gorvenal's headstall. 'Earl Renard's got a long journey to go come the morrow.' Hissing gouts of steam vapoured the air as he plunged the shoe into a kilderkin of cold water.

'Where then?' The apprentice fished into the scrip on his belt and fetched out a sticky brown object which he offered to the horse.

'Down to Ravenstow with the Countess first, so one o' the knights was telling me, then across east. Fenlands. 'Tis in payment of his feudal service to the King, and there's trouble brewing over there.' The older man's voice was constricted because he was doubled over, tacking on the horseshoe. 'Some bishop's turned rebel and the King's set to deal wi' him.'

'Can't Earl Renard get himself excused? He's got enough to deal with here.' The youth gave another of the brown, sticky lumps to the horse.

'Best to show willing in the early days,' the farrier straightened to pick another fistful of nails from his bench. 'What're you giving him there?'

The youth grinned. 'Dried dates. The Earl filched them from

the locked cupboard in the kitchens last night especially for this. He said it would sweeten him if he started acting up.' He groped in his scrip and tossed one over.

The farrier examined it dubiously. 'Looks like a piece of sheep-shit,' he pronounced, and throwing it back wiped his fingers on his leather apron and resumed his task.

'Tastes all right though.' The boy bit the date in two and offered half to the horse.

'Anything would taste all right to a glutton like you,' the farrier growled. 'Here, make yourself useful and throw me that rasp.'

Cup of wine in one hand, platter of bread and cheese in the other, Eleanor looked down at her sleeping husband and wondered if she should wake him up. It was long past dawn, but he had not ridden in from Caermoel until well after compline, and had not stopped to rest until he literally fell into bed somewhere around midnight.

She tip-toed round to the coffer and carefully put down cup and platter. The soft clink of pewter on wood caused him to stir and turn over. His hair needed cutting and he was bearded again, the growth a rich, beech-red that gave a markedly strange aspect to his appearance. He more resembled one of her shepherds than a marcher earl, but then she thought, glancing ruefully down at her own homespuns, she looked nothing like a countess, nor at this moment did she particularly want to be one. The last two months had been the most difficult of her entire young life and there was every indication that the rest of the year was set to continue in the same vein.

January had been spent of a necessity at Ravenstow. With so many people sick and the trauma of the Earl's death, it had resembled not so much a home as a staging post on the road to hell. Judith contracted the coughing fever and became seriously ill, her reserves sapped and her will to live a precarious spindle of flame that was only kept alight by the knowledge of duty. On her worst day, the one after Guyon's funeral, she had become delirious with fever and Eleanor had fetched John and pushed him urgently into his mother's chamber – not because he was a priest, but because he was the one who most physically resembled Guyon. Judith had pulled through, but as a grey husk of her former self that distressed Eleanor.

Renard had contracted the coughing sickness but thrown it off within a week, as had William. Harry was still barking like a seal when she left for Woolcot to supervise the lambing but was otherwise making a good recovery. The wound in his shoulder was much better too, although he still wore that arm strapped in a sling and would never have much use in it again.

Eleanor herself had not been struck by the contagion which was extremely fortunate since with the Countess so ill the responsibility for the domestic side of running the keep had devolved upon her slender shoulders. Heulwen had helped, of course, but the main burden had been hers.

Stephen had sent a message of condolence and half a dozen mares for Gorvenal. Ranulf of Chester had sent mercenaries to raid the Ravenstow lands, but Renard and William had tracked them down and destroyed them. It was a bitter but welcome outlet for grief.

Sighing softly, she put her palm on his exposed shoulder and leaned over him to kiss his throat below the prickly forest of beard. He raised his lids, looked sleepily bewildered for a moment, then focused and cupped her face to touch his lips to hers.

Eleanor wriggled away. 'It's like being kissed through a thicket!' she complained. 'And besides, it tickles.'

Grinning, he pulled her down on top of him. 'Does this tickle too?' he murmured after a moment.

She ran her palms over his naked chest and around the back of his neck, locking her fingers in his hair. Desire flickered through her, but more playful than imperative. It was high morning and the day was wasting. He stroked the small of her back, moved his hands to cup her buttocks, and pressed down.

She nipped his ear lobe. 'The farrier says he's finished shoeing Gorvenal. I've had the grooms saddle him up, and Bramble.'

Renard groaned softly. 'You're a hard task-mistress,' he complained. 'Aren't I entitled to any leisure?'

'Why, yes.' Eleanor struggled out of his arms. 'We'll escape from the keep and have the whole afternoon to ourselves. I want to show you the site for the new fulling mill and we can look at the herds. There's a sheltered place I know where we can stop to eat and ...' She let the remainder tail off suggestively.

Renard arched one brow. 'The promise of a sugared comfit to keep me in line?' he said, mouth tilting. 'What happens if I'd rather claim it now?'

'You'll have to catch me first!' she retorted, and before he could lunge at such provocation, had whisked from the room and sent in the barber to detain him. Renard narrowed his eyes at the curtain, then with a snort of laughter and a shake of his head picked up the wine and bread she had left for him.

The intended site for the fulling mill was close to the village, at its eastern end. The water to power it came from a broad stream that further down flowed into the River Alyn. The foundations for the mill were already being dug, and Renard dismounted to speak to the workforce.

Eleanor listened to him talking to the foreman in fluent, if accented English, watched him frown as he struggled to grasp a point of construction, then nod in understanding, his smile flashing brief and white. Her heart and loins both contracted and she lowered her lids lest he see her thoughts naked, for she knew that they made him feel awkward.

From the mill they rode to inspect the flocks, heavily popu-lated by proud mothers and their frisky, gleaming offspring. A shepherd obligingly captured one of the new rams in part responsible for the wealth of lambs, and Eleanor set about explaining to Renard the kind of fleece she was hoping to produce in the years to come.

Gravely examining top and undercoat and the general con-dition of the beast, Renard agreed with everything she said. She saw his eyes begin to wander, a slightly glazed expression in them. He stifled a yawn. Eleanor thanked the shepherd and turned to her mount.

'I'm boring you.'

Renard boosted her into the saddle. His eye corners crinkled. 'I would rather eat and wear sheep than look at them,' he admitted as he remounted. 'And I have a deal else on my mind. My sugared comfit for one.' His mouth smiled, matching his eyes, but it was a superficial amusement. Touching his heels to Gorvenal's flanks, he rode on towards a low slope half a mile away that was crowned by a coppice of hazel and hornbeam. Eleanor caught up her bridle and followed him.

'Have you ever been to the fenlands before?' Eleanor sat up in the tree-sheltered grassy hollow and started to fuss the knots out of her hair with her fingers.

Renard pillowed his head comfortably on his bent arms and watched her through half-closed lazy lids. 'Once,' he mumbled. 'With the court, before I was twenty. Nigel of Ely was one of us and he had a proud stomach even in those days. All this trouble now is because he was caught in rebellion last year with the other members of his delightful family and sent away with a flea in his ear.' He snorted softly. 'He's a greedy, vindictive bastard and it will serve him right if Stephen sits hard on him, bishop though he be.'

Eleanor digested this in silence while she finished with her hair. She disliked the thought of him being so far away from her in dangerous, marshy terrain, but had more knowledge of him now than to cling and ask anxious questions. It was the quickest way to turn him cold. She started to fasten up her disarrayed tunic. The seams were tight beneath her arms and when she closed the hooks and eyes, her breasts swelled together, her cleavage full. Gnawing her lip, she glanced at Renard, lying relaxed and contented in the aftermath of their love-making. No, she thought, she could not address him with that either. It was too early yet to be fully certain; too soon to burden him more, and she had a secret fear that once she did announce her pregnancy to him, he would cease to be as eager to lie with her.

The ghost of Olwen still haunted them both. Renard's pride, her sense of security. At the Christmas court it had been a minor scandal that blazed as hot and bright as a dry grass fire before burning itself out – Ranulf of Chester dragging off a dancing girl in the middle of a royal feast and throwing her on her back in the nearest stable. He had emerged from the encounter scratched, bitten and bloodily triumphant to confront the outrage with a boyish grin and a shrug that caused tolerant grins and shrugs in return. No one blamed him, indeed there was much envy. He had placated his wife with a new necklace and the promise of a Flemish tapestry to hang on the wall of her private solar. Olwen he placated with a pouch of silver and employment in his household so that she could dance for him or bed with him at his whim.

Renard had said very little on the matter, but sometimes Eleanor would see him staring into space and know where his thoughts were dwelling. On those occasions she would either interrupt him, or go away and absorb herself in some task until the panic and the anger had subsided. He had not revoked the Hawkfield charter, perhaps hoping that one day she would return. The tradition of a lamp in the window.

Reaching abruptly to the wine flask amid the remains of their meal, she poured herself another half cup. 'What about Caermoel? Is it safe to leave?'

Renard stretched. 'It's strong enough to withstand immediate assault. I've left William de Lorys in command. He's competent enough. Indeed, if he likes the post, I might make him constable.' Sitting up, he drew her cup hand to his lips and stole a swallow of wine. 'More stone is arriving this week from the quarry at Ledworth. It won't be long before the new sections of wall are finished.' Gently he plucked away a piece of twig that she had missed. 'By the way, did I mention that I'm taking a squire into my retinue once I've done my service in the fens.'

'No, you didn't,' Eleanor said, exasperated by his habit of casually springing surprises on her and expecting her to react with aplomb.

'Owain ap Siorl. He's half-Welsh, half-Norman. His father's dead, his mother's set to remarry, and he and his future stepfather don't like each other. Being as their lands are in my gift, I promised Lady Rohese I'd take Owain under my wing to train up. She'll be bringing him to Ravenstow around Easter time. Settle him in if you will.'

Eleanor's exasperation evaporated into empathy with the boy. She knew how it felt to be cast adrift in a strange household, even one that was warmly welcoming. 'Of course I will.'

'Harry can start showing him the basics now that he's on the mend. It'll stop him from brooding and perhaps even speed his recovery.' Sweeping on his cloak which had been used to cushion their bodies from the ground, he eased to his feet. 'We'd better be on our way home,' he added without any great enthusiasm, his mind upon the hauberk that was being scoured at Woolcut ready for his use on the morrow. Thirty pounds of rivet mail, a hot, heavy penance of responsibility.

Eleanor rose too and stood beside him, her lips at his shoulder. He slipped his arm around her waist, then pulled her round against him. She smelled of crushed grass and leaves, fresh and soft in his embrace. 'Oh Nell!' he said on a heartfelt sigh, and buried his face in her wild, black hair.

Judith drew her cloak close about her body to ward off the chill, full aware that more than half of it came from within – from the space where part of her soul was missing. The warm lining of her cloak was made of wolf skins from animals hunted by Guyon and their sons in times long gone. The wolves were all human now, two-legged and padding on the heels of death.

She crossed the ward to the plesaunce, her intention being to pluck some over-wintering sage to brew a herbal tea and to escape from the loving but overpowering vigilance of the other members of the household. Despite the cold wind, the sun was out and bright, bathing the soil beds in spring warmth. Against the southern wall, the pear cordons were in white, nostalgia-scented bloom and beneath them, still flowering, were the tiny white galanthus flowers that Renard had brought her from Outremer.

She went to the sage bushes. Ladybirds waddled in aimless industry among the leaves. Beyond, in the bay tree, sparrows were fighting over the best nesting sites. Judith picked a handful of medium-sized leaves and brushed them absently beneath her nose. Her gaze drifted to the rose arbour and turf seat there, empty and overgrown. The gardener had yet to shear it after the dormant winter season. She tried to imagine Guyon sitting there. Her eyes ached and began to water with long staring. Wandering over to the seat she sat down, brushing her hand over the damp, slightly prickly blades. It was sheltered and sun-warmed, and through a pang of desolation she was aware of feeling oddly comforted.

She sat there for a long time, lost in silence, and only came to with a small, guilty start when she saw Eleanor picking her way towards her between the herb beds. Judith regarded her daughter-in-law warily. In the first days of her loss when she had been weak and ill with the coughing fever and overcome with grief, the girl had taken over all responsibility and coped remarkably well, too well perhaps. Eleanor had proved herself a thoroughly capable chatelaine, and, as the new Countess, it was her right. Judith had lost that power when Guyon died. They all treated her now as though she was made of fragile glass. Her every move was watched. She was cosseted and coddled as though all of her soul had died and not just a part of it.

Eleanor sat down beside Judith on the turf seat. 'I thought you might be here,' she said. 'The sun's gone in now and it will soon be dusk. Will you come within?'

'No, I won't!' Judith snapped, feeling like a defiant small child. The sun had indeed disappeared while she sat lost in reverie and she was aware of the dampness from the seat invading her bones.

Eleanor folded her hands in her lap and stared at them in silence.

Judith gave her a look from her eye corners and sighed out hard. 'I'm sorry,' she said, and then slapped her hand down on her knee. 'I hate being treated like an invalid or a mad old woman. I know it is all kindly meant. Perhaps in the first days it was a welcome shield, but no longer. I swear I will become truly mad if I am not given some leave to think for myself!'

The scent of bruised sage leaves hung in the air. 'Have we really been that heedless?' Eleanor asked in consternation.

Judith moved her shoulders. 'No, not heedless,' she said on a softer note. 'Perhaps the change is in me. I need time alone now to grieve in peace. When I have need of company, be assured I will seek it out.'

Eleanor gave her a swift, sidelong long. 'Do you want me to leave you here then?'

Judith's lips twitched. 'Hoist with my own petard,' she said wryly. 'I'm stiff and it's growing cold, and that torchlight looks very welcoming.' Carefully she eased to her feet.

'I believe I am with child,' Eleanor said abruptly as Judith shook out her skirts. 'I missed my last flux and it is nigh that time of month again and there is no sign.' She touched her breasts. 'I am sore here and bigger than I was and I have begun to feel sick.'

'Oh, that is welcome news indeed!' Judith cried, kissing her. 'Does Renard know?'

Eleanor shook her head. 'It was only the merest possibility before he left for the fens.' She avoided Judith's eyes, staring instead at a clump of couch grass near her feet.

The latter pursed her lips thoughtfully. Despite her grief and illness she had heard what had happened at the Christmas court, both the politics and the scandals. 'Did you know about Olwen before Salisbury?' she asked.

To a listening stranger it might have seemed a complete *non sequitur*, but Judith was shrewd, and to Eleanor, thinking along the same lines, the question was a perfectly obvious progression. 'Yes, I knew,' she said tightly. 'I found out on my wedding night.'

Judith clicked her tongue sharply and raised her eyes heavenwards. 'Guyon and I seem to have bred up idiots in place of sons!' she said with exasperation.

'I made the first move,' Eleanor defended. 'I asked him.' She raised her head and fixed Judith with a suspiciously bright hazel stare. 'All the same, it was like being slapped in the face. We quarrelled, or rather I was shrewish and he was so reasonable that I started to think it was all my fault. We mended our differences in Salisbury and despite that whore the seams have held, but ...' She splayed her hand over her stomach. 'But sometimes I imagine him with her and I feel sick.'

Judith felt the moisture filling and stinging in her own eyes at Eleanor's anguish and at her own. She knew the feelings if not the answer, for anger was a part of her own raw grief. 'Guyon had a mistress before we were wed,' she said, a quiver in her voice. 'Heulwen's mother. They had been lovers a long time. I cannot number the nights I tossed in torment – not because he continued to lie with her, but because sometimes his eyes would go where I could not and I knew he was remembering.' She laid her hand lightly on Eleanor's shoulder. 'You must see it as experience and use it to your advantage. A man always needs a place of safe harbour after the hardships of the open sea.'

Each gave the other a wan, slightly watery smile as they left the dusk-shrouded plesaunce and went inside to the great hall.

CHAPTER 17

THE BOY STARED DOWN at his feet and shuffled them as if the concentration of eye alone was responsible for their motion. A shock of straw-coloured hair stopped just short of his thin, dark brows beneath which his downcast lashes were long and thick enough to be the envy of every woman within the keep.

'Owain?' said Eleanor gently. 'Look at me.'

He raised his head and then his lids. His eyes were as wary and dark as a deer's, his mouth set so firmly that it defied his will and trembled anyway. He had just watched his mother ride away from him in the company of his despised step-father-to-be, stranding him here among strangers, ostensibly for his own good, but he felt nothing but betrayed.

'How old are you?'

'Eleven, madam.'

'Almost a man then,' she flattered. 'Past time you began your training. Earl Renard won't be home for at least another month yet. You can use the time to grow accustomed to your new home. Is this your pony?' She indicated the sturdy grey gelding that was lipping at a clump of twitch spiking from the base of the wall.

'Yes, madam.'

'What's his name?' She stroked the pony's neck, noting that he was well groomed and cared for.

'Grisel, madam.'

'Well then, Owain, unlatch your saddle roll and come with me. We'll find you somewhere to sleep.' She beckoned to a groom. 'Kenrick will take care of Grisel for now. Other times he will be your responsibility.' She scratched the grey beneath his whiskery chin and fondled his velvet muzzle.

The boy relaxed slightly and began to unfasten his small bundle of belongings from the pony's crupper. He paused in mid-motion as more horses clopped into the yard, his expression becoming one of blazing hope before sinking once more into apathy as he saw that the newcomers were two men astride working coursers.

William lit down easily from his saddle and stood close to the second horse, ready to help Harry if he failed. 'Come on, you can do it!' he encouraged with exaggerated joviality.

'Shut up, I'm not a babe!' Harry snapped, nettled at his brother's tone of voice and completed his own move to the ground somewhat more clumsily. 'I've still got two good legs!' His face was white with strain as he fumbled the shield from his right arm. Retraining himself to fight left-handed, his damaged arm protected behind his adapted shield, was a process so difficult that in private he wept with the sheer frustration of his inability to co-ordinate. These were still very early days, he tired quickly, grew fractious, but was grimly determined to succeed.

Hands on hips, William took his gaze from his grumpy brother and rested it on Eleanor and a slender boy who was obviously dressed in his best tunic and scrubbed for some momentous event.

'Is this the new squire Renard was telling me about before he left?'

Eleanor nodded. 'Owain ap Siorl.' She put her hand on the boy's shoulder.

William considered him gravely, remembering what Renard had told him of the boy's recent past and the reasons for his placement here. He addressed him in Welsh. Owain looked doubtfully at Eleanor before replying in the same language, but his face visibly brightened, and once begun, an almost defiant torrent of words poured from his lips.

Eleanor exchanged a brief, meaningful glance with William over the top of the boy's head.

'Well, Owain ap Siorl,' the latter said, reverting to French for his sister-in-law's benefit. 'Let us go within and show you the surroundings of at least one of your new homes. Earl

Renard has three other stone keeps beside this one, you know, and more manors and lodges than I can remember.' He replaced Eleanor's hand on the boy's shoulder with his own, gave her a swift, conspiratorial wink, and drew the boy away in the direction of the hall, reverting back to Welsh as he walked.

Eleanor smiled gratefully after him, then turned back to Harry. 'Are you all right?'

He gave her a toothless smile, his complexion peaky. 'Just gaining my breath. Was that the lad's mother and her new beau we met riding out just now?'

'Yes.'

'Poor little beggar.' He avoided her eyes to watch the groom begin unsaddling the grey pony.

'He's better than he would have been had he stayed at home. He's very defensive of his father's memory; resents another man's encroachments on his mother's affections when it's not been a year since Siorl's death. That is how Renard reads the situation anyway.'

Harry grunted and started to turn away, fumbling at his sword belt and trying one-handed to unlatch it.

'Here, let me do it.' Eleanor came round to help him. The latch was fairly new and therefore stiff and she had to struggle to get it undone.

Harry's good hand clenched into a fist at his side. 'I can do it myself,' he rasped. 'I have to learn.'

'It's all right, it's coming now. You might as well let me finish.'

Harry muttered something beneath his breath, and without warning Eleanor suddenly found herself swept round on his good arm and pushed up against the stable wall. For the space of ten rapid heartbeats he kissed her. He was wearing neither mail nor gambeson, it being too early in his re-training for him to take that kind of weight, and she was fully aware of his body, the fact that he was swollen erect. His mouth ground down on hers, no finesse, just hard, desperate passion.

Eleanor tried to scream, her voice stifled in her throat, her lips crushed. She managed to wriggle one arm free and struck the side of his head with all the force she could muster. Harry let her go, the last of his breath spending itself in a groan. 'I'm sorry, Nell, I'm sorry,' he said wretchedly. 'God's love, don't look at me like that!'

'How else should I look at you!' she gasped, hand across her mouth. 'No, don't touch me!' Ducking under his arm, she fled for the safety of the keep.

Harry stared wretchedly at the stable wall and wished that the arrow that had maimed him had killed him outright.

'Can I come in?'

Eleanor glanced up at Harry, gestured reluctant assent, and continued setting pins into the gown she was making for herself – one that would accommodate her increasing girth in the coming months.

Harry cleared his throat and tentatively stepped just inside the sewing room doorway. He shuffled his feet as awkwardly as the new squire had done that morning and stared at the thongs fastening his soft indoor shoes.

Eleanor eyed him warily and kept to her side of the trestle, the sewing shears close to hand.

He raised his stubby ginger eyelashes. 'I came to apologise for this morning. If I could wipe it from the slate I would.'

'So would I,' Eleanor said grimly.

'I never meant to hurt or frighten you. It's just that . . .' He made a movement with his good arm. 'I tire easily and then things happen that I don't mean to happen. You were so close and . . .' He stopped and tugged viciously at his moustache. 'Christ's death, I can't even say I'm sorry without digging myself into a deeper hole!'

A wave of compassion stirred among the other emotions that were disturbing her with their intensity. This morning she had been shocked and frightened by his sudden assault. Having always viewed him in an affectionate, fraternal light, she had been horrified to discover that his own affections coursed through a different and potentially dangerous channel. Supposing Renard came to hear of it by rumour and misconstrued it? She had not yet told him about her pregnancy. Supposing he misconstrued that too? The implications were terrifying, both for Harry and for herself.

'You have said enough,' she answered him in as level a tone as she could muster. 'I do not think an explanation will benefit either of us.'

'Are you still angry?'

'I wasn't angry before, just very frightened. I still am.'

'So am I,' he said bleakly and leaned against the wall. His right arm, strained from the work he had forced upon it was resting in a linen sling. He crossed his left arm beneath it. 'God knows, it crept up on me unawares. I couldn't even tell you when it changed. I only knew it was there when I saw you and Renard together; the way you looked at him . . .' A choked sound came from him and he turned his head aside.

'Harry, stop it!' Eleanor quivered. She could not go to him and comfort him, neither could she pick up the shears and drive him from the room. 'I told you, you have said enough!'

'No, as usual, I have said too much.' His throat worked. When he spoke again, his voice was gruff but controlled. 'Apart from apologising, I also came to tell you that I'm going home to Oxley tomorrow. I'm mended enough for that now, and it would be too difficult if I stayed.'

Eleanor bit her lip and nodded. She pretended to busy herself with the length of cloth on the sewing trestle.

Harry remained in the doorway staring at her the way a hungry but well-trained dog might stare at a meal it was not permitted to have. 'I want to part as friends,' he pleaded softly. 'Will you forgive me?'

A small, darker coloured blot began to spread on the pale green linen beneath Eleanor's fingers, then another one. 'I forgive you,' she said, her throat constricted as she tried to speak and breathe without giving herself away. She dared not lift her gaze from the trestle, not for a long time, and when she finally did, Harry was gone and the first hint of dusk was beginning to deepen the shadows in the room. Free to cry, she found that she was no longer able.

CHAPTER 18

O N THE DAY OF Renard's return to Ravenstow, Eleanor had spent a long afternoon in the town itself, buying at the market and talking to the merchants – the cloth sellers in particular, and to an ambitious young packman who had recently become a carrier and wanted to expand his business yet again. She offered him a contract transporting cloth between Woolcot and the main villages beholden to Ravenstow. He leaped at the proposal, but proved himself shrewd by haggling the terms a little more towards his advantage without losing Eleanor's goodwill.

Satisfied with her own end of the bargain, a little amused at the young man's sharp wit, Eleanor let Owain help her into the saddle, and turned Bramble for home. Sir Thomas d'Alberin, leader of her escort for the forty days of his feudal service, watched her with a long-suffering look on his heavy features. It was raining, his gouty foot was throbbing against his stirrup iron and he had heartburn from eating too many spiced shrimp pasties at the pie-sellers booth while he waited for Eleanor to complete her business with the cocky young upstart who called himself a carrier on the strength of the two moth-eaten ponies he had purchased to replace his haversack.

Sir Thomas had considered Eleanor a sweet little thing when he encountered her at her wedding in November, but as with all the Ravenstow women, that first impression had been a sugar coating, disguising a concoction that he was only too pleased belonged in Earl Renard's cup and not his own.

He glanced at her as she drew the hood of her cloak over her veil and cast a hazel grimace at the gathering rain clouds. Unlike the dowager countess, she did not snap or turn sarcastic when angered. Her tone remained level and calm, but her full mouth would tighten around the words and her eyes would narrow, as they were narrowing now, in response to the rain, leaving him in no doubt as to her displeasure.

Sir Thomas signalled the escort to increase the pace and thought with new longing of his own plain, plump wife. Guard duty at Ravenstow was always an adventure into a different, brighter world, but after a time the colours jarred his eyes and the struggle to meet expectations frazzled his nerves. The situation this year was also exacerbated by the fact of a new earl, his absence at war, and this dangerous quarrel with Ranulf of Chester. Not only that, but the son Thomas had brought with him, hoping that the lad would make a good impression, had done nothing but behave badly, particularly towards the new official squire.

By the time they arrived at the castle, the rain was tipping out of the leaden clouds like water from a leaky bucket. The thick new coat of limewash applied to Ravenstow's walls during the past few weeks was sluicing in white runnels into the tussocky rocks upon which the keep was built. Mingled with the thud of the rain, Eleanor heard the rush of the river, still high with the spring spate. Bramble's hooves squelched on mud and thudded onto the planks of the drawbridge. The mare picked her ears at the familiar smell of home and, unbidden, increased her pace to a trot, nudging the wet, sleek rump of the horse in front.

The bailey was already busy, every available groom and lackey attending to destriers, palfreys, rounceys and baggage nags. Two supply wains were leaning against a wall and other servants were toing and froing between them, the armoury and the hall as they unloaded their contents. Eadric, the head groom, who was leading a black stallion with familiar star and long white hind stockings towards a clean stall, paused and touched his forehead to Eleanor. 'We weren't expecting 'em, my lady,' he excused with a nod at Bramble. 'I'll only be a moment with this 'un.'

Puffing, Sir Thomas helped her down from the mare. Rain dripped from the nasal of his helmet into the groove of his upper lip. He blew upwards, spraying droplets. 'Lord Renard's home,' he announced unnecessarily and not without a certain degree of relief. And discovered that he was talking to thin air.

The great hall was crowded with armed men and stank of unwashed bodies and wet wool just beginning to steam rankly in the hall's smoky fug. Firelight flashed off rust-speckled hauberks and sword hilts, and the tankards that were being thirstily drained. A flustered serving girl was pushing her way among the men with two slopping pitchers of cider.

Eleanor tapped a huge, broad-shouldered knight on the back. 'Ancelin, where's Renard?'

He swung round. His blond hair was greasy from crown to cheek hollow and the ends hung in wet strings upon his coif. There were tired pouches under his eyes but his smile was as broad and genuine as ever as he looked down on her from an advantage of a full twelve inches. 'In the solar, my lady.' He pointed with his cup, then, with a sudden bellow of joy, rose on tip-toe and extended one brawny arm, affording her a whiff of rank armpit as he snatched a chicken leg off a loaded tray a maid was trying to bring to a trestle.

'Is he all right?' Eleanor felt a pang of fear for she knew that Renard was not a lord to hold aloof from his men without good reason.

'More or less,' Ancelin said indistinctly through a massive mouthful of meat. 'A trifle bad-tempered with the pain, but if you can bear with him, you'll not find him too sorely wounded to greet you fittingly.'

'Wounded!'

Ancelin chuckled and wiped his lips on the freckled back of his hand. 'And not even in the thick of battle . . . excuse me.' He broke away from her to dive after a wide wicker basket of hot bread.

Eleanor gathered her damp skirts and ran inasmuch as it was possible down the hall to the solar. She knew that Ancelin would not be guzzling with such joyous abandon if Renard was seriously hurt, but nevertheless it was with a heart full of apprehension that she drew aside the hanging across the solar archway and stepped inside the room.

Renard was sitting in a high-backed chair, one leg propped

on a footstool, and Judith was bent over, carefully examining his exposed foot. 'They're not broken,' she said doubtfully, as if not quite sure, and turned round as his gaze flickered to the curtain where Eleanor stood as white as a ghost.

'It's all right, he isn't going to be crippled for life, just a few weeks,' Judith said by way of reassurance. Leaving him, she went out, touching Eleanor lightly on the shoulder as she did so.

Renard raised the small cup of usquebaugh near his elbow and drained it in one fast gulp.

Eleanor advanced on him. Like Ancelin's, his hair was long and unkempt, and through a grizzle of beard his face was harsh with pain and fatigue. She looked at his foot. The skin was broken here and there and across his toes the swelling was a magnificent conglomeration of shades ranging from thundercloud black, through purple and magenta to a bright, angry red. 'What happened?'

He made an impatient sound under his breath. 'A baggage wain stuck in the mud at a ford this morning. I dismounted to help push it free, spoke to the driver about the damage to a wheel, and his cursed nag took fright at a coney flushed from cover by one of the dogs and shied sideways onto my foot!'

Eleanor bit her lip. It did no good. She covered her mouth with her hand. He glared at her. 'I'm sorry,' she said in a choked voice. 'It looks as though it hurts dreadfully.'

'It does,' he growled.

Contrite, she stooped over to kiss him. He relaxed slightly and curved his arms around her waist. The damp end of her braid tickled the back of his hand. He became aware that she was only a little less wet than he was himself. Her lips were cold and tasted of rain, but then everything did — rain or river or stagnant weed. Sighing, he released her.

'Did Bishop Nigel get his comeuppance then?' she asked.

He tipped back his head and closed his eyes. 'After a fashion, I suppose. We built a bridge of boats and hurdles to cross to Ely where he was holed up at Aldreth. A local monk with a grudge against him guided us through the marshes. We took dear old Nigel by surprise from the rear.' He lifted one hauberk-clad shoulder. 'Unfortunately he escaped – to Bristol we think, but we captured some of his knights and most of his treasure. There's a necklace in my baggage – that's a personal present from the King to you. Apparently you made a good impression on the Queen at Christmas.'

'Did I?'

'She likes strong-minded women who rule their men,' he said dryly and raised his lids to flash her a look full of brooding amusement. 'I was not altogether flattered, although I suppose it might be true. You're just not as obvious as Mama, are you?'

Eleanor was slightly taken aback. It had never occurred to her that she might be able to rule Renard, or that the Queen might think her capable. 'She had the advantage of your father's devotion,' she said, and began to pluck at the sodden leather laces of his coif.

'Ah now, that is fishing with either a very subtle or a very foolish bait, Nell,' he smiled, and wrapped his fingers around the thick rope of one of her braids to draw her down to him again, adding just before he kissed her, 'I've missed you.'

Her palm was against his throat and she felt his pulse surge rapidly against it. He slipped his hand beneath her cloak to stroke her body, revelling in a luxury that had been six weeks absent from his life. The camp whores had proved no trial to celibacy. Most of them stank worse than the surrounding fetid marshes and had been so well used that Ancelin had remarked feelingly that they were all hole and no target. Besides, he was still smarting too much from the wounds Olwen had inflicted on his pride to seek a whore for the mere easing of boredom.

He closed his eyes again, savouring. Eleanor's lips were as soft and cool as damp silk. Her fingertips traced a delicate, fiery pattern over his throat and her body, pressing upon his, set up a pulsing ache in his loins. 'Oh Jesu, yes, I've missed you,' he whispered against her mouth.

Eleanor caught her breath and swallowed, her senses swimming. From the way he had taken fire at such preliminary stimulus, she surmised that he had not been with other women whilst on campaign, and that acted as a fillip to her desire.

'Me?' she asked. 'Or this?' And boldly sought beneath the heavy slit skirts of his hauberk and gambeson. At which embarrassing juncture Judith returned. Eleanor snatched her hand away, her face becoming poppy-scarlet.

Renard was sufficiently graceless to guffaw for all that he tried to stifle it behind his hand.

'You will do that on the other side of your face!' his mother warned. 'I've had Elflin prepare you a tub in your chamber and to get there you'll have to walk on that foot – unless of course you intend hopping across the hall like a mad sparrow.' Ignoring his scowl, she turned to Eleanor. 'Don't fret, child. Myself and his father were often interrupted on occasions far more intimate than this one. If my mind had not been so full of housing and feeding that untimely rabble out there, I'd have given you due warning.'

Her words had been meant to comfort, but made Eleanor realise that in her haste to reassure herself of Renard's safety, she had been remiss in her duties as chatelaine. 'I'm sorry, I shouldn't have left it all to you. I'll . . .' She started towards the doorway.

'No, no, don't apologise.' Judith waved her hand. 'Your place is with your husband, undeserving wretch though he be, and it helps to keep me busy.'

'Rabble?' Renard protested indignantly as he levered himself carefully to his feet, assisted by the two women. He had seen Eleanor's hesitation and the pain underlying his mother's response, and knew when to steer the conversation into less turbulent channels. 'They've been working their backsides off for the last six weeks and in conditions only a frog would enjoy. Don't salt your tongue too liberally while you see to them, Mama.'

Judith's lips twitched. She held them firm. 'As if I would!' she declared.

By the time Renard sank into the steaming tub that had been prepared for him, he was grey-faced with pain, all thoughts of chaffing anyone completely erased from his mind and muffled curses the limit of his ability. Through a throbbing haze he was aware of Eleanor and his mother consulting low-voiced about the best method of bandaging his damaged toes. Squeezing his eyes shut, he gasped.

Judith departed. Silence fell, punctuated by the small sounds of Eleanor returning to his coffer the few items of clothing in his baggage that did not require laundering or discarding.

The pain eased. His knotted muscles relaxed in the hot, herb-infused water. Eleanor came to the tub and examined him with a critical eye but could see no other signs of injury on his body. There was a shallow scratch on his face between eye socket and beard, but it looked like a scrape from a tree branch that would heal quickly of its own accord. Unstoppering the jar of staves-acre lotion she was holding, she knelt beside the tub and handed him a cloth. 'Cover your eyes.'

The smell of the lotion was pungent and familiar. He did as she bid and said in a muffled voice, 'I hope you have plenty. We're all alive with lice.'

'Heulwen had a surplus. She sent some over last month knowing how likely it would be.' She worked the lotion into his hair and left it while she barbered off his beard and its occupants.

'I didn't see Harry when I arrived,' he remarked, and when she did not reply, lowered the cloth and looked at her piercingly. 'Gave himself away did he? I thought he might.'

Eleanor paused in her ministrations to lean back and return his stare. 'You knew?'

'I've known since our wedding day.' And then, defensively, 'Well, what was I supposed to do? Swell into a jealous rage and swathe you up in black cloth like an infidel would do to his wife? Throw Harry half-dead with wound fever out of the keep?' The bath water churned. Somewhat grimly he set about the motions of a wash. 'What happened?'

There was a huge lump in Eleanor's throat, making her voice husky. 'He was struggling to undo his swordbelt. I went to help him and he grabbed me. It was an impulse. I . . . I fought him off and he stopped at once. I think he was horrified and ashamed of what he had done. Later, he came to apologise, and then he left.'

Renard sighed heavily and shook his head.

Eleanor swallowed. 'What are you going to do?'

He squeezed shut his eyes against the sting of the staves-acre lotion. 'Nothing. I daresay he'll come round in his own good time. Certainly I'm not going to chase after him rubbing salt into a bleeding wound. Let him heal a little first.'

Eleanor took the cloth from him to wash his back, positioning herself so that without a violent contortion of his body he would not be able to see her face. 'I never dreamed for one moment that Harry felt more than brotherly towards me,' she whispered.

'He always was shy with women,' Renard said slowly, feeling his way towards understanding. 'I suppose he has known you since childhood and therein lies the difference. He has long been familiar with you in a family atmosphere.' A heavy frown rested between his brows. 'My father should have betrothed him years ago before the mould became too firmly set.'

'But he betrothed you instead – to me.'

Renard tried to swivel and look at her, unsure of her slightly breathless tone, but found that with his injured toes propped over the far edge of the tub, it was not physically possible. 'Yes,' he answered, the frown deepening. 'Are you going to make an end of this before I die of discomfort?'

Eleanor made allowances for his grumpiness, and murmuring assent made herself meekly busy. She required a respite to think and rationalise. She knew how Harry felt because she felt it herself; more so, for while Harry could only look longingly like a starving man at a forbidden loaf of bread, she at least was permitted to gnaw at the crust, discovering too late that it was not enough. She wanted the soft, fragrant interior, and to gorge until she was replete.

'That is not all I have to tell you,' she said hesitantly when Renard was finally de-loused, dry, and dressed for comfort in a loose robe, his injured foot smeared with salve and bandaged.

'Ranulf of Chester hasn't . . .?'

'No,' she reassured him quickly. 'There has been some minor raiding, but more opportune than of any grand design. You'll have all the reports as soon as you're ready for them.'

'Then what else?'

Eleanor looked down at her clasped hands. 'I'm with child.'

He stared at her, his surprise reserved not for the fact of her pregnancy – sooner or later it was bound to happen – but because he read more apprehension than excitement in her expression and the tone of her voice. 'That's excellent news,' he pronounced with guarded enthusiasm. 'When?'

'Mid-autumn I would guess.'

Renard continued to study her. He remembered that her mother had died in childbirth when she was very small. Even women who longed for children and had a strong maternal instinct could be terrified by the prospect of giving birth, for it was also the prospect of death if anything went wrong. 'Come here, Nell,' he said gently.

Obediently she came, and sat down as he indicated, but when he set his arm around her, he could feel the violent vibration of her body. 'What's the matter? Are you afraid?'

She buried her head suddenly against his shoulder and breast. He felt her lips against his throat and the flutter of her eyelashes like small moth wings. 'Only of losing you. A ram takes little interest in a ewe save to keep other rams away once she is in lamb.'

'You think that of me?' he asked, stricken.

'I *fear* that of you. It is foolish and jealous I know, but I cannot stop myself.'

He tightened his embrace. 'If you were ever a duty, Nell, you're much more than that now,' he told her. 'If I call you love, or sweetheart, it is because I mean it.' He sought her lips and kissed her, tenderly at first, but with a growing tension that was interspersed with murmured endearments and then breathless entreaties. Eleanor yielded herself to the sweeping needs of her body and his, and thought with a pang that the difference was that while he called her sweetheart, she called him her soul.

'Here.' Renard presented Eleanor with a key and indicated the iron-bound donkey-skin chest that a puffing servant had just set down on the rushes.

'What's in it?'

'Plunder.' He grinned and gestured. 'Some of Nigel of Ely's ill-gotten gains. Mine now. Mostly it's silver which I'll use at Caermoel, but you can have the gee-gaws. Wear them or melt them down. The necklace for you from Stephen's in there too.' He darted a glance aloft to show what he thought of the King's taste in jewels.

Eleanor knelt by the chest. Clasp, hinges and keyhole were all rusty from the damp fenland spring and it took a strong effort from the cushion of her thumb before the lock gratingly yielded. Within, protected by a waxed cloth, lay bag upon bag of silver pennies, innocuous lumpy rows of coarse leather, and riding upon them, like gem-stoned ships on a grey ocean, were two decorated cups, a flagon, odds and ends of jewellery, and a collar of ostentatious gold squares, each one the size of a small griddle cake and adorned by rough-cut red stones.

Renard's grin became an outright guffaw at the look on her face as she raised the collar to the light. 'I don't know which is the more priceless!' he japed. 'That thing, or your expression!'

Eleanor wrinkled her dainty nose at him. She turned the object this way and that and a thoughtful look came into her eyes. 'It's not so bad,' she said consideringly. 'I'm sure I can find a use for it.'

'As long as it's not embroidering it into one of my tunics, I don't care what you do with it.' He rubbed his jaw. 'I have something else for you too, but it's down in the bailey, a personal gift this time.'

'In the bailey?' Locking the chest she clambered to her feet. Her stomach churned and for a moment she compressed her lips, waiting for the nausea to subside.

'What's the matter?' He looked at her with sudden anxiety.

She managed a wan smile. 'Just the sickness of the early days. I should not have risen so quickly. It will pass.' The smile warmed. 'I'll race you if you like.'

Renard looked from her white complexion to his damaged foot and laughed.

The bailey was a morass of churned mud, dung and greenish puddles after the previous day's downpour. Planks had been bridged across the filthiest parts. A flooded store shed was being swept out by two chattering women, forearms bare, besoms working in rapid, long strokes.

Eleanor raised her skirts to her shins and splashed in her pattens beside Renard. He had borrowed a quarterstaff from one of the soldiers, and with its aid was managing to limp along at a commendable pace.

Rounding a corner near the swept-out mulch from the stables, he halted before the pen that usually held stray animals waiting to be reclaimed by their owners on payment of a quarter penny fine. Today, instead of old Edward's cow which was almost a permanent fixture due to her propensity for wandering and his reluctance to pay, the pen was occupied by a score of sheep. Ten ewes all with lambs at foot, and a handsome shell-horned young ram.

'Longwools.' Renard gestured towards their full, curling fleeces, colloped with mud after yesterday's rain. 'I thought you might find a use for them on that low land at Woolcot where the Alyn floods every spring. They're marsh-bred and not susceptible to hoof rot, or so I was informed.'

Eleanor looked at the animals and swallowed the lump that came to her throat. Any man could have offered his wife jewellery – the more decent probably did – but Renard seemed to have an intuition that ran much deeper, touching the quick. He brought his mother bulbs from Antioch that flowered bravely in the face of winter. He brought her sheep and craftsmen, making light of it when she knew that it meant more to her than a hundred ostentatious gold collars.

'They're from the Bishop's own personal herd. Some of Stephen's less disciplined and hungrier troops had a preference to slaughter them, but I persuaded them otherwise.'

'They're in excellent condition.' She looked beneath the caking of mud at the bright eyes, sturdy legs and solid bodies. The lambs were frisky and inquisitive.

'Better than me and the men,' he qualified. 'They seem to thrive in the wet with the joy of mushrooms!'

A ewe bleated at him as if in thorough agreement and he laughed. Eleanor turned into his arms and impulsively kissed him.

His balance wobbled. He grabbed her around the waist to steady himself and then kept hold of her, bending his head to seek her lips.

'You crazy half-Welsh whoreson, let go of me!' screamed a high-pitched, panicking voice. The sheep bunched nervously together. Renard jerked up his head and stared at the two boys wrestling in the mud, dung and straw on the edge of the stable midden.

A tawny head came uppermost, narrow arms flailing, an obscenity in Welsh snarling from writhed-back lips. His adversary warded the blows on pudgy, raised forearms and threshed his feet with the frantic incompetence of a corpse on a gibbet.

Eleanor started towards the boys. Renard bellowed a command at them and was ignored, the antagonists being locked in their own private battle and deaf to all else.

'Owain, Guy, stop it now!' Eleanor cried, circling them in search of an opening to try to drag them apart.

Renard limped across the path of a kitchen maid yoked with two buckets of well water, unhooked one of them from the rope, and returning to the brawl, hurled an icy deluge into its midst.

The boys broke apart, spluttering and suddenly breathless with shock. Renard put himself between them and regarded both without favour. It was useless to ask what had happened or who had started it. Boys of their age had usually perfected the art of lying, or at least of seeing the truth from a totally different angle to that prescribed by the harassed adult.

'You're Guy d'Alberin, aren't you?'

The pudgy boy twitched his soaking shoulders. 'Yes, my lord,' he said through chattering teeth. A fresh breeze swooped around the open spaces of the ward, catching unawares those who were not wearing cloaks.

'And you are?'

'Owain ap Siorl, my lord.' The other boy jutted his chin proudly at Renard. Blood was trickling from his nose, but he was pretending not to notice.

'It was his fault, he started the fight!' accused Guy d'Alberin. 'He can't take the tiniest joke without going wild!'

Which told Renard everything he wanted to know, particularly when the Welsh lad tightened his lips, eyes dark with fury. 'Suffice it is that you both have the time and energy to indulge your tempers,' he said coldly. 'It will not happen again. I know that for a certainty because I am going to see to it myself. Guy, go and find your father and send him to me. After that, do the same with Sir Ancelin.' He turned to fully peruse the slighter youth. 'Owain ap Siorl, get yourself cleaned up and changed, then saddle up your own mount and the blue roan for me.'

The boys, frightened of the quality of Renard's presence rather than the strength of anything he had said, sheepishly vanished on their separate errands.

Eleanor sighed and shook her head. 'Guy d'Alberin's a bully,' she said. 'The older boys just laugh at his airs and ignore him, so he takes his revenge on the newest member of the household. Owain's so sensitive about his Welsh blood and his mother's remarriage that he's his own worst enemy. Also, I think that Guy's jealous of the fact that Owain is to be your squire.'

'Fancies himself in that role does he?' Renard thoughtfully stirred the end of the quarterstaff in the mud as if mixing porridge.

'Unfortunately so.'

'Might do him good.'

'But not you.' Eleanor pulled a face.

'Oh, undoubtedly not in the beginning, but he's the heir to Farnden. If he isn't tempered before he inherits, he's going to be about as much use to me as a sword made of raw dough! The other lad requires tempering too but in a different way. Guy d'Alberin has to acquire a cutting edge; Owain already has one but needs the nicks of misuse honing out.'

'And you see all that from one small encounter?' Eleanor eyed him sceptically.

'I see the probability.' He went to lean across the top of the sheep pen and murmured in a voice so low that she hardly heard him, 'Perhaps I too have been recently tempered.'

CHAPTER 19

Westminster
Pentecost 1140

MATILLE WATCHED Ranulf and his half-brother, William de Roumare, cradling their wine and their sour, power-hungry hatreds, and with an impatient click of her tongue retreated behind the leather curtain into the sleeping chamber.

She knew how it would go, round in a vicious circle, ever-decreasing as the drink took effect. The earldom of Carlisle and how it should be theirs by right of birth instead of belonging to David of Huntingdon, son of Scotland's king. Then various curses would be aimed in the latter's direction, degenerating to all Scots in general and the Welsh too for good measure. Plots and plans to regain Carlisle and plant King David in the ground would follow.

Sighing, Matille bid her maid fetch her jewellery casket, and opening it up, began selecting some earrings to wear to the King's feast at court. Ranulf would expect her to drip with jewels tonight, would expect her to outdo the Queen. His tastes were crude. He would not see the vulgarity in such a gesture, only the necessity of displaying his wealth and power. In some ways Matille was not averse; she disliked the Queen, but she preferred to be less blatant than her husband. And these days Ranulf was blatant in all things – his contempt for Stephen, his contempt for his fellow barons, and the flaunting of his blonde, foreign whore who went by the improbable name of Olwen and whom he had set up handsomely in a house on the Southwark side for the duration of their stay in London.

Matille held up a pair of engraved gold discs, punched and

hung with gold wires upon which were threaded freshwater pearls, five to a strand. They had been a betrothal gift from Ranulf and were one of her favourite items. There were other, newer gifts in her casket, payments to keep her sweet and salve Ranulf's tardy conscience while he dallied with his dancing girl. Matille was slightly piqued at his fascination, but it went no deeper than that, indeed she was even grateful to the slut for taking the edge from his sexual appetite. Accommodating Ranulf had always been one of the less pleasant marital duties.

Apparently the girl was now pregnant and claimed that Ranulf was the father of her child. It was possible of course, but Matille was sceptical. Ranulf, for all his eagerness between the sheets had never got any of his previous mistresses with child, and on her he had only fathered the two girls and a third pregnancy that had ended in miscarriage. If the dancing girl was pregnant, then for Ranulf it was swift work, and probably to be repented at leisure.

Matille had not approached him on that matter directly lest he see it as jealous carping, but nevertheless, with a word here and there in the right quarters, she had ensured that the seeds of doubt were sown in his mind, growing as did his leman's belly. While Matille was indifferent to raising Ranulf's bastard among their vast household, she drew the line at raising some ditch-begotten pedlar's brat with no blood claim whatsoever. If the babe came early then Ranulf would doubt his paternity. Even if it didn't, knowing him, he would still be suspicious, and that suited Matille perfectly.

'The pearls,' she confirmed to the maid, and signalled her to remove the casket.

'All right,' said William de Roumare, jutting his bluish jowls at his half-brother and with one eye to the edge of the curtain that was blowing slightly in a draught, lowered his voice. 'We'll deal with Henry of Huntingdon as you suggest and use him as a lever to wrest Carlisle from his father.'

Ranulf nodded and rolled the goblet between his damp palms. 'We can arrange the details tomorrow. I know several useful men who love money as much as they hate the Scots.'

Roumare grunted and leaned back in the chair. It creaked

against his solid weight. 'Carlisle,' he said softly, fondling the word.

Ranulf smiled. 'Then Lincoln and Ravenstow,' he said as if listing the delicacies spread upon the table of an anticipated feast.

Olwen sat near the open shutters, listening to the night sounds of the Southwark streets. Behind the houses the afterlight was a luminous teal-green pin-pricked by the first stars. She could smell the closeness of the river and the vinegary odour of cheap ale and wine from the bath house next door. Laughter was emanating too, loud and high-pitched. The Southwark stews. The other side of the river where men kept their mistresses and appointments with the seamier side of life. Not hidden, but separated, and the chasm was far deeper than that carved by the muscular grey river flowing between the two.

She pressed her hand to the slight mound of her belly where the baby was kicking vigorously — far too vigorously for a child begotten at Christmastide. The superb tone of her dancer's muscles made her look less pregnant than she actually was — four months instead of the six she knew to be fact.

Sometimes the potions and the preventatives did not work. That last time in November with Renard they hadn't and by the time she had realised her dilemma it had been too late, she was already established in Ranulf of Chester's bed. Now she had to pray the child would come late and that Ranulf could be led to believe that it was his. The small size of her abdomen thus far and the fact that she was still being sick had worked in her favour. The fact that she had announced her pregnancy within weeks of the Christmas feast had not.

She had thought about returning to Renard but could not bear the thought of mouldering in that draughty little manor house, knowing that not five miles away at Ravenstow he was there and that he would fight his will to exhaustion rather than visit her. He had said at the outset that it would destroy one of them and now she understood what he meant. At the Christmas court she had wanted him to fight for her, take a knife to any man who dared to lay hands on her, and had almost had her wish fulfilled. But his wife had stepped in his way and he had taken her outside. Olwen had seen the way of it then. The way of it was slender and black-haired with the eyes of a forest nymph and a sweet face. Wholesome as new bread.

She rose abruptly from her seat and turned to pace the room like a caged animal. It was a well-appointed cage with hangings on the walls and a clothing pole and laver. There were thick, scented rushes on the floor and animal pelts either side of the bed. She flounced down again on the latter and in self-mockery adopted a sultry pose. Picking up an exquisite silver-backed hand mirror she regarded herself, decked out as Ranulf preferred in her dancing clothes, her face painted. She knew all about his preferences now. For all his power he was subject to his lust, and her own power lay in her ability to both feed and satisfy it.

Amid the sound of sporadic, loud laughter from the bath house, other approaching voices intruded upon her consciousness. Ranulf's wine-thickened growl and his brother's slurred reply. Ranulf and Roumare liked to share. Suddenly Olwen could not bear to look at her face any more. She put the mirror face down on the coffer, locking herself within it, and it was the reflection that went with a smile on its face, brittle as glass, to open the door.

CHAPTER 20

RENARD STOOD IN THE TILT YARD at Caermoel, squinting against the bright June sunshine and watching his two squires sparring with sword and shield. Owain was as nimble as a flea but guarded so wide that all his speed was channelled into extrication not attack. Guy d'Alberin was much slower, but he learned the lessons surprisingly well. Literally battered into his body, the knowledge was becoming ingrained for life. He would never carry off prizes in a tourney, but he would be solidly capable of holding his own. He and Owain were easier with each other now, bonded by a mutual dislike of Ancelin who worked them so hard that they had no time to quarrel except like this in a tilt yard, spare time being reserved for precious sleep.

Turning his attention away from the boys, Renard stared at his youngest brother who had just announced that Ranulf of Chester and William de Roumare had tried to force Stephen's hand in the matter of Carlisle by attempting the kidnap of Henry of Huntingdon on his journey home from Westminster to his father's court in Scotland. 'You're jesting!'

'I wish I was.' William let a groom take his sweating horse to the trough where a handful of Milnham men were already clustered with their mounts. Distantly from the area where the new well was being dug, came the clink of hammer on stone.

'De Gernons must either be mad or very sure of himself to try a trick like that!' Renard signalled Ancelin to continue instructing the boys and set off through the inner bailey to the hall.

'*He's* not the one who's mad, it's Stephen!' William helped himself to a cup of cider from a jug on the table where the steward and a scribe were working at a pile of tally sticks. He

211

hitched himself onto the board. On his braced forearm, a heavy gold bracelet caught the light. 'I'm renouncing fealty to Stephen and heading for Bristol to do homage to Mathilda,' he announced with a hint of uneasy defiance and took a stiff gulp of the cider.

'Oh yes?' Renard arched one eyebrow. 'What makes you say that?'

'What, that Stephen's mad, or that I'm going to give my oath to Mathilda instead?'

'Both.'

William banged his cup down on the trestle. 'Stephen's mad because when his spies told him about the plot against Huntingdon and sent him warning, he turned on de Gernons and Roumare, reddened their ears with a load of moralising clap-trap, and rewarded them! God's death Renard, rewarded them! "Sorry, you can't have Carlisle, but here's Cambridge instead and a few other honours to pad it out!"' William's eyes were brilliant with anger. 'That man couldn't organise a drinking session in an ale house, let alone rule a kingdom!'

'What makes you think Mathilda's any better?'

'Well she certainly cannot be any worse!'

Renard rested one elbow on his folded arm and pinched his upper lip. 'I'll agree to differ with you on that count, but give my regards and regrets to Uncle Robert when you see him.' Uncle Robert being their mother's half brother, the Earl of Gloucester, and Commander-in-chief of the Empress' Army.

'You're not going to try and argue me out of it then?' William asked suspiciously.

Renard shot him a bleakly humorous look. 'Is that why you're here?' He poured himself some of the cider.

William glowered at him for a moment before shrugging himself into a grin. 'No, my mind's made up this time. You can't keep me in tail clouts for ever. I came to tell you about de Gernons, since one of the men responsible for foiling the plot is a friend of mine. I suppose I want to justify myself too.' He fiddled with the narrow rope of gold on his sinewy wrist. 'I know you think I've some scapegrace ways about me, but I have thought long and hard about this, not least

212

the possibility of facing you across a battlefield.'

Renard gestured a dismissal at the steward and scribe. 'That would be a pity wouldn't it?' he said sarcastically as the two men gathered together their bits and pieces and adjourned elsewhere.

'I would not fight you.' William gave him a weak imitation of his usual incorrigible grin. 'You're bigger and far more experienced. I'm going to offer my services to the Empress as a scout and forager with the proviso that she does not ask me to do any of that scouting and foraging on your lands.'

'Oh, very noble!' Renard said through his teeth and raised the cup, then seeing William's expression, lowered it again. 'Well what do you want me to do? Pat you on the head and send you off with my blessing? Christ, William, grow up! Mathilda's not like Stephen. You go to her and she'll toss you on the altar of her ambition and cut out your heart! You won't be able to pick and choose when and where you scout like some finicky old nun demanding a boneless portion of fish!'

A dusky flush crept beneath William's summer-browned skin. 'I have the skills to make myself invaluable enough to be worth such a concession,' he said stiffly.

Renard said nothing, just drank, his eyes a sidelong flicker more eloquent than words.

'Look, I'm much closer to the rebels than you are. I've got Miles of Hereford breathing down my neck and my lands are just the right size to make inviting fodder for a quick raid. It's not safe to support Stephen any more!' William thrust out his lower lip. 'Besides, our oath was to Mathilda originally anyway.'

'Papa's oath, not mine,' Renard reminded him in a harsh voice. 'And sworn under duress. Mine was given freely to Stephen at Christmas.' And then on an exasperated, slightly weary note, 'You can stop puffing up like a frog. If your heart is set on it, then go to the Empress, just don't expect my approval. I presume you intend staying the night here at least?'

William let out the swift breath he had drawn. 'Aren't you afraid that I might take note of all these new defences you're adding and relay them all to Aunt Mathilda?'

Renard's eyes darkened, but he suppressed the urge to grab

William by coif and surcoat and hurl him into the rushes. Show restraint now and it would be easier later when one or the other of them was forced to back down. 'Are you insulting yourself or me?' he asked, and succeeded in keeping his voice on the level.

William chewed his lip. 'Sorry,' he said. 'I didn't mean it. I told Adam I was going over to the Empress too. He said I was a fool and he wished he was coming with me.'

Renard snorted. 'That sounds like Adam.'

'There was some more news about Chester too – gossip, nothing serious.' William leaned forward to remove his spurs, then flicked an upward look at Renard. 'His mistress is with child.'

'Oh?' Renard made his tone indifferent, although he felt his gut tighten and turn. He could go for weeks without thinking of Olwen, but now and again, unbidden, she would haunt his memory or his dreams with a knife and tear open the healing wounds.

'Conceived in the winter,' William added, pressing his thumb down on the tip of the spur. 'From what I heard, she's carrying it to full term this time.'

'I suppose Ranulf's bragging to all who will listen.'

'Not really. He doesn't trust her.'

Renard laughed sourly. 'Then he and I have found common ground at last.' A noise behind him made him turn round to find Eleanor standing there. She had been resting, and her face, framed by her loose black hair, was still rosily flushed, her eyes a sleepy, luminous green-gold. Something stirred within him, as painful as thoughts of Olwen, akin to physical desire but possessing increased texture and depth.

'William!' Eleanor hugged her brother-in-law delightedly and kissed him.

Returning the embrace he back-stepped to look her up and down. 'You're blossoming like an orchard, Nell!'

'Why thank you!' Laughing she laid her hand lightly on her stomach where for two weeks now she had been feeling the baby's fluttering movements. 'But fruiting is the more appropriate word I think!'

William grinned. 'Still planning a huge brood? I remember you used to have some impressive ambitions of motherhood when we were little.'

'I did, didn't I?' She blushed round at Renard.

He smiled in a slightly preoccupied way and squeezed her thickened waistline, his mind obviously far distant from the light banter of the moment.

Eleanor turned to William. 'How long are you staying?'

'Just overnight.' He looked at Renard.

She sensed constraint in the atmosphere. 'Is there any special reason for your visit?'

'Folly of the most serious order,' Renard answered before William could speak.

The latter hooked his thumbs in his belt. 'Stephen's folly, not mine,' he retorted. 'You'll discover it soon enough.'

The summer progressed in hot somnolence. A peace treaty between the two opposing forces was mooted, discussed, and abandoned. War drifted across the land like August thunder, sometimes passing over, sometimes deluging an area in brief destruction and misery. Crops burned. People and livestock roasted. Storm-coloured smoke mingled with storm-coloured sky.

William went foraging and raiding with the Empress's troops. By turns he found himself exhilarated by the joy of his abilities and the tensile strength of his young body, and sickened by the strewn aftermath of a raid and what some of his companions considered sport. He learned, he matured, and stubborn determination did the rest.

In early September Olwen was brought to bed of a son at Chester.

'A fine boy, my lord,' said the nurse, plucking the bawling infant from his cradle and presenting him to the Earl. 'Born yesterday dawn.'

Ranulf declined to hold the baby, and pushing down his coif stared suspiciously at the red, unprepossessing features. There was nothing to commend or recognise, but then at one day old both his daughters had looked remarkably like wizened turnips too.

'We did not think he would live at first, he nearly drowned in the birthing fluid. Father Barnard christened him Jordan because he had a vial of Holy water from the river.'

Jordan FitzRanulf. It had a reasonable ring to it, but how did he know that FitzRanulf was the correct appellation?

'He's big and strong,' added the nurse with a sly look at Ranulf. Men liked to hear things like that about their sons, and sometimes paid silver for the compliments.

Ranulf grunted at the woman and turned round to the bed. Too big and strong for a child delivered three weeks early? Olwen's eyes were closed. Heavy smudges purpled the delicate skin beneath them. Otherwise she was waxen, her lips shockingly pale because he was so accustomed to seeing them painted scarlet. A difficult birth so the midwife had said, but she could have been lying in hopes of a higher payment.

'Is he mine?' he said to her.

Olwen's eyes remained closed, but he saw the infinitesimal flutter of her lashes. Putting one knee on the bed, he braced his arms either side of her.

'Damn you, answer me!'

The heavy lids half-opened, revealing a glimpse of hazed dark blue iris. 'Yours?' The faintest of smiles played around the word she formed. 'Yes, he's yours.'

'Hah!' Abruptly he jerked away from the bed to look ferociously at the infant who had now settled hungrily at the wet nurse's ample breast.

'Bought, but not begotten,' she whispered, assailed by a terrible, seeping weariness. She had never dreamed in her life that such pain existed, that it could surge so relentlessly and for so long and culminate in a pushing, splitting agony beyond all her control.

Ranulf had not heard her thread-thin whisper. He was too occupied in watching the child, his expression a mingling of longing and doubt.

Olwen turned her face towards the wall and closed her eyes

216

again, but it did not stop the tears leaking from beneath her lids.

The Michaelmas fair at Ledworth went unaffected by the strife elsewhere and made an excellent profit for Renard from the tolls he was entitled to levy on all the booths and all the transport in and out of the town. Some of the proceeds he donated to the widening of the road approaching the town from Shrewsbury and also to a hostel for those seeking a night's lodging. Laughing, he returned Eleanor the half-penny fee that her own carrier had paid to bring the bales of Woolcot cloth into the fair. Woolcot and all it produced belonged to Renard, secured by the act of marriage, but he had gifted the herds and all profit from them back to Eleanor in the form of a 'morgengab' or 'morning gift', the ancient custom of presenting a bride with a gift should her husband be satisfied with his wedding night.

The product of Eleanor's morning gift, the finely woven, soft and gorgeously dyed woollen cloths, had been sold right down to the last ell on the last bolt, for it was of comparable quality to Flanders cloth and cost much less. Eleanor decided to reserve at least two thirds of her clip from the following year and begin building up the flocks at Ravenstow, Ledworth and Caermoel.

A little before the commencement of the Martinmas slaughter, Eleanor was delivered of her own son. Her waters broke as the bell was summoning the pious to morning mass. Shortly after prime, she pushed the baby smoothly into the world – 'With no more effort than using the garderobe,' Alys said later, when asked.

Hugh, named for his maternal grandfather, was a large-boned, well-developed baby and amazed everyone by how little trouble his birth had caused his smug, smiling mother. Strong-willed and extremely loud from the moment he emerged bawling into the world, he was also a definite throwback to his Norman-Viking ancestors, displaying scarcely any traits of the Welsh strain at all. By the time of his christening feast on Twelfth night, he possessed a respectable amount of sandy-blond hair and from between lashes that were almost white regarded the world with vivid, light blue eyes.

'Hugh suits him,' Judith said to Eleanor. 'He resembles your family.'

Eleanor smiled and agreed. She knew that Judith had been somewhat hurt at first that she and Renard had decided upon Hugh, not Guyon for their firstborn son, but as the baby's colouring and features had developed over the ensuing weeks, Judith's attitude had altered. 'He looks like my brother Warrin,' Eleanor added. 'Particularly around the eyes don't you think?'

The fine lines at Judith's mouth corners deepened slightly. Eleanor's brother had died in a street brawl in the city of Angers over twelve years ago. The circumstances had been decidedly murky and Adam and Heulwen somewhere involved. No one had ever prodded a spoon too deeply into that particular bowl of stew for fear of discovering putrid bones. 'Renard seems to beget the red hair,' she remarked instead of agreeing. 'Roslind's little girl was copper, and there's more than a hint in Hugh's. It only ever showed up among Guyon's in Heulwen. I'm glad you asked her and Adam to be godparents as well as Lord Leicester.'

'One for policy, one from the heart,' Renard said, edging his way between his wife and his mother.

Judith scowled at him. 'I wish you wouldn't creep up on people like that.'

'You're going deaf,' he retorted disrespectfully and lightly kissed her cheek before turning to Eleanor. 'Are you coming to dance with me, Nell, or now that you're a staid matron is it forbidden to show me a quick glimpse of ankle?' He held out his hand, inviting.

'If I show you my ankle, you'll want to see other things too!' she laughed at him.

'Yes,' he admitted cheerfully.

She blushed. Hugh's christening had coincided with her churching and purification which meant that she and Renard were permitted to bed together again. It was also Twelfth night, the feast of all fools and laden with wild merriment like a bandage stretched tight over an open wound, and the blood, despite all efforts, gradually seeping through. Sometimes Eleanor thought that they were not just living close to the edge, they were already over it.

She let him whirl her among the laughing, swirling dancers, was passed from hand to hand, swung round, lifted, turned. Her milk-tender breasts started to feel sore. Ancelin slobbered a kiss on her cheek and trampled on her toes, his eyes as glazed as misted glass. From the corner of her eye she saw Judith unobtrusively retiring as the roistering reached a new pitch.

She was spun back into Renard's embrace. He had seen the longing direction of her gaze, and squeezing her waist, stooped to murmur against her ear, 'Let's go to bed.'

Eleanor felt her face grow warm and her loins weaken. She would never accustom herself to just walking out of a room full of people to lie with him, aware that everyone was looking – making assessments, even wagers on how long it would take them.

'There's Hugh,' she prevaricated. 'He needs feeding.'

'Go and fetch him from Alys then and bring him up,' he said practically, and then as she looked at him, 'Oh in the name of Christ, Nell, I'm not about to pounce on you and ravish you! I just thought that you looked in need of respite from this wild horde.' He gestured around and grimaced. 'I know I am.'

She remembered the times when his laughter, the lightness of his remarks had been a cover for much deeper thoughts and emotions. She remembered the checked wildness in his eyes and body and him saying *'What I need to ease the pressure is ...'* And was suddenly contrite. 'I'll fetch Hugh,' she said, and turned to weave her way among the gathering.

It was strangely quiet and calm upstairs in the main bed-chamber, no sound, no hint of the revelry below, just the sputtering crackle of the alder logs in the hearth and the wind whining against the shuttered window slit. Hugh, as usual, guzzled with the speed of a sailor hitting the first ale house after three dry months at sea, and choked in his frantic haste.

Renard sat down on the coffer, legs outstretched, spine propped against the wall, and watched Eleanor and the baby. Only a few candles were burning on the small pricket, their glimmer diffusing into a dull, grainy gold. Eleanor's exposed skin gleamed softly. The baby's hair had the sheen of pale, pure gold against Eleanor's jet black, of which a strand was clutched tightly in Hugh's small fingers.

Renard swallowed. It was a sight to gladden the eye, but somehow it brought a lump to his throat, and not all of it was paternal tenderness. 'I thought Harry would have come,' he said in a tired, desultory voice. 'The weather has been clear, and I expressly invited him.'

Eleanor glanced from her absorption with the baby. 'Perhaps the wound is still too deep and new,' she suggested. 'Perhaps to see me with a child . . .' She left the sentence hanging in mid-air.

He twitched one velvet-clad shoulder. 'Maybe so. I thought that by now he would have come around. William's in the enemy camp but he still managed to send good wishes and a christening gift through a Welsh carrier.'

'Distance and differences of opinion do not separate the similarities between you and William,' she said shrewdly. 'You and Harry, even when you were smiling at each other never really scratched beneath the surface.'

Renard snorted and looked away, but was well aware that she spoke the truth. 'Even so,' he reiterated heavily, 'I thought that he would come.'

She watched him sit down before the hearth in the chair that had been his father's. His face was expressionless, but there were fine lines bracketing his mouth corners where he had been smiling without being in the least amused. She could sense the tension in him, straining on a taut leash.

'It's too quiet, Nell,' he said, eyes on the flames.

'But you just said below . . .'

'No, not up here. I'm talking about the war. Stephen, Mathilda and Ranulf de Gernons. No matter what Chester is given, he still wants more, and when one side has nothing else to give, he'll turn to the other.'

Hugh had fallen asleep at her breast. Carefully she lifted him away and went to put him down in his cradle, then turned round again to Renard. She had not bothered to hook up her bodice and she saw his eyes flicker to the ripe curve of her breasts. 'You think he will really leave Stephen?' she asked, not because at that moment she really cared, but because she felt too awkward to just boldly walk up to him and sit down on his knee. Absence of such contact had increased the shyness as well as the longing. It was not a familiar action any more.

'Undoubtedly. He has no reason to stay, has he? Hands smacked off Carlisle again, and Lincoln denied too, not to mention Caermoel.' His laugh was brittle.

'Do you wish you'd stayed in Antioch?' She was closer to him now. Very tentatively she laid her hand on his shoulder. The side of her hand grazed his throat and she felt the sudden leap of his pulse.

'Sometimes,' he sighed. 'But there it is an even more fractured mosaic of power-hungry war lords. I suppose I was always too low in the hierarchy to be much affected.' Slanting one arm around her waist and hip he did what she had hoped he would do and pulled her down into his lap. Then he kissed her and all conversation stopped.

They had reached the bed and a state of breathless, urgent half-undress when Owain cleared his throat raucously on the other side of the curtain and announced that Lord Harry had arrived and that he wanted an immediate word with Renard.

Renard closed his eyes and pressed his lips into the silky hollow of Eleanor's shoulder. His whole body was taut, reaching towards a release that was rapidly retreating, leaving pain in its wake. 'Judgement on me,' he groaned through his teeth to Eleanor, levering himself up. 'All right Owain, tell him to come up.'

'Yes, my lord.'

Renard sat up on the edge of the bed and fumbled his tunic back on with unsteady hands. He looked round at Eleanor, at the rapid rise and fall of her dark-tipped breasts and the loose hair spread abroad. 'Wishes have a fickle habit of exploding in your face, even while they're being granted,' he said wryly. 'Best cover yourself, love, unless you want to start a fight.'

Still dazed by the passion of a moment since, Eleanor was acutely aware of the soft beaver skins against her shoulder blades, of a liquid prickling in her womanhood, of Renard's eyes and the mingling of expressions on his face – staunched need, exasperation and reluctant humour. Her eyes went lower, travelling down over his body.

'Why do you think I put my tunic back on?' Breathing out hard, he left the temptation of the bed and walking to the window slit stood in the draught from an ill-fitting shutter.

Eleanor dragged her skirts decently down, shrugged her gown back onto her shoulders, and with fumbling hands hooked up the bodice. Her hair she could do nothing about except grab a comb, tidy it quickly and place a circlet on top to hold it away from her face.

Owain drew the curtain aside and Harry strode into the room. Rain sparkled on his cloak. Eyebrows and moustache were frosted with it and his eyes were the colour of a rain-swept river bank. He had regained some of the flesh he had lost during his convalescence, but his bones were harder now, stripped of the last malleable vestiges of infancy.

'I thought you had decided not to come,' Renard said quietly and returned to the hearth where his brother had now thrown off his cloak to reveal a leather hauberk, the kind of thing worn by foot soldiers and serjeants when they went to war, and by barons when they were preparing for it.

Harry flexed his good shoulder. 'I would have been here sooner, but I had some business with an armourer in Shrewsbury and whilst there I heard some very disturbing news.... Eleanor.' He spoke her name in a stiff greeting, averting his eyes, and advanced on the cradle to regard his new nephew. 'I've brought him a christening gift. Over there by the wall in the oiled cloth.' Stooping over the baby, he made the usual adult gesture of putting his finger in the baby's fist. Even in sleep the fingers curled and gripped. Harry's expression became less tense and he managed a smile.

'Strong,' he said, which was also an inevitable part of dutiful adult admiration.

Renard drew aside the covering from Harry's christening gift and looked at the shield leaning there. A black leopard rampaged across a golden background in direct imitation of

Renard's own shield, but it was only half the size, suited to a child who one day, far too soon for his mother, would leave the safety of maternal skirts to learn the warfare skills, his life depending on how well he learned and how well he was taught.

Eleanor could see that Renard was both surprised and moved by the gift and the thought behind it. Men watched their sons' development with more pride than fear. Indeed, it was the custom in every warrior household that a child's first solid food should be taken from the tip of his father's sword so that he developed a taste for the steel. She managed to smile, however, and thanked Harry warmly.

Behind his moustache, Harry's mouth twisted. 'My nieces and nephews are the nearest I'll ever come to children of my own. I ...' He swallowed and looked very quickly at her and away again. 'I have no wish to marry and I'm no great catch except to fat merchants' daughters who are hoping to add a title to their wealth. No, one day this little fellow will inherit Oxley, or I hope he will.' He cleared his throat, his colour high and his demeanour awkward.

Renard glanced up from his admiring examination of the superb craftmanship of the small shield. 'You mentioned news from Shrewsbury?' he remarked before the atmosphere became too difficult.

'The sheriff's mustering a force. Ranulf de Gernons has finally turned rebel and seized Lincoln castle from the King's custody.'

'What?' Renard's gaze sharpened and struck like a dagger. 'When?'

'First day of the Christmas feast. Ranulf and Roumare sent their wives into Lincoln castle to talk with the constable's lady, pass the time of day and courtesies. When it came time for the women to leave, Chester and his brother wandered into the keep with a small escort as if to fetch them away, but rounded on the garrison instead and held the castle until their reinforcements hastened from their hiding places. The whole of Lincoln's in an uproar. The citizens have sent to the King for help, and the call to arms has gone out. Likely you'll have it by official letter in the next couple of days.' There was a certain amount of satisfaction in Harry's tone because for once he had the advantage over Renard.

The latter looked eloquently at Eleanor. 'I said it was too peaceful, didn't I?'

Eleanor nodded woodenly. Her throat was too tight to speak. Renard was going to war again. It had not been peaceful at all, just the calm bordering the violence of a storm.

'I suppose,' said Renard with a sigh, 'that I've had a year's grace for Caermoel. If it doesn't withstand war now then I might as well break my sword over my knee.'

'I'm sorry to be the harbinger of bad tidings.' Harry looked between his brother and his brother's wife who was icily pale, her hands clenched tightly in the folds of her gown, and her green-gold eyes fixed on Renard in anguish. *Oh Eleanor*, he thought, and felt as if the pain would crush him.

'Nay,' Renard moved to clasp him on his good shoulder. 'I'm glad to see you, truly glad. How's the arm?'

There was genuine concern in Renard's voice without the bored note that so often crept into their discussions. Harry raised and flexed his right arm and his fingers. The movement was sluggish because he was still cold and numb from his ride, but at least there was some feeling present and a reasonable degree of control. 'I manage,' he said with a bleak smile. 'As ever, not well, but I manage.'

CHAPTER 21

Lincoln
February 1141

RENARD FITZGUYON to his dearest wife Eleanor, greetings.

Does it ever do anything but rain on this side of the country? I think not. My hauberk should be fashioned of fish scales not iron rivets. Owain and Guy have worn their fingernails to the quick keeping it clean of rust.

Our quarry is absent, chasing support in the south and has gallantly left his wife to defend Lincoln castle against us. It is not as foolish as it sounds. As you know, Matille is Gloucester's daughter and he's a fonder father than Ranulf is a husband. Whether it will force him through this sleet and wind to her aid I do not know, but she is conducting a spirited defence as if she well expects to be succoured.

The King is using the cathedral itself as a base from which to conduct the siege and we are encamped between it and the castle, well above river level, thank Christ. In several places it has burst its banks and flooded folk out of their homes.

I do not know how much longer we will be constrained to remain here in Lincoln. Two more weeks at the very least I suspect, by which time I will need more silver to pay the men. Send me two bags from the strongbox at Ravenstow. I need not tell you to ensure that it is well escorted. Include too, if you will, a hogshead of Anjou. The stuff here tastes like river water and even getting too drunk to care about our current discomfort is an unwholesome task. Harry manages it very well, through recent long practice I suspect.

I spoke to Adam yesterday. He is reluctant to be here, but resigned. Although his sympathies lie with the Empress, they most certainly do not lie with Ranulf of Chester. He gives you his greeting and asks that you ride over to Thorneyford and show Heulwen and the children this letter – you know the difficulty he has in setting quill to parchment.

I pray that this siege is finished soon, for if it is not, I swear I shall go mad with nought to do but crouch in a draughty tent, watching everything grow mould or becoming rusty while I huddle in my cloak and try to keep warm. Well I remember other ways of keeping warm with you and I cannot say whether the remembrance is a pleasure or a pain.

Written at Lincoln this first day of February, year of our Lord, eleven hundred and forty-one.

Renard finished writing, discarded the quill which had started to split, and sent Owain from his task of oiling an iron lance head out into the gusting sleet to find a messenger. Across the tent, as he sanded the parchment and set about melting wax to seal it, Harry clinked pitcher to cup again and focused on him with the owlish scrutiny of the well drunk.

'Did you ask Eleanor for more wine?'

Renard shot his brother a cool look. 'Yes.'

Harry took several loud gulps. 'Good.'

Renard added pointedly, 'Whether I actually get to drink any myself is another matter.'

The smell of hot wax mingled with the other musty, pungent odours of the tent. Harry wiped his gambeson sleeve across his mouth. 'You don't begrudge me an odd measure here and there do you?'

'The odd measure, not at all,' Renard said in the same, cutting voice. Of late Harry had been resorting to entire flagons.

''S all right then,' Harry said. 'Wine numbs the pain from my wounds ... all of them.' He pointed at the letter. 'Have you told her everything?'

Renard wrapped the letter in a square of waxed cloth and tied it up deftly, cutting the string with his dagger. 'Such as?' he said evenly as he concentrated on the task in hand.

'Such as that little yellow-haired wench who came scratching round the tent last night?'

Renard looked surprised. 'Why should I tell her about that? She knows full well that whores and sluts abound in an army's tail and that they proposition every man in sight. If I made mention, she would think me guilty.'

'And aren't you? I saw what she was doing.'

Renard rested his palms on the table. 'If you hadn't fallen down drunk, you'd have seen me push her away. I wasn't that desperate.'

Harry sneered. 'You must think I'm an idiot!'

'Jesu, Harry, just get out,' Renard said wearily as if to a truculent child. 'Take the flagon if you want. I doubt there's more than dregs left in it anyway the way you've been swilling it down your throat!'

Harry lurched to his feet. Unbalanced by drink and his damaged right side, he almost fell, clutched at the table for support and knocked the pitcher sideways. Renard was right. Little more than dregs did remain to trickle away into the floor. Harry felt the blood scorching into his face. Embarrassment made him clumsier than ever, and that in its turn led to rage. 'Perhaps I am an idiot!' he sobbed raggedly as he regained his feet. 'But I do not need to be made to feel like one!'

The tent was very quiet after he had gone. Renard uttered several terse obscenities at the canvas side of the tent and stared unseeingly at a clump of black mould sporing there. It was not about a yellow-haired whore at all. It was about everything that he possessed and Harry did not.

He swore again, and the messenger just entering the tent in Owain's wake baulked, stared for an instant and quickly dropped his gaze to the sheepskin hat in his hand. It was not Earl Renard's usual habit to blaspheme at his servants and call their ancestors into disrepute, but the tensions of the siege and the depressing state of the weather were beginning to mar even the steadiest of tempers.

Renard pinched the bridge of his nose. 'It wasn't personally intended ... Martyn.' It took him a moment and an effort to recall the messenger's name, but a good memory and a thorough training in the art of handling men made it just about possible. Smiling bleakly he lowered his hand and picked up the neatly sealed package. 'I want you to take this to the Countess, wherever she may be. Try Ledworth first.'

Martyn took the letter, noting that there were some fine beads of liquid on the waxed linen. He brushed them away on a calloused fingertip and saw that it was not rain as he had first thought, but wine. Then he noticed the shards of a pitcher on the floor. The squire stooped and began to pick them up.

'Now, not tomorrow,' Renard said sharply to the messenger. 'Take the bay gelding. He's not fast but he's got the endurance for this kind of weather.'

Martyn dipped his head, crammed his hat down around his ears and went out into the dripping, silvery sleet. Owain silently gathered the broken pieces of pitcher and put them in the empty chamber pot so that he could bear them away to the midden pit. 'Shall I bring you a fresh jug, my lord?'

Renard shook his head and drew another piece of parchment towards him, indicating that he wanted to be left alone. The parchment too was beaded with wine, the colour of rain-diluted blood. He shovelled his thoughts impatiently to one side like an over-worked groom attacking a pile of soiled straw, and with brisk decision trimmed another quill.

Moments later Owain burst back into the tent, Guy d'Alberin hot on his heels and both boys as quivering and wide-eyed as a pair of young deer. 'Lord Renard, come quickly! The scouts have sighted the rebel army drawing nigh the river!' cried Owain. 'Thousands of them!' A rapid swallow garbled the last word.

Renard dropped the quill, left his stool and the doubtful warmth of the brazier, and went outside. Cold needles of sleet stung his face and the ground underfoot was as treacherous as a butcher's shambles. Men were leaving tents and watchfires to view the approaching army, their faces a mingling of expressions ranging from bored 'seen it all before' cynicism, through frank, fairground curiosity, to excitement and gut-wrenching dread.

Owain's 'thousands' proved to be a vanguard of less than thirty mounted knights with perhaps twice that number of footsoldiers, and all of them spreading out along the far bank of the swollen Witham, searching for a suitable fording point. Renard narrowed his lids the better to see the shapes busying themselves below, industrious as aphids colonising an orchard leaf. Tents were being pitched and more men were riding to join them through the gathering late afternoon murk.

'How's the fire in your belly, Renard, hot enough for a battle?' asked Ingelram of Say, one of his fellow barons.

'What fire?' Renard hunched more deeply into the thick wolf-skin lining of his cloak. 'To whom do that lot belong?'

'Robert of Gloucester, so the rumour flies.' Ingelram sleeved a drip from his narrow beaky nose and sniffed loudly. 'Alan of Richmond's sent a detail down to guard the ford. I hope he's chosen doughty men or we'll have that lot over our side of the river faster than a whore can lift her skirts for business.' He jerked his head at the cathedral. 'Are you coming to the King's Council of War? Give your penny worth of advice to our beloved sovereign for how much notice he will take?'

Renard bestowed the garrulous Ingelram a tepid half-smile. 'In a moment.'

Ingelram shrugged at him and disappeared. Renard stared through the drizzle at the activity below and saw a figure on a raw-boned, spotted horse pacing along the river bank. The soldier, helmeted and grey-clad, was indistinguishable from any other of his kind, but the horse was all too sickeningly familiar.

Overnight the sleet turned to snow, a white curtain hissing silently into the spated river, blanketing one side's view from the other, as it had always been. In a freezing dawn, breath wreathing the air, feet stamping to preserve some vestige of circulation, Stephen's barons gathered in the cathedral, first to celebrate a special Mass commemorating the purification of the Virgin Mary, and then, that dealt with, to hold another Council of War and plan their next move now that it was known for certain that a huge rebel army was gathered on the opposite bank of the Witham and seeking a way across.

The candles were as cold in the hands as stalagmites, the wax inferior and as flaky as scurfy skin. Stephen's had a ghost in it and his flame sputtered with blue flickers of impurity as he followed Bishop Alexander up the nave. Cloth-of-gold shimmered on ivory and crimson wool in the gleaming, icy darkness. Jewels and link mail alternately twinkled and extinguished as the procession moved. Supplicating breath chanted heavenwards, sweetened with incense that blocked the more earthly smells of last night's wine and garlic-seasoned salt-fish stew.

Renard uttered the familiar responses through chattering teeth. The candle wobbled in his frozen fingers, the flame fluttering in panic. He managed somehow to steady it. The vast, cold, vaulted glory struck no answering chord from his soul. Bishop Alexander of Lincoln was a man too bogged down by temporal concerns to enthuse a spiritual uplifting in others similarly bogged down, beset by chilblains and varying lacks of piety.

The incense tickled Renard's nose. He stifled a sneeze before it could disturb the chanting or blow out the precarious, coddled flame of his candle. The Mass progressed, and responses learned by rote left his mind free to wander.

The besiegers besieged. Matille, behind her battered but still intact castle walls must be celebrating this mass with a heart as light as thistledown. Her husband, whatever his faults, was a good soldier and strategist when not over-reaching himself with ambition. What might have seemed like over-reaching this time was now shown as an audacious gamble about to pay its reward.

Renard slipped a surreptitious glance at some of his fellow barons. Alan of Richmond caught his look and gave him an uneasy smile and a half-shrug in return. William of Aumale, Earl of York stared stonily at the altar, the candle in his huge fist as steady as a rock. Renard knew without looking further round that Harry was not among the lesser barons thronging the nave. The duty of guarding the fording point had fallen to him, his men and a detail of Richmond's knights.

Renard had tried to speak to Harry before he went down to the river. Still on his pride, temper wearing the residue of drink, Harry had shrugged him gracelessly away, accepting his attempt at conciliation with an inarticulate mutter, his movements jerky as he buckled on his swordbelt. Renard had well recognised that it was not the right moment, but with a battle looming on their threshold, there might never be another one, right or otherwise. In the end, he had embraced Harry and been forcibly rebuffed. No les than he expected, but it had still hurt.

The King's candle sputtered in a draught from an open doorway. Stephen tilted the taper to try to make it burn better, but only succeeded in dripping the glossy, boiling wax onto his hand. Reacting instinctively, he dropped the candle with a choked oath. It hit the flags, spat, flared and died. The King sucked his burned flesh and stared. One of his squires bent to pick up the offending article and rekindle it from his own flame, and discovered that it was impossible. Stephen's candle was jaggedly broken in three places.

Men exchanged looks, the more superstitious among the company already reading evil portents into the incident. Richmond, not one of them, took a pace forward and calmly presented Stephen with his own clean-burning taper, bowed and turned away to take a fresh one from one of Bishop Alexander's chaplains.

Stephen inhaled deeply. The lines between nostril and mouth corner were more deeply engraved than usual, perhaps a trick of the flickering light, but his hands were steady on the fresh taper, even if one of them did display a hot red streak, overlaid by an opalescent film of wax.

No difference could be detected in the Bishop's demeanour, but as his habitual expression was that of a shocked rabbit, that was no reassurance. He continued the mass smoothly enough, however, and lulled, men began to sigh out the nervous breaths they had drawn, and to relax a little.

It was entirely the wrong thing to do. Whether by accident or design, and Renard very much suspected the latter, one of the silver-gilt chains suspending the pyx above the altar gave way, and the whole thing came crashing down. Sacramental wine splattered into the King's face and stained the Bishop's ornate vestments. A gilt candlestick fell over and fire suddenly

231

licked along the embroidered edge of the altar cloth.

Renard doused his own candle and ran to beat out the flames before they could take proper hold. Already he could hear the rumours winging forth from the cathedral – of how the pit of hell had opened up immediately beneath the King's feet as he celebrated the Mass.

The stink of singed linen overrode that of incense. The pyx was badly dented and the wafers it contained were strewn everywhere like giant flakes of snow. Had the light within the cathedral been less gloomy, Stephen's pallor would have been obvious. As it was, apart from the rapid rise and fall of his chest he displayed few outward signs of being perturbed, but then he could not afford to, and besides, his courage was famous. Even his enemies admitted so much.

Renard righted the candlestick and stepped back from the altar. Bishop Alexander was fussing over the pyx like a parent over a badly injured child. There was no doubting his intent to make the King pay full reparations.

Alan of Richmond looked sideways at Renard. 'At least we're in a cathedral,' he murmured from beneath the cover of his full, russet moustache 'It's as good a place as any to pray for our lives.'

'Or to claim sanctuary?' Renard said.

The assault by the rebels on the guarded ford was swift, brutal, and entirely effective. The men attacking were either adventurers and routiers out to line their own pockets, or the bitter dispossessed who had nothing to lose and everything to gain.

Harry had been spared the watery death of the common soldiers because someone had decided that his clothes were rich enough to make him a reasonable gamble for good ransom money and because the leaders of the rebel forces wanted information. Consequently he was knocked senseless, disarmed and sent backwards through the lines.

If Harry's skull had been splitting with a drink megrim before, when he opened his eyes now, he felt as though his brains had burst through the top of his head. He felt so sick that he dared not move. To move was to retch. To retch was to increase the agony to unbearable proportions.

'Christ's arse, when's he going to wake up?' snarled a dangerous voice that he thought he recognised and hoped against hope that he did not.

'Your knight should not have hit him so hard.' This was a woman's voice, throaty, rich and bored.

'When I want your opinion, I'll ask for it!'

Skirts swished petulantly and a strong, spicy scent wafted and caught in Harry's throat. He struggled valiantly not to be sick and through narrowed lids caught a swirl of blue embroidered fabric and a woman's hand clutching it free of a stamped mud floor. Her fingers were long and graceful with manicured sharp nails. The Empress Mathilda he thought hazily, and, despite himself, widened his gaze to see if he was correct. As usual, as in all things, he wasn't. The woman was tall and slim like the Empress, but her curves were more pronounced and her hair was not brown, but the colour of sun-bleached corn, and flowed abundantly to her hips. Their eyes met and he had the briefest instant to see what an incredibly lush blue they were before she tossed her head and turned away. She said nothing about his conscious state to Earl Ranulf, but then she did not have to. The movement of his eyes to meet hers had been too much for Harry's stomach. He raised himself up and vomited.

'Welcome to my hospitality.' Ranulf's sarcastic growl was that of a wolf personified. 'Perhaps when you have finished the preliminaries you might like to tell me a few things. Drink?' He raised a pitcher.

Harry wiped his mouth and gingerly sat up. Then he put his face in his hands, welcoming the darkness. 'No,' he said indistinctly through his fingers.

Ranulf studied him, aware that he knew him from somewhere, but for the moment unable to put place and name together. 'Suit yourself.' He shrugged his powerful shoulders. 'We have taken the ford, you know. No casualties on our side, but all of your lot swept away like twigs on flood water. We're going to take the castle just as easily.' He spiralled a moustache strand around his forefinger. 'Do you know who I am?'

233

'The devil,' Harry croaked without taking his hands from his face.

That amused Ranulf into a brief chuckle. 'I suppose I am to those who get on the wrong side of me. You'll do well to co-operate if you want to be ransomed whole to your kin and not sold back by the portion.'

'I would rather die than be ransomed.' Harry's voice was dull.

'That too can be arranged. Whether there is an unpleasant interlude along the way is for you to decide. I need to know some things ... numbers, morale, intentions.'

Harry raised his head. 'I do not know, and that is the truth. Most of the time I have been too drunk to know my own name.' He glanced across the tent to the woman. She had picked up a small baby from the pallet in the corner and put it against her shoulder. It stared at him with dark blue eyes and sucked loudly on its fist.

'Which is?' Ranulf studied him like a hawk.

Harry's wits might have been displaced by the rattling they had taken, but he was still aware enough of the danger should Chester recognise him as a member of the house of Ravenstow. 'Henry de Rouen,' he said, using the name of the town in Normandy from which his family had originated.

It meant nothing to Ranulf. He jerked on his moustache and wondered if this was going to be a waste of his time. Some minor cog that helped to turn the main grindstone but never actually saw it in operation. 'Drunk most of the time is not all of the time. Tell me what you know!'

Harry swallowed. His mind darted and found nothing but blankness. No knowledge and no lies to replace knowledge. He wished he had listened to Renard instead of stoppering his ears with pent-up bitterness. The baby paused sucking its fist to wail and bump against the curve of the woman's cheek. He saw that its hair was an unusual shade of red, dark as beech leaves. 'Nothing,' he said, closing his eyes. 'I cannot think.'

With an impatient oath, Chester kicked him to the floor, then kicked him again, solidly in the ribs. 'Perhaps this might help you!'

Harry curled up. The pain came, but he had suffered pain before and had learned to endure it. 'I don't know!' he reiterated. He heard the woman sigh heavily. Chester strode to the tent flap and shouted. Two guards came at his summons and Harry felt himself grabbed and thrust roughly back against the Earl's pallet.

'Strip him,' commanded Ranulf.

Harry briefly struggled but his bones were made of lead, his muscles of wool, and all without co-ordination from his concussed mind. He flopped almost lifelessly against the rough handling of the guards. The Earl fetched the pitcher of water used for sluicing hands and face and threw it over Harry's naked form. 'Remember anything now?' he demanded, kicking him again.

Olwen had seen enough. She went to the tent entrance.

Ranulf daggered her a look. 'Where do you think you're going?'

She raised an indifferent shoulder. 'I am taking Jordan to his nurse; he's hungry.' And then favouring Harry with the kind of look a sympathetic stranger might give a dying animal, 'It is obvious that he knows nothing. Either put him out of his misery now with a blade, or return him to the other prisoners so that he can be ransomed.'

'You're paid to lie on your back with your legs open and your mouth closed!' he snarled. 'I could throw you out just like that!' He snapped his fingers.

Olwen gave him a scornful look, not in the least intimidated, and went outside. It was still snowing, but the flakes were huge and wet and punctuated by flashing silver drops of rain. She heard the dull sound of blows from within the tent and Ranulf's voice rising from anger to rage. She understood that kind of impotence because she had experienced it herself, only hers had never been so acute as to lead her to commit murder.

Jordan mewed on her shoulder as she stalked around the camp fire and the Earl's guards towards her own smaller tent. Their eyes hungered over her body, but she ignored them. They were no more to her than the irritation of a swarm of summer midges.

Two mounted soldiers squelched past her, clearing the way for the richly dressed man riding behind. Olwen recognised Robert of Gloucester. His eyes, an indeterminate greyish-blue, hesitated on Olwen and the baby, then slid away to his mount's forelock as though the twist of coarse black hair was of enormous fascination. He flicked at it unnecessarily, taking refuge in pretended preoccupation. The other night he had watched her dance and she had seen the lust glitter in his eyes, followed by the denial. Apparently his marriage, although political, was also happy, and he had no intention of jeopardising it.

Olwen's next move stemmed from irritation at being ignored as if she was something doubtful that had just crawled out from under a stone, and from anger at Ranulf for the way he had spoken to her. Turning round, her cloak sweeping the mud, she came across the bows of Gloucester's horse, and with her free hand grasped the bridle.

'A word, Lord Robert,' she said in her spicily accented French.

'Let go,' he said, wrenching at the reins. His courser backed and jibbed.

'I thought you might want to know that my Lord of Chester is torturing one of the men taken prisoner at the ford. The man has no information. He is a knight and should be put up for ransom with the others.'

Gloucester scowled. The correct and haughty response to the presumptuous slut was that Ranulf's actions were his own affair, and that he had no interest whatsoever in her tale-carrying. The problem was that he did have an interest, since he wanted to question the man himself, and preferably in a reasonable state of mind and body. 'Let go,' he said again.

Olwen did so, and half-smiled as he turned the horse aside towards Ranulf's tent.

In her own tent, she handed Jordan to his wet nurse and watched him hungrily begin to feed. He was a good-natured baby, swift to smile, slow to fret, robust and mostly uncomplaining, although when he did lose his temper, the resulting screams were spectacular.

Olwen had never really come to terms with the fact that he was hers. Pregnancy was a hazard of her profession. She had tried to protect herself against it, a child being no part of her design, but it had happened and now she had Jordan as well as herself to think about. He bore no marked resemblance to his father except for his hair, and no one would notice that similarity unless Renard grew a permanent beard – and perhaps his build also was going to be his father's. Whereas Ranulf was compact and powerful, his neck disappearing into his shoulders which in turn disappeared into his body, Jordan was long-boned, the kind of child who would be all gangling legs and elbows, that would develop into a fluid, cat-like elegance as his body came to manhood.

Sometimes, looking at him, she felt so resentful that it frightened her, and sometimes the pangs twisting her heart were of love, so deep and hard that they were the most frightening of all. Occasionally she thought of leaving him with the women and running away, but there was nowhere to run except back over the same ground, and besides, Ranulf could not be trusted with the child. He still questioned Jordan's paternity and his feelings towards him were ambivalent. Indeed, the other day he had deliberately dropped him. The baby had not been hurt beyond bruises and Ranulf had been guiltily contrite, but Olwen had seen the warning signals. It was not going to get any better. As the boy grew, so too would the doubts and the violence.

Outside she heard shouting. Ranulf, in his usual inimical style was trying to out-bellow Earl Robert and failing. Earl Robert was insisting on his right as commander-in-chief of his sister's army to take the prisoner into his own custody before he died of a surfeit of Ranulf's hospitality. There was disgust amidst his rage, and a ragged edge of pity.

Olwen heard the snarl in Ranulf's response and knew that tonight there would be no pleasing him. Bruises, blue and yellow mottled her upper arms which were still sore to the touch where he had held her down two nights ago. With Renard it had been a game – if he left bruises it was by her consent and the result of heedless, molten passion. Ranulf hurt her deliberately for his own gratification. His political power was swiftly losing the aphrodisiac qualities that had made him seem so attractive. She was beginning to loathe him.

Rising, she went to the tent entrance and looked out. Ranulf, hands on hips, face puckered with temper, was glaring at the unconscious, cloak-bundled man and the two guards who were hauling him across the saddle of a handsome bay stallion. 'The horse is mine,' Ranulf growled, 'and the ransom. Your nephew or not, I'll have you acknowledge that before you take him anywhere!'

Olwen saw Gloucester's lips thin and tighten, islanded from his face by a rim of checked white rage. 'I should never have let you talk me into giving you Matille to wife,' he gritted out. 'Sometimes I think you're capable of anything.' He jerked on the reins and clapped his heels vigorously into his stallion's sides. Olwen watched him leave, then fastened her gaze on the inert young man draped over the bay. Blood was clotted in his sandy hair and streaked like red rain over his lax features. His nephew, Gloucester had said. Renard too was Gloucester's nephew which meant that he and the prisoner must either be cousins . . . or brothers. She thought about asking Ranulf, saw the look on his face, and decided that later would do.

Across the river, the cathedral bells started to toll.

CHAPTER 22

THE BATTLEFIELD ON THE PLAIN was to the west of the city, two armies faced each other. The King, against the advice of many of his barons, had descended the hill to meet the rebels head on instead of allowing them to besiege him. His temper was up, his fighting blood hot, and he intended coming to grips with Robert of Gloucester and the treacherous Earl of Chester.

Rhetoric was spouted from both sides. Robert of Gloucester made a grand speech for the opposition in which he maligned every one of Stephen's senior barons. He was gentler with Renard's reputation than the others, merely decrying him as a short-sighted, misguided fool and thanking God that his father was in his grave and unable to see him now.

Renard listened expressionlessly and stared across the coarse winter meadow, bleak green against scudding brain-grey clouds, at the host armed against them. He was in the centre section guarding the King, along with Baldwin FitzGilbert, Ingelram of Say, Richard FitzUrse and Ilbert de Lacey who was a far distant relative of Adam's. Adam himself, although forced to Lincoln itself by feudal duty, had no intention of fighting against the rebels with whom his sympathies lay. He had developed a 'fever' and cried off the battle, remaining within the city itself to prepare the remains of the royal camp for rapid retreat if need be. Stephen had been annoyed, but had seen the sense in Adam's offer of organisation, and realising perfectly well the underlying cause of the 'fever', had not pushed him too far. Better to have half a man than no man at all.

Beside Renard, Ancelin wiped his moustache nervously on the back of his hand and stared at the mass of Welsh levies howling on the enemy flanks and almost drowning out what Gloucester was saying about the King. 'Do you think Lord William's among that lot?' he asked.

'It seems likely.'

Ancelin sucked his teeth and glanced at Renard. Behind the implacable mask there was anguish. Brother facing brother across the battlefield, and another already lost. The bodies of the slaughtered from the skirmish at the ford had been returned under a banner of truce. Harry's had not been among them, but more than half the men had drowned in the river itself, dragged under by the weight of their mail. Others had been mutilated beyond recognition, and there had been no word from the enemy camp as to whether any prisoners had been taken for ransom. Probably Harry was dead, but without certainty the spark of hope was like a honed prick spur digging into an open wound. They needed to grieve and yet they could not.

Ancelin hefted the long-handled broad axe that had been passed down in his family, father to son, since before the Battle of Senlac when his great-grandfather had been a thegn of some importance. After the great battle the remnants of his line had taken service under Renard's grand-sire, Miles le Gallois, then under Earl Guyon, and now under Renard, the loyalty bred in the bone. Le Gallois's wife had been Saxon, and her blood, although diluted by strains of Welsh and Norman still ran in Renard's veins. And in William's and Harry's too, waiting to be spilled. He caressed the smooth, ashwood haft with loving, troubled fingers and wished that he too had a fever.

Renard, checking the position of his men, could see Stephen a little beyond them. The King's gilded helmet, clipped blond beard, and the fluttering red and gold of his standard marked him out as he listened to Robert of Gloucester's speech and now and then dipped his head to murmur to Ingelram of Say. It was not just the wind that was whipping slashes of colour across his broad cheekbones. From the set of the royal face, Renard could see that Stephen was close to one of his famous but infrequent rages. Perhaps some of it was due to the knowledge that among the rebels stood his brother, Henry of Winchester, who he had loved and trusted above all other men.

Even as he smiled and reassured his own soldiers, Renard felt his gut queasily tightening. His own experience of war was mostly of light skirmish and brawl rather than the full weight of a pitched battle, and he was accustomed to fighting on horseback, not on foot as Stephen had chosen to do for his centre.

A shout went up from the flank commanded by Alain of Brittany as several of his knights broke formation to challenge some of the rebel knights to joust. Renard, his hand on the shoulder of a young Ledworth footsoldier, felt a tremor writhe through the quilted leather he was clutching.

'I'm going to be sick,' the youth whispered, face grey.

Renard looked at him, knowing that each man in his mind's eye was seeing the moment of his own death, and knowing that he was trapped, the wheel set in motion. 'Best do it now lad,' he said, tightening his fingers. 'You won't have time later.'

The shouts of challenge that had floated on the wind changed suddenly to howls of outrage and one scream of agony. Raggedly, like the edge of a rainstorm, Gloucester's troops clashed with the Breton and Flemish flank. All thoughts of chivalry dissipated faster than the scent of expensive perfume into a gale as the rebels displayed their preference to fight in deadly earnest.

The youth vomited. Stephen bellowed something that was lost in the roar and clash of first battle. Renard hastened to Ancelin, unsheathed his sword, and brought his shield down onto his left arm, preparing for the assault of Earl Ranulf's vassals and levies.

Later, he was to recall very little of the ensuing battle, only that men who should have known and reacted better fled the field in the face of an opposition whose bark was twice as ferocious as its actual bite. They fled because they were afraid to lose the battle, because after yesterday's ill omens in the cathedral they expected to lose, and in fleeing they sealed the prophecy.

Earl Ranulf's contingent went for the throat, attacking the footsoldiers holding Stephen's centre. With no protection from the cavalry on the flanks, it was inevitable that they should be torn to pieces. Stephen fought like a man possessed. In a sense he was – possessed by the rage of despair and given the strength of three men by its violence. None could touch him. Renard, guarding him, was merely despairing. Being young, agile and the owner of a mail coat of superb quality, he had managed thus far to avoid any serious wounds, although he had taken his share of nicks and bruises. The pain from his overworked right shoulder kept shooting all the way down to his hand, cramping his grip on the hilt of his bloody sword.

Lungs burning, he leaped over a back-handed slash aimed at his knee and retorted rapidly inside his opponent's guard, cutting him down. Beside him he heard Ancelin grunt with effort as his axe swung and carved. Both men drew back and panting stood shoulder to shoulder. There was time for the briefest exchange of glances, a rueful acknowledgement that this was the tightest corner they had ever been in, and probably their last, before another wave rolled over them, aiming for the King, and spearheaded by the Earl of Chester himself.

Ancelin killed three men in rapid succession and went down beneath a fourth before he could recover to swing his axe again. Renard made the mistake of bellowing his name and trying to go to his aid. He was struck a bone-shattering blow with a mace that was only half-absorbed by his helmet. His knees gave way. He was struck again, and the sky turned black.

The blackness was still with him when he returned to his senses, but it was not this time of the open sky but of enclosing bare stone darkness somewhere in the undercrofted bowels of Lincoln castle. Blackness and the pulsating throb of pain that jolted through his skull with every stroke of his heart.

His cheek on dusty straw, he became aware of small noises; rustlings and movements not his own, groans, voices in low conversation, someone retching up blood. He realised that the darkness was not as complete as he had first thought. A sliver of night-blue from a narrow grilled window punctuated its finality. Hardly a ray of hope, but distantly comforting never-theless.

Beside him someone was shivering and moaning feverishly.

He raised his head, but slumped it immediately back down with an oath, the pain crashing unbearably around and through his mind, robbing him of the ability to think. He lay still until the worst of it subsided. His hauberk was gone, and his gambeson, leaving him only shirt, braies and chausses. Thirst encroached upon his other discomforts as awareness returned. He knew that he was locked up, probably within the castle itself, but at whose auspices he baulked to think.

He discovered that the desire for a drink was of the moment less overwhelming than his dread of sitting up, and closed his eyes again.

The next time he opened them, the slit of light above his head had paled to a dull, rain grey. His skull was still throbbing fit to burst and his thirst was now too severe to be ignored. Gingerly he looked to one side. The man who had threshed and cried out beside him before stared back with filmed eyes, dried blood staining his mouth corners. Renard recognised him as one of Stephen's squires. He was dead.

Slowly, very slowly, Renard raised his head and pushed himself to a sitting position. The cell wavered and wallowed before his eyes, giving him the impression that he was sitting under water. Bright flashes of colour like strange fish swam at the corners of his vision and threatened to encroach. 'Jesu!' he gasped, and put his hand up to cover his eyes, encountering as he did so a swollen, tender line of clotted blood. Above it, his flesh was as puffy as risen bread dough, contracting his vision to a tight slit.

'Welcome to hell,' croaked Ingelram of Say, dragging himself across the rushes to Renard's side. Then he recoiled and stared. 'God's blood, I don't know which looks worse, my leg or your face!'

Renard glanced at the blood-soaked bandage wadded around Ingelram's right leg.

'Shattered knee cap. I'll never fight on foot again, thank Christ or the devil!' He tried to laugh, but the sound fell far short of humour. 'What happened to you?'

'I don't know. I saw Ancelin fall and tried to cover him. I think I was struck from the side.'

'Regular mess it made of you too. You'll not be charming women with that face for a while.' He looked dismally round the cell then at the dead young man beside them. 'If ever again.'

'Is there any water?'

'No, but there's ale. Richard, pass us the jug.' He shrug-smiled at Renard. 'There's some dried bread too, but by the looks of you, you'd kill yourself if you tried to chew on it.'

'I'm not hungry anyway.' Renard watched another knight who was pouring liquid from a glazed stone pitcher into one of the ubiquitous black leather soldiers' mugs. The sound it made was musical torture, but when it was handed to him, he took the mug with careful effort, forcing his limbs to function, and, equally as carefully, drank.

'Earl Ranulf said to make us go without, but Gloucester overruled him.'

Renard let the cold, slightly bitter liquid trickle down his parched throat. 'Earl Ranulf would,' he muttered. 'What of the King? Is he dead or taken prisoner?' He did not mention escape, for in the given situation of the battlefield, it would have been impossible.

'Knocked senseless like yourself in the midst of hand to hand combat with Earl Ranulf. One of the Earl's men with an eye to the main chance threw a stone at the King and got him straight between the eyes. A pity his aim was so good. Stephen had Earl Ranulf down on the ground about to spit him like a coney on a skewer when he was hit. I saw it all, helpless to do anything.' Ingelram touched his knee again and winced.

Renard stared around the cell. His companions were mostly knights and minor barons, the nucleus of Stephen's bodyguard. Being himself an earl and the Empress's nephew, he was the highest ranked among them, and also the one who would fetch the most ransom money.

'As soon as they've finished making it all secure here, we're all to be brought to Gloucester to await Madam Empress's pleasure.'

'Gloucester?'

'Afraid so. Best prepare yourself to grovel. At least with this leg I've the advantage over everyone else. Ever tried pissing when you can only stand on one leg? Incidentally, the bucket's in that corner over there.'

Renard glanced and caught his breath at the renewed jolt of pain. His helmet had saved him from certain death, absorbing most of that first blow, but the edge of the mace had caught and cracked his cheekbone. He tried not to imagine the kind of reception that awaited him at his aunt's hands. In a space of silence he thought about Adam and hoped that he had been able to evacuate the camp in time and get the boys clear. Then he thought of Eleanor and his infant son, and bowed his head.

Ingelram noticed how violently he was shivering. 'Aye, 'tis cold,' he said. 'I asked them for blankets when they brought us the bread and ale, but all they did was curse at me ... whoresons.'

'Blankets won't warm my kind of cold,' Renard murmured bleakly. 'When I think ...' He stopped speaking and looked at the door as the heavy draw bar was pulled back.

'Perhaps I was wrong,' said Ingelram. 'Perhaps these are the blankets now.'

Torchlight flared on high, revealing half a dozen men-at-arms, two with swords drawn and wearing full hauberks, the others in the regular footsoldier's armour of couir bouille. Supported between them, as floppy as a necked chicken, was another prisoner. Ingelram's optimistic remark about the blankets was proven premature. A question asked received a growled insult and a twitch of the foremost man's sword arm. His weapon was obviously not his own, but plundered from a richer man on the battlefield, for the hilt was set with gems and the grip was of plaited silver wire. Somewhere Renard knew that his own weapons and hauberk would be similarly adorning one of the victors.

The new prisoner was thrown down in the straw among them and lay unmoving. The door closed and the torchlight receded, leaving them once more in their grey, cold purgatory. Renard stared at the inert form on the straw and his chilled blood froze solid, immobilising him. The empty cup slipped from his fingers. 'Christ!' he said softly, voice cracking through the layer of ice that held him prisoner.

Richard FitzUrse stooped beside the newcomer and felt for the pulse at his throat. 'Alive,' he announced. 'Just. And he's as hot as the pit of hell. Wound fever. Look, he's been whipped.'

'My brother,' Renard swallowed. 'He's my brother. I thought he had drowned.' And went to where Harry lay.

'Harry?' Renard stared at the rents in his shirt and the crusted, suppurating weals they exposed. Harry's hair was matted with blood, his breathing harsh and his pulse thundering. He was not, however, unconscious beyond recall, for at the sound of his name and the familiar voice his eyelids fluttered.

'Harry, for God's love, can you hear me?'

Another groan and flicker. Harry's fingers tightened upon the straw beneath them. 'Renard?' he mumbled thickly. 'Why is it so dark? Are we at Ravenstow?'

'We're prisoners in Lincoln. Stephen lost the battle.'

'Lincoln? Oh yes, I remember. Is it still snowing?' Harry finally managed to lift his lids. His eyes vacantly wandered the cell's dank darkness before alighting on Renard.

'I do not know. Who did this to you?'

Harry's mouth cracked in the sour approximation of a smile at the sight of Renard's anger. They might have nothing in common apart from their blood, but in a crisis, blood was always thicker than water. 'Earl Ranulf lost his patience and his temper when I could not answer his questions. Your whore it was who saved me from being beaten to death.'

'Olwen!'

'I never knew her name, only that she deserted you for him. She has a son now. Red hair . . .' Harry's voice trailed off. He closed his eyes again, his face pale and sweat-beaded.

FitzUrse retrieved the cup that Renard had dropped and splashed it a third full of ale. Then he knelt at Harry's other side. Between them, he and Renard managed to raise Harry's head and tip some of the liquid down his throat. It was difficult because he was lying on his stomach and they dared not turn him over because of the wounds from the lash. Harry gulped convulsively, choking and spluttering, but at least some of it

246

went down. He re-opened his eyes. 'Uncle Robert was passing,' he said huskily to Renard. 'The woman hailed him – not for my sake, I was of no more significance to her than an ill-treated dog, but she was riled at Earl Ranulf for threatening her.'

That rang true of Olwen. Many times over the last year Renard's thoughts had returned to her like the tongue to an abscessed tooth. This time the pain was diminished, replaced by a certain wry admiration. 'But if Robert of Gloucester rescued you from de Gernons' clutches, why have you been thrown in here?'

'Uncle Robert's got too much on his trencher just now to remember me unless pushed directly under his nose.' Harry's voice was weak and fumbling as the fever sapped his strength, replacing it with poison. 'When they moved his things from tent to castle, his chaplain "tidied" me away in the hopes I'd be forgotten ... die somewhere else than at his lordship's feet.'

'Save your strength Harry, don't talk.' Renard laid a calming hand on his brother's racing pulse.

'What for, so that I can be taken out and whipped again? What will happen to us all if we live beyond the moment?'

'We're to be taken to Gloucester,' said FitzUrse. 'To await the Empress's pleasure.'

'Which means we'll be killed, disinherited or banished and our families and lands sold to the highest bidder. I'd rather die now.'

'Stop talking about dying!' Renard snapped. 'You're wounded, that's all, and not even as badly as last time!'

Harry grimaced cadaverously. 'Thought I was the one full of delusions,' he muttered. His lids dropped and he turned his head away.

Renard stared at the matted sandy hair in frustration, knowing that he could not reach him, that there was nothing he could do for him except perhaps speed him on his way, and, because it would have been all too easy, he shied from it with revulsion.

A sense of dreadful inevitability began to worm itself into his mind. Until recently, Renard had never had occasion to feel helpless or inadequate, and for him it was the most difficult tempering of all, the point at which the blade was either broken or perfected. Kneeling in the straw of Lincoln's castle dungeon with his brother, Renard felt the molten hammer beat of a three-fold pain – body, mind and soul.

CHAPTER 23

Stuffing himself back into his braies and straightening his tunic, Ranulf looked with malicious satisfaction at the woman on his bed. Her pale hair was tangled over her breasts and shoulders. Upon the smooth, honey skin, new bruises bloomed like dark flowers. Hatred and defiance glowed in her eyes. Even now she would not acknowledge him her master. In a way it quite amused him, as when one of the hound pups bared its milk teeth at him.

'Get out.' His manner was brusquely indifferent now that his lust was spent. 'I'm expecting company.'

Olwen rolled onto her stomach, turning her face from his while she controlled the expression it wore. What she most wanted to do was take her knife and cut off not only his long, braided moustaches, but that other thing dangling between his legs. In keeping with the rest of his character it was all vulgar show and no finesse.

She pulled on her shift. The linen dragged over her bruises and a row of blood-filled tooth marks on the upper swell of her breast. She might be the mistress of the most powerful man in England, but just now she felt like a used trencher after a meal. For an instant the resentment rose in her so strongly that she almost whirled on his complacency in a fury of teeth and nails. The knowledge that he was as strong as a bull and would relish the opportunity to bruise her more held her back.

'Am I not to be paid?' she asked instead, in a low, honeyed voice. 'I need linen to replace the shift you tore in your haste.'

'You presume.' There was a cold gleam in his eyes, but he slipped a silver bracelet from his arm and tossed it on the bed. It was the same bracelet that had lain across her windpipe, cutting off her breath as he took his pleasure in rape. 'Here, buy yourself a dozen shifts,' he said contemptuously.

Olwen picked up the incised silver band and quickly put it on before she gave in to the temptation to throw it back in his face. Full lips pursed, she tugged on her overgown. Outside the room she heard the sound of laughter and bright Welsh voices.

'Hurry up!' Ranulf snapped. 'I've some more Welsh whores to pay for their favours yet.'

By which he was referring to his own Welsh levies she knew. She had seen their leader once from a distance. Cadwaladr ap Gruffydd, younger brother of Prince Owain Fawr of North Wales. 'I doubt that anyone ever performs you a service for free,' she retorted snidely. He lunged at her, but she was prepared, and in one smooth dancer's motion rolled off the bed, leaving him clawing at thin air. Not waiting to see him recover, she shot through the curtain onto the stairway and collided with Cadwaladr ap Gruffydd.

He caught her arm as she slipped. She cried out in pain as his fingers gripped on one of the bruises Ranulf had inflicted. She felt the wiry strength of him and saw the admiration flicker in his eyes, followed by the scorn.

'Fleeing the devil?' he asked in heavily accented French.

She tossed her head and looked him in the eyes, a feat not difficult because she was tall for a woman and he a little less than average for a man.

'The devil's attention would be more welcome!' she spat with a look over her shoulder, then let herself yield a little in his grip. Her lids came down. Her silky lashes lay like fans on her cheeks. She made her expression a demure contrast to the state of her garments and the manner of her exit. Virgin and whore embodied in one woman. The paradox never failed to excite. She heard him swallow, could feel the heat of his gaze, and judging the moment precisely, broke from him.

'Lord Ranulf is waiting for you,' she panted. 'At least I presume it is you. He said that I was not the only Welsh whore he had to pay tonight for services rendered. *Nos da fy arglwydd.*' And left him staring after her, not knowing whether to believe her or ignore.

Outside as she emerged into the bailey and blinked into the sleety wind, a young man wearing the inconspicuous garb of a Welsh scout rose from his crouch beside a semi-sheltered fire and advanced on her with sauntering, but definite purpose. It was only after he had circled behind her and to one side like a dog herding a sheep, and taken hold of her arm, that she recognised Renard's youngest brother from the time she had seen him at Hawkfield. She had thought him handsome even then, much more so than Renard. Another year of maturity had only carved more character into the beautiful proportions of his bones. His eyes were the blue-green of a summer dusk with gold striations raying from the pupils. Just now, however, there was naught of summer in their depths, only cold, hard, determination.

'I need to talk to you,' he said abruptly and drew her away into a store shed that was being used as extra stabling for the overflow of the army's horses, his own spotted stallion among them.

'Why?' she mocked. 'Are you lonely?'

William's outdoor brown skin took on a ruddy hue. 'Not that lonely!' he scathingly declared.

'Then what do you want?' Arching her brow, she regarded him with a half-smile on her lips and arms set akimbo.

'I want you to help Renard before it is too late — before we begin moving out for Gloucester.'

Olwen stared at him. 'And how pray should I do that?' she demanded incredulously. 'Beg Earl Ranulf on my knees so that my tears melt his iron heart with pity? Bed the guards into exhaustion and steal the prison keys? I fear you have been listening to a surfeit of minstrels' tales! No, let go of me or I'll scream Ranulf's guards down on us!' She prepared to kick him.

William sucked a breath through his teeth and released her, although he still blocked her way. 'You have access to his bedchamber,' he said.

'Oh, I see. I murder him in his sleep and Renard disappears in the confusion?' she cooed.

He chose to ignore her sarcasm, his cause too urgent for a

bout of repartee. 'You take his seal, the one which gives authority to his documents, and you bring it to me. I will have ready a parchment authorising Renard's release. The seal will give it credence and I'll have him out of that hell-hole and on the Fosse Road faster than Earl Ranulf can braid his moustaches!'

Olwen's gaze remained hostile. 'Why should I?' she asked coldly. 'What gain is there to me in such risk?'

William ran his hand lightly down her arm. She winced and stiffened. 'More gain than remaining as his mistress.' He touched the broad, silver bracelet. 'How many bruises did you trade for this?'

Olwen snatched her hand away, but withdrew no further. Full underlip caught in her teeth, she thought about making Ranulf look an utter fool and doing him out of the joy of having Renard an impotent prisoner. Not only that, but she would be putting Renard forever in her debt. The idea made her feel both malicious and gleeful at one and the same time. Like a cat that has just groomed its ruffled fur into sleek order, Olwen recovered her aplomb. 'So,' she murmured, gently patting William between her paws, 'I do it for a passion gone cold and to avenge my bruises on Earl Ranulf?'

'I don't give a damn why you do it,' William said, his lips so stiff that he was barely articulate. Behind him, Smotyn pawed the straw and nickered to him, demanding a tit-bit. Rummaging in the pocket of his sheepskin jerkin, he brought out a heel of bread saved from the breaking of fast and offered it to the horse on the palm of his hand. It gave him a focus other than the woman, and at least Smotyn was predictable. 'I don't give a damn why you do it,' he repeated less tensely. 'Only that you do.'

'You could be an earl in Renard's place,' she answered in a provocative, smoky voice that her former lover would have recognised all too well. 'It is yours for the taking.'

William's forced control broke from him in an explosive oath. 'Christ forbid!' he cried. 'I would rather be a landless beggar than yoke myself to that particular plough! Renard's welcome to it!'

Olwen arched her brow at his horror. A man who spoke of

power with contempt. A chill scuttled down her spine. She wondered briefly how it would be to lie with him and quickly dropped the thought as if it were a scalding ingot. Far too seductive and dangerous. Cadwaladr ap Gruffydd was a much safer prospect and liable to lead her to an introduction to his kinsman, Owain Gwynedd, Prince of North Wales.

'Supposing I take this tale to Earl Ranulf?' she purred. 'What might it be worth to him? I know that his hatred is not just centred on Renard. He would hang you from the nearest tree if he found out.'

William shrugged. 'I'm a scout and tracker. I could go to ground faster than a deer in the morning and not be seen again this side of the Welsh border. How else would I get Renard beyond the hue and cry?' Returning her look with one of his own, he slapped Smotyn's neck, fuzzy in its winter coat. 'And you would never feel safe in the dark of night again.' He rested his other hand lightly on his dagger hilt for emphasis.

Warned, but uncowed, Olwen considered him steadily before breaking her gaze to stroke the horse. A spark kindled within her and radiated ripples of warmth through her veins. It was a feeling akin to that which she felt when dancing for men, the awareness of the power she had over them, as she had the power now.

Her eyes came back to William, darkly luminous as a hunting cat's. 'You do not need to threaten me,' she said softly, and suddenly her smile was filled with self-mockery. 'For a passion not as dead as I would wish it to be, and to avenge my hurts on Lord Ranulf, I will do as you ask.'

Renard measured the span of time by the changing colour of the spear of sky trapped in the narrow window high above his head. Some of that span he fitfully slept, but most of it was spent in a relentless awareness of cold, pain and impotence, the latter the most intense of the three. Watching a man die was never pleasant. Watching your own brother when there were added currents of guilt, pity and a sense of having failed, was sheer hell.

The dull grey of morning had dimmed beyond an early dusk

into the pitch darkness of night. The wind whined eerily through the unshuttered slit of light, bringing with it the tantalising discomfort of the smell of rain and raw cold without. The guards had come to empty the bucket and bring the by now familiar bread and ale. This time too, as a grudging afterthought, some dirty horse blankets had been tossed in upon them.

Harry alternately burned and shivered beneath Renard's blanket and his own. The lash stripes smothering his back had been bathed in ale for want of anything better, but it had been of no use. His wounds had suppurated beyond all healing and the fever had continued to mount relentlessly. Another knight had already died of the wound fever. His body, along with that of the dead squire had been dragged out that evening.

'Gloucester tomorrow,' said Ingelram, whose knee, despite all the odds, was not festering. A crippled leg he would carry to his grave, but precluding execution, he was not yet worm fodder. 'He won't survive the journey, Renard. Looking at him, I doubt he'll last the night.'

Renard swallowed. 'He's had the wound fever severely in the past and survived,' he objected.

'With this kind of nursing?' Ingelram disparaged. 'The signs are on him. He hasn't pissed since well before noon and I can feel the heat of him from here.'

Renard gave him a vicious glare.

'It's the truth,' Ingelram said stubbornly, 'even if you don't want to see it.'

At which juncture Richard FitzUrse, out of pity, pulled his insensitive companion away.

It was still dark, the blackest part of the night immediately before dawn and Harry still clinging by the fingertips to life when the draw bar was shot back and a voice impatient, autocratic and very angry, snapped at the guards.

'Authority?' it demanded incredulously and there came the sound of parchment being struck vigorously with the back of a hand. 'Is this not authority? The Earl of Chester's own seal! Look at it, clod! He wants the most important moved out by dawn, and it will go more than hard with you if I'm not on that road within the half hour!'

There was a pause and then a weak stammer. 'We've had no orders, my lord.'

'What do you think these are – morning rations?' And then with a further virulent spurt of sarcasm, 'or perhaps you would rather interrupt Earl Ranulf's slumbers and ask him yourself?'

'N . . . no, my lord.' The door slowly creaked inwards. The prisoners put up their hands, squinting against the sudden intrusion of torchlight, or else groaned and turned over, huddling away like hedgepigs curling against danger.

A knight attired in a full coat of the best rivet mail, burnished mirror-bright, stepped among them. His head was protected by a helmet hammered from a single piece of iron, the most expensive type to make, and his boots as he trod the soiled straw were gilded up the sides with figures of bowmen and deer, and adorned with silver-gilt prick spurs. He exuded wealth and authority.

'Where is he?' he demanded, gaze roving the cell, one hand resting on his polished sword hilt, the other on his exquisite belt.

The guard nervously indicated Renard. 'They say he fought like a leopard on the battlefield, my lord, but he's too sorely wounded and fretting over t'other one to have given us any trouble.'

Renard turned to face the light and the moment was suddenly fraught with more than just danger as from the boots upwards he traced a path to the knight's face, and recognised William. The Norman war gear sat on his brother most gracefully considering he so seldom donned it. All kinds of thoughts flashed through Renard's mind and were gone without cohesion. 'William?' The utterance was more breath than sound.

'Holy Christ!' William muttered. He had expected to find Renard battered about and bruised – a man seldom came unscathed from the heart of a battle – but he had not been prepared to see his brother still blood-caked and mired, bones gaunt beneath the swollen flesh of injury, and haunted eyes dull with exhaustion. Added to the nausea of excitement, William now felt the nausea of horror too.

The senior guard at his shoulder hovered, looking between the two of them, and William emerged rapidly from his shock to realise that Renard had spoken his name and that if he were not to end up in this cell beside him or kicking on the gallows, he had to carry through a convincing pretence.

'When last we met I warned you what would happen if you stayed with Stephen!' he said harshly for the guard's benefit, spat in the straw to clear the fluid from his mouth, the gesture looking contemptuous, and then nodded brusquely to the two serjeants standing in the doorway. They marched into the cell and hauled Renard to his feet. He staggered and then locked his knees, bracing himself against their rough grip.

'I'll not leave without Harry.' He looked William in the eyes and then deliberately away to the blanketed mound near his feet.

'You have no choice!' growled the senior guard. 'This parchment is for you alone.'

William stared in dawning, appalled comprehension at the sick man in the straw. Crouching, he set one hand on the huddled shoulder and peered round into Harry's face. Not just sick but dying. He had seen the wound fever often enough to realise that Harry was over the edge. 'Mary, mother of God,' he muttered under his breath, and waited until he had control of his expression before he stood up and faced the guards. 'This man needs a priest, not a cell,' he said roughly.

'There is one to attend the prisoners, my lord....' began the senior serjeant, and was laughed down bitterly by Ingelram of Say.

'Oh yes!' he spat. 'One exists no doubt, but if so, he's not seen fit to soil his sandals on our souls for shriving or anything else. Two have died already without comfort of the Church. He's probably abed with his whore and a flagon of Anjou's best!' There was acid sarcasm in his tone as he spoke of Anjou.

A guard moved to club him silent, but William stopped him with a sharp command. 'If this is true, it is damning upon your own soul that you have not vouchsafed a priest for these men.'

'Oh, it's all true,' Renard said hoarsely. His eyes, cold as the dungeon stone, nailed the senior serjeant. 'But then corpses have no need of adornment, do they? Stephen's squire for example. A pity to bury such a fine gilded belt with a corpse. What will you do with my brother's thumb ring? Cut it off him before he's cold? Do I disappoint you because I'm bound out of here?'

'It's a lie!' The serjeant thrust out his jaw, but it was not the torchlight that yellowed his complexion. 'I never took the belt and it ain't my fault if the priest don't come when he's summoned.'

William's mind, momentarily paralysed by the shock of seeing Renard and Harry in such poor case, was beginning to function again with gathering rapidity. He realised that Renard, by accusing the serjeant of stealing from the dead, had thrown him an excellent reason to have Harry out of here too, orders from above or not.

'Time is wasting!' he snapped. 'Time I don't have. Since you cannot vouchsafe a priest for this man, and since he is Robert of Gloucester's own nephew, I'm removing him from your custody. If you have any complaint, you can take it to the Earl of Chester come full light.' And then to the two gawping soldiers, 'See to it.'

'My lord, I'm not sure that . . .' The serjeant started to protest.

'See to it!' William interrupted, blue eyes incandescent.

The serjeant lowered his own gaze to the expanse of belly bulging over his broad belt, fortunately not the one he stood accused of stealing. That was searing a hole in the bottom of his coffer. 'Yes, my lord.'

'And while you're about it, I'll advise you that there's no ransom for crows' meat. This place stinks. Get it cleaned up and see that these men are treated decently. God's teeth, why must it always be me who is sent to deal with the idiots!' He glanced heavenwards, more than half of his expression relief at the serjeant's capitulation.

Renard did not speak as he was led from the cell into the stark air of Lincoln castle's bailey. The wind had changed direction and the moon its phase, bringing with it clearer, much colder weather. Frost crackled around the edges of the bailey puddles and the air was almost painful to breathe and bore upon it the acrid smell of burned dwellings. Like a knife the wind cut through Renard's flimsy garments and probed the wound on his cheekbone. Dangling between the guards, Harry moaned and shuddered as he was drag-carried to the waiting wain and lifted within. Then it was Renard's turn. He was escorted by two of William's soldiers – Ashdyke men whom he well recognised.

William mounted his horse, not Smotyn, for his colouring was too easily remembered, too conspicuous, and he had traded him with one of Cadwaladr's men for a sturdy brown hack. For Renard, he had obtained a Cleveland which awaited the right moment among the remounts.

The whip cracked over the backs of the two horses drawing the wain, and after a brief hesitation, while they took the strain, the iron-shod wheels started to rumble and turn. The torchlight transformed all breath to red vapour and reflected tints of fire upon horseflesh and mail. Dawn barely a glimmer in the eye of night, William led his precious load out of the castle and wound his way down through the devastated town to the ford. The Earl of Chester's seal and the knowledge that the prisoners were due to be moved that day granted him an easy passage, if ripe with more casual curiosity than he would have liked. It was not the deepest of his worries. Turning in the saddle as they passed the churned mud of the recent battleground, he bid one of his men go aside and fetch a priest.

Ranulf of Chester slept late, the result of too much wine and an exhausting night of bedsport. He had intended to pass the night with his wife, but his mistress had had other ideas and they had been so novel and exciting that he had succumbed, and succumbed again, and finally been defeated by the wine and the masculine limitations of his own body.

He awoke to find one of his squires bending anxiously over him, hand cupped around a candle to prevent it either from going out or dripping hot wax all over the disarrayed sheets. Of Olwen there was no sign, only the distinctive smell of her perfume. Ranulf rolled over and groaned into the pillow, his head feeling as though a war horse had kicked him in the temples.

'Piss off,' he muttered through his teeth.

'My lord, Earl Robert has already started moving the prisoners out of the city and wants your opinion on some matters.' The youth did not add any of the pointed remarks made by the Earl of Gloucester concerning the disgusting morals and behaviour of his son-in-law.

Ranulf half-turned to cock a bleary red eye. 'What hour is it?'

'Nigh to prime, my lord.'

'Impossible!' With as much alacrity as his thundering headache permitted, he sat up and stared around the room. The shutters were closed to keep out the weather and it was not possible to judge the time of day by the state of any natural light.

'I am sorry, my lord, but it is. I saved you some bread from the breaking of fast ... and some small beer too if you want it.'

Ranulf compressed his lips at the thought of food. 'Clothes,' he said, and held out his hand.

His squire carefully put the candle down and gathered up from the floor various garments including a woman's red silk hose garter. Ranulf snatched his crumpled shirt from the youth and dragged it on. His head became tangled in the laces and he half-strangled himself before he managed to right matters. 'The prisoners?' he queried. 'Does that include the King?'

'I think Earl Robert was waiting for you, my lord, before he consigned him to the road. Renard FitzGuyon went early, before the dawn as you commanded.' The squire briskly dusted off his master's fur-trimmed tunic as he spoke.

The silence from the bed was palpable.

'My lord?'

'I gave no such command,' Ranulf whispered huskily.

The squire's eyes widened. 'My lord, a young knight brought a parchment to the prison serjeant. It bore your seal and ordered the release of the Earl of Ravenstow into his custody for the journey to Gloucester.'

'What!'

'The serjeant told me himself.' Prudently, the youth stepped away from the bed. Earl Ranulf was apt to be violent when beset by bad tidings, and if the colour of his face was any indication, these were not just bad, but catastrophic. 'Apparently the knight was harsh with him and threatened to report him to you. He was scared witless and wanted to plead his own version of events first, so he attached himself to me like a leech when he saw me crossing the bailey.'

'What was the knight's name?' Ranulf rumbled with all the menace and tension of an imminent volcano.

'I'm not sure, my lord.' The squire screwed up his face. 'The serjeant did tell me ... William le ... yes, William le Malin.'

An obscure nick-name that meant nothing. 'No title or place-name?'

'No, my lord.'

'Bring that serjeant to me immediately, and start a search through the camp for anyone who knows of a knight by the name of William le Malin.'

The squire made his grateful exit and escape, leaving the junior lad and Ranulf's chaplain to bear the brunt of the eruption.

The brunt actually arrived about a candle notch later in the presence of Robert of Gloucester. The cringing senior serjeant in command of the prisoners had been hauled from his post with knocking knees and flung down before his simmering liege lord.

'But it had your seal on it!' he pleaded in a cracked voice, eyes darting anxiously between the tight-lipped Earl of Gloucester and the scarlet-faced near-apopleptic de Gernons. 'And Sir William was richly dressed and spoke with authority. I had no cause to doubt he was genuine!'

'You'll have cause to regret now!' Ranulf growled.

'How did your seal come to be upon that parchment in the first place?' asked Gloucester with a puzzled frown. 'Do you not keep it locked in your strongbox with your immediate silver? Whoever took it must have intimate access to your bedchamber.'

Ranulf's body servants all made heated protests and denials. No one had been in his chamber without their knowing, and they would all swear oaths on the holiest relics to prove their own innocence. Besides, the key to the strongbox was about the Earl's person, and no one could remove it without his being aware.

Gloucester gave his son-in-law a weary look. 'What about the woman?'

Ranulf looked blank. 'What woman?'

'The dancing girl you persist in bedding even under your wife's long-suffering nose. Don't you have brains above your belt, Ranulf?'

'Why in Christ's name should she want my seal?' he scoffed, thinking of the previous night when she had been all over him, full of the demanding submission that he so enjoyed.

'I'll tell you why,' said William de Cahagnes, a hard-bitten baron who had been listening to the conversation with more than a glint of malice at Chester's discomfort, 'because she used to be Ravenstow's mistress. He brought her home with him from Antioch.'

The words fell like red-hot stones into a trough of cold water.

'Whaaat?' roared Ranulf, jerking round as if scalded.

'One of my men served at Ravenstow last year as a mercenary, and he recognised her the moment he saw her in your retinue. Apparently she only dances to her own tune. I think you will find that she is gone, and whatever joy you had of her last night was paid for by your seal.'

Near to choking on his rage, Ranulf was incoherent.

'You had better check your strongbox,' Gloucester suggested wearily. 'If your seal has gone, then God knows what other documents might be forged with its aid.'

Swallowing, Ranulf fumbled in his scrip for the key. 'Fitz-Guyon's whore!' he gagged out, thinking of how much she must have been laughing at him.

A swift investigation confirmed the worst. The seal was

missing from his chest and the guards sent to apprehend Olwen returned empty-handed, their only lead a rumour that she had ridden out before first light with a departing band of North Welsh. She had taken the baby with her. Either his son, or Ravenstow's cuckoo. While this was being reported, another detail came back having failed to find any trace of a knight by the name of William le Malin – William the cunning.

That was when the volcano erupted and men scattered for cover. Flagons, cups, two roast pigeons and an expensive and heavy carved chair were hurled indiscriminately across the room.

Gloucester, while not approving, was accustomed to his son-in-law's excesses of temper, and waiting until Ranulf had run out of immediate objects to throw, said into the panting respite, 'For Christ's sake, Ranulf, and mine, control your tantrum and put it to some use before you do more damage to this keep than Stephen did in six weeks of siege! Send out men after them and a messenger to your lands, telling your constables to beware of anyone bearing parchments with your seal and in the meantime have a new one cast. God's blood, surely I do not need to lecture you like I would one of my squires!'

Ranulf glared at him with eyes that threatened to pop out of his skull. His fists clenched and unclenched spasmodically, but even while the rage ran like molten lava, its core was cooling into a reasoning anger. He managed a curt nod at his father-in-law. 'You do well to recall me to my duty,' he said, and swung to the door.

As he reached it, Gloucester cautioned him. 'Remember that Renard is my nephew, and Mathilda's. Keep that temper of yours in check.'

'I'll bear it in mind.' There was more than a hint of ambiguity in Ranulf's reply.

CHAPTER 24

O N THE ROMAN ROAD TO Newark, one of the wain wheels lurched into a rut for the hundredth time, tossing Renard and William about like podded peas in a housewife's bowl. Harry, strapped to his pallet, made no sound beyond a sawing effort to breathe. Just outside Lincoln, a priest had been found to shrive him and had been given a generous donation to his church in the hopes that he would hold his silence. Whether or not he would was open to conjecture.

'We're travelling too slowly,' William said with an anxious glance at Harry. 'We need to be on horseback and cutting across country by now, not stuck on the main road for all to see and for Chester's knights to capture as easily as a bratch would seize a lame hare. And we'll never get this great solid thing across the ford with the river as high as it is.'

Renard stared back at William with dull eyes. He knew what William wanted him to say and the responsibility dragged on his shoulders as heavily as the mud sucking at the wain wheels. Opening his mouth he obliged, for it was inevitable, and their escape was not.

'Leave the wain at the ford,' he said, 'and load whatever we need onto one of the horses. Harry can ride with someone holding him in the saddle. It cannot make any difference to his condition except perhaps bring him a mercy nearer death.'

William's shoulders relaxed and he breathed out. 'It is the only way,' he agreed.

Renard grimaced. 'Have you any usquebaugh?'

William had. It was inferior stuff and as rough on the throat as a punnet of horseshoe nails, but Renard was not drinking for pleasure.

'There's bread and sausage too,' William added. 'You can

soften the crust in the rain as we ride.'

Given less grim circumstances, the pragmatic remark would have made Renard laugh. Of the moment his mood outmatched the weather, and besides, the usquebaugh had closed his throat. Wordlessly he handed William the flask.

William took a short gulp and choked. 'God's death!' he gasped. 'No wonder the man I bartered it from was so pleased to be rid!'

'How did you come by that parchment to get me out?'

William lowered the flask and darted him a bright blue glance. 'I wrote it myself.'

'But the seal, how did you come by that?'

William reached inside his jerkin, rummaged, and brought out a disc the size of a large coin. 'This you mean?' He tossed and caught it and put it in Renard's hand. 'I found the glimmer of gold within your dancing girl's heart of stone.'

Renard gaped at him in astonishment. 'Olwen got it for you?'

'More to please herself than any favour for me.' He rubbed the side of his thumb along his jaw and looked rueful. 'Jesu Renard, she's feral. I thought she was going to eat me alive!'

Renard lowered his eyes and examined the bronze disc and the mounted knight, sword raised, incised upon it. 'He will kill her if he discovers what she has done.'

'He will have to catch her first.' Admiration glinted in William's tone. 'She took to the road with Cadwaladr ap Gruffydd even as we did, although you didn't see her, being enclosed in the wain. In the disguise of a Welsh youth she was. Best bare legs I've ever seen on a boy. Cadwaladr seemed to think so too by the direction of his eyes! Mind you, she's only playing with him. My guess is that she'll try to hook her claws into Prince Owain himself.'

'Did she take her child too?'

'Yes, slung in her cloak.'

'Then Ranulf will stop at nothing.'

William shook his head. 'I don't know. Apparently Matille has worked diligently to sow doubts in his mind. He's not entirely sure the child is his.' He took the seal back from

Renard, and his eyes sparked with an irrepressible gleam. 'Think of the havoc we can wreak with this before he's able to put a stop to it.'

From somewhere, Renard actually found the semblance of a smile. 'You know that you have risked your own future with that little gee-gaw,' he nodded at the seal.

'It was too high a price to have held back.' William's brightness faded somewhat. 'You were fortunate in one way that you were thrown into prison. You didn't see what Chester's men did to the people of Lincoln for their resistance.' He made a swift gesture as Renard tried to speak. 'No, I'm not that green about such matters. A little plundering goes not amiss — it's necessary if you want to keep and control your men, but to let them run wild shows no control at all. They end up believing they can do as they please.' He took another drink from the usquebaugh flask. 'Did you know that Robert of Leicester's gone over to the Empress? He's in Gloucester already, making private arrangements of his own.'

'No, I didn't know.' Renard was surprised, and a little dismayed, but not outrightly horrified by such news. 'Leicester might have gone courting, but I cannot believe that he intends going further than flirtation. He's one of Stephen's closest friends and advisers.'

'But fonder of his own skin. There is a hair-thin line between holding firm for the sake of honour and sheer pig-headed folly.'

'Is that an indictment?'

'Perhaps.'

The usquebaugh was starting to burn through Renard's veins, making him feel light-headed. 'If Stephen's commanders had shown more determination to "hold firm", then the battle for Lincoln would never have gone the way that it did!' he growled.

'A hair-thin line,' William repeated.

'Thick as the goddamned River Witham!'

They glared at each other, although William's anger was the less intense, laced as it was with relief that Renard still had enough fight left in him to argue.

The wain jolted to an abrupt halt at the approach to the ford and the small cluster of daub and wattle huts lining its banks. William broke the deadlock by leaving the wain and gazing with hands on hips at the fast-flowing murky water. A rope had been stretched across the river, secured by stout poles on either side, affording a hand grip to those either courageous or mad enough to want to cross on foot. Probably it was easy in high summer, but now, after a season of heavy rainfall, the water churned and frowned to the limit of both banks.

Inside the wain, Renard finished the usquebaugh. Harry breathed with stertorous effort, the noise all-pervading, drowning out every other sound, including the rushing of the river. Unable to bear it any longer, Renard lifted the canvas flap and followed William outside. For a moment as he stepped from platform to ground, he was so dizzy that he had to clutch the side of the wain and grip until the wood scored his hand.

Two dogs appeared from among the cluster of dwellings, and weight upon their hindquarters, forepaws braced, barked a loud warning at the strangers. They were followed more sedately by an old man leaning on a hickory stick and wearing a cloak made of moth-eaten wolfskins and homespun. Calling the animals to heel, he regarded the small entourage curiously.

'You'll not get that thing across yon water,' he observed, fondling the dogs with the hand that was not holding the stick. 'Deep as the height of a man in the middle it is.'

'We're not taking the wain over,' William replied and looked round at Renard who was shivering against its canvas side. 'You can have it if you want in exchange for some hot food while we load the pack horses.'

The peasant sucked his motley collection of teeth and considered the group. Usually armed Normans took the direct route through Newark. Abandoning a stout wain like this rather than head for the town spoke of great haste and the need for stealth. The man propped shivering against the cart had a new wound on one cheekbone and looked exhausted.

'Not stolen is it?' he asked as William gestured to his men and they started to unhitch the horses from the wain.

'No.' William checked the cinch on his mount's girth. 'It

was paid for by the Earl of Chester himself – his own seal on the transaction.'

Renard was taken with a sudden fit of coughing.

'See what I can do.' Whistling to his dogs, the old man stamped back towards the houses.

In a short while, two women emerged from one of the dwellings to serve the men with watery soup that resembled the river in both colour and texture, and fresh but gritty maslin bread. Renard took the wooden bowl that was handed up to him and thanked the woman in English. Her eyes widened, for although marred by a French accent and of a different dialect to her own, he spoke clearly enough for her to understand, and it was seldom indeed that the aristocracy bothered to learn the native tongue.

Renard sipped her offering. It tasted much better than it looked, hinting of leeks and mushrooms, but then after the deprivations of Lincoln anything short of midden sweepings would have tasted like manna. He dipped the bread into it to soften it and managed tolerably well to eat it.

'Rumour says that there has been a big battle in yonder town and the King taken prisoner,' she ventured after a moment, emboldened by his use of English and his enjoyment of the hot soup.

'Rumour speaks true.' He was aware of her gaze dwelling on the rough state of him, lingering on the bruised, clotted mess of his cheekbone.

'Fought in it, did you?'

Renard gave her a look that made her realise that although he spoke English, it brought him no nearer to being one of them. 'Yes,' he said stiffly. 'I fought in it.' And returning the bowl to her, went to untether the Cleveland from the rear of the wain.

She clicked her tongue and set her hands on her hips, but deferred total umbrage in the interests of observing the soldiers as they prepared to cross the ford. Some of the other women brought out hot griddle cakes which were devoured in a flash and paid for with a scattering of silver. She watched them gently bring an injured man out of the wain and craned for a better view. There was not really a great deal to see, only that his face was waxen with approaching death, and that he was too young to be meeting it. Crossing herself, she muttered the traditional response as he was lifted from his bed of latticed hides and straw.

'Give him to me,' said the man whom she had served with the soup and who was now sitting in the pillion position behind his saddle.

'Are you strong enough?' demanded the young, handsome one who was wearing some very fine armour.

'For this, yes,' came the grimly determined reply, and after a hesitation, the sick man was manœuvred carefully into the empty saddle where he slumped, held in place by the man seated behind.

'Hah!' cried Renard to the horse and kicked its flanks. A northern-bred working saddle mount, it stolidly obeyed the command, and with not so much as a back-flicker of its ears, plunged into the rapid water. Spray surged over shoulders, belly and haunches, soaking Renard's and Harry's legs. The horse fought forwards against the kick of the current, muscles bunched into hillocks and ravines. Behind him, Renard heard the splash of other horses entering the water, and one neighing a refusal.

On the bank, the woman looked for a moment longer, crossed herself piously again, and turned away. She took one pace towards her cot and stopped, rooted by shock, and then fear at the sight of a new group of mounted knights charging down the village track towards the ford. The shriek she let out would have put a banshee to shame as they came on hard.

William, last to cross, and in mid-stream, swivelled to look. Swearing, he spurred the brown. On the far bank, Renard too had heard the scream and seen what it heralded. There was not a chance in hell of out-running such a group, or of out-fighting them, for they were properly armed, and William's men were either plain serjeants or lightly clad Welsh ... Welsh bowmen.

'Help me,' he said to the soldier at his side, and together they managed to lower Harry from the saddle to the ground. It was wet, cold and muddy, but there was nothing else they could do. 'Now, train that bow of yours on the ford. Don't aim for the riders. Arrows will only bounce off helms and shields, and if their mail's any good, it will stop the serious damage. Bring down their destriers. Is that bow on your saddle roll spare?' He held out his hand for the weapon and began rapidly to string it.

William's horse reached the shallows at a lunging gallop, false-footed, and somersaulted mane over tail. William was pitched over the pommel, landed hard, and was momentarily knocked out of his senses. The hack threshed to its feet and wallowed onto the bank where it stood bleeding and trembling. A Welshman shouldered his bow and hastened to catch its bridle and tug it out of the way. Renard and the man whose bow he had borrowed ran to the water and, knee-deep, grabbed hold of William to pull him out before he drowned. His hauberk weighed almost thirty pounds, and beneath it the quilted gambeson that protected his body from the bruises of impact and the chaff of the rivets was fast becoming water-logged. Renard and his companion struggled. Across the ford, less than sixty yards away, the first horsemen sprayed into the water.

Renard's fingernails ripped back to the quick, although at the time he felt nothing, all sensations of pain, all physical and mental exhaustion, extinguished by the upsurge of the survival instinct.

'Shoot in God's name!' he bellowed over his shoulder at the men on the bank who were staring hypnotised at the approaching horsemen. Aided by William's groggily returning senses, the two men succeeded in pulling him clear of being drowned and abandoned him on the bank like a piece of stranded flotsam.

Paying scant attention to the blood running down his fingers, except to be irritated that it might foul his grip, Renard wiped his hands on his water-sodden cloak, set an arrow to the nock, and trained his eye on the broad bulk of a knight astride a dun destrier.

The man's sword cut the air with a grey glitter. His feet were thrust well down in the stirrups and his horse was breasting the water with the smooth power of a sea monster. A little to one side an arrow hit the following horse obliquely. It reared up with a scream of pain and came down awry. Its rider was thrown into the mid-depths of the river and dragged under by the weight of his armour as had almost happened to William.

The dun began to emerge from the water. Renard released his arrow and saw it sing into the destrier's throat. The horse ploughed forward, knees buckling, then smashed over on its side, crushing its rider and fouling the path of another horse. Hit by an arrow but not mortally so, the destrier shied and bolted into the path of the oncoming riders.

The knights following the first onrush found that they were sitting targets for the small cluster of archers, unable as they were to cross the ford and come to close-quarter grips with them. With the range so short, only an inexperienced fool would have missed, and these were Welshmen, trained to shoot from birth. The knight in the forefront hesitated in his decision to turn back a fatal moment too long. Three shafts of plumed death buckled his horse beneath him. He managed to leap clear and seize hold of the crossing rope, but without his shield was as vulnerable as a snail half out of its shell. The bravest of the rest spurred to where he clung and gave him a hand into his own saddle, then hastened out of arrow range, back to the village side of the ford, in the wake of his companions.

'Where's the next crossing point?' Renard asked, lowering his bow. The stave was printed and smeared with blood from his torn fingernails.

'Newark I think. Lord William knows.'

'Yes, Newark,' William groaned, sitting up. 'Too far for them to catch up, and we can leave a couple of the lads here with their bows to dissuade them from trying this way again. . . . God's teeth, I feel as if I've been through the paddles of Eleanor's fulling mill! Is the horse all right?'

'Bruised and grazed, but still rideable.' Renard crouched beside his brother. 'Obviously the news of my escape is well abroad.'

'Bound to be.' William's teeth chattered together. 'There's a new Augustinian priory at Thurgarton, no more than two hours' ride. We can dry out and fortify ourselves for the rest of the journey ... Your hands are bleeding.'

'Have you ever tried dragging a hauberk-clad body out of a river?' Renard said ruefully. His limbs were starting to tremble in the aftermath of effort and he forced himself to stand up before it became too easy to stay down. Holding out his hand, he pulled William to his feet too, then fetched the bay and went to Harry's blanket. Sodden with water, William squelched to collect his own mount from the soldier holding it.

Renard stared down at Harry, then suddenly he stopped and laid his bloodied fingers against his brother's throat. The skin was clammy and still warm, but there was no life beat, and his face was as grey as the sky, his eyes half open and fixed on eternity. 'Christ's mercy, no,' Renard said softly.

William looked round from inspecting his mount's grazed legs. 'What is it?'

'It doesn't matter the pace we set now.' Gently Renard closed Harry's lids and covered his face. It was not the River Trent they had crossed, but the Styx, gateway to the under-world.

William stared. His throat worked and he shook his head. To live with the imminence of death was still not to be prepared at the moment of knowledge. 'We can put him over one of the spare horses.' His voice was a croaked whisper.

'Yes.' Renard's expression was blank as he stood up again. 'Like a sack of grain or a dead roe buck. I suppose Harry would see no wrong in it.' His voice cracked. 'He's been used to making do all his life.' He took the Cleveland's bridle, but instead of mounting up, he bunched his fist and crashed it into the trunk of the nearest tree in a futile protest against a futile waste.

CHAPTER 25

The Welsh Marches

THE METALLIC CLINK OF METAL on stone in rhythm with the heartbeat of some mason invaded Eleanor's consciousness and brought her from a restless, dream-haunted sleep into the awareness of a bleak winter dawn. Shivering, she sat up, called out to her maids and taking her bedrobe from the foot of the bed, put it on over her shift.

In the cradle beside her, Hugh was still asleep, although soon he would be awake and greedily demanding like the ravening Vikings to whom, in a far distant past, he owed his bright Norse colouring. Her breasts were hard and pleasantly sore with milk. The constable's wife had suggested that she obtain a wet nurse, but Eleanor guarded jealously the privilege of feeding her son. His infant years were all that she would have of him. The moment he could sit his own horse and point a toy lance at a quintain, he would enter a man's arena and break the thread that attached him to the distaff. Besides, Eleanor knew from Judith's careful instruction that women who fed their own babies were far less likely to conceive again in the early months while their bodies were still recovering from the birth of the previous child, a fate that had overcome and subsequently killed her own mother. Eleanor, much as she desired children could see the sense in not producing them at the rate of one a year.

Not that there had been or was likely to be much opportunity to tempt fate, she thought, glance flickering to the coffer and the parchment lying there – Renard's last letter from Lincoln, written two days before the battle. She knew it by heart and had no need to read the words because they were indelibly printed on her mind as was the news of the disaster that had overtaken King Stephen's forces.

The letter had been followed a week later by Adam's appearance at Ravenstow along with Renard's two frightened squires and the evil tidings. Having been forced to flee before it was too late, Adam had known nothing of what had transpired after the battle, apart from the fact that Lincoln had been sacked. The smoke had cast a pall over the city, visible for miles around. He had told her and Judith, in the courtyard, the moment he dismounted. Looking past him, they had seen Gorvenal being led away by a groom. The stallion had been blanketed, without rider or decorated high saddle. Seeing him thus had brought Adam's news home to roost with all the impact that his words had been unable to convey. Not just the battle lost, but perhaps the rest of their lives.

Judith had drifted away to the plesaunce in a daze and remained there until nightfall, sitting upon the turf seat and talking to herself. Both Renard and Harry were missing on the losing side of a battle. Her other son, scapegrace and half-wild, was somewhere among the victors, unless he too had been lost in the fighting. It was too much to bear, and she told Guyon so over and over again.

Adam had stayed awhile, but only to ensure there were no outright hysterics from Judith or Eleanor. The latter, left in sole command of the keep because of Judith's mental withdrawal, had mastered her grief and panic in an outward display of calm that was reassuring to everyone but herself. Lulled by her wan smile and stubbornly lifted chin, Adam went home. His own lands needed attention, and then he was bound for Gloucester, to do homage to Mathilda and intercede on Eleanor's behalf for Ravenstow. From what Renard had told her of the Empress, Eleanor doubted that she would be persuaded to show clemency.

Two days after Adam's visit, Sir Thomas d'Alberin arrived with a straggle of Ravenstow men, having made their way from the disaster at Lincoln by hazardous by-ways. Sir Thomas was a shadow of his former bulk, and were it not for the haggard story written on his face, would have looked twice as healthy as when he set out. From him, after he had sobbed with relief and reaction all over his son, Eleanor and Judith had learned that the King had been taken prisoner, the victim of a minor head wound, and probably Renard with him, although Sir Thomas could not be quite sure. As to Harry, he was probably dead, but there was no final certainty.

Eleanor shivered and hugged her arms as her maids came from the antechamber in response to her summons. Renard might or might not be dead. He might or might not be a prisoner. It was traumatic not to know. She could not eat, or concentrate on anything. Leaving Judith at Ravenstow, she had come up the march to Caermoel to warn the garrison of possible attack by the Earl of Chester or his Welsh levies, and to hearten the men by her presence. Five days she had been here now. Five solitary, frightened days that were filled with the banging of masons' hammers, the rapid, loud sawing of the carpenters, the slap of trowel upon mortar, and the rumbling of wain wheels as they delivered the supplies vital to a keep that might soon be under siege. Sounds echoing in a vast, vaulted emptiness.

'Madam?' questioned the maid.

Eleanor folded her shaking hands in the sleeves of her bedrobe. 'The blue gown,' she said, the surface of her mind functioning efficiently and belying the turmoil beneath. 'Have some hot honey and wine ready for after mass.'

'Yes, madam.' The maid went to Eleanor's clothing pole to find the requested gown. Another maid, yawning behind her hand, fed charcoal onto the brazier. Hugh woke up and began making his usual loud demands for sustenance.

Eleanor took her son and put him to her breast. She watched him as he suckled, his tiny fingers kneading the source of his pleasure, and his jaws working steadily. Eleanor was overwhelmed by pangs of love and terror so fierce when she thought what might become of him that she began to sob with the pain of it. This impeded her flow of milk and Hugh sucked furiously in disbelief, released her nipple and howled his indignation to the world. This only made Eleanor cry the harder herself.

In the end she had to give him to one of the maids who had

her own baby and a surplus of milk in her breasts. The storm of tears left her exhausted and in possession of a splitting headache, but at least in a temporary state of numbed calm. White-faced with strain, she went to mass, lit candles and prayed for deliverance. The floor was cold and her mind remained a remote observer of all her actions, as though she moved in a dream.

On emerging from the chapel into the bailey, she was greeted by small, wind-floated feathers of snow. One of the guards on the wall walk, his voice full of excited alarm, cried out a warning of approaching troops.

It was the worst moment in Eleanor's entire life. Paralysed with terror she stood and stared up at the great, grey walls. Suddenly they seemed no protection at all. If she could have moved, she would have covered her ears with her hands and run to hide in the smallest, darkest recess that she could find.

William de Lorys, Renard's companion in Antioch and now the Constable of Caermoel, responsible for its defence, followed Eleanor from the chapel in time to hear the cry from the walls. 'It's too soon to be de Gernons,' he reassured her. 'The whoreson will still be down in Gloucester persuading the Empress of his sincerity in the hopes of being given Carlisle.'

Mind and body jolted back into awareness with a single hard stroke of her heart, and then the latter commenced pounding like one of the masons' hammers. 'But she won't give it to him,' she said through stiff lips. 'She'll give him Caermoel instead.'

'My lady, your cloak.' Alys set Eleanor's wool and marten mantle around her shoulders as de Lorys left them to mount the battlements and discover more.

Mechanically Eleanor stroked the sleek fur trimming of the cloak and thought that something always had to die in order to gratify others. Alys was trying to usher her inside to warmth, muttering about the cold and the growing yellowish heaviness of the snow clouds.

'Let me be,' she commanded in a voice that would have better belonged to Judith, or even the termagant Empress herself. Shaking herself free of her maid's solicitous arm, she followed de Lorys up to the battlements.

The wind snatched at her veil, whipped strands of hair free of her braids and stung her eyes as she tried to focus on the advancing troops below. Miniature men on miniature horses with pack ponies in tow. They did not hesitate at the ford, but splashed straight through it, heading for the steep pathway that wound its way around Caermoel crag and up to the twin baileys and keep crowning its summit.

'Not sufficient numbers for the enemy.' De Lorys sucked his teeth. 'Looks like they're coming straight up; seeking hospitality I would guess, or else they're some of our own from Ravenstow or Ledworth. Pox take it, I can't make out their shields.' He scowled at the now heavily falling snow that was obliterating their vision.

For a moment Eleanor slumped against the merlon, weak with relief. A shout drifted on the wind and guards in the outer ward suddenly began pulling back the heavy draw bar that secured the gatehouse door. Eleanor turned and standing on tip-toe, strained her eyes. Through a whirl of banking, shifting white, she saw that the leading horse was a black with white hind stockings. Its rider's shield, momentarily glimpsed, was blazoned with a rampant black leopard upon a flame-coloured background.

'It's Renard!' she shrieked. 'God be praised, it's Renard, he's alive!' Whirling to de Lorys, her eyes feverishly ablaze, she kissed him hard and impulsively on the cheek. He staggered, and then grinned his own delight and relief. Without waiting for him, Eleanor ran pell mell down to the bailey, snapping at a loitering maid she encountered to hurry to the kitchens and warn the cook of extra mouths and a celebration. Another was ordered to see to the arranging of a bath tub in the bedchamber. The grooms and other pertaining servants were alerted.

Nervous excitement shivered in the air as the first horses came through the open gateway, and emerged from the guarded passage into the ward. Eleanor watched Renard dismount. His cloak was scaled with snow, turning haddock-silver at the edges as it melted. It was agony crossing the bailey to him. She knew that she must not run among the highly bred destriers in case one kicked out, but all she wanted to do was fling herself upon him – hold and taste and know that he was solid and real, not some figment of her yearning imagination.

Renard spoke to one of his companions, then to the groom with an instruction about the horse, and thus did not turn until Eleanor had almost reached him. She stopped in her tracks as though hit by a crossbow quarrel, and gasped. The words of welcome stuck in her throat, for the picture she had carried in her mind's eye for the past two months bore no resemblance at all to the man confronting her now. Renard's face was gaunt, pared to the bone, and along one of those bones was a livid, half-healed scar, angry red against the sallow final remnants of a Middle Eastern sun. His mouth was a hard, narrow line, slightly down-turned, but he succeeded in giving her the slightest of bitter smiles.

'Commendable,' he said. 'My mother fainted.'

Eleanor swallowed, but the words still remained in her throat. She was never good at dealing with him when he was defensively sarcastic. The more he hid behind it, the more she floundered and stammered. 'What happened?' Even to her own ears the words sounded stupid and she would have retracted them if it had been possible.

'My barber's careless,' he snapped acidly as he removed his helm and stuffed his gauntlets inside. 'The battle for Lincoln, what do you think?'

'We thought . . . We did not know if you were . . .' Eleanor stopped, totally unnerved by his flat, granite stare. 'Do you want to bathe?'

'Do I what?' His voice rose incredulously.

Eleanor burst into tears, and instead of casting herself into his arms as she had first intended, she gathered her skirts and fled.

Renard stared after her rapidly disappearing figure and swore roundly. He knew that it was not fair to vent his temper on her just because she still looked all eager innocence when he had been through the pit of hell, but he had been unable to stop himself.

'Welcome, my lord,' said de Lorys with a touch of irony.

277

Renard responded by thrusting his helm into the knight's hands. 'Hold this,' he said, and hastened in pursuit of his wife.

He caught up with her just beyond the gateway to the inner bailey – not because he was any faster. The fact that she was hampered by her skirts was offset by the weight of his mail, and it was only because she had twisted her ankle and leaned against the wall for a moment that he was able to catch her.

Weeping, she fought to break free. In part she was angry with him, but the main source of her chagrin was her own flustered response. She ought to have stood her ground, not run like a panicking hen.

Renard clamped his arm around her waist and held her immobile against the bailey wall. She felt the stones grinding into her shoulder blades and buttocks and Renard's mailed weight crushing her there. For a wild instant she wondered if he was going to strike her, then all wondering stopped as he did, with his mouth, and all pain was suspended.

It was a harsh, demanding embrace, brooking no resistance. Not that after the first tremor of surprise Eleanor had any intention of resisting.

'Christ!' he muttered, surfacing briefly. 'Do I want to bathe? For all your cleverness, I sometimes think that your head is stuffed with feathers!'

'I only, I . . .'

'I can think of better ways of drowning,' he muttered and cut off her stammering with another hard kiss.

The snow fell in a thick, white curtain. Eleanor clung to him, her fingers in his hair, her lips parted and starving. Despite the cold, her body felt as warm and pliant as sunlit willow. His embrace softened, but the core of urgency remained. One hand went to her breast, fumbling with the hooks of her bodice, the other fanned over her hip. She felt the flutter of snow on the upper swell of her breast, then the cold touch of his lips and the heat of his tongue. A broken cry rippled from her throat and she pressed herself against him. Renard was aware of her action, but the sensations he craved were inhibited by the various layers of clothing he was wearing and the discrepancy in height between himself and Eleanor. He wanted her feminine softness to flow over and engulf him so that at least for a while he could forget.

'Let's go within,' he muttered against her ear, and then with an effort stood back, straightening her dishevelled gown and drawing her cloak together. Then he swallowed and touched her cheek. 'Nell,' he said softly. 'Jesu God, Nell, you can't imagine the hell I've known ...' And broke off, a groove of muscle straining on the good side of his face. Taking her hand, he led her to the hall and through it to the adjoining bedchamber.

A steaming tub adorned the centre of the room. Renard eyed it speculatively.

'Shall I get rid of it?' Eleanor blushed, wishing that she had never given orders for it to be prepared in the first place.

'No, just the maids.' He jerked his head.

Eleanor nodded at Alys and the other two women. They curtseyed and left, taking Hugh with them. Renard's eyes dwelt briefly on the child, but for the nonce, all his interest was centred on Eleanor and the scalding congestion in his loins. He could not, did not want to think – desired only oblivion and a release from thinking.

Faintly from the hall Eleanor heard a man's voice raised in laughter and realised it was the first merriment she had heard since Renard went to Lincoln. He flickered a look towards it and she thought that he grimaced, but then his eyes returned to her and devoured. Closing on her, he pulled off her chaplet and her veil, then unhooked the last fastenings on her bodice with predatory fingers. Eleanor swayed towards him and retorted by reaching to the buckle of his sword belt. The thickness of the new leather and stiff latch frustrated her, and Renard had to stop undressing her to do it himself. Removing his surcoat and, with an effort, his encumbering hauberk, he dropped them on the rushes, then kissing her, pulled her to the bed, uncaring of control, driven by white-hot need.

Eleanor gasped and subdued a cry as he entered her, but the initial pain swiftly subsided. She shifted beneath him, arching her hips to meet the downward thrust of his, her breathing rapid and erratic. She remembered a frosty night at Salisbury and her wistful longing for Renard to want her as badly as this, without time for dalliance or finesse. She clutched him, the triumph sweeping over her like a tidal wave.

With a muffled groan he buried his face against her throat, and she felt his fingers grip with the pleasure-pain of his release. She was swept onto the crest of it herself, her body shattered and convulsed by ripple upon ripple of sensation like the rings created by stones flung into a pool.

His breathing eased a little. He nibbled the lobe of her ear and the corner of her jaw. She turned her head to return the compliment. Her fingers moving in a caress touched his face, and then the healing wound on his cheekbone. He jerked and winced.

'I'm sorry, I forgot!' She was immediately contrite.

'So did I for a moment.' Renard raised himself up. She wriggled, reluctant to end their union, but made uncomfortable by the rucked skirts bunched beneath her. A slight murmur of protest did leave her lips as he withdrew, but she quickly realised that it was only so that he could continue the task of removing their clothing at a more leisurely pace. She sat up as he dictated and let him take her shift.

'You don't want to get it wet,' he murmured, a sudden glint in his eyes.

'Wet?' Eleanor looked at him blankly, then her stare flickered to the tub and widened. The first heat of passion had been vented in mere moments and the tub still steamed. It was of the upright cask variety. Room for two perhaps, but a very close fit – very close indeed.

The glint spread from his eyes to become a mischievous smile. His gaze dropped to her full, brown-tipped breasts, then lower still. 'No sense of adventure?' he teased, and tilting her chin on his forefinger, kissed her. 'Pleasure me,' he said softly. 'God knows, if I could have had control of my dreams these past few weeks, they would have been of this.'

His expression became bleak, almost desolate. All doubts and hesitations left Eleanor. Willingly she went with him to the tub.

Pulling her ivory comb down through the wet tangles of her hair, Eleanor listened in appalled silence to Renard's brief summary of the Lincoln campaign and its disastrous results, of the price paid so far and the price yet to be exacted.

'Mama says that she is going to endow a convent at Ravenstow on that piece of meadow just outside the town,' Renard said in that same, careful voice he had used throughout the narrative. 'She wants to dedicate it to my father, and Harry, and Miles. You never knew my oldest brother, did you? He drowned on The White Ship. Stone, she says, will be there long after she's gone ... long after we've all gone.'

Eleanor put the comb down on her coffer. 'Poor Harry.' Her voice wobbled and her eyes filled with tears.

'That is what we have all said about him throughout his life. I suppose he'll have more dignity when the stone carver has finished with his effigy. Mama intends Nottingham alabaster. She has it all carefully planned.' He laced his shirt and pulled on a tunic of wine-coloured wool. 'Probably we'll all need effigies if Mathilda gains the throne. Either that or hasten into exile. I suppose I could hire my sword to Prince Raymond again.' Picking up his indoor shoes of soft, embroidered deerhide, he stared at them as if he did not know what they were and said wearily, 'Christ's blood, I'm sick of it, Nell, to the back teeth.'

She blinked the tears from her eyes and looked at the tub, the water now merely tepid and much of it splashed on the floor. Her body still ached and tingled. 'Will Earl Ranulf come against us?'

'Of a certainty. I'm a rebel now.'

'Can you hold him off?'

'I do not know. It depends upon so many things – how he is received at Gloucester, how Mathilda's fortunes progress, and how quiet the Welsh remain.'

She tried to nod sensibly, but found it impossible. 'How long do we have?' she asked instead, her voice thin and frightened.

Renard finished dressing and came to lay his hand on her shoulder. 'Again, I do not know. As long as this snow lasts we are secure. Beyond that ...' He sighed heavily. 'Look, Nell, I don't want to talk or even think about it – not for today at least. I have told you all that you need to know, and that was grief enough to recount.' He kissed her mouth and lightly strayed his hand between her breasts, bringing it to rest on her waist.

'Now, before I yield to temptation again, let me see my son, and is there anything to eat?' he asked plaintively, using the mundane as a safe path through a vast quagmire. 'I broke fast at Woolcot but that seems ages ago and it was no more than rye bread and weak ale.'

Eleanor toyed with the leather dagger sheath at his belt. 'There is only pottage.' She raised to him a smile both tremulous and teasing.

'Do you remember that night at Salisbury?' He gave a small shake of his head. 'That seems ages ago too. I wish that time had stood still.'

CHAPTER 26

THE SNOW FELL HEAVILY for the next two days, and intermittently for the three after that. Hushed beneath a sparkling quilt the world held its breath. Animals had to be dug out of drifts. Some were not found until the snow had melted, and among the victims was an old packman who had been caught out in the first blizzard.

Whether their dwelling was in castle, cottage or hovel, people stayed close to their hearths – mending tools, telling tales, sewing, weaving, drinking, quarrelling, fighting and fornicating. That year there were several new births celebrated around the Christmas period, many a Noel or Christmas owing his or her life to the late snowfalls of February and March.

Renard spent the first blizzard days either in bed or very close to it, and most of that time he slept, restoring his drained physical and mental reserves. In his waking periods, he took the opportunity to play with his infant son and enjoy the soothing balm of Eleanor's company. The knowledge that this interlude was only a respite, that there might never be such an opportunity again, made the time spent even more precious, each moment savoured to the full.

Gradually, however, a degree of restlessness returned to his spirit, a need to go beyond passive pleasures. Eleanor discovered suddenly that she could no longer beat him at tables and she had to exert every ounce of wit and concentration to hold him at nine men's morris. They had a wild snowball fight in the bailey that was adjourned, minus snowballs and amid much giggling, snatched kisses and horseplay, to the bedchamber.

That same night upon the wall walk, gazing out on the black and white emptiness of moon, sky, forest and snow, their hackles were raised by the howling of wolves. 'Human or four-legged,' Renard murmured to Eleanor who was wrapped inside the warmth of his cloak, body pressed close to his. 'They may cry at our gates all they wish, but if they bite, they will find it is more than they can chew.'

The next day he had a grindstone fetched from the armoury and set up in the hall. While Eleanor plied her needle through soft coney fur slippers for Hugh, he occupied himself in sharpening his meat dagger and hunting knife, and oiling the razor-keen edges of his sword. He had lost his own at Lincoln, it having become a spoil of war. His mother, eyes liquid, chin firm, had given him the one that had belonged to his father. The hilt was set with Lothian garnets and the grip of slightly worn, shrunken leather still bore the pressure marks of his father's hand. It had originally belonged to Renard's great grandfather, Renard le Rouquin, after whom he had been named, and the Lombardy steel was still as bright as the day on which it had been forged more than a hundred years ago. One day, if it too did not become a spoil of war, it would belong to Hugh.

Judith had also given him his father's hauberk since his own had been lost at Lincoln. It fitted him well, had needed only minor adjustments to compensate for his being slightly taller and a little less broad. It had been a wrench for his mother, he knew. Piece by piece the fabric of her young womanhood was being unravelled, leaving her threadbare to the world and there was nothing he could do about it. If cozened, she would bristle, reluctant to be openly affectionate except to her grandchildren. While giving him his father's arms and accoutrements, her voice had been brisk and practical, warning him not to dare sentiment.

Eleanor had wept openly when he showed her the sword, and put her arms impulsively around him, for which he loved her. With Eleanor there was never any need to banter, fight or pretend.

The snow started to melt and recede. Eleanor fretted that she had missed lambing time at Woolcot. Renard closeted himself with de Lorys and the senior knights of the garrison to devise strategies for resisting siege. He sent patrols out and rode down to Ledworth and Ravenstow himself, returning via Woolcot with the reassurance to Eleanor that the lambing had gone well despite the late bad weather.

Adam visited them with the expected news that Renard had been stripped of his lands by the Empress and declared rebel, his earldom promised to Ranulf of Chester. 'Although she did not give it to him outright,' Adam had qualified. 'That awaits her coronation.'

'Oh,' Renard said sarcastically. 'That's all right then.'

Adam shrugged. 'It won't stop Ranulf from anticipating the promise, I grant you, but the way Mathilda keeps treating her supporters as if they were serfs, she'll be queen of nothing. More than one man walked away from an audience with her harbouring second thoughts, myself included. I have known for a long time that she is mettlesome, but with so much iron in her pride, she is riding for a fall.'

'At the hands of Stephen's queen?'

'Perhaps.' Adam pursed his lips. 'Certainly those who fled at Lincoln have returned to her in shame and are doing what they can to rally support behind her, but it is Mathilda's own high-handedness that will bring her down. As I said, she treats men of rank like serfs. Naturally they take offence, but how much higher is the insult to the burghers and freemen of the towns when they come suing for peace and she treats *them* like serfs.'

'What do you mean?'

Adam spread his hands. 'To us, a serf is a serf, too far removed from our own situation for a comparison to do more than astonish. To a burgher or freeman, a serf is a symbol of what he once perhaps was, or what he might become if his business fails or his crop is blighted. Too close for comfort in other words. Mathilda does not understand, and it may well be her undoing. Also she has quarrelled on several occasions with the Bishop of Winchester. She needs him more than he needs her, but she's refusing to see it, and when people try to tell her, she goes into a sulking tantrum.'

Renard looked thoughtfully at his brother-by-marriage. Adam had frequently moved in Angevin circles in the past and knew the Empress by past acquaintance. He it was who had been sent by King Henry to bring her back from Germany when her first husband, the Emperor, had died. Adam's reading of political situations was shrewd and seldom wrong. 'So, if I can weather whatever Earl Ranulf throws at me and bide my time, I may yet come out of this crisis with little more than storm damage?'

'It is possible.' Adam looked doubtful, as if he wanted to add that all things were possible given miracles. 'But for safety's sake, if you want, I'll take Eleanor and the babe down to Thorneyford when I leave. Heulwen would love to see them.'

'Thank you. I was going to ask that boon of you anyway.' Renard looked relieved.

Eleanor, not consulted, just informed of the decision, was both reluctant and angry, and displaying the stubborn part of her nature above common sense, refused to comply. An evening's persuasion resulted in frayed tempers. Renard bellowed at her. She shrieked back at him as she had never shrieked at anyone before and threw a cup at his head. Astonished and diverted at this wild outburst, Renard forgot to argue and took her to bed instead, thereby losing the battle outright.

When morning came, he knew that they need not have bothered fighting, for soldiers were gathering at the foot of Caermoel crag in the growing light, and preparing to lay siege to the castle.

Renard and Adam ascended one of the new towers and gazed down the precipitous slope at the armed men below, small as animated wooden toys. Among them, conspicuous and well out of bow range, Ranulf of Chester sat a muscular grey stallion, and beside him was the mercenary who had tried to abduct Eleanor on her way to her marriage.

'He'll lose too many men if he tries a direct assault,' Renard said. 'This tower guards the most vulnerable part of the approach path. If they want to avoid arrows in their gizzards, they'll have to climb the rock face, and by the time they've reached the top of that, they'll be as easy to pick off as wasps from a conserve.'

'Supposing they come up at night?'

'The guards will either have their eyes skinned or be skinned themselves. It's impossible to muffle the sound of a grapnel or climb that crag in silence. I tried it last week.'

'What, up there?' Adam looked at him sidelong.

Renard grinned and made a small movement of his shoulders. 'The hand and footholds are easy enough to find, it's just the way it goes up, hard and steep that makes it so difficult. By the time you get to the top, you're gasping so hard that even a child could kick you back over the edge, particularly if you're hampered by arms and weapons, which I wasn't.'

Adam's stare was open-mouthed and comical.

'It was exhilarating,' Renard added, a glint of remembered enjoyment in his grey eyes.

'If you had fallen, you would have been killed!'

'I knew what I was doing.'

Adam gave a derisory snort. Renard might have matured beyond the out and out wildness of first manhood, but a seam of it still remained to surface and terrify everyone bar the culprit. 'And Heulwen calls *me* reckless!' he said with heartfelt injury.

'You should have heard what Eleanor said to me. You'd think she was as sweet as honey to look at her, wouldn't you?'

Adam grunted. Renard did not appear much set down by his wife's remonstration if the humour crinkling his eye corners was any indication. 'I am sorry. I was too late to get her and Hugh away,' he said seriously.

'It might have been a sop to my conscience,' Renard admitted, sobering 'But it will cost Ranulf de Gernons more than he can afford to take this keep. It won't be easy for us, but our difficulties will be as nothing compared to his.'

'You sound very confident.'

'I am.'

Adam leaned on his sword belt. 'Look, the new tower guards the approach, I grant you that, but what's to stop him undermining it using a cover of withy screens and green hides? It is what I would do – what every siege commander would do.'

'For a start, he'd be mining through solid rock,' Renard said and gently rubbed his thumb along his scarred cheekbone. 'For another . . .' He turned to the steps down. 'Come with me. I want to show you something.'

At the foot of the tower there was a large, iron-studded trap door that gave access to an oubliette – a windowless chamber that could be used either as storage space, or more grimly as a place to put offenders to suffer. Out of sight and out of mind until the victim himself was sightless and mindless too. Adam peered down into the darkness and by the brand sputtering in the cresset saw a wooden ladder descending to a dirt floor and half a dozen dusty, brown barrels. He eyebrowed a question at his brother-in-law.

'Greek fire,' Renard said. 'Olwen was not the only volatile item in the baggage I brought home from Antioch. I took it in lieu of silver from Prince Raymond.'

Adam whistled softly. His glance flickered nervously to the torch to make sure that there was no likelihood of it sputtering near the barrels. Greek Fire. Its effect was devastating and the secret of its composition jealously guarded by the Byzantine Greeks who were the only ones who knew how to make it, and thus it was a rare, much coveted and feared weapon of war. Once it adhered to something it did not stop burning until there was nothing left. Damp and water only made it all the more combustible.

'Withy screens and green hide are no protection against this,' Renard said grimly. 'It will burn his siege machines into the soil and roast his soldiers alive within their armour.' Carefully he closed the trap and dusted his hands. He and Adam looked at each other sombrely, for a moment, their breath smoking in the cold air, and then went back up into the ward.

Hamo le Grande listened to the desultory talk of the soldiers seated around the nearest watchfire. Most of it was grumbling. It was a warm spring night, but their purses were empty and even had they been full of the money they were owed, there was nothing up here in the Welsh border wilds to spend it on. The supplies of ale were low and women non-existent.

Gambling was banned because last week a fight had broken out over a disputed dice throw, resulting in two deaths and a severe wounding. They were an army under siege themselves from boredom, dissatisfaction and loss of morale as all their efforts foundered against the solid stone confidence of Caermoel's walls.

They could not even vent their frustration on raiding the surrounding area since it was deciduous woodland, inhabited by a few woodcutters, charcoal burners and foresters. The game was elusive, requiring trained men and dogs to catch it. Sport for the Earl of Chester, but hardly for his men. The parts that were not wooded were populated by sheep; a diet of mutton soon became monotonous and there was no thrill in the chase.

'When will Earl Ranulf be back, sir?' asked Lucas, one of Hamo's seconds. His predecessor had fallen during the abortive attempt to capture Eleanor de Mortimer which had so nearly succeeded and then ended in bloody failure. She was Eleanor, Countess of Ravenstow now and already the mother of a seven-month-old son.

'Later tomorrow.' Hamo scowled at the keep. They had been trying to locate the source of its water in order to send poison through the system, but it seemed likely that at least one well was fed by an undefileable spring rising straight from the rock and secure within the walls.

'Do you think Prince Owain will agree to help him take this place?'

'How should I know?' Hamo snapped. Earl Ranulf had ridden off to a meeting with his sometime enemy, sometime ally, Owain Gwynedd, for the broad intent of general parley and the narrower purpose of persuading the Prince to co-operate in laying siege to Caermoel. 'You never know which way the Welsh are going to jump.'

'Nor FitzGuyon,' Lucas said with a pained grimace at Caermoel's walls. The last attempt at assault had been met by a barrage of small, clay pots, seemingly innocuous until they shattered on impact with the ground, or a man, and burst into the deadly flames of Greek fire. Since then there had been a noticeable reluctance in the men to go anywhere near the walls.

'FitzGuyon!' The word left Hamo's lips like a red-hot coal. He remembered the fight in the forest and its ignominious conclusion. The blame was his own. He should have pushed on for home. In stopping to rest the horses and make sure of his prize, he had lost it, and the way this siege was progressing, Caermoel was not going to be his restitution. He spat again and stalked in the direction of his tent. Lucas followed, the grimace still on his face.

Somewhere in the distance a dog fox barked thrice and was answered. The sound floated clearly on the calm night air. Above the watchfires of the camp, on the keep's outer wall walk, metal clinked and boots scraped on dusty stone as a guard left his post. The fox barked again and a vixen yammered an answer. Hamo growled a curse at the noisy mating habits of the local wildlife and splashed some cloudy ale into his leather cup.

Renard too was drinking – a pleasant, slightly tart wine from his brother's vineyards down at Milnham-on-Wye. Caermoel's hall was built against the inner curtain wall and the single row of windows facing the bailey were unshuttered to the balmy evening air.

Eleanor sat beside a double candlestick and close to one of the windows where she had been catching the last rays of light. Her needle flew nimbly in and out of a piece of fabric like a bird darting to and from its nest. Renard lounged in a pelt-spread chair, his tunic removed, shirt open and smutty from the forge where he had been helping the armourer to make lance heads. Standing on the trestle beside his cup were a cluster of wooden toys carved and polished smooth, and seated on his knee, resting in the crook of his arm was Hugh.

The child should have been long abed, but the sudden hot turn to the weather and a sore gum had kept him awake, crying and fractious, until his father in passing had plucked him out of his cradle and brought him to sit in the hall. Hugh's distress had subsided so quickly that Renard had been forced to laugh at the almost smug expression on the baby's face as he settled back against his arm.

Hugh gnawed experimentally on the wooden dog he was holding, then threw it down and decisively reached a chubby hand towards the belt that Renard had removed with his tunic, round eyes intent upon the decorated hilt of his father's eating knife.

Adam, who was playing chess with Renard, rolled a pawn between his palms and chuckled. 'You've a warrior on your hands there.'

Renard smiled, albeit grimly. 'Learning early the skills he will need.' He picked up the belt and let the baby play with the haft, keeping his hand around the sheath to prevent Hugh from drawing the blade. Then he lifted his attention from his son and fixed it on the soldier who was running up the hall towards him.

'My lord, the signal has come. Three barks of the dog fox repeated. It could not be mistaken!' the man panted.

'You know what to do?' Renard was suddenly as tense as he had been relaxed.

'Yes, my lord.' The soldier saluted and left again at a rapid trot.

Eleanor abandoned her sewing. Her heartbeat thundered deafeningly in her ears and her stomach churned. The sensations were not new to her; she had been enduring them every single day of this siege. Permanent fear. Fear that de Gernons would breach their defences, fear that Renard would be maimed or killed by the stones that periodically flew from the siege machines and crashed into the ward, fear for her son, fear for herself.

She rose to meet Renard as he handed Hugh into her care. Her throat closed and the words she wanted to say beat like prisoners against the walls of her skull. All she could show to Renard was a wide, mute pleading.

'Better rouse the cook, love,' he said. 'We'll need hot water for the wounded and food for later.' There was an irrepressible gleam in his eyes as he stooped to kiss her cold lips. 'Best tell him to make it pottage. I don't know how many men William has brought with him.' Then he gave her a squeeze and hurried after Adam.

Hugh squealed and held out his hands towards his retreating father. Eleanor bowed her head over his silky blond-red hair and struggled for a moment. The fear sucked out her insides, leaving a husk to wander somewhat unsteadily out of the hall and into the kitchen building to which it was annexed, the baby clutched tightly to her breast.

In the stables everywhere was harness and chaos as the grooms and drafted servants worked furiously to saddle up the destriers. One of them mishandled a cinch on Gorvenal's girth and received a hefty kick. Gorvenal plunged and rolled a white eye. Renard caught his bridle and led him out into the open bailey. Owain completed the girth and ran back into the stables to help elsewhere. Adam mounted his red-chestnut destrier, the progeny of the stallion he had lost before Eleanor's wedding, and mustered his own half dozen knights. Renard had another ten and himself. Then there were eight serjeants who had experience of fighting horseback, and another twenty on foot.

'Ready?' Renard enquired of Adam. The torchlight shone on his helm, on the rivets of his mail, and on his smile which was more than half-snarl.

Adam saluted him briefly and returned his hand to the bridle to control his restive horse.

Renard gestured to the guards in the gatehouse and the double portcullises were smoothly raised. There was no sound. Renard had had them thoroughly greased and checked over for this very occasion. The draw bars on the huge gates were run back and noiselessly they swung inwards.

Silence. On the slopes the watch fires burned and the guards lolled at their posts. It was true dark now and the camp was asleep apart from those few men involved in illicit dice games and other less savoury vices. From the direction in which those alert enough to take interest had decided there must be a fox's lair, an owl hooted softly and closer to hand.

'That's the attack,' Renard muttered to Adam. 'We count to a slow fifty, then we go.'

Adam nodded and fastened his ventail, glad that he was not

one of the men about to be ground like corn between two crushing millstones.

He had reached forty when the first bellow of alarm was throttled short and the sound of a single sword blade scraping across a shield reached them. There was silence again, suspended like a rain drop trembling on a thread, and suddenly exploding outwards into confusion.

Renard adjusted his grip on his shield straps and unwound the morning star flail from his saddle bow, his lips silently counting. The weapon was much less refined than a sword, but its effect was devastating and excellent for lashing out at men in the darkness when it was difficult to see where to slash and thrust. Behind him he could feel the restlessness of his men, their eyes boring into his spine, holding on his command. In the darkness beyond the gates a shriek of mortal agony rose above the battle clamour. 'Now!' he said, and squeezed Gorvenal's flanks between his knees.

It was not a full charge which would have been suicidal down a haphazard rocky slope in darkness, but Renard took the men down as swiftly as he dared. There were no guards to cry warning of the new assault because they were already caught up in the chaos of the first battle. Awareness only came as Renard hit the outskirts of the fighting.

A soldier attacked Gorvenal with a lighted brand plucked from one of the fires. The stallion shied. Renard altered his grip on the reins and brought the horse under control and round in a semi-circle. The soldier fell beneath the vicious lash of the studded ball on the end of the flail. Renard rode over him, leaning over Gorvenal's withers to take up the brand himself and set fire to the nearest tent. A coughing soldier bolted out of it and Renard struck him down. More tents flared, blossoming the night with fire. Illuminated smoke billowed away towards Wales. The battleground resembled a portrait of hell from the quill of an imaginative priest. A cluster of pitch barrels caught fire and exploded with lethal results. Supplies were trampled, wains overturned and horselines cut. Men panicked, broke and fled. Those who did not run fast enough or mistook their direction, died. Hamo and Lucas were not among them. Both had sufficient experience of saving their own skins to make the correct decisions rapidly.

Panting, Renard drew rein. Gorvenal sidled and half-bucked, a raw patch on his rump where a fragment of molten pitch had burned the hair away. Another knight rode up alongside on a handsome liver chestnut, its hide made red by the reflection of the fires. William, his face smoke-streaked and ablaze with a triumph as high as the flames, slapped Renard's mail-clad sleeve. '*Cadno!*' He used the Welsh word they had agreed upon to determine friend from foe in the thick of the fighting. 'They're running like coneys from a fox.' His eyes gleamed with humour at the joke, for *cadno* was the Welsh term for fox.

Renard coughed, his throat rough with smoke. 'What took you so long?' he demanded. 'I was expecting you by last week at the latest!'

'Business elsewhere.' William gave a maddening shrug. 'Earl Ranulf's not among this rout, you know.'

'It had not escaped my attention,' Renard answered huffily, and then his glance focused hard. 'And that was no idle remark. You know where he is, don't you?'

William glowered. 'I can't keep anything from you, can I?' he said, almost irritated.

'Well?'

'He's up the border and across it, meeting with Prince Owain.'

'Is he now?'

'One of my men has a brother in the Prince's service, so I receive regular reports, the most recent only a few hours old. Ranulf asked the Welsh to combine with him in attacking Caermoel.' He flicked at his horse's mane, drawing the moment out.

'All right, have your revenge,' Renard said impatiently. 'Just don't make me wait all night. What did Prince Owain say?'

Grinning William told him.

CHAPTER 27

THE FOREST WAS A PALE GREEN froth of tender new leaves spotted and rayed with sunlight. Here and again a complete shaft of gold would illuminate the place where a tree had fallen and was rapidly being colonised by a multitude of forest opportunists, while its sapling offspring scrambled frantically towards the hole of light it had bequeathed in the ancient canopy.

It was late April and hot enough to be a full month later. Ranulf of Chester was cooking inside his armour like a lobster being boiled alive in its shell. His destrier's hide was patched with sweat and its head was carried low. The jingle of harness was loud, the atmosphere somnolent, almost oppressive, as if a thunderstorm was just about to break. Ranulf's shoulder blades itched and not just because of the sweat trickling down between them. He knew that the Welsh were not far away and it made him uneasy. Even the most civilised of them were as unpredictable as the wild boar and wolves with which they shared the forest.

Colour flickered between and behind the trunks. Ranulf put a nervous hand on his sword hilt. Welsh soldiers were riding parallel with him and his men. They made no move to approach, but nevertheless ensured that they were seen. Ranulf clenched his teeth and swallowed the urge to bellow at them to come out, aware that they would only laugh and he was tired of being laughed at.

The awareness that he was about to be made to look a fool had begun on the day of his arrival at Caermoel when he first inspected the new stone defences. His spies had informed him that Renard was building the site up, but he had not expected to see so much and so professionally accomplished. It was a nasty shock. Renard had always been a wild one at old King Henry's court, unable to settle at anything for long.

Revising the time it would take to capture Caermoel and the coin he would have to spend, Ranulf had begun his preparations. Trees had been cut and siege machines fashioned — night sorties by the garrison had twice razed these to the ground and wrought havoc among Ranulf's camped troops. When he finally did manage to get the rams and ballistas constructed and brought up to the walls, they had been destroyed by Greek fire, along with the soldiers manning them. Ranulf had started to realise with a leaden sickness that without extremely heavy expenditure in terms of silver, men and time, he was never going to take Caermoel.

Leaving Hamo le Grande seeking the source of the keep's water with a view to poisoning it, and soaking the latest battering ram and pick in vinegar in the hopes of proofing them against the dreaded Greek fire, he had come to this meeting with Owain Gwynedd. After that, he was bound for the Empress's court in Gloucester. Stupid, sullen bitch. He almost thought he preferred Stephen, whom at least he could run rings around while fleecing him of lands and titles.

An increasing number of Welsh flanked him and his men as the trees began to thin out. The sense of oppression eased, although not the tickling sensation between his shoulder blades or the feeling of anticipation.

Beyond the forest stretched a broad, green meadow, usually sheep-grazed to judge by the closeness of the grass and the crumbly evidence of old droppings. Waiting for him in the middle of the meadow, seated upon an elegantly carved stool that was set upon a sheepskin rug, was a wiry young man. He was brown-haired and brown-eyed and robed in an incongruous yet fitting mixture of rich velvets and rough hides.

Rising unhurriedly, he advanced to greet Ranulf as he dismounted. Ranulf returned the greeting warily. The lack of height and the boyish good looks were traps. There were lines of experience at the eye corners and the full, brown moustache was lightly scattered with grey. Compared to Owain Gwynedd, Mathilda and Stephen were political innocents.

They talked and ate sweet young mutton and white bread washed down by mead and accompanied by the gentle, unobtrusive music of a Welsh harp. The flies were a nuisance and the sun was very hot, but Prince Owain was better at pretending not to notice and thus gained an immediate advantage.

Towards the end of the meal, Ranulf raised the subject of Caermoel and enquired as to whether Prince Owain would be interested in helping him take it.

The Welshman widened his deceptively innocent eyes. 'You mean you are unable to do so by yourself?'

Ranulf cleared his throat and scowled. 'It is taking too long, that is all. Your aid would bring it to a swifter conclusion.'

'I see.' Owain stroked his moustache and pretended to think. 'And if I gave it, what then?'

'We could share the spoils and you would be free to raid down into the Ravenstow lands.'

Owain was unimpressed. 'Until you re-garrisoned,' he pointed out. 'It would suit me better if Caermoel were torn down, stone by stone.'

'You talk of the impossible. Its position is too strategically valuable.'

'Then you have my answer, my lord.' The Prince spread his hands and stood up, indicating that as far as he was concerned, the meeting was at an end.

'Ravenstow is rich in herds and flocks,' Ranulf said persuasively. 'The finest destrier stud in England, and sheep by the thousand. Think of the wealth grazed on lands that were once Welsh.'

Owain raised a cynical eyebrow. Most of Chester's earldom had once been Welsh land too. 'If your troops garrison Caermoel, we'll never get past it except as corpses to behold such bounty. It is not in your interests to let us raid the best from estates you are hoping to claim.'

'It is in my interests while their revenue is of benefit to FitzGuyon. Once the earldom is mine, we would have to negotiate of course.'

'Oh, of course,' said Owain with bridled sarcasm and snapped his fingers at the young groom holding his horse. 'I will have to think on it. I'm not prepared to commit myself here and now.'

Ranulf glanced towards the youth, drawn by something familiar about the tilt of the head and the straight-backed stance. The lad was slender and wore a cap set at a jaunty angle on his head to protect him from the glare of the sun. Handing the reins to the Prince, he lifted his head and bestowed a freezing glance upon Ranulf. His eyes were as dark blue as the sea in shadow.

Ranulf choked.

Prince Owain smiled benevolently at his guest's mottled complexion and swung the horse around. 'Whatever your Normans take, it always returns to Welsh hands,' he said.

The youth mounted his own cream mare, deliberately revealing a lithe expanse of leg.

'You treacherous bitch!' Ranulf howled furiously.

'Like will know like,' she answered with contempt and started turning her own mount in pursuit of Owain's.

Ranulf leaped at her bridle. A Welsh spear barred his way and suddenly the situation was ugly as his own soldiers reached to their hilts.

'Ease back,' Owain commanded his own men, and swung his horse alongside Olwen's. Spears rattled and hesitantly retreated.

Ranulf subsided, breathing hard. He glared at Olwen. 'Where's my son?' he demanded.

She gave him a small, cool smile. 'Your son?' she laughed. 'What makes you think he's yours? I'd have swallowed black-spurred rye before I'd have given life to a child of your siring.'

'Olwen, enough!' Owain commanded as Ranulf's colour faded and he began to shake as though he had an ague. The grinding of his teeth was audible.

'He owes it to me,' she replied. 'And he always did want to know. Well, now he does.' Her hand twitched. Responding, the cream mare broke into an ambling glide.

Ranulf coughed and spat. 'Whose?' he croaked as if he was being strangled. 'Tell me, you conniving whore!'

She kept on riding, did not answer.

'Mine now,' said Owain as he followed her. 'By right of

conquest. You Normans understand all about that, don't you?'

Olwen lay across Owain's chest and played an idle game with the wiry mat of curls beneath her fingers. The glade where they dallied was sun-dappled, warm as a caress, and silent except for the sound of their horses cropping the grass.

'Woman, you're dangerous!' he chuckled ruefully.

Olwen tasted the salt in the hollow of his throat with a pointed tongue. 'Why is it that men always accuse or blame the woman for their own weaknesses?' she demanded.

'We're hardly going to accuse or blame ourselves are we!' he retorted, the laughter deepening. He wound a silken coil of her hair around fore and middle fingers and held it up to watch it sparkle in the sunlight. 'I suppose that we should be on our way,' he added, but made no effort to move.

'Will you do as Ranulf de Gernons asks?' She lowered her eyes to her gently playing hand and watched the rise and fall of his chest. Neither breathing nor heartbeat changed, but she was aware of the intensity of his gaze. When she flashed a glance at him, he was admiring the lock of hair between his fingers.

'Was your passion just now by way of bribery?' he enquired of the tress. 'If so, you are wasting your time.'

It was Olwen's breathing that changed, and hearing it, he smiled coldly. 'I do not respond to that kind of bargaining, *cariad*. Learn it now, learn it fast and well, or seek another man's hearth.'

Olwen bit her lip. 'It wasn't bribery.'

'Not entirely,' he allowed, 'but you are like a falcon, my Olwen. You only come to my fist because I feed you. It is not unconditional. You want me to refuse the Earl of Chester, don't you?'

'It matters not to me, my lord,' she shrugged indifferently.

Owain saw through it immediately and laughed at her. 'Oh, I think it matters very much indeed,' he contradicted and half sat up, bracing his weight on his elbows and the flat of his upper arms. She had hidden her face from him, a pitiful defence, and in response he took pity. 'What he proposes is an excellent idea in principle,' he said, 'but Ranulf de Gernons is about as genuine as a piece of the True Cross bought from a huckster at Ravenstow Fair. If I helped him to take that keep, he'd have it re-garrisoned faster than I could say the paternoster, and he would use it to raid into my territory. FitzGuyon's use of it so far has been defensive. I leave him alone, he leaves me alone, and at least his blood is part Welsh.' He slanted a thoughtful glance at Olwen. 'Perhaps you still hold him in some degree of affection, *fy curyll fach*?'

'He was good to me by his code – more than I deserved.'

'Then why in Christ's name did you leave him for a toad like Ranulf de Gernons? . . . No,' he said as she flounced away from him. 'I truly want to know.'

Olwen tugged at the moist blades of grass beneath her fingers. 'I wanted Renard because he was different, a challenge, but the only way to win that challenge was to lose. I had heard all about Ranulf de Gernons – how important and powerful he was. I wanted to show Renard how high I could rise if I so chose, far beyond what he could give to me. The pleasure was never important, except when it got in the way.' She tossed her handful of grass into the air and watched the green blades scatter down.

He was silent for a time, digesting this and seeing a glimmer of the reasons for her flying to his fist like a lost hawk sighting a falconer's glove. 'And the child that came of this challenge?' He sat up further and linked his hands around his upraised knees. 'Does Renard of Ravenstow know that he has sired him?'

Olwen laced up her shirt and picked her hat off the grass. They had rolled on it in their passion and the jaunty peacock's feather in the brim was broken. She shook her head. 'No, he doesn't know.' She plucked at the feather.

'Do you want him to?'

Olwen gnawed at her bottom lip, then shaking her head, raised her eyes to meet his. 'Jordan is mine,' she said. 'Perhaps when he is older . . .'

Owain arched his brow. He watched her dust off the hat and set it back on her head. No stranger to women, he found her

300

exquisitely beautiful, intricate and intriguing, worth every moment of the time he had spent coaxing her to the lure. His gain that the other two had been fools. 'He's better fostered in my household than in any *saeson's*,' he added. 'Come to think on the matter, we probably share several common ancestors through the FitzGuyon line and that's reason enough to take and raise him.' He stretched in a loose-limbed, satisfied manner and rose to follow her to their cropping mounts. 'Although I'd have taken him without that for the sake of his mother,' he said, and kissed Olwen.

He saw that her eyes were bright with tears.

CHAPTER 28

'JOHN!' ELEANOR HASTENED TO embrace her brother-in-law as he dismounted from his palfrey in Woolcot's courtyard. 'This is indeed a welcome surprise!' She hugged him hard, cheek pressed to the rough black wool of his cassock, then stood back to look into his eyes, fear present even in the midst of her delight lest he bear evil tidings. His face, however, was open and smiling, the only lines on it those around his eyes from constantly narrowing them in order to focus.

'Where's my newest nephew?' he asked as she led him across the bailey towards the keep.

'Crawling after dog bones in the hall and leading Alys a merry caper! You won't recognise him for the scrap you baptised at Christmas.' She looked along her shoulder. 'Have you ridden far?'

'Only from Ravenstow. Mama told me that she thought Renard was here?' He squinted around as they walked. She had to grab his arm and steer him around a pile of dirty rushes that had recently been forked from the hall. He said ruefully, 'When I write letters for Lord Leicester, I look through a glass orb of water to see the page better. If there was some way of carrying such a thing around on the end of my nose, I might be able to see where I was going.'

Eleanor laughed at the image he conjured and patted his arm. 'You've missed Renard by less than an hour. He's gone up to Caermoel to sift reports and sit at the manor court. I'm here to supervise the wool clip, and then we're travelling down to Ledworth for the Lammas feast. He's due back at the end of the week. Do you need him urgently?'

They had reached the hall. John stared myopically around.

He had seldom visited Woolcot and was unfamiliar with its layout. It was much smaller than Ravenstow and Ledworth, but sturdily built for all that and made comfortable by Eleanor's domestic wiles. Bright hangings abated some of the damp from the walls and the central hearth was well tended so that it burned cleanly without enveloping the hall in a smoky miasma. 'Yes, I do.'

'So urgently that you cannot stay to dine?' She propelled him in the direction of the dais.

'Oh plenty of time for that, Nell,' he assured her, patting his stomach, 'but I won't stay overnight.' He gave her a smile. 'There's no need to look like that. It's urgent, but cause for relief, not alarm.'

She wrinkled her nose dubiously, a habit of hers when she was unsure of herself, and leaving him went down the hall, returning a moment later with Hugh whom she deposited in his lap. The baby took his usual exception and yelled.

'He's definitely louder than I remember from Christmas,' John said wryly, 'although even then I marvelled at the power of his lungs.'

'Renard says that even if you put his cradle in the undercroft, you'd still be able to hear him on the battlements,' she laughed and poured him wine.

John snorted and put the baby down on the floor to watch him crawl, which he did with great determination. 'Lord Leicester sends his greetings to you and his godson and hopes to make you a visit soon.'

'I thought he was with the Empress.'

'Was,' John emphasised, taking a swallow of the wine. 'Only he grew so disgusted at her haughtiness and so impressed with Stephen's fortitude in captivity that he's returned to the Queen's party as meek as a washed lamb, and that is only half the good tidings.'

'Oh?'

'The Londoners have rejected the Empress too. They let her into the city on midsummer day, reluctantly resigned to giving her the crown. She needed to handle them as delicately as blown eggshells but instead she demanded money from them –

said it was not her fault if they were hard-pressed to pay, they should not have squandered their coin on a perjurer like Stephen.' He shook his head over the folly he was reciting. 'Both sides left the meeting in high dudgeon. My lady went to eat her dinner; the mob went to fetch their weapons. She escaped by the skin of her teeth, which never did take a bite of her food. Fled to Winchester so I hear, shedding supporters like autumn leaves.'

'There is hope then?' The gold flecks in Eleanor's eyes were suddenly very bright against the green.

'More than there was last month, certainly.' John's voice constricted as he leaned from the midriff to rescue his nephew from crawling too far. 'Apparently the Bishop of Winchester has shut his palace against her and refuses to see her. She won't give him an inch of ground and it's beginning to play on his conscience that he betrayed Stephen. After all, they are brothers, and until recently they were very close.'

'We had heard from William that Winchester petitioned her to let Stephen's son keep his father's Norman lands.'

'It was refused. And then to add insult to injury, she went and put Stephen in chains. Men are saying that it is disgraceful to treat him thus. My Lord of Leicester would have no more to do with her after that. He helped her to escape from the London rabble as a matter of courtesy, but he took the road to Kent, not Winchester.'

'And Earl Ranulf?' She took Hugh back from him.

'Cursing his decision to turn rebel in the first place. Expect him back in the marches full of spleen, but more concerned to defend for the nonce than attack.'

Eleanor looked down at her son, at the chubby hand grasping at one of her gilded braid fillets. She felt him heavy and warm in her arms. 'John, it frightens me,' she murmured. 'I wish there could be peace between us and Chester. I know that Renard fought him off at Caermoel, but it has not stopped the raiding. He sends his routiers to strike at our vulnerable parts and we strike back – ripping out each other's entrails for the Welsh to feed upon and grow fat.'

'What does Renard say?'

'That the blaze is not of his making and that he is not the one who keeps feeding it with branches. I suppose it is true, but neither will he make any move towards peace.'

'You cannot blame him for that,' John said quietly. 'Not after what happened to Harry at Lincoln.'

'I don't blame him, I just wish there was a way.' And pretended that the sudden moisture in her eyes was caused by the baby tugging sharply on her braid.

A heavy silence descended. A maid set a deep bread trencher before John and put a steaming dish of pigeons in saffron sauce upon the table and a savoury accompaniment made of bread, herbs and onions.

Eleanor sat down with him, giving Hugh a crust to suck, while she picked at her own trencher, a deep frown almost linking the delicate arches of her eyebrows.

'What's the matter?' asked John. A maid leaned over him to pour wine into his cup.

'Nothing ... I ...' she hesitated. 'I ... I was thinking that sometimes it is possible for a woman to tread where even angels fear.'

'You mean go to Earl Ranulf yourself?' His hand paused, half way between mouth and trencher and his eyes grew round with alarm. 'That would be walking into a lion's den and asking the lion to eat you!'

'I was thinking of his wife. She is your cousin and not ill-disposed towards Ravenstow. I've met her before and I think that she would probably agree to help bring this petty warring to a truce.'

John continued to stare at her. After a moment he remembered to put his food in his mouth.

'Would you carry a letter if I wrote it?'

He swallowed his mouthful convulsively and almost choked. 'What, behind Renard's back?'

Eleanor bit her lip. Then she looked at Hugh and the mess he was making of the crust. 'Yes.'

'Are you strong enough to face him when he finds out?'

She thrust her jaw at him. 'Yes.'

John concentrated on the meal and said nothing until he was

305

washing his hands in the fingerbowl. Then he leaned back and folded his arms. 'A year ago I'd not have believed you, but then a year ago you'd not have answered yes to either question.'

'A year ago I knew neither Renard nor myself.'

'And now you do?'

'I know Renard,' she said with quiet surety.

John rubbed his chin and noted absently that he needed to shave, knew without feeling that his tonsure would be fuzzy too. 'Have it written down,' he said, not at all sure that he was doing the right thing. 'And I will do my best to deliver it to Matille.'

'Thank you.'

They looked at each other sombrely, as if their thoughts were made of lead.

To throw off the guilty feeling of conspiracy and ease her mood, Eleanor had her mare saddled, and when John left, rode with him a little way in order to show him the fulling mill and the weavers' cottages that now existed in Woolcot village.

John was impressed by the industry and bustling enthusiasm of the operation. Cloth was being cleaned and felted by the pounding of hammers driven by the mill's water wheel, and some village women were delivering hanks of distaff-spun yarn to be woven into cloth on the Flemish looms. Another shed housed dye troughs and the frames on which the wet, newly dyed cloth was stretched to dry, secured by tenterhooks. In a final building, Eleanor showed him a pile of finished bales.

'This is homespun for the cottars. Some of the women take their wages in cloth.' She plucked out a corner of a plain, fairly coarse tawny weave, then two smoother ones in green and russet. 'This is slightly finer, the sort of thing a craftsman or merchant would wear to mass. And for the merchant or wealthier freeman who would like to look as if he wears Flanders cloth but baulks at the price –' she gestured and Master Pieter, her manager, tugged a dark blue cloth from the foot of the pile. It was fine and soft to the touch with a slightly glossy appearance '– Woolcot weave. Half the price of Flemish cloth and twice the quality.'

Mouth open, John stared at her. Then he spluttered and put his palms across his mouth. 'Eleanor, you sound like a huckster at a fair!'

'I'm proud, that's all,' she said defensively and blushed poppy-red. Then she looked at him through her lashes and smiled.

'And rightly so.' John's doubts concerning the letter he carried were at one and the same time increased and diminished by this little episode. Eleanor's nature was like amber. It did not give off its glow until it had been warmed, and then heaven help the recipient if he was not prepared.

They returned to their mounts. Guy d'Alberin boosted Eleanor into the saddle, while John, distracted and thoughtful, set his foot in the stirrup.

'Have a care to yourself,' she said. 'And come back soon.'

'I will. And I'll send a message to let you know when I've delivered the letter to Cousin Matille.'

She nodded and smiled rather apprehensively before she kissed him farewell.

He started up the track that led over the hill and down to the main road. Eleanor shaded her eyes to watch him and his small escort of serjeants, and resisted the urge to tear after him and take back the letter she had written to the Countess of Chester. For all that she had proclaimed herself capable of standing up to Renard's wrath, she was nevertheless afraid.

A shout floated on the wind from the direction of the horsemen just gaining the top of the rise and Eleanor saw them suddenly wheel around and come galloping back down towards her, the foremost man frantically gesticulating. She saw the twinkle of his spurs as he raised them and drove them hard down.

Master Pieter came to Eleanor's bridle and stared. 'Trouble afoot,' he said brusquely. 'Best go, my lady.'

Eleanor drew Bramble's reins through her fingers. On the brow of the slope several more riders appeared. Sun flashed on armour and drawn swords. 'Holy Mary!' she whispered and swallowed convulsively. Memory flooded her mind even as the bile flooded her throat. Her kidnap, the assault that had so nearly ended in rape. Horsemen tearing out of nowhere and ripping the world apart.

Thus far Woolcot had escaped lightly from the Earl of Chester's raiding. To reach it, his men had to get past the garrison at Caermoel. Twice at least since the siege they had attempted it and twice been beaten. The only other approach was from the east, across Harry's former lands at Oxley, unoccupied now except for a harassed constable who did his best but was not really fit for the task in hand. Renard had had scant time to give his attention to Oxley, the defence of Caermoel and the earldom being his first priority. It was their Achilles heel and now it lay exposed.

'The church!' she cried, whirling to Master Pieter. 'Get everyone into the church!' It was no guarantee of safety, but it was all they had. 'I'll ride back to the castle for aid!' Turning Bramble, she dug her heels in hard, slapped the reins against the mare's neck and shrieked in her ear.

Unaccustomed to such rough handling, the little mare took exception and broke into a gallop. Eleanor clung for dear life, but when Bramble started to slacken pace, she kicked her again and shouted, wishing fervently that she were a man and accoutred with spurs. Sheep scattered in bleating panic before woman and horse. The ground became tussocky and started to slope. Bramble stumbled and Eleanor was pitched onto her neck, lost her hold and fell off. The softness of the ground broke her fall, but even so the breath was knocked from her body and she was momentarily too stunned to do anything but lie on the prickly-soft grass, heartbeat and blood roaring in her ears, blackness before her eyes.

Gradually she became aware of shouting and the clash of weapons as the men of her escort and John's attempted to hold the routiers while the villagers and cloth workers were evacuated to the church. Eleanor sat up and collected her wits. Her body, although bruised, appeared to be in one piece. She staggered to her feet, hampered by the drag of her skirts. Her legs felt as though they were made of wet hemp. Bramble had stopped several yards away and was looking at her with nervously flickering ears. Not daring to turn around lest she see some of the routiers galloping after her, Eleanor whistled to the horse and extended her hand coaxingly. Bramble sidled, her nostrils wide, drinking in the smell of smoke.

'Good girl, Bramble, good girl,' Eleanor crooned, a tremor in her voice. Lifting her skirts clear of her shoes, she advanced on the mare. Bramble tossed her head. Eleanor's familiar scent filtered through the mare's nostrils as she approached, warring with the instinct to run from the pungency of the smoke.

Eleanor closed her fingers round the reins with a gasp of relief. Her limbs were weak and trembling but she knew that they had to serve her to remount. Bramble was trembling too, on the verge of bolting. Eleanor set her foot in the stirrup. There was no groom to boost her into the saddle, no mounting block to stand upon, and nothing in sight she could use as one. Bramble stood less than fifteen hands high, but suddenly she seemed enormous.

Sobbing through clenched teeth, Eleanor struggled. She grabbed a handful of Bramble's cropped mane, pressed the heels of her hands into the brown, sweating neck and somehow scrambled crabwise across her back. The pommel dug into her abdomen and she had to fight to breathe, but the congestion eased as she came upright and shifted her weight backwards. The mare plunged and circled as Eleanor searched for the right stirrup iron.

The smell of the smoke was increasingly strong. Eleanor caught a glimpse of the cottages, flames bursting in the doorways with their thatches alight as men armed with brands and weapons ransacked and then torched. Her eyes were suddenly blinded with tears of grief and rage. 'No,' she sobbed, 'oh no!' The reins slackened in her fingers, and Bramble took the bit between her teeth and bolted, this time in earnest.

Woolcot's priest was elderly with eyesight poorer than John's own and a hazed mind. Eleanor had bought a corrody for him at a nearby priory, but it had yet to be implemented and a new priest found to replace him. Confused and querulous at the sudden invasion of his church when as far as he recalled no one had recently been born, betrothed or died, Father Edwig wrung his hands and tearfully demanded that they all get out.

John, still panting from the exertion of his rapid ride, took the old man's arm and sat him down on a bench along the nave wall. 'There are routiers coming,' he gasped. 'Hell spawn. The people have gathered here for sanctuary.'

'Routiers?' Father Edwig quavered. 'Have they come to confess?'

'Crime first, confession later,' John replied, more than a hint of Renard ringing in his tone. 'Are you strong enough to go up the bell tower and toll out the excommunicat?'

The old man regarded him dimly. 'Have you come from the Bishop?'

John hesitated. Then he said, telling the lie with a face as open and candid as a child's, 'He sent me personally. You go aloft, take this brawny young fellow with you, and ring out the excommunicat as hard as you can.' Beneath John's hand, Father Edwig's shoulder was light and bony. Hardly the strength to lift a halter, let alone peal down the wrath of heaven and hell upon a troop of hardened mercenaries.

The old priest stared hard at John. Sunlight poured through an unshuttered window and Edwig's fuzzy vision detected a golden nimbus haloing John's tonsure. An expression of awe filtered onto his slack face. A dribble of saliva ran down his chin. Convinced that he was in the presence of God's messenger, he let a burly young hayward help him to his feet, and in a daze shuffled off with him towards the belfrey stairs. When he looked over his shoulder, John's figure was shrouded in an aureole of sunshine so that he was impossible to look upon. 'A miracle,' he whispered to the hayward. The latter humoured him.

John, less convinced about the possibility of miracles, stepped from the shaft of sunlight and turned to the gathered workers and villagers. Several of the men were armed with pitchforks, spades and hoes. One even had a sword that had been handed down through his family for several generations. The women had their distaffs and brooms. Their array was brave, but scarcely impressive and probably quite laughable to the kind of men now plundering and burning their homes.

John set about calming and reassuring them. Help would

come very soon. He had a rich, bass voice that he knew how to control so that it enfolded the frightened villagers like a comforting, fleecy blanket. His arm around a weeping, pregnant woman, he listened to the triumphant yells of the raiders and the first ominous crackle of flame and wondered if he could remember the damning words of the excommunicat. He had never had occasion to use them before. From the bell tower, the tocsin stuttered into life and was unevenly sustained, although John was unsure if the sequence was quite correct. The roar of flames grew louder as more of the village was put to the torch, and then they all heard the heavy thump of a sword hilt against the barred church doors.

John told the villagers to go and kneel before the altar, the women in the centre, the men protecting them in an outer ring, and the armed men of his escort and Eleanor's standing slightly forward. John himself stood alone in the nave by the font to face the door as it trembled beneath the blows rained upon it. He heard snarls and threats, as though a pack of wolves yammered outside. A final blow and the hinges gave way and the doors reeled inwards, revealing a vision of hell.

'Silence those bells!' howled the foremost routier, sword blade dripping with what John hoped was nothing more serious than animal blood. 'Now, priest, before I cut off your head and stuff it up your arse!'

Eleanor and Renard might have recognised Hamo le Grande. John had never encountered him before, but he recognised the type well enough. The Earl of Leicester kept such men in his own employ and for a similar purpose. Ministering to them was generally a waste of time unless they were dying and in fear that they would do so unabsolved of a lifetime of atrocity. Killing a priest on holy ground while the excommunicat rang out might daunt them, but it depended how hardened they actually were.

John filled his lungs, pointed a finger, and channelled all the charisma he possessed into his powerful voice as he began the Latin words that would damn the routiers to eternal hell.

★

Renard had ridden less than a third of the way to Caermoel when Gorvenal started to limp. Cursing, he dismounted and ran his hands down the stallion's foreleg. It was cool to the touch and felt sound, no sign of swelling at fetlock or cannon. He picked up the hoof to examine that and immediately the source of the problem became obvious. A stone had lodged in the tender frog. Gorvenal laid his ears back and tugged against the bridle that Owain was holding close in to his head. Another knight dismounted and helped the lad to hold the horse. Gorvenal's hatred of having his feet picked up was notorious, and this time Renard had no dried dates to sweeten him.

Unsheathing his meat dagger, Renard braced his body against the jarring shocks of the stallion's attempts to plunge, and tried to gouge the stone from the hoof without sticking the point of the knife into the sensitive frog which would have driven Gorvenal uncontrollably wild.

He succeeded, but not without a deal of swearing, both at the horse, the stone, his squire and the knight. By the time the stone finally did fly out onto the grass, tempers were boiling, limbs weak, and the stallion's hide was creamed with sweat. Renard wiped his hands on his surcoat, his brow on the sleeve of his gambeson, and sat down on the tussock to regain his breath.

'Do we ride on, my lord?' hesitated a young knight.

Renard restrained the urge to be sarcastic. 'I think we'll eat first,' he said. 'It'll give the horse – and me – a chance to recover. It's only a bruised frog, nothing that will hamper him. Owain, mount up and stand lookout on that hill up there.'

The boy left. Renard rose and went to Gorvenal. He gentled the horse with soft words and fondling, unslung his wineskin from the pommel and took a packet of food from his saddle roll. There was cold fowl, bread and cheese. Leaning against the horse, he ate and drank. A skylark bubbled. Renard squinted into the cloud-ridden blue and sought it out – a tiny, dark speck with a song ten times as loud and spectacular as its drab, brown plumage. He was reminded of Eleanor and smiled.

Temper forgotten, Gorvenal swung his head to butt Renard and demand a chuck of his bread. The stallion's full, black tail swished at the flies. His glossy hide shivered. Renard scratched his withers and enjoyed the peace of the moment, culled from the midst of uncertainty and war.

Following the aborted siege of Caermoel, hostilities between himself and the Earl of Chester had ceased for a while, and then, like a cry cast into a well, the echoes had resounded, on and on for ever. Ranulf, having learned his lesson, did not attempt another siege or blockade. Instead he used Welsh tactics and struck out at the small and vulnerable targets. Timber and wattle manor houses, and villages. Wanton, indiscriminate destruction. Renard retaliated with equal savagery, but sometimes, looking at earth that was scorched instead of growing with young crops, or at slaughtered plough teams, he was physically sickened. Watching the skylark now, he wondered if Eleanor understood. Perhaps.

The lark plummeted like a stone. Owain came down the hill at a gallop, shouting something that was snatched away by the wind. Renard dusted off his hands. Stoppering the wine skin, he looped it quickly back around the saddle, and mounting up, cantered to meet the squire.

'It's Woolcot!' the boy gasped out. 'Woolcot's burning!'

Renard spurred Gorvenal to the crest of the hill to look for himself. A thick, grey coil smudged the horizon, too large to be a midden bonfire or anything legitimate concerned with Eleanor's weavers and dyers. He wrenched the horse around and sent him flying back down to his men. Owain had already passed on the news and they had remounted, food abandoned, and were looking to him for confirmation.

'Yes!' he cried. 'The whoresons have hit Woolcot, but they've reckoned without us being so close. Gerard, when we get there, sweep round by the mill with half the men. I'll take the other end. We can talk as we ride!'

It was a little more than three miles back to Woolcot and Renard and his men covered the distance as though they were racing each other on the Smithfield coursing ground rather than bumpy sheep terrain. As they neared the stricken village they heard the tolling of the church bell and the smell of the smoke thickened and gouted on the wind. Added to it came the stink of charring meat. It caught in the lungs and cut off breath. It stung the eyes with more than just the irritation of smoke.

Garden crops were burning, dwellings were on fire. Animals lay where they had been slaughtered. The main street was an avenue of fire, every building alight. The roar of the flames was like the breath of a ragged, mythical beast, stalking and destroying in the wake of the perpetrators. Of them there was not a sign except for one body trapped beneath the hulk of a dead ox.

Gerard de Brionne split away from the main group and took a handful of men round by the fulling mill. That too was on fire, although not yet as wildly ablaze as the houses. Torches still held aloft, three men were backing away from the building, shouting gleefully to each other. Gerard and his companions rode them down, dousing both brands and men in the fast-flowing river beside the mill. Their armour pulled them under. Those who floated were encouraged to sink. Renard's knights removed their cloaks, saturated them in the river and set about beating out the fire.

Renard came round to the church by way of the village pond where incongruously, amid all the destruction and chaos, a pair of ducks still dabbled with a total lack of concern. The church itself, stone-built by Eleanor's father, was untouched by fire, but the doors hung drunkenly wide, and clustered around them were a group of routiers in mail hauberks or gambesons of boiled leather. From the belfrey, the excommunicat resonated, tolling amid the drifts of windblown smoke. The wind veered and the bells faltered and suddenly died. Within the church a child wailed.

'Hah!' Renard cried and spurred Gorvenal. The horse passed the pond at a canter. Renard leaned forward, left fist curved around the hand strap of his shield, right around his sword grip. The child's wail became a full scream, and above the roar of the flames, Renard heard a man's voice thundering in Latin. John, he thought, recognising it even as it was cut short.

He spurred Gorvenal again, frantically, and they galloped into the churchyard. Without stopping, Renard took the stallion straight up the path to the broken church doors. A routier stared. His mouth widened to yell a warning. Renard stood in the stirrups and clove him like a bacon pig. Gorvenal dealt with a second man, a lashing kick doubling him over, and Renard finished it. Then he was riding into the church, horse-shoes clattering hollowly on the stone flags of the nave.

Hamo le Grande turned and gaped as a vision from the hell the priest had just promised him bore down the nave. A horseman of the apocalypse, his sword edge dripping blood and his horse wild-eyed with crimson-lined nostrils. At Hamo's feet, John used his good arm – the one that the mercenary had not slashed to the bone, to grasp Hamo's ankle and pull hard. The mercenary threw out his arms to save himself, but was too late. The cry of surprise on his lips rose to a scream of agony as he landed without cushioning on the hard flags. They all heard the crack of bone as his spine broke. And yet he was still alive to suffer the agony. Unable to move, he watched Renard slow the horse and pace him up the nave, finally drawing rein before him.

Renard looked down implacably. 'Take him out,' he com-manded to the men waiting behind. 'And hang him . . . slowly.'

Hamo's screams as he was dragged outside the church faded to background insignificance. Renard dismounted. Owain appeared to take charge of the horse and lead him outside. Renard knelt beside John who was ashen with pain and his habit-sleeve saturated in blood.

'Not as bad as it looks,' he tried to jest. 'His blade was blunt.'

'Let me see.' Renard drew his knife and ripped the material. The wound was deep and sluggishly oozing, but not so deep that it would not mend or damage the arm's function. 'It's nasty,' he said, 'but it won't kill you. Eleanor will be able to stitch it and pack it with a mouldy bread poultice.' While he spoke, he worked to temporarily bind the wound with strips from the linen shirt that Master Pieter had obligingly sacrificed.

'Eleanor?' John grimaced. 'Eleanor rode back to Woolcot to fetch help from the garrison . . . She was here in the village showing me the wool sheds and seeing me on my way.'

'What!'

'She was gone before they struck.'

Renard sprang to his feet just as the brawny youth came up the nave, Father Edwig's body borne in his arms. 'He's dead,' the young man said in a wondering voice. 'Just suddenly dropped at the bell rope, but see, he's never looked so happy!'

People gathered to marvel or weep over the serenely smiling old priest. Renard left the church at a run, snatched Gorvenal's bridle from Owain and vaulted into the saddle.

'There are some men from the keep looking for you,' the boy said. 'Sir Oswell and Sir Randal.' He pointed down the churchyard, his young face frightened.

Renard rode over to the garrison force. A little beyond them several corpses swung on a gibbet, their entrails still steaming on the ground, and their faces black with strangulation. 'Where is Lady Eleanor?' he demanded brusquely.

Sir Oswell looked troubled. He wiped his hand over his beard. 'I do not know, my lord.'

'What do you mean, you don't know?'

'Her mare came into the bailey all sweated up and riderless about the same time that we heard the bells and saw the smoke. We rode here first, thinking perhaps to find her, but ...' he gestured bleakly at the burning village.

Renard coughed as he inhaled a gust of smoke. His gut felt cold and queasy. 'Oswell, stay here and organise the villagers into putting out the fires and cleaning up. Randal, take half a dozen men and search the area between village and keep.'

'Yes, my lord.'

Renard wheeled Gorvenal and rode in the direction of the castle. On all sides of him the rough pasture stretched. Grazing sheep raised their heads and stared at him with wary indifference, jaws circling busily. The wind veered and buffeted, bringing the stink of burning with it, hot and strong. It was difficult to remember a time when that smell had not pervaded his every waking moment and stalked him through his dreams.

Across the moorland he and his men searched without finding a single sign of Eleanor and with each piece of ground unfruitfully covered Renard felt the apprehension tightening in his belly. What if she had been caught in the fire? What if the horse had bucked her off in the village and run home to her stable riderless all the way? The thought was unbearable, but once it had insinuated itself into his mind it would not leave him alone.

Unknowing, he passed the place where she had first fallen from the mare, and then the place where a second time she had lost her seat in the saddle. Nothing. He halted Gorvenal and stared at the wind-whipped moorland until his eyes stung.

'Hola!'

Renard turned in the direction of the shout and saw a shepherd and dogs running towards him. The man was waving his arms, and a molten flicker of hope coursed through Renard as he rode to meet him.

'My lord!' the shepherd saluted him, then had to stop to gather his breath, quite unable to speak.

The suspense was impossible for Renard to bear. 'Is it about Lady Eleanor? Is she all right? Tell me, man!'

'I ... I think so, my lord ... She were a bit shook up at first, but my wife's looking after her.' He gulped and gasped, pressing his hand to the stitch in his side. 'At first we thought her ankle was broken, but I do believe 'tis only a nasty strain.'

'Where is she?'

'My hut ... over yon.' He pointed to a small dwelling a few hundred yards away. 'I carried her like I would a wounded sheep. It weren't far and my wife had just brought me som'at to eat.' He straightened slightly and creased his eyes at Renard. 'Is it true the village is burned to t' ground? I can smell smoke. Dogs are restless.'

'Yes, it's true.' Renard left the shepherd and galloped to the hut, dismounting even as he drew rein. Tethering Gorvenal to a hook protruding from the dung and wattle wall, he ducked inside the hut. It took a moment for his eyes to adjust to the single, tiny room, but Eleanor's glad cry brought his gaze immediately to the place where she lay, tended by the shepherd's wife who was pressing a cold compress onto her swollen ankle.

'Praise God!' Renard said. 'We've been searching every-where for you!'

The woman stood up, dried her hands on her gown and, bobbing a curtsey, went outside the hut.

Eleanor struggled up from the shepherd's narrow bed of bracken and sheepskins and as Renard knelt in the woman's place flung her arms around him. 'You smell of smoke,' she tried to say lightly, but the words cracked and broke up, and she buried her face in his surcoat, sobs shuddering through her.

Silently, tightly, he held her, as much for his own comfort as hers.

'I suppose the village is in ruins?' she asked at length, her voice wobbly and choked.

'More or less. Gerard saved the mill I think, but everything else bar the church is gone.'

'The people . . . I tried to get help, but Bramble took fright at the smoke and I could not control her.'

'The people are safe,' he reassured her, and told her every-thing that had happened, adding in a growl at the end, 'If de Gernons thinks that an atrocity such as this will go unavenged, then he was never more mistaken.'

Eleanor clung to him, her fingers clenched in the em-broidered velvet of his surcoat and her knuckles pressed against the unyielding rivets of his hauberk. 'No, let it lie!' she cried vehemently. 'You have hanged the men responsible. If you raid on his lands you will only continue the circle. It needs to be broken, don't you see!'

'If I do nothing, he will think I have weakened.'

'He will think nothing of the sort. His routiers are dead or scattered. Call it even!'

'I do not think you have seen the extent of the damage,' Renard said grimly. 'Everything is gone – every last bale of your cloth, and that cannot be rebuilt as quickly as the houses'

'It can never be rebuilt if you keep raiding tit for tat. Renard, promise me you'll hold your hand, I cannot bear it any more!'

'I will promise nothing of the kind!' he muttered, and then swore as she began to weep again. His defences were not up to dealing with Eleanor's grief, nor could he understand her insistence that he must not retaliate. Part of him wanted to stand up, walk away, pretend none of this was happening. He disliked being pushed into emotional corners, but he was in one now and if he escaped from it by thrusting her away, he knew he would feel guilty for the rest of his life.

'The only promise I'll make is to think about it,' he temporized, running one hand down her braid. 'Don't push me further than that, Nell.' He tipped up her chin and kissed her tear-streaked face, then he sighed. 'Come on, I'll take you to the keep before I go back to the village and see what's to be salvaged.'

Eleanor put her arms around his neck as he lifted her up. She kissed him back and he felt the corner into which he was backed growing smaller and tighter. Ducking under the low door arch, he carried her out to Gorvenal.

CHAPTER 29

Chester
November 1141

RANULF DE GERNONS STOOD in his wife's chamber, hands on his hips, and watched her fussing with their younger daughter's tiny braids. They stuck out at right-angles from her head, were shorter than his own moustaches, only half their thickness and of a light, mousey brown that no amount of adorning would enhance. Her sister, three years older, was sitting on her mother's bed, playing a counting game with some carnelian beads.

'Is there any news of my father?' Matille looked at him anxiously.

'Only that he's being treated well and the Queen is refusing to bargain. They want Stephen in exchange for him or nothing.' He scowled, revealing what he had thought of that particular idea. The smallest child climbed into her mother's lap and hid her face against Matille's grey silk gown. Ranulf's scowl deepened. Thus far Matille had borne him three children − two girls, alive and healthy, but the all-important boy miscarried. She was pregnant again. God willing this time she would give him what he desired. To that end he had been unduly gentle with her these past three months, particularly during the last one that had seen the Empress's forces reduced to chaos at the siege of Winchester and the subsequent capture of her father, the Earl of Gloucester.

Ranulf had quickly distanced himself from the Empress, had returned to his marches to wait out events like a spider lurking in the bushes beside its web. Lincoln had been the Empress's pinnacle. Since then, everything had begun to slip away. At Winchester, Bishop Henry had turned against her, and

Stephen's queen had appeared with her army beneath the city walls. Overwhelmed, deserted by many of her supporters, she had been forced to flee towards Oxford. During the rout, Matille's father had been captured and now Queen Malde wanted to exchange him for Stephen. Negotiations were in slow progress, but it was obvious to Ranulf that whatever came of them, the best course was to do nothing until he saw which way the wind blew for certain.

'But he is well?' Matille persisted.

'Better than for a long time,' Ranulf grunted. 'He hasn't got that sulky bitch bleating in his ear. Why won't Lucy look at me?'

'You frighten her, Papa,' said Adela, his eldest, looking up from her game. 'She doesn't like it when you shout.'

'Hah!' Ranulf said, dismissing the comment, although inside it hurt him. It always did. He had the power to make people do whatever he wished – except love him, and he was aware of that lack most strongly when he tried to be at ease with his wife and children.

'Ranulf, I've been thinking about Lucy,' Matille said hesitantly.

'Indeed?'

'Have you any plans for a betrothal yet? I know you have for Adela, but . . .' She broke off and cuddled her whimpering daughter. Her stomach moved queasily. Some of the nausea was her new pregnancy. As usual she was not carrying well, but the rest was caused by her fear of Ranulf. These days he was as unpredictable as a wild bull, but if she could arrange a favourable marriage for her daughter and help the Countess of Ravenstow into the bargain, then she was willing to brave his temper.

'Whom did you have in mind?'

Matille swallowed. 'Ravenstow's heir.'

Ranulf's bellow almost blew the shutters off their hinges. 'God's balls, woman, you dare to suggest that to me!' he roared.

Lucy screamed in terror and the older girl stopped her game, her eyes becoming round with fear in case their father should use his fists.

321

'I only thought that an alliance with Ravenstow might leave you free to deal with the Welsh and pay more attention to your other concerns,' she said far more calmly than she felt. Her heart jumped and jumped and the sickness almost made her heave.

'I'd rather have her wed to a gong farmer than joined to that kind of blood!' Spittle flecked his moustaches.

'Ranulf, please don't shout, you're making me ill,' she gasped.

He cleared his throat. The red mottling faded slightly from his face and throat and he looked at her anxiously. 'The answer is no,' he growled.

'Heir to Ravenstow means heir to Caermoel,' she said, after a moment, a sly look in her eyes.

Ranulf turned away and stared out of the open shutters at the vista of autumnal colours. Golds and oranges and woodsmoke grey. The news of the burning of Woolcot had pleased him, but the cost had been high. He had lost almost a full mercenary troop. This was gradually being replaced although not yet up to full raiding strength. Thus far Renard had not retaliated, but his patrols had tightened up considerably, and he too had been hiring men.

The fighting was indeed tiresome. Ranulf had looked forward to rubbing Renard's nose in the dirt, to humiliating him, but had discovered quickly that it was an ambition not to be realised. He was realistic enough to abandon the attempt to take Caermoel, but sufficiently vindictive to continue raiding.

A marriage alliance. He discarded his first, gut reaction and looked at it objectively. Yes, it would leave him free to deal with the Welsh, with Prince Owain, the presumptuous cocky bastard. It would stop him from having to constantly patrol the border with Ravenstow, and if, as Matille said, Ravenstow's son was also Caermoel's heir, his grandchildren would inherit the land, and there was scope for manipulation and appropriation there in plenty. The fact that Renard's son and Lucy were second cousins would require a dispensation, but that was no real barrier, and an escape route should a more propitious marriage offer come his way.

'Heir to Caermoel,' he mused, and looked round at the child. It would only be an agreement to a betrothal anyway. Both parties were much too young to even begin to lisp the words of acceptance. It would be saving face with certain, implicit advantages.

'I'll make up my mind later,' he said, just to let her know that he was the master, and stalked out of the room.

Weak, soaked with perspiration, Matille leaned back against her pillows and fought her nausea, but mingled with it was the relief that he had gone, and the triumph that she knew he would do what she had suggested.

CHAPTER 30

Leicester
November 1141

T HE DAIS TABLE WAS ADORNED with a solid gold aqua-
manile in the form of a horse. There were candlesticks
of silver gilt, flagons set with rock crystal and amethyst
and goblets that matched. The napery was of the finest
pounded, bleached linen, except where someone had knocked
over a cup of wine, leaving a blood-red stain. The only real
blood in evidence was that oozing from a haunch of under-
cooked venison. It sat in front of Eleanor's place, reminding
her of how matters might have been had not Chester's offer of
peace been accepted by Renard – the price, their son in a
marriage alliance.

Renard was wearing his wedding tunic for this event on the
neutral ground of the Earl of Leicester's main keep, always a
sign that he felt in some way constrained. His eyes were as
opaque as flints and frequently concealed behind lowered lids.
At least, she thought, he had been brought to agree to burying
the hostilities – not by her, but by Robert of Leicester and
the more powerful persuasion of Welsh aggression along the
marches as Prince Owain sought to extend his own borders.

Leicester, chief witness to the strained proceedings, was blus-
teringly jovial, decidedly on edge, but then a natural manner
would have been very difficult to maintain given the parties
involved and the differences between them.

The children were elsewhere with their respective nurses.
Lucy was a year older than Hugh, but that scarcely mattered.
She was also sweet and shy and obviously terrified of her father.
As tradition demanded, she would be given to Eleanor at about

the age of nine to grow up in the household into which she would later marry, with only short visits home. Eleanor could not find it in her to be angry with Matille for manipulating her plea for an end to the hostilities.

Matille seemed unaffected by the atmosphere at the high table, but then she had every reason to celebrate. Her father, captured in the flight from Winchester, had been released in exchange for King Stephen and was none the worse for his ordeal. Ranulf was not as pleased, but that made him all the more eager to form the alliance with Ravenstow. Stephen was likely to have a sore head about Lincoln, so it behoved Ranulf to keep loyalist company for a while at least.

The haunch of venison was evocative to Renard too, reminding him of what continued war with the Earldom of Chester would mean. Leicester had not had to persuade him very hard to see reason, and the Welsh threat had quickly done the rest. He was amenable to the suggestion of a truce, particularly as the agreement to a betrothal had an escape clause in the form of consanguinity between Hugh and little Lucy. What was galling him at the moment was having to sit at the same board as Ranulf de Gernons and endure the interminable courses of a celebration feast. Hypocrisy of the worst order. Both of them knew where they wanted to stick their eating knives, and it was not in that haunch of venison. Grimly he endured and counted down the candle notches until the moment he could decently retire. Soon, he thought, as the various marchpane subtleties were served and the barely touched deer haunch was removed to a sideboard.

The musicians who had played harp and crwth during the main meal now made way for the entertainers. Renard reached for his goblet, discovered that it was empty, but declined a refill from the squire serving the high table.

A group of traditional dancers replaced some jugglers. Robert of Leicester, well lubricated by the wine he had been drinking to carry him through this ordeal, grinned and nudged Renard. 'Different to the last lot of dancing we all witnessed together, eh?' he chortled. His voice was loud and carried to include Ranulf in the remark. Comically, Leicester then realised his mistake. 'Oh,' he said. 'That's put my foot in the subtlety hasn't it?'

The words fell into an awkward silence.

'She was nought but a faithless whore!' Ranulf snarled, shattering it.

'Who nevertheless kept faith to her own code,' Renard defended.

'Hah, you know she's bedding Owain Gwynedd now?' Ranulf's light eyes were dangerous.

'Yes, I know, and I wish them well.'

Ranulf's look narrowed, became almost crafty. He wondered whether to tell Renard about the child. In the same moment as the thought was born he decided against it. She had never said the boy was Renard's, although he well suspected it was so. Let him grow up among the Welsh and perhaps one day put a goose-fletched arrow through his own father's heart in some wet border woodland. 'I hope they both die of Syrian pox,' he said, hunching his shoulders.

Renard could feel Eleanor quivering beside him, could see the strain on Leicester's face. He swallowed down an inexcusable retort of his own and instead reached down to his belt.

Ranulf thought that he was going for his recently sheathed knife and whipped his own dagger from where it had been thrust upright in a loaf of bread. Leicester caught his arm to hold him back as retainers leapt up and the mood suddenly turned very nasty indeed.

Remaining calm, Renard held out a flat bronze disc on the palm of his hand. 'I was in two minds whether to return this to you or not, but you might as well have it for the sake of the treaty between us.'

De Gernons subsided onto his chair. He was scarlet in the face as he took from Renard the seal he had lost at Lincoln.

'Call it a gift of good faith,' Renard added dryly. 'Let it be a token of the esteem in which we hold each other.' Inclining his head, he drew Eleanor to her feet and left the dais and the speechless Earl of Chester.

★

'Renard?'

'Mmmm?'

'I . . . I've got a confession to make.'

'Oh? And what sort of penance should I exact from you in payment?'

The bracken stuffing rustled and Eleanor felt his weight shift on the lumpy mattress. His hand came lightly down upon her body, smoothing over her belly and cupping her breast. She knew that he had been angry earlier, but his mood had since lightened, so that now, in the bedchamber they had been allotted for their stay at Leicester, she knew even in the darkness that he was smiling.

'I do not know,' she said apprehensively. 'Either you will beat me black and blue or you will never speak to me again.'

'A serious sin then,' he murmured, nibbling at her mouth and chin and throat, his fingers busy.

'It is . . . Renard, please!'

His lips left the jumping pulsebeat on her collar-bone. She felt him prop his head on his hand. It was pitch dark and she could not see a thing. 'Tell me then.'

Eleanor swallowed. 'I . . . this meeting between you and Earl Ranulf. It was not his idea.'

'I know, love.'

'You do?'

'Of course,' his voice held a note of smug contempt. 'It was his wife's. You don't think he would have done it of his own accord, do you? It shows too balanced a reasoning, and I know that Matille's desperate to foster the girls somewhere that they'll be loved for themselves even while they're being pawns.'

'It wasn't Matille's idea. She only improvised on what she was given . . . It was mine. I wrote to her and John carried the letter. He was carrying it on the day that Woolcot burned to the ground.'

'Yours?' he repeated blankly, and remembered her begging him in a shepherd's hut not to seek revenge – because revenge would have spoiled her hopes for a truce. Even in the midst of losing everything for which she had worked, she had held herself to discipline.

'Renard . . .?' She touched his face, but was unable to tell what expression it held, not without the benefit of rush-light.

There was a long silence in which she waited, scarcely daring to breathe. Renard's own breath emerged suddenly on a deep sigh and was followed by a very reluctant snort of wry laughter. 'Thus am I served justly for my conceit. What did I say about balanced reasoning?'

'Are you angry with me?'

'Angry?' He considered the word. The mattress moved again. 'I'm trying very hard,' he admitted. 'For the sake of my pride, I'm trying, but I cannot quibble with the outcome. Still,' he added severely, 'erring wives must know their place . . . which is firmly beneath their husbands.'

Eleanor dutifully accepted her punishment.

Some time later, Renard sat up in the bed. He was uncomfortable, he had no real desire for sleep, and besides, he was starving. Feeling around for tinder and flint, he lit the night candle and began pulling on his clothes.

Eleanor watched him and swallowed. 'I won't do it again, I promise.'

'Was the punishment so terrible to bear then?' he grinned facetiously.

'No, I mean go making bargains behind your back. I've been so frightened these past few weeks in case you never trusted me again, but I had to do it, for Hugh's sake.' And her expression suddenly hardened.

'And saddle him with one of Chester's brood for a wife,' he retorted as he pulled on his shoes, and then, on a gentler note, 'You were right, Nell, and Ranulf and I were wrong. It is easier for a woman to back down than a man. Perhaps we've both learned lessons from this.'

'Where are you going?'

'To find something to eat. I might have made an alliance with Ranulf but sitting at the same board as him still curdles my appetite, and now I'm starving.' He picked up her shift. 'Do you want to raid the kitchens with me?'

Smiling, she took the garment from his hand. Their fingers

touched. 'Perhaps there'll be some pottage on the fire,' she teased.

He laughed and kissed her.